Did I Mention I Love You?

Estelle Maskame started writing at the age of thirteen and completed her DIMILY trilogy when she was sixteen. She has already built an extensive and loyal fanbase for her writing around the world by sharing her work in instalments on the digital platform Wattpad. Estelle's trilogy will now be available for the first time in book and e-book formats. The news of her publishing deal has now gone viral, and her fans are eagerly anticipating publication. Books 2 and 3 in the DIMILY trilogy will be published in 2016.

Advance Praise for *Did I Mention I Love You?*

"It's a safe bet the films will be out by 2017." – *The Guardian* (*Observer*)

"Maskame's followers are voracious readers and the Scot has had to grow accustomed to every plot twist being feverishly discussed." – *The Herald*

"[The books have] received pretty much universal acclaim from her 125,000 followers." – *The Times*

"A beautiful, compelling novel. I found it almost impossible to put down. I strongly believe this could be the next big YA novel of 2015." – Emma, YA Bookseller

"I loved this. I thought it was written really well, full of romantic will-they-won't-they tension, and it kept me hooked until the end. This is the first book in a trilogy with Book 2 (*Did I Mention I Need You?*) and Book 3 (*Did I Mention I Miss You?*) coming soon. You will be counting down the days once you've finished this one, it's so addictive! It's hard to believe the author is only seventeen, I can't wait to see what's next from her. This is the next big thing in teenage fiction, the book that everyone will be talking about, it's amazing! A perfect summer read." – Stevie, YA Bookseller

Did I Mention I Love You?

ESTELLE MASKAME

HARPER

First published in India in 2015 by Harper
An imprint of HarperCollins *Publishers*
4th Floor, Tower A, Building No. 10, Phase II,
DLF Cyber City, Gurugram, Haryana -122002
www.harpercollins.co.in

P-ISBN: 9789351775843
E-ISBN: 9789351775850

2 4 6 8 10 9 7 5 3 1

First published by Black & White Publishing Ltd, UK

Typeset in 11/14.75 Plantin MT Std by
Iolaire Typesetting, Newtonmore

Printed and bound at
Manipal Technologies Limited, Manipal

To my readers from the beginning,
because this book isn't mine, it's ours.

1

If movies and books have taught me anything, it's that Los Angeles is the greatest city with the greatest people and the greatest beaches. And so, like every girl to ever walk this earth, I dreamed of visiting this Golden State. I wanted to run along the sand of Venice Beach one day, to press my hands on my favorite celebrities' stars on the Walk of Fame, to one day stand behind the Hollywood Sign and look out over the beautiful city.

That and all the other lame tourist must-dos.

With one earphone in, my attention half on the music humming into my ear and half on the conveyor belt rotating in front of me, I try my hardest to find a spot clear enough for me to haul my luggage. While the people around me shove and chat loudly with their partners, yelling that their luggage just went past and the other yelling back that it wasn't actually their luggage, I roll my eyes and focus on the khaki suitcase nearing me. I can tell it's mine by the lyrics scrawled along its side, so I grab the handle and yank it off as quickly as I can.

"Over here!" a familiar voice calls. My father's astoundingly deep voice is half drowned out by my music, but no matter how loud the volume I would probably still hear him from a mile away. His voice is too irritatingly painful to ignore.

When Mom first broke the news to me that Dad had asked me to spend the summer with him, we both found ourselves in a fit of laughter at the sheer insanity of it all. "You don't have to go anywhere near him," Mom reminded me daily. Three years of hearing nothing and suddenly he wanted me to spend the entire summer with him? All he had to do was maybe start calling me once in a while, ask me how I was doing, gradually ease himself back into my life, but no, he decided to bite the bullet and ask to spend eight weeks with me instead. Mom was completely against the idea. Mom didn't think he deserved eight weeks with me. She said it would never be enough to make up for the time he'd already lost with me. But Dad only got more persistent, more desperate to convince me that I'd love it in southern California. I don't know why he finally decided to get in touch out of the blue. Was he hoping he could mend the relationship with me that he broke the day he got up and left? I doubted that was even possible, but one day I caved and called up my father to tell him that I wanted to come. My decision didn't revolve around him, though. It revolved around the idea of hot summer days and glorious beaches and the possibility of falling in love with an Abercrombie & Fitch model with tanned skin and an eight-pack. Besides, I had my own reasons for wanting to get nine hundred miles away from Portland.

So, I am not particularly thrilled to see the person approaching me.

A lot can change in three years. Three years ago, I was three inches shorter. Three years ago, my dad didn't have noticeable graying strands throughout his hair. Three years ago, this wouldn't have been awkward.

I try my hardest to smile, to grin so that I won't have to explain why there's a permanent frown sketched upon my lips. It's always so much easier just to smile.

"Look at my little girl!" Dad says, widening his eyes and shaking his head in disbelief that I no longer look the same as I did at thirteen. Oh, how shocking that, in fact, sixteen-year-olds do not look the same as they did when they were in eighth grade.

"Yep," I say, reaching up and pulling out my earphone. The wires dangle in my hands, the faint lull of the music vibrating through the buds.

"I've missed you a lot, Eden," he tells me, as though I'll be overjoyed to know that my dad who walked out on us misses me, and perhaps I'll throw myself into his arms and forgive him right there and then. But things don't work like that. Forgiveness shouldn't be expected: It has to be earned.

However, if I'm going to be living with him for eight weeks, I should probably *try* to put my hostility aside. "I've missed you too."

Dad beams at me, his dimples boring into his cheeks the way a mole burrows into dirt. "Let me take your bag," he says, reaching for my suitcase and propping it onto its wheels.

I follow him out of LAX. I keep my eyes peeled for any film stars or fashion models that might happen to brush past me, but I don't spot anyone on my way out.

Warmth hits my face as I walk across the sprawling parking lot, the sun tingling my skin and the soft breeze swaying around my hair. The sky is mostly clear apart from several unsatisfying clouds.

"I thought it was going to be hotter here," I comment,

peeved that California is not actually completely free from wind and clouds and rain that stereotypes have led me to believe. Never did it occur to me that the boring city of Portland would be hotter in the summer than Los Angeles. It is such a tragic disappointment and now I'd much rather go home, despite how lame Oregon is.

"It's still pretty hot," says Dad, shrugging almost apologetically on behalf of the weather. When I glance sideways at him, I can see his growing exasperation as he racks his brain for something to say. There is nothing to talk about besides the uncomfortable reality of the situation.

He draws my suitcase to a halt by a black Lexus, and I stare dubiously at the polished paintwork. Before the divorce, he and my mom shared a crappy Volvo that broke down every four weeks. And that's if we were lucky. Either his new job pays extremely well or he just chose not to splurge on us before. Perhaps we weren't worth spending money on.

"It's open," he tells me, nodding at the vehicle as he pops the trunk and throws my suitcase inside.

I move around to the right side of the car and slide my backpack off my shoulder, opening the door and getting in. The leather is scorching hot against my bare thighs. I wait in silence for a few moments before Dad edges in behind the wheel.

"So, did you have a nice flight?" he asks, engaging me in a generic conversation as he starts up the engine and backs out of the spot.

"Yeah, it was okay." I tug my seatbelt over my body and click it into place, staring blankly out the windshield while holding my backpack on my lap. The sun is blinding, so I open up the front compartment of my bag and pull out my shades, slipping them over my eyes. I heave a sigh.

I almost hear my dad gulp as he takes a deep breath and asks, "How's your mom?"

"She's great," I say, almost too enthusiastically as I try my hardest to emphasize just how well she's getting on without him. This is not entirely the truth, though. She's doing okay. Not great, but not bad. She's spent the past few years trying to convince herself that the divorce is an experience that she can learn from. She wants to think that it's given her a life-affirming message or filled her with wisdom, but honestly, the only thing it's done is make her despise men. "Never been better."

Dad nods then, gripping the steering wheel firmly as the car peels out of the airport grounds and onto the boulevard. There are numerous lanes, cars racing down each one, the traffic heavy but moving quickly. The landscape here is open. The buildings are not leaning, towering skyscrapers like those in New York, nor are there rows of trees like the ones back home in Portland. The only satisfying thing I discover is that palm trees do really exist. Part of me always wondered if they were a myth.

We pass under a collection of road signs, one above each lane, outlining the surrounding cities and neighborhoods. The words are nothing more than a blur as we speed under them. A new silence is forming, so Dad quickly clears his throat and makes a second attempt at holding a conversation with me.

"You're going to love Santa Monica," he says, smiling only briefly. "It's a great city."

"Yeah, I looked it up," I say, propping my arm up against the window and staring out onto the boulevard. So far, LA doesn't look as glamorous as it does in all those images I saw on the Internet. "It's the one with that pier thingy, right?"

"Yes, Pacific Park." A glint of sunlight catches the gold wedding band around my dad's finger where his hands grip the steering wheel. I groan. He notices. "Ella can't wait to meet you," he tells me.

"And I her." This is a lie.

Ella, my dad informed me recently, is his new wife. A replacement for my mom: something new, something better. And this is something that I can't understand. What does this Ella woman have that my mom doesn't? A better dish-scrubbing technique? Better meatloaf?

"I hope the two of you can get along," Dad says after a moment of suffocating silence. He merges into the farthest-right lane. "I really want this to work."

Dad might really want this to work, but I, on the other hand, am still not completely sold on the whole reconstituted-family-model idea. The thought of having a stepmom does not appeal to me. I want a nuclear family, a cereal box family made up of my mom, my dad and myself. I don't like adjustments. I don't like change.

"How many kids does she have again?" I ask, my tone contemptuous. Not only have I been blessed with a lovely stepmother, I have also been graced with stepbrothers.

"Three," Dad shoots back. He is growing irritated by my obvious negativity. "Tyler, Jamie and Chase."

"Okay," I say. "How old are they?"

He talks as he focuses on the stop sign only yards ahead and slows the car down. "Tyler just turned seventeen, Jamie's fourteen and Chase—Chase is eleven. Try to get along with them, honey." Out of the corner of his hazel eyes, he fixes me with a pleading stare.

"Oh," I say again. Until now I just assumed I'd be meeting a couple of toddlers who could barely string sentences together yet. "Okay."

Thirty minutes later we're driving through a winding road in what appears to be the outskirts of the city. Tall trees decorate the parkway on each sidewalk, their thick trunks and crooked branches providing shade from the heat. The houses here are all larger than the one I live in with my mom back home, and they're all uniquely designed and constructed. No two houses are alike, neither in shape nor color nor size. Dad's Lexus pulls up outside a white-stone one.

"You live here?" Deidre Avenue seems too normal, as though it belongs in the middle of North Carolina. LA isn't supposed to be normal. It's supposed to be glitzy and out of this world and totally surreal, but it's not.

Dad nods, killing the engine and closing his sun visor. "You see that window?" He points to a window on the second floor, the one right in the center.

"Yeah?"

"That's your room."

"Oh," I say. I wasn't expecting my own room for the eight weeks that I'm here. But it looks to be a pretty big house, so I'm sure spare rooms are plentiful. I'm glad I won't be sleeping on an inflatable bed in the middle of the living room. "Thanks, Dad." When I try to push myself up, I realize that wearing shorts has proven to have both pros and cons. Pro: My legs feel fresh and cool in this weather. Con: My thighs are now stuck to the leather of Dad's Lexus. And so it takes me a good long minute to actually get myself out of the car.

Dad heads around to the trunk, collecting my suitcase and placing it on the sidewalk. "Better head inside," he says as he yanks out the handle and begins wheeling it along behind him.

I take a wide step over the parking strip and follow my dad along the stone path. It leads up to the front door: mahogany and paneled, just like the doors to houses owned by the rich should be. All the while, I'm just staring at the Converse on my feet, taking a moment to let my eyes run over my scrawling handwriting, which decorates the sides of the white rubber. Just like my suitcase, there are lyrics written in black Sharpie. Staring at the writing helps keep my nerves at ease: slightly, just until we reach the front door.

The house itself—despite being an obnoxious symbol of consumerism—is very pretty. Compared with the house I woke up in this morning, it may as well be a five-star guest house. There's a white Range Rover parked in the driveway. *How flashy*, I think.

"Nervous?" Dad asks, hesitating outside the door. He smiles reassuringly down at me.

"Kind of," I admit. I've tried not to think about the endless list of things that could go wrong, but somewhere within me there is a sense of fear. What if they all absolutely hate me?

"Don't be." He opens the door and we head inside, my suitcase trailing behind us, its wheels scraping along the wooden flooring.

In the entryway we're immediately overcome by an overwhelming scent of lavender. In front of me there is a staircase leading upstairs and a door to my right leading, from what I can see through the crack, to the living room. Straight ahead there is a large archway into the kitchen: a kitchen from which a woman is approaching me.

"Eden!" the woman cries. She swallows me into a hug, her

extreme bustiness getting in the way a little, and then takes a step back to examine me. I return the favor. Her hair is blond, figure slim. For some absurd reason I expected her to look similar to my mom. But apparently Dad has altered his taste in women as with his living standards. "It's so nice to finally meet you!"

I take a slight step back from her, fighting the urge to roll my eyes or pull a face. Dad would surely drag me straight back to the airport if I ever displayed such disrespect. "Hi," I say instead.

And then she blurts, "God, you've got Dave's eyes!" which is possibly the worst thing someone could ever say to me given that I'd much rather have my mom's eyes. My mom wasn't the one who walked out.

"Mine are darker," I murmur in disdain.

Ella doesn't push the subject any further and instead turns the conversation around in a completely different direction. "You'll need to meet the rest of us. Jamie, Chase, get down here!" she yells up the stairs before turning back to me. "Did Dave tell you about the get-together we're having tonight?"

"Get-together?" I echo. A social gathering was certainly not on my Things To Do While In California list. Especially when it's strangers who are doing the gathering. "Dad?" I glance sideways up at him, willing myself not to fire a death glare in his direction, and arch my brows.

"We're sparking up the barbecue for the neighbors," he explains. "No better way to kick off the summer than with a good old barbecue." I really wish he'd stop talking.

Quite frankly, I hate both large groups of people and barbecues. "Awesome," I say.

There's a series of thuds as two boys come jogging down

the staircase, their footsteps pounding against the oak as they jump down two steps at a time.

"Is that Eden?" the eldest of the pair whispers to Ella as he reaches us, but I hear him anyway. He must be Jamie. The younger one with the wide eyes must be Chase.

"Hey," I say. My lips curl up into a beaming smile. From what I remember of my conversation in the car, Jamie is fourteen. Despite being two years younger than me, he is about the same height. "What's up?"

"Just hanging out," Jamie answers. He is so totally Ella's child. His sparkling blue eyes and shaggy blond hair make this connection clear. "Do you want a drink or something?"

"I'm good, thanks," I say. From his straightened posture and his attempt at good manners, he seems mature for his age. Perhaps we'll get along well.

"Chase, are you going to say hi to Eden?" Ella encourages.

Chase comes across as very reserved. He too has inherited Ella's flawless genes. "Hi," he mumbles, not quite meeting my eyes. "Mom, can I go to Matt's?"

"Of course, honey, just be back by seven," Ella says. I wonder if she's the type of mom who grounds you for dropping crumbs on the living room carpet or the type who doesn't mind if you disappear for two days. "We're having the barbecue, remember?"

Chase nods and then brushes past me, swinging open the front door and closing it again just as quickly without even a whisper of a goodbye to any of us.

"Mom, do you want me to show her around?" Jamie asks the second his brother is gone.

"That'd be great," I answer for her. Jamie's company will surely be better than my dad's or Ella's or both of them combined. I don't quite see the point in spending time with people I'd much rather be nowhere near. So for now I'll stick to my new, wonderful stepbrothers. Surely they are finding this entire thing just as foreign as I am.

"That's nice of you, Jay," Ella says. She sounds grateful at the idea of not having to be the one to tell me where the bathroom is. "Let her see her room."

Dad gives me a clipped nod and grins. "We'll be in the kitchen if you need anything."

I try to refrain from snorting as Jamie takes my suitcase and begins hauling it up the staircase. Right now, the only things I need are tanned legs and fresh air, which I most certainly won't get from lingering inside with my dad.

As I turn to follow Jamie upstairs, I hear my dad hiss, "Where's Tyler?"

"I don't know," Ella says.

Their voices begin to fade as we all distance ourselves from each other, but not far enough that I can't hear Dad reply with, "So you just let him leave?"

"Yes," says Ella before we move out of hearing range.

"You're right across from me," Jamie informs me as we reach the landing. "You've got the coolest room. The best view."

"Sorry." I laugh lightly and try to keep a smile on my face as he makes his way over to one of the five doors. But I can't help but pause to glance down to the hall below, my eyes focusing on the back of Ella's blond hair as she disappears through the archway into the kitchen.

I figure she's the type who doesn't mind if you disappear.

2

If I could only use one word to describe my new room for the summer, I would use basic. There is no other word for a bed against pale walls and a simple dresser. And nothing else. It's also incredibly hot.

"I like the view," I tell Jamie, despite being nowhere near the window to even see what my view is.

Jamie laughs. "Your dad said you can make the room yours."

I walk around this room of mine, circling the beige carpet and checking out the built-in closets. The sliding doors are mirrored. Much cooler than my tiny closet back home. And there's an en-suite bathroom too. I peer inside the door, raising my eyebrows in satisfaction. The shower looks as though it's never been used.

"Do you like it?" Dad asks from somewhere behind me. I spin around to the sound of his voice and he greets me with a grin. I don't know when he entered the room. "Sorry it's a little hot, I'll turn on the AC. Give it five minutes."

"It's fine," I say. "I like the room." It's almost twice as big as my bedroom in Portland, and so, despite how basic it might be, it is most definitely impossible not to like.

"You hungry?" It seems that questions are the only thing

Dad is great at these days. "You've been traveling all afternoon; you're probably starved half to death. What do you want?"

"I'm good," I say. "I think I'm gonna go for a run. Stretch my legs, you know?" I don't want to ruin my daily running schedule, and taking a quick jog seems like a good way to explore the neighborhood.

I watch the hesitation cross my dad's aging face. For a moment or two he frowns and then sighs as though I've asked him to buy me pot.

"Dad," I say firmly. I tilt my head and force out a gentle but fake laugh. "I'm sixteen; I'm allowed to go out. I just wanna look around."

"At least take Jamie with you," he suggests. Jamie's eyebrows shoot up in curiosity. Or surprise. I'm not sure which. "Jamie," Dad says, "you enjoy running, don't you? Will you go with Eden and make sure she doesn't get lost?"

Jamie glances over to me, offers a knowing, sympathetic smile, and then says, "Sure. I'll get changed." I suppose he understands the struggle of having overprotective parents that treat you like you're five.

So, taking all of this into account, I figure that I'm off to a great start here in Santa Monica. It's only day one and already the awkward tension between my dad and me is close to unbearable. Day one and I'm already being forced to attend a barbecue with a crowd of strangers. Day one and I'm already being escorted while going out for a simple jog.

Day one and I already regret coming here.

"Don't go too far," Dad says, and then leaves the room without closing my door, even after I call after him to do so.

Jamie heads over to it and places a hand on the frame, but not before asking, "You wanna go right now?"

I shrug. "If that's okay with you."

With a quick nod, he makes his way out of my room. He remembers to shut the door.

I would rather not waste too much time inside, especially when the air conditioning doesn't seem to be working, so I haul my suitcase up onto the soft mattress and unzip it. I'm happy to discover that my belongings—ranging from my laptop to my favorite underwear—have all arrived safe and intact. Usually my suitcase arrives with half its contents spilling out of it because baggage handlers tend to be lousy. So I dig through my surprisingly sturdy suitcase, straight to the bottom, because my workout gear was one of the first things I packed.

As I'm prancing into my lavish bathroom to freshen up a little and get changed, my phone vibrates to kindly let me know that it's about to die pretty soon. I remember Amelia asking me to call her when I landed. Setting down my running shorts and sports bra by the sink, I sit down on the sparkling-clean toilet seat and cross my legs. My best friend is on speed dial, so the call starts connecting in a matter of nanoseconds.

"Hello there," Amelia answers in a goofy voice that sounds something like a cross between a cartoon character and a sports commentator.

"Hello," I say back, mimicking her tone. I laugh but then sigh. "This place sucks. Let me come spend the summer with you."

"I want you to! It feels super weird already."

"As weird as meeting your new stepmom?"

"Not that weird," Amelia says. "Is she okay? She isn't like the creepy-ass stepmom in *Cinderella*, right? What about your stepbrothers? Have you been put on babysitting duty already?"

I shake my head even though she can't see me. If only she knew it's the other way around. "Actually, they're not even kids."

"Huh?"

"They're, like, teenagers."

"Teenagers?" she echoes. Before I left, I complained for two weeks straight about how terrified I was of meeting my new stepbrothers, because I have a low tolerance for children under the age of six. It turns out they're all much older than that.

"Yeah," I say. "They're okay. One of them is sorta shy, but he's the youngest, so I get it. The other is a little older and I think we'll get along. I don't know. His name's Jamie."

"I thought you had three brothers," Amelia says. "You said you had three."

"Well, I haven't met the third one yet," I explain. Until this point I had forgotten that I do actually have three new stepbrothers to judge me rather than just two. "I'll probably meet him later. I'm about to go for a run with Jamie."

"Eden," Amelia says, her voice stern yet gentle. "You just got there. Chill out. You look fine."

"No." I press my phone to my ear with my shoulder and reach down to slip off my shoes. "Have they said anything else about me?" I ask slowly, despite however much I'd rather not know. But there's always that interest, that curiosity that eats away at you—and the inability to handle it. And I always give in.

Silence radiates across the line. "Eden, don't think about it."

"So that means yes," I state, mostly to myself. It's almost a whisper, so quiet I don't think Amelia could have heard me. My phone vibrates once more. "Hey, look, this is about to die. I have to go to this lame barbecue tonight. If everyone sucks, I'll text you the entire time so they know I do actually have friends."

Amelia laughs, and I picture her rolling her eyes straight to the back of her head like she usually does. "Sure. Keep me posted."

My phone bails on me before I even get the chance to murmur goodbye, so I toss it onto the sink counter and reach for my clothes instead. Running is great for clearing your head, and clearing my head is exactly what I want to do right now. I change into my running gear effortlessly—I do it so often I could most likely do it in my sleep—and head back downstairs to enter the kitchen for the first time. I'm greeted by black gloss counters and white gloss cabinet doors and more black gloss flooring. Everything is very, very glossy.

"Wow," I say. I glance down at the water bottle in my hand and then to the spotless sink by the window. I'm almost terrified to use it.

"Like it?" Dad asks, and it's only then that I realize he's even in the room. He keeps appearing out of nowhere as though he's following my every move.

"Was it installed yesterday or something?"

He chuckles, shakes his head at me and then walks over to flick on the faucet. "Here. Jamie's waiting for you out front. The kid's stretching."

I shuffle around the island to awkwardly fill my bottle until it overflows, and then I swivel on the lid and get the hell out of there before my dad has a chance to say anything more. I don't know how I'm supposed to survive eight weeks with him.

Jamie is shuttling up and down the sidewalk when I finally head outside to meet him. He stops and grins. "Just warming up," he says.

"Can I join you?" When he nods, I take a quick sip of my water and then step parallel to him, and we slowly jog around the lawn a couple times. And then we set off, making our way through the beautiful neighborhood at a comfortable speed.

It's the first time in a long time that I've run without music as my companion, but only because I figure it would be rude to completely block Jamie out. We engage in brief conversation and the occasional "Let's slow down," and that's about it. But I don't mind. The sun is beating down on us, almost as though its rays have grown stronger over the past hour, and the streets here really are lovely, with their residents walking dogs or cycling or pushing strollers. Perhaps I will fall in love with this city after all.

"Do you hate your dad?" Jamie asks out of nowhere as we retrace our route back toward the house, and it's so sudden that I almost trip over my own feet.

"What?" is the only response that finds its way to my lips. I collect my thoughts and settle my eyes on the sidewalk ahead of me. "It's complicated."

"I like him," Jamie says, or pants. I'm surprised he's still keeping up with me.

"Oh."

"Yeah, but it seems kinda awkward between you and him."

"Yeah," I say, gnawing at my lip while I try to figure out a way to change the subject. "Hey, how cool is that house over there?"

Jamie completely ignores me. "Why is it awkward?"

"Because he sucks," I finally answer. This is true: My dad does suck. "He sucks for walking out. He sucks for not calling. He sucks because he sucks."

"I get it."

Our conversation wraps up there and we jog back to the house, stretching on the lawn before heading inside to shower. Dad doesn't forget to remind us about the barbecue in two hours' time. Jamie and I split up and go into our own rooms.

By this point I feel sweaty and gross, so, after plugging my phone in to charge, the first thing I do is throw my body into the sparkling shower. The water feels amazing and I stay in there for thirty minutes, spending most of the time simply sitting down and basking in the steam. Showers back home were never this good.

I end up taking the remaining hour and a half to get ready. If I could, I'd turn up on the patio in sweats. But I don't think that would go down well with Ella, so I rummage through my suitcase and pull out a pair of skinny pants and a blazer. Smart casual. That should do.

I get dressed, dry my hair, curl it into loose waves, and then apply a fresh layer of makeup. I'm just spraying some body spray when I inhale the waft of . . . well, barbecues. It must be nearing seven.

I head downstairs, following the scent into the kitchen. The two glass patio doors are slid open, and I realize the get-together is already in full swing. So, correction, it must be after seven. There's music playing from speakers somewhere, groups of adults milling around the yard, and everything else that makes social gatherings awful. I spy Chase in the pool with some kids around his age. I also spot Dad flipping burgers on the barbecue over in the corner while attempting to carry out a dance move from the '80s. He looks lame as hell.

"Eden!" a voice calls. When I turn around, I'm irritated to discover that it belongs to Ella. "Get out here!"

Maybe if I fake a seizure I'll get to escape back to my room, or, better yet, home. "Sorry I'm a little late. I wasn't checking the time."

"No, no, you're fine," says Ella. She pushes her sunglasses up to the top of her head as she steps inside for a moment to pull me out onto the grass. "I hope you're hungry."

"Well, actually I—"

"These are our neighbors from across the street," she interrupts, nodding toward a middle-aged couple standing in front of us. "Dawn and Philip."

"It's great to meet you, Eden," Dawn says. It's clear either my dad or Ella or both of them have been informing everyone that I'm here. Philip offers me a half smile.

"You too," I reply. I'm not sure what else there is to say. *Tell me your life story? What are your plans for the future, Dawn and Philip?* I smile instead.

"Our daughter should be coming by too," Dawn continues, which immediately makes me feel unsettled. "She'll keep you company."

"Oh, cool," I say. My eyes drift away from the pair. Clicking with other girls has never been one of my strong points. Girls are terrifying. And meeting new ones is even worse. "Nice to meet you," I say with a farewell smile.

I make a quick escape from them and Ella, hoping to avoid any more awkward introductions. It works for the first forty minutes. I linger by the fence and screw my face up at the awful mainstream crap that's echoing from the speakers at the opposite end of the yard. It's embarrassing to even be here. At least when the food is finally cooked and everyone begins digging in, the noise of their voices helps drown out the horrendous pop music. I pick at the bun of my burger for a few minutes and then end up tossing the entire plate into the trash. And just when I think I've successfully avoided Ella for the night, she decides to haul me around each individual or couple or family and introduce me to them as her new stepdaughter.

"Here's Rachael now!" she says as she's leading me over to another batch of our neighbors.

"Rachael?" I repeat. If it's someone I've been introduced to already then I don't remember. I've been given so many new names to learn within the space of an hour that I've started blanking them all out instead.

"Dawn and Philip's daughter," Ella informs me. She nods over my shoulder, and before I even get the chance to turn around, she's calling, "Rachael! Over here!"

Ugh. I take a deep breath, convince myself that she'll be friendly and nice, and then I plaster the fakest smile I can across my face. The girl joins us and steps around me. "Oh, uh, hey," I blurt.

Ella beams at the two of us. "Eden, this is Rachael."

Rachael smiles too and we end up looking like a trio of serial killers. "Hey!" She shoots Ella an awkward grin.

Ella gets the memo. "I'll leave you guys be then." She laughs before striding off to engage in even more boring conversations with boring people.

"Parents make everything awkward," Rachael says. I immediately like her based on this statement alone. "Have you been stuck here the whole time?"

I wish I could say no. "Unfortunately."

Her hair is long, blond, and definitely not its natural shade. But I'll let that slide simply because she doesn't seem to hate me yet. "I live right across the street, and you probably don't know anyone here, so we can hang out if you'd like. Seriously, come over whenever you want."

I'm surprised yet grateful for the suggestion. There's no way in hell I'm spending eight weeks stuck in the house with my dad and his new family. "Yeah, that sounds good . . ." My voice tapers off as my attention is reeled in by something out front.

I can almost see the road through the gaps in the fence by the side of the house, and I squint through. There's music playing. More like blaring. I can hear it over the crappy music that's already bouncing around the back yard, and as a sleek white car speeds up to the edge of the sidewalk and skids against the curb, I grimace in disgust. The music cuts off the second the engine is killed.

"What are you looking at?" Rachael asks, but I'm too busy staring to even attempt to answer.

The car door swings open roughly, and I'm surprised it doesn't fall straight off its hinges. It's difficult to see clearly through the fence, but a tall guy gets out and slams the door shut just as aggressively as he opened it. He hesitates for a moment, stares at the house, and then runs a hand through his hair. Whoever he is, he looks super wound up. Like he's just lost all his life savings or his dog just died. And then he heads straight for the gate.

"Who the hell is this jackass?" I mutter to Rachael as the figure nears us.

But before either of us can say anything more, Jackass decides to hit the gate open with a fist, drawing the attention of everyone around us. It's like he wants everyone to hate him. I figure he's probably that one neighbor that everyone despises, and he's only here in a fit of rage because he wasn't invited to the lamest barbecue get-together that's ever been hosted.

"Sorry I'm late," Jackass comments sarcastically. And loudly too, with a smirk on his lips. His eyes flash green as emeralds. "Did I miss anything besides the slaughtering of animals?" He throws up the infamous middle finger to, from what I can see, the barbecue. "I hope you guys enjoyed the cow you just ate." And then he laughs. He laughs as though everyone's expressions of disgust are the most entertaining thing he's seen all year.

"More beer?" I hear my dad call out to the silent crowd, and as they chuckle and return to their conversations, Jackass heads through the patio doors. He slams them shut so hard I can almost see the glass tremble.

I'm stunned. I have no idea what just happened or who that was or why he's just entered the house. When I realize I'm slightly slack-jawed, I close my mouth and turn to Rachael.

She bites her lip and pushes her sunglasses down over her eyes. "I'm guessing you haven't met your stepbrother yet."

3

I don't know exactly what I was expecting before I arrived in Los Angeles, but I can say this: I did not expect to have a lunatic for a stepbrother.

"He's the third one?" I spit as the guests around me ignore what just happened. I, on the other hand, simply can't shake the bizarre scene from my mind. Who does that guy think he is?

"Uh, yeah," Rachael says, and then she laughs. "I feel for you. And for all of the heavens above, I really hope your room is nowhere near his."

"Why?"

She looks slightly flustered all of a sudden, as though I've just uncovered her deepest and darkest secret and it just so happens to be the most embarrassing thing in the world. "He can be really annoying to be around, but hey, I really shouldn't say anything. It's none of my business." With her cheeks flushed and a lopsided smile playing on her lips, she quickly changes the subject. "Are you busy tomorrow?"

My mind is still dwelling on what she said about my room. "Yeah—wait, no. Sorry, I don't know why I said yeah. Um." *Way to be awkward, Eden.*

Thankfully Rachael doesn't write me off as a complete idiot

just yet. Instead she laughs again. "Do you wanna hang out? We could go to the promenade or something."

"Sounds good," I say. I'm still a little distracted and a little confused and a little irritated by Jackass's rude entrance. He couldn't have just come in through the front door? Was it necessary to even say anything?

"It's amazing for shopping!" Rachael continues to talk, occasionally flicking her blond hair over her shoulders, the strands whipping my face each time. Eventually she stops babbling about the promenade and says, "I've got a bunch of stuff to do, so I'm gonna head home. Sorry I can't stay longer. Mom wanted me to drop by on my way back to the house to say hey. So hey."

"Hey," I say. She tells me she'll see me tomorrow, and then departs just as quickly as she arrived, leaving me alone with a semi-drunk group of adults. And Chase.

"Eden," he says as he approaches. He says my name so slowly and so carefully that it's obvious he's testing it on his lips. "Eden," he says again, this time much faster and blunter, "where's the soda?" His friends slowly edge toward us, their wide eyes innocent and anxious. *Right*, I think, *because I am oh-so-intimidating.*

"Probably on the table," I suggest. "Ask your mom."

"She's inside," Chase says. And then one of his friends shoves him forward, laughing as though it's the greatest prank in the world, and Chase bumps into my body with a soft thud. He reels back immediately and is, quite obviously, a little embarrassed. It's then that I realize my tank top is damp. "Sorry," he blurts. He glances down at the empty plastic cup in his hand. It was a quarter full a second ago.

"It's fine," I say. In fact, it's great. Now I get to head inside and escape this terrible barbecue while I change my shirt. I make my getaway then, almost gleefully twirling into the house. Hopefully Dad will have one beer too many and won't notice if I decide not to head back out there for the rest of the night. I'll hang out in my ever-basic room and call my mom or video chat with Amelia or maybe break both my legs. Any one sounds better than standing alone outside.

I heave an exhausted sigh—it's been a hell of a tiring day—and make for the staircase. But I've barely set foot on the first step when I hear explosive yelling bouncing from the walls of the living room. And I'm too curious, too intrigued to even think about ignoring it. So I don't. I edge toward the small gap in the door.

From my limited view, I see Ella close her eyes and bury her head in her hands as she rubs her temples. "I'm not even late," a male voice says from somewhere at the opposite side of the room. His tone is harsh and I immediately realize it belongs to Jackass.

"You're two hours late!" Ella yells, and I find myself taking a slight step back as her eyes snap open. I'm afraid she'll spot me.

Jackass laughs. "You really think I'm gonna come home to watch a damn barbecue?"

"What is your problem this time? Forget the barbecue," says Ella, and she begins to pace back and forth across the cream carpet. "You were acting like a little kid before you even got out of the car. What's wrong?"

He's a little out of breath as he clenches his jaw and angles his face to the side. "Nothing," he says, his teeth grinding together.

"It's clearly not nothing." Ella's tone is stern and scolding, which is a far cry from the sweet tone I was offered just fifteen minutes ago. "You just humiliated me again in front of half the neighborhood!"

"Whatever."

"I shouldn't have let you leave," Ella says, more quietly this time, as though it's herself she's mad at. "I should have just made you stay, but no, of course I didn't, because there I was, trying to cut you some slack, and you throw it back in my face as usual."

"I would have left anyway," Jackass retorts. He steps into my view, shaking his head as he chuckles at Ella. His back is turned and it gives me a chance to get a half-decent look at him—he stormed past us all so quickly the first time that I barely had a chance to take in anything. "What are you gonna do? Ground me again?" His voice is deep and husky and his hair is almost jet black. It's tousled yet neat, and his shoulders are broad, and he is tall. Very tall. He towers over Ella by several inches.

"You're impossible," she states through gritted teeth. But as she says this, her eyes flicker over his shoulder for a split second and she fixes her gaze directly on me.

My breath catches in my throat as I scramble away from the door, desperately wishing that she hasn't actually seen me, that perhaps she was glancing toward the door and not the person hiding behind it. But my wishing proves to be a waste of hope when the door swings open seconds later, before I've had the chance to make my escape.

"Eden?" Ella steps into the hall and her eyes drop to mine, for I'm half sprawled across the staircase. My pathetic attempt to quickly clamber upstairs hasn't worked out that well.

"Um," I say. If my arms weren't frozen stiff, I'd be face-palming right now.

And then the worst thing in the world happens. Jackass sticks his head around the door frame and moves out into the hall beside us, and that's when I get a good look at him up close for the first time. His eyes are emerald—too bright to be considered a mere green and too vibrant to be considered normal—and they narrow at me in a way that sends a shiver down my spine. His jaw clenches again, wiping the smirk completely off his face.

"Who the hell is this chick?" he demands, his eyes flashing sideways to Ella as he awaits an explanation for why there's a clueless teenager on his staircase looking like she's doing aerobics.

I can see the hesitance cross Ella's features as she carefully considers how to reply. Gently, she reaches for his arm. "Tyler," she says, "this is Eden. Dave's daughter."

Jackass—or, more formally, Tyler—snorts. "Dave's kid?"

I push myself up a little and get to my feet, but he's still looking away. "Hi," I try. I'm about to hold out my hand, but then I realize how stupid I'll look, so I interlink my fingers instead.

His eyes finally move back to mine. He just stares at me. Stares, and stares. It's like he's never seen another human being before, because to begin with he appears confused, and then angry, and then perplexed again. His sharp eyes make me feel uncomfortable as he studies me, so I drop mine to his casual brown boots and jeans for a second. When I steal a lock at him, he slowly swallows and glances at Ella. "Dave's kid?" he repeats, this time his voice much quieter, laced with disbelief.

Ella sighs. "Yes, Tyler. I already told you she was coming. Don't act stupid."

He's facing Ella, but out of the corner of his eye, he's looking me up and down again. "Which room?"

"What?"

"Which room is she staying in?" It feels odd hearing him talk about me like I'm not even here, and judging by his reaction, I'm guessing he wishes that was the case.

"The one next to yours."

He dramatically groans, exaggerating his annoyance at knowing I'll be near him, and then turns back to fully look at me. Now he's glaring. Does he think I want to be living in this house with this pathetic excuse for a family? Because I don't.

Once he's glowered at me, as though to make a statement, he nudges Ella to the side and then barges past me and storms upstairs.

For the several long seconds that it takes for us to hear a door slam, Ella and I remain silent. Waiting for him to slam a door before talking again seems like it must be a daily occurrence in this house.

"I'm sorry," Ella apologizes. She genuinely looks stressed and mortified, and I find myself feeling sympathetic. Maybe even empathetic. If I had to deal with as big a moron as him every day, I'd probably have three breakdowns every twenty-four hours. "He's just . . . Look, let's head back outside."

No thank you. "Actually, Chase spilled his drink on me, so I've got to change my shirt."

"Oh," she says. Her eyebrows arch as she studies the damp stain on my tank top with a slight grimace. "I hope he apologized for it."

As she makes her way back to the yard, I finally move up the staircase—swiftly this time, without looking deformed—and collapse into my room, breathing a sigh of relief the second I get the door shut. Alone at last, with no one to irritate me.

For exactly eight seconds, until music starts blasting from

the room next door so loud I fear the wall might collapse. Rachael said she hoped my room was nowhere near Tyler's. Forget being near—I'm next door. I feel speechless and annoyed and tired as I stand in the center of my room and stare at the far wall. On the other side of it, a moron sleeps at night.

Thankfully after about five minutes the music dies down until it's silent again, the only noise the sound of a door opening. Perhaps my stepbrother has calmed down by now. And it's this hope that draws me toward my own door, pulling it open slowly to meet the fierce, far-from-calm eyes outside.

"Hi," I try again. If this person is now a permanent fixture of my new "family," I need to at least make an effort. "Are you okay?"

Tyler's emerald eyes laugh at me. "Bye," he says. With the same red flannel shirt on his back and brown boots on his feet, he smoothly descends the staircase and heads out the front door without a single person noticing his departure besides me. He is quite clearly grounded, but it seems he couldn't care less.

I simply sigh and shuffle back into my room. At least I tried, which is far from what he did. I slip off my blazer and haul off my tank top, dropping it on the floor before collapsing onto my new bed for the first time. The foam mattress engulfs my body, and once I develop the ability to tune out the faint pumping of music laced with drunken laughter, I stare at the ceiling and just breathe. I breathe even when an engine growls to life outside and catapults a car down the street. Presumably Tyler.

I use the next hour to call Amelia, emphasizing just how agonizing the barbecue was and how lame my dad is and how much of a douchebag Tyler is. I offer my mom a similar summary.

"Eden." Dad's voice echoes through my door a little while later when I'm half asleep. He opens my door and walks in before I even give him the right to. "That's the neighbors all pretty much headed home," he says. He smells of burnt meat and beer. "We're going to hit the sack. I'm done for the day."

I offer him a quick goodnight and then roll over to face the wall, burying my head in my comforter as he leaves. People say it's either very easy to fall asleep in a foreign bed or very, very difficult. And right now, despite the fatigue overcoming every inch of my body, I'm beginning to realize that it's the latter. I roll back over and press a hand to my forehead. The day's heat is trapped in my new room, and the AC still hasn't come on. I can't decide if it's broken or if Dad has just completely forgotten about it. Either way, I'll mention it in the morning.

It takes me a good hour of tossing and turning and testing my will to live before I do finally fall asleep. For exactly forty-seven minutes. Nothing seems to last long in this house before it gets interrupted.

I'd assumed if anything were to waken me it would be the scorching heat in my room, not the sound of drunken wails bouncing through my open window. The moans and groans and occasional cursing make my ears prick up and my eyes widen. I creep across the floor on my bare knees, slowly and on high alert. I steal a peek over the window ledge. The cool night air feels great against my face.

"No," a drunk Tyler tells the air. "No." His expression is completely solemn. A hand is pressed firmly to the lawn.

"What the hell is going on?" As he talks to no one but himself, his voice is hushed. I figure he must have walked home, since his car seems to be nowhere around, which reassures me that he does have some common sense. Driving under the influence is too idiotic even for him. "When did it pass midnight?" A tremendous laugh escapes his lips and into the air.

"Hey," I whisper-yell out the window as I sit up and push it open a little wider. "Up here."

It takes Tyler's rolling eyes a good few seconds to locate my voice, and when he spots me up on the second floor he blesses me with a glare. "What the hell do you want?"

"Are you okay?" Once the words leave my lips, I realize how pointless the question is. He is clearly not okay.

"Open the door," he says. His words are slightly slurred as he talks. With a single nod, he advances beneath the slanted roof and out of my view, but not without swaying.

Because I've stripped down to nothing but my underwear in an attempt to cool down, I quickly grab the first pieces of clothing that find their way into my hands and pull them on as I jog down the staircase. I'm careful to remain silent. I keep the lights off and my steps quiet. The outline of his figure is sharp through the glass panels of the front door.

"What am I doing?" I whisper as I play around with the lock. The jackass who has done nothing but irk the hell out of me is asking me to let him into the house, and I'm doing it? Yet without hesitating, I pull open the door the second I hear the lock click.

"You took your damn time, huh?" Tyler mutters as he barges past me. He carries with him the charming scent of booze and cigarettes.

I close the door and lock it again. "Are you drunk?"

"No," he says. His grin is wide and it soon quickly falters into a smirk. "Is it morning yet?"

"It's 3AM."

He chuckles to himself and then attempts to get upstairs, but it involves a series of stumbles and trips. "When did these get here?" he asks as he pats one of the steps. "They weren't here before."

I ignore him. "Do you want water or something?"

"Get me another beer," is his answer. Through the darkness, I see him reach the landing and then disappear into his room, thankfully without slamming the door this time. Surely Ella would have him murdered if she saw him right now, drunk and unable to hold himself up for more than a few seconds.

I swiftly follow suit, creeping upstairs and into my own room, hauling off my clothes again and strewing them carelessly across the floor. The room is still unbelievably hot, so instead of crawling back into bed and dying of heat exhaustion, I sit down by the window. I press my face to the cool glass and breathe in the night air. There's a crushed beer can by the mailbox.

Jackass.

4

When Rachael said she would talk to me in the morning, I didn't expect her to turn up at my dad's front door at 10:04AM. Waking up, never mind socializing, before noon during summer is an absurd thing to do. It's against the norms of society for any sane teenager. I shoot Rachael a heavy glare the second I descend the staircase.

Dad holds the door open with one hand, a coffee mug in the other and a grin on his face. "Here she comes now!"

"Bye, Dad," I say gently, and throw in an eye-roll too. He continues to beam down at me—it's like I'm in kindergarten again and I've just made my first friend—and then finally shifts through to the living room. "He's so embarrassing."

Rachael laughs. "So's mine. It must be a rule that all dads have to be lame."

"Yeah," I say. Still half asleep, I'm surprised I'm even able to string words together. "I didn't realize we'd be leaving so early."

Rachael's eyes widen as she smiles in a this-girl-is-so-stupid sort of way. "It's Saturday; if we're going to the promenade, we need to go super early, because it's gonna be packed!" I don't even know what a promenade is.

"Ohhh." I pause for a second (or four) to run my eyes

over Rachael's outfit. She's wearing cute shorts and a cream button-down blouse and aviator sunglasses and a whole collection of jewelry. And I'm wearing an oversized T-shirt with cartoon alpacas on it. "I'm gonna go get ready. Do you want to come in and wait or . . .?"

"Just come over to my place when you're ready," she says, and then adds for clarification, "It's that one." She points to the house across the street. Before heading back over, she politely asks me to hurry up.

It takes me thirty minutes to get ready. I skip breakfast, spend six minutes in the shower, pull on an outfit similar to hers, leave my hair down, and apply a light layer of makeup. Nothing too complicated and nothing too time-consuming.

"I'm going out now," I tell Dad as I stick my head around the kitchen archway after following the sound of his voice.

He stops mid-conversation with Ella. "Be careful and don't stay out late. Where are you going?"

I shrug. "Somewhere called a promenade or something like that, I think."

"Oh! Tyler's at the promenade too," Ella comments. I'd forgotten about that moron until now.

Dad automatically turns to fix his eyes on her. "Isn't he grounded?" he asks, his tone a little harsh. It seems he can't stand the guy either, and I really can't blame him. Tyler isn't the warmest of people. "Stop cutting him so much slack. You need to stop backing down."

"Have fun," Ella says to me and smiles, completely ignoring my dad's fuming expression. It's like his words completely bypass her mind.

The awkwardness grows and I get out of there as fast as

I can. I don't want to keep Rachael waiting. Pissing off my new friend on the second day of knowing her isn't something I particularly want to do. Thankfully, when I arrive on Rachael's driveway at 10:37AM she doesn't seem annoyed, despite clearly having been waiting for me—no one rushes out of a house this early for no reason.

"It's gonna be hot today," Rachael says. She throws her head back to the sky as she exhales. Admittedly, yes, the weather is much hotter than it was yesterday. And it's not even 11AM yet. "Alright, let's go." There's a red Bug parked by us on the drive, and she pulls out a set of keys and unlocks it.

I'm a little skeptical before getting in. "When did you pass the test?"

Rachael arches a brow and sighs as I unintentionally stall her journey to the promenade. "November," she answers. I stare at her. "I know what you're thinking: It hasn't been twelve months yet. But around here no one follows all those bullshit restrictions, so come on and get in."

Ignoring the fact that it's illegal for me to get in the car with her, not twenty, I settle into the passenger seat. I take extra care to ensure my seatbelt is secure. "So you're seventeen?" I guess. Rachael backs out onto the road.

"Yeah, I'm about to be a senior," she says, but her attention is clearly focused on the street ahead as we pull away ridiculously fast. "Same age as Tyler. We go to school together. You?"

"Junior." Only two years left of high school before I hopefully get to pack up and head for the University of Chicago. The wait is taking forever, and I've already started filling out my Early Action application, because I'm just that desperate to get in. My heart has been set on Chicago ever since freshman year, and although Mom would much rather I applied for Portland State University, I feel Chicago has the better psychology program, and psychology is all I've ever been interested in. I'm curious about people.

"Junior year is the worst," is the advice Rachael gives me. "You're gonna hate it!" She switches on the radio then, and it blasts to life in a way that's almost deafening as we hurl along Deidre Avenue and turn left. Rachael sings along.

As we drive for five minutes, I can't figure out if I feel nauseous because of Rachael's terrible driving or because we're heading to a social spot with hoards of people. Hoards that include Tyler.

"Meghan's coming too, by the way," says Rachael as she lowers the volume of the music. She pulls up by a pale-bricked house on the corner of the street and honks her horn. I play anxiously with my fingers.

A few moments later, an Asian American girl with glossy dark hair half jogs over to the vehicle. She slides into the backseat behind Rachael, saying, "Hey, guys!" in a soft voice.

Rachael starts up the engine. "Hey, Meg. This is Eden, Tyler's sister."

"Stepsister," I correct. I tilt my head over my shoulder to meet her eyes. "Nice to meet you."

"You too," Meghan says, offering me a wide smile as she pulls on her seatbelt. "You're here for the summer, right?"

"Yeah."

The music blows up again, leaving no room for conversation, and I'm grateful. We soon emerge from the residential side of the city and head into the more industrial area, passing motels and cafés and office buildings. Soon we're crawling through traffic.

"I hate trying to find a spot to park," Rachael complains, despite pulling into a parking structure, accelerating up three levels, and then pulling into a free spot—diagonally. "Now let's hit the stores!"

I still don't know what a promenade is.

We make our way back down to the ground while I trail slightly behind. Rachael and Meghan are walking way too fast, and I'm quite happy with walking slow to take in my surroundings. I follow them around the corner and onto the next street. And it's then that I discover what a promenade is—it's a huge pedestrian-only street cluttered with designer stores and expensive restaurants and flashy movie theaters, and it's the kind of overrated entertainment complex that I usually hate.

"Eden, meet Third Street Promenade!" Rachael says, and I cringe. "My favorite place in the whole of Los Angeles. You can't beat it."

"Same," Meghan adds. They must both be either insane or just extremely mainstream and cliché. Of course they love this wonderful, fantastic promenade, because they are girls. Pretty girls. It's only natural for them to grow attached to a place like this, for it to become their safe haven.

"This is so cool," I say. My voice is so dry that it's blatantly obvious I'm lying. I attempt to chirp up, so I clear my throat and keep going. "How far does this place stretch for?"

"Three blocks!" Rachael glances at her watch and then waves her hands around erratically. "Now come on, we're wasting shopping time!"

God. Shopping is one of the worst pastimes to ever exist,

unless it's scouring the shelves of a bookstore. I don't think Rachael and Meghan are into that type of shopping. This is confirmed when they pull me into American Apparel.

"You're basically a tourist," Rachael says, "so you should probably knock yourself out. I need a new pair of pants, so I'm gonna go find some."

"I need a new bra," Meghan comments.

They both strut off without another word, leaving me alone in this huge store to do something I hate—shop. Admittedly, I could do with some new outfits for the summer, so I man up and begin rummaging and sifting through racks and rails of clothes. Eventually I find a cute skirt and an Aztec-print top that can both pass as acceptable. I decide to try them on for size, and I groan when I discover the line by the fitting rooms.

"Eden," Rachael says as she approaches out of nowhere. "Get outta this line."

I stare at her. "What?"

"Because—" she says, but then stops when the woman in front of me turns around to look her up and down. Rachael grasps my elbow and pulls me away. "Because," she says again, "there are fitting rooms at the back of the store that are closed, but we always use them anyway. Beats waiting in line. C'mon, I'll show you." With a pile of pants over her arm, she directs me through the store to the very back corner. "I need to finish looking, so just come find us when you're done or whatever."

When she twirls off again, I find myself staring at a white door with a sign informing me that it is, indeed, closed to all customers. I don't know if Rachael is playing a joke on me or something equally as cruel, but I glance all around to make sure the coast is clear before slipping inside. I feel scandalous.

I'll try the items on quickly and then get out of here as fast as I can, before I get caught. It's quiet besides the sound of the lame store music, and I slip into the first cubicle I come to. My heart is racing and I have no idea why. Reaching for my shirt to pull it off, I hear a giggle from the cubicle next to mine, and my entire body freezes as my breath catches in my throat.

"Stoooop," the voice whisper-giggles. It's so light and so quiet that it's barely audible. It definitely belongs to a female.

"Babe," a male voice murmurs, low and firm. There's the sound of lips smacking. Or skin and lips. I can't tell the difference.

"What is that you're wearing?" the girl asks. More smacking noises. "Is that Montblanc? It smells like it."

"No, it's Bentley," the guy answers. I sniff. There is an amazing scent of cologne lingering in the air. "Come here." Even more smacking. A body thuds against the wall of my cubicle, and I try not to exhale as my hands hover in mid-air.

The girl laughs. "What are you doing?"

"What?"

"Whatever it is you're doing right now. It feels nice."

"Of course it does."

My face contorts with disgust and I press a hand to my mouth as I shake my head. This is the most awkward thing I've ever experienced. In fear of these people glancing down and seeing my feet through the opening at the bottom of the divider, I silently step up onto the chair. I'd try to leave without them ever knowing I was here, but the thought of me making a sound and them discovering my presence is keeping me glued to the spot. I tilt my head to the side and let my eyes fall to the floor. They may not be able to see my feet, but I can certainly see theirs. Sky-blue flats and brown boots.

"Tyler," the girl gasps as she pulls her lips away, "we're not doing that here."

I don't know what it is that they're not doing here, but I do know that those brown boots and the voice and the name Tyler click in my mind all at once. Please, God, no.

It's then that I almost throw up, and it's also then that I hear Rachael call, "Eden, are you still in here?"

Without waiting a second longer, I snatch the clothes from the wall and leap off the chair, throwing open the curtain and fixing Rachael with a frantic stare. I make my way toward her, half jogging as I wave my hand around in an attempt to let her know that we need to get the hell out of here.

"Shhh," the girl says sharply, and then, louder, "Who's here?"

I try to push Rachael out the door, but she stops. "Tiffani?"

"Rachael?" The curtain of the cubicle next to mine slides open, and a tall, platinum blond girl takes a step out. Her cheeks flush with color and she bites her lip. Half the buttons on her blouse are undone. "Um, I didn't know anyone was in here."

Clearly, I think.

"What are you doing?" Rachael asks, raising her eyebrows suspiciously. "Tyler, are you there too?" We wait for a response.

"Yeah, I'm here." Tyler steps out around the curtain just as he's pulling on a faded gray T-shirt, and then he runs his hand through his hair. Admittedly, he looks a lot better than he did in the early hours of the morning. "Ever heard of privacy?"

"Ever heard of not hooking up in the middle of American Apparel?" Rachael shoots back, her voice even, her nose wrinkling. "That's gross."

Tiffani's perfectly arched brows and high cheekbones and plump lips all fall to the floor. At first she appears abashed at being discovered, but then her expression hardens as she quickly closes up the buttons on her blouse. I have to look away.

"What the hell are you guys even doing here?" Tyler asks, locking his attention on me. His sharp eyes fix on me for several seconds, and a shiver surges down my spine as I worry about what he might say next.

"Trying on clothes," Rachael answers tersely, "which is a normal thing to do in fitting rooms."

Tiffani throws her a death glare before locking her eyes on me, clearly pissed off. She tilts her head. "And you are?"

"Eden," I murmur. I'm struggling to meet her eyes, partially because I feel so small and partially because the circumstances are awkward. I look to Tyler instead. "His stepsister."

"You have a stepsister?" Tiffani's tone softens only briefly as her eyebrows knit together. She flashes her eyes at Tyler.

He just shrugs. "Apparently."

She blinks at him for a few seconds, as though a stepsister is some sort of mythical creature that only exists in fairy tales. When she eventually comes to terms with it, she glances back over to me, her eyes narrowed. Her tone is sour. "Why were you in here? Were you spying on us?"

"Chill, babe," Tyler tells her, saving me from having to muster up an answer, and reaches for her arm. "It's not even a big deal. Stop tripping out."

Tiffani's eyes grow wide as she parts her lips, appalled at his lack of care. She folds her arms across her chest and sulks. "I'm just saying."

"Yeah, well, don't," he says. He presses his lips together,

shrugs again. "She doesn't care. Let's just go. I need to go to Levi's." He throws his arm impatiently over her shoulders and pulls her against his body, but she heaves a sigh and stands her ground, pausing to meet Rachael's eyes.

"I'll see you on Tuesday," she tells her. "You're still coming to the beach, right?"

"Yeah," Rachael says, and then glances at me. In that second I know exactly what she's thinking, and I pray she doesn't say it loud. But, of course, she does. "Eden can come too, right?"

Ugh.

Tiffani's features harden again as she exhales slowly, evidently having a mock debate with herself on whether or not she should allow the intruder to invade her beach plans. Eventually, she just murmurs, "I guess."

And then she allows Tyler to pull her away, his arm slung around the back of her neck. She's semi-mortified and semi-irritated. It'll probably take several hours before the rose tint fades from her cheeks.

I stare at Rachael in the new silence that appears once they leave, arching a brow in curiosity. "Girlfriend," she tells me. "They've been dating since freshman year. You're probably scarred for life."

I shake my head and breathe for the first time in ten minutes. "He's such an asshole."

"He's Tyler Bruce," Rachael says. "He's always an asshole."

5

In all honesty, my afternoon at the promenade with Rachael and Meghan wasn't that bad. They didn't spend too long in the same store, they didn't blow their entire allowances on shoes, and surprisingly they both love coffee, which I discovered when we stopped at a small, minimalist coffee shop just around the corner on Santa Monica Boulevard. It was called the Refinery and it served the best latte I've had in a long time.

"Are you sure you're not coming?" Dad asks for the eighth time now as he pops his head around my door.

I'm in the process of painting my toes a bright sapphire, but I pause to glance over my shoulder to the irritating human being behind me. "I'm sure," I say. "I still don't feel too great." I return to my nails and keep my face down. I'm an awful liar, and back when I was younger Dad used to know whenever I was lying just by looking at me. Hopefully it's not that noticeable anymore.

"There's food in the refrigerator if you get hungry."

"Okay," I say, and he leaves the room.

Perhaps avoiding a family meal is an unsociable thing to do, but just the thought of spending Saturday evening with my reconstituted family is enough to give me a migraine. In the two hours that I've been home from the promenade, Dad has done nothing but pester me about attending this horrendous event. I am consistently rejecting the offer.

Finishing off my nails and tidying up after myself, I prance around my room on the balls of my feet and then head out onto the landing when Ella calls up the staircase that they're about to leave. I've barely begun to descend the stairs when Tyler emerges from his room.

His eyes narrow the second he sees me, and for a long moment he just glares at me. Me and my sweatpants. "Aren't you going?"

"Aren't you?" I shoot back. He's wearing a navy hoodie with the hood pulled up. There's an earphone dangling from one ear.

"Grounded." He snorts and rubs his temple. "What's your excuse?"

"Sick," I lie. I turn around and make my way downstairs to the hall, but I feel him close behind me. "And that's weird: Being grounded didn't stop you from going to American Apparel," I throw over my shoulder in a hushed voice.

"Shut the hell up," he hisses.

When we reach the hall, Dad is waiting by the front door with Ella by his side. Jamie and Chase look bored as hell. Being younger, it must be harder for them to get out of these sorts of atrocious social events.

"We won't be too late," Ella says. She fixes Tyler with a firm look. It's almost as though she's worried to leave him alone. She should be. "Don't even think about leaving."

"Mom, I wouldn't dare," he says, but the sarcasm is dripping from his voice. He leans against the wall and folds his arms across his chest.

"Can we go now?" Chase asks. I'm thankful I don't have to go through what he's about to. "I'm hungry."

"Yes, yes, let's go," Dad says. He opens up the door, tells Chase and Jamie to go to the car, and throws me a sympathetic glance. "I hope you feel better, Eden."

I just smile. "Bye."

"Behave yourselves," Ella warns. She still looks apprehensive, but they all leave nonetheless.

When they shut the door behind them and the house falls into an odd silence, it occurs to me then that I'm left alone with the moron next to me. For the entire evening. I turn to face him. His eyes are already on me. "Um," I say.

"*Um,*" he mimics in a voice that sounds absolutely nothing like mine.

"Um," I say again.

"I'm gonna grab a shower," he tells me. "That's if you'd get out my way."

I step to the side of the staircase and he barges past me, the same way he shoved past yesterday, like I'm merely an obstacle in his path. "Rude," I mutter under my breath. In the forty-eight hours I've been here, he hasn't said one nice word to me. He doesn't appear to have any manners, either. I'm thankful I won't have to talk to him for at least five minutes.

Bored already, I head for the living room and get comfortable on the couch. The truth is, when you're new to a city and have zero friends, you end up spending your Saturday night alone in your stepfamily's immaculate living room watching reruns of *Keeping Up with the Kardashians*, because the only thing to do when your life sucks is to watch someone else's. Admittedly, Amelia would kill me if she knew I watched this show. It's not that I actually like it or anything. Well, maybe a little, but I'd never tell her.

During my time in front of the TV, I also bombard my mom with several texts containing nothing but complaints about Dad. She agrees with each one.

I'm looking at my phone when a female voices calls "Hello?" from the hall. The front door clicks shut. I stop moving and pause the TV. Surely it's not Ella. It's only been thirty minutes and I doubt they've even eaten their appetizers yet.

"Hello?" I call back.

"Who the hell is that?" the voice explodes, startling me to the point where I retreat back into the couch. A figure swings open the living room door and enters with her lips pressed firmly together. It's Tiffani. She breathes a sigh of relief when she sees me. "Sorry, I thought . . ."

"You thought what?" I prompt as I stare back at her blankly.

"Nothing," she says quickly. "Where's Tyler?"

That is the moment when I become no longer interested. I turn back to the TV, taking it off pause and continuing with the episode. "I haven't seen him since he went to take a shower."

"Thanks." She leaves the living room, and I listen to the sound of her footsteps as she jogs up the staircase as though this were her own home. I slowly lower the volume of the TV and wait, admittedly attempting to eavesdrop.

For a good three minutes I can't hear anything, but then their voices grow louder as they head downstairs together. I press the back of my hand to my lips and stare at the door in curiosity.

"Chill out," Tyler says. "I was gonna head over in an hour, like you said."

"You could have at least answered my calls," Tiffani says.

"I couldn't hear them over my music." They both come to

a halt in the hall and I stare at them through the open door. Tyler notices. "Now what the hell is your problem?"

"Geez," I say.

Tiffani shakes her head disapprovingly at him. It makes me wonder how she puts up with him. "Shut up, Tyler."

"Whatever," he mutters while turning his back to me, his face nothing but a rigid scowl. "Let's just get outta here."

"Actually . . ." Tiffani's voice tapers off and her bottom lip juts out as she glances up at him from beneath her eyelashes. Tyler doesn't take her smug expression lightly.

"What now?"

Tiffani enters the living room and steps in front of the TV. I'd call her out on it, but I'm not quite yet in a comfortable enough position to be able to argue with these strangers.

"New plan," she says, and I notice how she begins glancing between both Tyler and me. I feel inclined to listen. Rightly so, because what she says next takes us both by surprise. "Austin's throwing a last-minute party and we're going. You too, Eden." She fixes her eyes on me. "It's Eden, right? You don't really look the partying type, but Rachael says I have to invite you along. So come."

"Back up a second," Tyler orders, furrowing his eyebrows and marching over to her. In a hushed voice, he murmurs by her ear, "I thought we were going to your place. You know . . ." But it's not hushed enough, and it's clear what their intentions had been.

"Reschedule that," she whispers. Clasping her hands together, she steps around him and raises her voice again. "Okay, so you're coming, Eden. And you too, Tyler. You're coming and you're not getting wasted for once."

"The fuck?"

"Rachael and Megs are already at my place getting ready, so come on, let's go!" She pulls a set of car keys from her back pocket and makes for the door, but I quickly call her back.

"Wait, I need to get an outfit," I blurt. I get to my feet and glance up at the ceiling. Maybe if I'm lucky it'll collapse on me. "Give me five minutes to find something." Right now I'm wondering why I keep finding myself in these awful situations, but for some reason I just can't seem to say no.

Tiffani laughs, reaches for my arm, and pulls me toward her. When she talks again, her voice is laced with pity. "You can borrow something of mine. Now come on! We're leaving in two hours." Letting go of me, she twirls away and heads outside. Tyler shoves his way in front of me and also makes for the front door.

"I thought you were grounded," I say.

Turning around, he stares back at me evenly, smirking in a way that is far from friendly. "And I thought you were sick."

That shuts me up.

The drive to Tiffani's house is nothing but a journey full of anxiety. I can think about one thing and one thing only: I haven't shaved my legs. This fact torments me for the entire ten minutes that I'm in stuck in the sporty vehicle, crammed into the tiny backseat with my knees shoved into my chest because Tyler selfishly decides to push his chair as far back as it can go. Neither of them includes me in the conversation. Not that I care, anyway. They're only talking about the latest drama and gossip in their high school. Apparently Evan Myers and Nicole Martinez broke up, whoever they are.

Tiffani's house is on the edge of the neighborhood on a large piece of land, and it's made of the kind of marble that suggests she probably has a butler to wait on her. But when we pull up and get inside, there are no butlers and no servants. It's just a regular house made of very expensive material.

"Your mom's still out, right?" Tyler asks. His previous intentions are even clearer now.

"Yeah," Tiffani says. "There's beer in the kitchen. Kick back down here while we get ready, but take it easy." She shoots him a warning glare. There's music echoing loudly from upstairs. She grasps my hand and begins pulling me in the direction of it. We ascend the staircase—marble, of course. "We won't be long!" Tiffani calls over the banister.

"Tiff?" Rachael's disembodied voice calls from the room at the end of the long hallway. The music dies at the same time. "Tiffani?"

"I'm back!" Tiffani pushes open the closed door and waltzes in. I trail behind.

"Eden!" Rachael immediately gets to her feet, despite being in the process of doing Meghan's hair, waving the curling iron around in mid-air and grinning at me. "You came!"

I didn't really get the chance not to, I think. "Are you sure it's okay for me to come?" I ask no one in particular.

"I guess so," Tiffani answers. It's not very convincing. She heads over to her closet—which is merely an archway leading into a section of the room overflowing with clothing—and glances over her shoulder at me. "Rachael says you're only here for the summer, right?"

"Yeah."

"Right, so you've got to make the best of it, I suppose."

"She's right," Meghan says from her position on the floor, draped in a silk dressing gown with her hair only three-quarters curled. "We'll make sure your summer doesn't suck."

Too late, I think. *It already does.*

"Come pick a dress!" Tiffani squeals, but the enthusiasm sounds fake. "I say go for black. Black or red. You'd suit that. And tight. Yeah. Wait, Meghan, you're wearing red, aren't you? Okay, tight and black. Let's go for that." Despite just asking me to come pick a dress, she hands me one before I even get the chance to look at it, but then she immediately draws it back. "Actually, this one might be too tight on you," she murmurs as her eyes run up and down my body, and I can feel myself shrinking beneath her scrutiny. Did she just imply I'm chubby?

I'd like to believe it wasn't intentional, that she didn't mean it in such a way, but it still hurts. I try my hardest to let it bypass my mind, but it's already too late. It repeats itself over and over again, endlessly and agonizingly, even while Tiffani is piling new dresses into my arms and bubbling with more of that same forced enthusiasm. I try to breathe in. I try to deceive myself into believing that she's wrong.

With a stack of outfit options in my hands, all black dresses, she leaves me to get ready, and I start by letting my hair down and borrowing her hot iron to straighten it. Meghan offers to do my makeup for me. Tiffani finds a pair of platform heels that match the dress she's given me, because fortunately we share the same shoe size. And when the time comes for me to actually put the dress on, I confide in Rachael about my unshaven leg hair. After a brief moment of laughter, she sends me into Tiffani's grand and glorious bathroom to fix myself up, giving me clear instructions on where to find the disposable razors.

I'm just finishing up and slipping into the dress—the very, very tight dress, which only makes me feel worse—when I hear Tyler enter Tiffani's room. I step back into the room to find that all of us are now dressed and ready to leave. But even though Tiffani, Rachael and Meghan's dresses all look as tight as mine, I still feel awfully inappropriate. I can feel it clinging to every inch of my body.

"Alright, can we head over there now?" Tyler asks, quite blatantly bored. He's been waiting around for two hours with beer as his only companion, and this is evident in his unsteady balance. "Dean and Jake are already there."

"Do I look good?" Tiffani asks, twirling around in a slow circle to ensure he gets a good look at her body. Her dress is white, and despite its tightness and shortness it creates an aura of elegance.

"Baby, you look fine," he slurs. He takes one final swig from the beer in his hand before setting it down on the dresser and stepping forward. "Real hot." He clasps her waist and pulls her body toward him. And as though there aren't three other people in the room, he rams his lips against hers in a way that looks almost painful, one hand grazing her ass and the other pressing against the small of her back. She doesn't pull away.

I throw Rachael a disgusted glance and she rolls her eyes. All I can hear is that horrendous smacking sound again. Tyler and Tiffani: the world's worst couple when it comes to PDA. "Are they always like this?" I mutter in a hushed voice, because interrupting their intimate moment for a second time isn't exactly something I want to do.

Rachael just shakes her head. I think it's in commiseration. "All the time."

I glance back over to the pair. They don't seem to be stopping anytime soon, even when Meghan nudges them to the side so that she can step out into the hall. You'd think they hadn't seen each other in three years. They're that engaged in one another.

And so Tyler may be irritating, and Tiffani may be obliviously rude, and I may be chubby. But at least my dress isn't as clingy as those two.

6

Just after 8PM, Meghan takes us all over to this party that I'm dreading beyond words. I'm dreading it so much I wish I'd gone out to the family meal with Dad and Ella. Surely forcing overpriced food down my throat would be better than the bitter taste of cheap liquor.

We pile into the silver Toyota Corolla as the darkness begins to filter through the setting sun in such a beautiful way that I find myself gazing down the street toward the horizon before Rachael calls shotgun and nudges me to the side. I unwillingly get in the backseat with Tyler seated in the middle between Tiffani and me, beer in his lap and vodka by my feet. There's an overwhelming combination of body spray and perfume and Tyler's cologne, not to mention the music that's increasing in volume with each passing second. The car rolls down the street at, thankfully, a safe speed. Meghan drives with her body rigid and huddled over the wheel, and she doesn't say a word. It's like she's terrified of getting distracted, so while she concentrates hard on the road, Rachael and Tiffani do enough talking to make up for her silence.

"If Molly Jefferson is at this party, I swear to God, I'm leaving," Rachael states without glancing up from her phone.

She's texting extremely quickly, her fingers moving so fast that I just watch in amazement.

"Why would that loser be there?" Tiffani lets out a laugh as she adjusts her hair, running her fingers through it until she's pleased with the way it's sitting. "Austin's a total creep, but at least he has standards. No losers." For a moment, she leans forward an inch to peer at me over Tyler, but then she smiles and gets comfy again.

As we travel across the city, I steal a glance to my left. Tyler's arms are folded across his chest and he doesn't quite look comfortable, his eyes fixed on the handbrake, his face tight. He must notice my eyes on him, because he quickly glances sideways at me and then looks away just as fast. So I angle my body to the side and train my eyes on the passing buildings outside the window instead, but it does little to help how awkward I feel. Every few minutes I can sense Tyler's eyes on me again, but each time I look back over to catch him in the act he's already looking in the opposite direction.

"What about that Sabine girl? Sabine . . .?" Rachael glances up from her phone and presses a finger to her lips as she thinks for a moment. She twirls around in the seat and squints at Tiffani through the gap in the headrest. "You know the one I'm talking about, right? The German exchange student?"

"The girl who stole my seat in Spanish class? Sabine Baumann."

"Yes!" Rachael shrieks as she slumps back in the seat. "I hope she's not there either. She's always staring at Trevor."

"And you, Tyler," Tiffani adds. Beside me, I feel Tyler shrug, but it's obvious this Sabine girl isn't her friend. She presses her lips together and scoots closer to him.

The two of them discuss other potential party guests, with the rest of us offering little input: Meghan because she's too busy trying not to kill us all; Tyler because he's focusing so hard on staring at nothing in particular; and me because I honestly couldn't care.

So fifteen minutes and a lot of hair adjustments and bitchy remarks later, we arrive at the party, which appears to be in full swing. There are several people loitering in the front yard and more arriving, the music loud and echoing as we step out of the car, which Meghan has managed to awkwardly squeeze into a spot between a beat-up truck and a convertible. We grab the booze and I end up carrying in a pack of Twisted Tea and a bottle of vodka, and suddenly I feel like an alcoholic. I bet the neighbors are peeking through their blinds with the cops on speed dial. It's so obvious that we're all minors. I have no idea where Tiffani, Rachael and Meghan got any of this from or how they managed to get it, but like every other teenager in this country they must have their ways. There are always ways.

"Hey, Tyler!" a voice yells across the lawn. A shorter guy with a buzz cut and a Budweiser in his hand approaches him and they greet each other with a fist bump. "Glad you could make it."

"Yeah," Tyler says. He nods to the crate of Bud Light under his arm. "Kitchen?"

"Yeah," the guy says, jabbing a finger out toward the house. "Dump it and come join us." Tyler disappears inside, greeting a number of people on the way, his steps uneven.

"Hey, Austin!" Tiffani says to the same guy—the host of the party. I tag along behind her, with Rachael and Meghan by my side, and I can't help but feel entirely out of place. I don't know any of these people, yet here I am, turning up at a party and praying that no one will notice the stranger among them.

"Enjoy yourselves, girls," Austin says, and there is so much lechery underlying his tone that it makes him repulsively gross. "Nice dresses."

"I know," Tiffani says. She rolls her eyes over her shoulder and down to her ass, biting her lip. But I notice. "By the way, Eden's here too."

"Eden?" Austin's eyes drift past her, darting from Rachael to Meghan and then finally to me. "Crashing my party, Eden?"

Before I can drop dead right there and then, Tiffani steps forward and presses her hand flat against his chest. She leans in close by his side, murmurs, "Eden is Tyler's stepsister," and then leans back to fix him with a hard look. "And you don't want to get on the wrong side of him, so . . ."

Austin's expression immediately falters and he takes a step back, replacing the smirk on his face with a wide smile. "Welcome to the party! Turn up or go home." He raises his beer to the sky, whistles for a moment, and then walks away.

"You heard him," Rachael says. She unscrews the cap of a bottle of vodka she's holding in her hand and takes one huge gulp, drinking it straight without her features even shifting. She must do this a lot. "Turn the hell up!"

The sky darkens and Tiffani leads the way inside, and I've figured by now that she's the alpha female of the trio. The trio of friends plus me, the tagalong from Portland. And with being the tagalong come anxiety and nerves and the awareness that I'm not welcome here.

The house is pretty much packed from one wall to the

other, be it with bodies or crates of beer, and it is very, very hot. The music is loud and the alcohol doesn't seem to be in short supply. The majority of the people here are already tipsy, if not wasted, and there are only a few who are still standing steady. By the time we weave our way through to the kitchen, Tyler is already gone. His box of beer is lying among the overflowing collection of alcohol that covers the table and every worktop. Used shot glasses decorate the floor, and I carefully step around them before sliding the pack of Twisted Tea and the vodka onto the edge of the table.

"S'cuse me, Rach," a male voice says from behind us, and when I glance to my right there is a guy moving Rachael to the side by guiding her with his hands around her waist. "I was wondering if you'd show up tonight."

"Trevor!" Excitedly, she throws herself into his arms and pecks his lips.

Trevor moves around her and fetches himself a beer as she gazes at him the way a three-year-old gazes at a puppy.

"Boyfriend?" I mouth to Meghan, but she shakes her head.

"Catch up with you guys later!" Rachael yells, despite being right next to us all. "Have fun, Eden!" The two of them head out of the kitchen together, Trevor with a beer in his hand and Rachael with the vodka still in hers.

"Rachael's a total lightweight," Tiffani says while lining up two new shot glasses, her back to us. "She's been drinking cocktails since the second she turned up at my place." True, Rachael did slip out to the kitchen every so often while we were getting ready. Until now, I thought she was just making excessive toilet trips.

Closely, I watch as Tiffani fills the glasses with tequila. "Who's that Trevor guy?" I ask.

"Her party fling," she answers in monotone, as though it's no big deal at all. "They hook up at parties and that's all it is. Okay, here." She twirls around, her lips quirked up into a huge grin, and she hands me a glass of Cazadores tequila. I glance at Meghan for help, but she shrugs and holds up her car keys.

I've tasted tequila a couple times before, back home in Portland with my limited group of acquaintances, but it didn't do anything for me besides leave a sour, bitter taste in my mouth. "Oh," I say as I study the glass. It's filled to the brim. From the corner of my eye, I notice Tiffani licking the back of her hand. "Oh?"

Meghan laughs softly and rolls her eyes as she reaches for the random salt shaker lying on its side on the worktop. She passes it to Tiffani. "Have you done this before?"

"Tequila?" I ask.

"Tequila done right," she corrects, arching her brows. "You know, with the lime and all."

"Oh," I say again. Back home, all we drink is beer and rum. "Our parties aren't so . . ."

"Cool?" Tiffani smirks. She pours some salt onto the back of her hand. "You can teach them this when you go back. Now lick the back of your hand between your thumb and forefinger."

I feel dumb all of a sudden. It's like I'm in freshman year all over again, where I'm subject to scrutiny by the much older, much cooler students. But this isn't high school and they aren't other students. This is a party and they know exactly what to do and what to say and how to fit in. I, on the other hand, have no clue. "Okay," I say, and lick my hand. I feel ridiculous, and I'm beginning to wonder if Dad and Ella are home yet.

"Salt." Tiffani passes me the shaker and I pour a small amount onto my skin, mimicking her. It sticks. "Okay, there's gotta be limes somewhere."

"Tiff, they're right there," Meghan says, and laughs as she points to the basket of limes that has clearly been provided for this exact purpose. I don't even like limes.

Tiffani presses her hand to her forehead and then sighs. "I haven't even had one drink yet and I'm already going blind. Alright, grab a slice. Eden, hold it in the hand with the salt."

I do as instructed, placing the lime slice between my thumb and forefinger and then staring back at her, waiting to hear what my next move should be. "Now?"

"Salt, tequila, lime," Meghan answers instead. She steps back to examine Tiffani and me, and when Tiffani nods, she cheers, "Go, go, go!"

I panic but lick the salt anyway and throw my head back as I attempt to force the tequila down my throat. I fight the urge to gag. It's so gross and so bitter. I remember the lime in my hand and bite into it, despite how screwed up my face is, but the juice only squirts all over my cheeks and I make a dive for the kitchen sink, spluttering the drink all over it.

When I get home, I am so dead.

"You know what they say," Tiffani says with a grin. I must look horrified, and she quickly passes me a can of beer, as though it'll help to clear the taste. "One tequila, two tequila, three tequila, floor." Several people file into the kitchen to top up their drinks, and she decides to seize this opportunity as her getaway. "I'm gonna go find Tyler. You guys have fun."

The music gets louder all of a sudden, bouncing from the walls and drilling into my ears. The intense beat drops are giving me a headache. Meghan reaches for my free hand and pulls me out of the kitchen and into a large—but cramped—living room. She talks to a couple people on our way, but thankfully none of them ask her why there's a loser by her side.

A bulky guy approaches us from the opposite side of the room, and Meghan instantly yells "Jake!" over the sound of the music.

"Hey, Megs," Jake says. He's wearing a black T-shirt with a huge slogan scrawled across the front of it, which I don't bother to read, and his blond hair is gelled messily in all directions. "Where are Tiff and Rach?" Jake, I discover, likes to cut names short.

"Rachael's with Trevor," Meghan says, and she rolls her eyes, as does he, "and Tiffani's looking for Tyler. Seen him?"

I notice the way Jake's expression hardens slightly. "Yeah," he says a little stiffly. "Doing what he does."

Meghan glances sideways at me, bites her lip, and then moves the conversation on. "Where's Dean?"

"He was looking for you guys." Jake laughs, his expression softening as he takes a sip of his beer. As he swallows it, he stares at me. "Who's the new girl?"

"Eden," I answer before Meghan can. I already know which questions are coming next, so I go ahead and throw the answers out there before Jake can even ask. "I'm Tyler's stepsister. I'm here for the summer." There go his hardened features again. He shoots Meghan a glance, and she shrugs in return. "What?"

"Um," Meghan says. "I'm gonna go check on Rachael. Gotta make sure she doesn't get knocked up."

"Want some rubbers to give 'em?" Jake smirks. He pats his pockets in a joking manner and then chuckles. Meghan giggles, adjusts her hair, and then leaves. "So you're Tyler Bruce's stepsister?"

I want to shake my head no, but that would be bullshit, so I murmur a quick "Yeah," and then change the subject as quickly as I can. I ask him the first thing that pops into my head. "Are you all seniors?"

He tilts his head. "Aren't you?"

"Junior," I say quietly. Yet another reason why I'm so out of place here. I'm a junior attending a senior party. There's no way Amelia is going to believe this. In Portland, seniors refuse to associate with the rest of us. The guys are too cool for us, the girls too busy acting like adults. It's almost as though they believe they're a superior race. Kind of like New Yorkers.

"Where did you say you were from again?"

I reel my attention back to Jake. "Um, Portland."

"Portland, Maine?"

"Portland, Oregon," I correct. Jake takes another swig of his beer, and the silence and blunt conversation is making the entire thing awkward. "Sorry, where'd you say Tyler was again?"

He stops drinking and raises a brow. "Why does it matter?"

Because I want to go home and we just so happen to share the same one. "I've got to get a beer for him." Sold.

Jake hesitates for a long moment before finally saying, "He's out back. Watch yourself."

"Thanks." I take a quick sip of my own drink and head out into the hall, following it down toward the back of the house and through the mass of bodies. Bodies that do not include Tiffani and Rachael and Meghan. And right now, I could really do with having them with me. I've been abandoned among a crowd of strangers in a brand-new city and it certainly doesn't feel great.

At the end of the hall, there's a back door left open with people slipping in and out of the house, so I squeeze by and step outside into the yard, laying my beer down on the patio table. There's a guy throwing up by the fence and a girl passed out on the lawn. I contemplate helping her, but my attention is immediately diverted to the eruption of laughter from the shed in the corner. The laughter sounds as though it belongs to a group of guys, so I build up some courage and head over there. If I don't, I'll be stuck at this party until some unearthly hour of the morning.

As I get nearer, I notice the smoke in the air. There's no window and the door is shut, so I reach for it and pull it open. Immediately I'm hit with the most overwhelming smell of weed, so overwhelming that as the smoke escapes into the night air all at once tears whelm in my eyes. I clasp a hand to my mouth and cough, squeezing my eyes shut and taking a step back.

"Is that weed?" I blurt.

"No, it's cotton candy," someone shoots back, and the shed rings with howls of laughter. But there's nothing funny about this at all.

I open my eyes again as the air clears and I find four guys staring back at me. One of them is Tyler. There's a joint in his hand and he's attempting to hide it behind his leg, but it doesn't make a difference. I can still see it, the same way I can see the panic and alarm crossing his features. "Are you serious?" I ask in disbelief.

"Dude, get this chick outta here," someone mutters. I don't even know which one of the other three is talking. I don't care about the others. My eyes are locked on Tyler. "Unless she wants to come in here and keep us company."

"Bro," Tyler says, but it's hard to ignore the shake in his voice as he swallows and forces a small laugh to escape his lips. His eyes are glazed, pupils wide. "You really want that kid in here?"

There's more laughter, but Tyler doesn't join in with the combination of chuckling and coughing. He's just gnawing on his lips and glancing between me and his friends, not quite sure of the best way to handle the situation. For starters, he should get rid of the joint that's still in his hand.

"Who the hell is she?" the same guy asks. More smoke wafts toward me as someone exhales, but I quickly wave it away from me. "Has no one taught her the rules?" I squint through the dispersing plume of smoke until I spot the pair of bloodshot eyes struggling to focus on me. The black guy that they belong to is grinning. "No interrupting, babe. Get the fuck out of here unless you're here to ball with us." He takes a step forward and holds up the glowing joint in his hand. It's almost burnt out, but he offers it to me nonetheless.

As though I'd actually consider taking it from him, Tyler steps in between the joint and me. He licks his index finger and presses it to the cherry of his own joint, extinguishing it and then stuffing it into his pocket before straightening up and glowering at the guy in front of him. "What the hell are you doing?" he asks, nodding to the jay in his hand. "C'mon, Clayton, where's your common sense?"

Clayton moves the hovering joint back to his lips, drawing on it for a long moment before exhaling the smoke toward Tyler's face. "Offering her a hit *is* common sense. It's called good manners. It would be rude not to," he says. He peers at me over Tyler's shoulder. "Am I right, new girl?"

The other two guys stifle a laugh again, but they're not

paying too much attention anymore. I think they're too baked to even care. They're just standing around at the back of the shed, laughing, grins wide. Tyler, on the other hand, is not so easily entertained.

"Dude, take the damn hint," he hisses. He takes a step backward and his body nudges against mine, forcing me to back away too. "She doesn't want it. Look at her." He glances over his shoulder at my repulsed expression, and he ends up staring at me for a moment longer than I feel comfortable with. Even when Clayton speaks again, Tyler's just looking at me.

"Alright, alright," Clayton says. "Just get her outta here then. Why do we have some random kid in here anyway?"

"I'm wondering the same thing," Tyler murmurs. Suddenly he turns to face me. Completely disgusted by the smoking, I shake my head at him. I wonder if Ella knows about this. Is she aware that he's out here spending his night getting high?

Tyler takes a step toward me, but as he shifts, his curled-up fist knocks against something. His eyes fall to his right and my stare follows until it lands on a small metallic table and the tiny lamp perched on the corner of it. I'm about to look away when I notice what's on that table and beneath the light. There's a stack of dollar bills and some credit cards scattered around, and, most importantly, a row of neat lines. White powder lines.

"Oh my God," I whisper, blinking as fast as I can, because I have no idea if the smoke I've just inhaled is having an effect on me or if I'm really seeing what is truly there. "Oh my God?"

"Dude, seriously, I'm not kidding." It's Clayton. "Get her out of here before she calls us out to the cops or something."

"Yeah, yeah, she's leaving," Tyler replies. At the same time he reaches for my elbow, gently pushing me away from the shed. I'm surprised he follows, pulling me across the yard until we're away from everyone else and out of hearing range.

"You're unbelievable," I hiss while I shake his hand off me. "Coke? Really, Tyler?"

He appears helpless before me, like this is the first time he's ever been confronted about it, because he just presses his hands to his face and groans. "This isn't the place for you," he says once he drops his hands. He stuffs them into his pockets and kicks at the grass. "You should—you should go back inside."

I grind my teeth. I've never been in a situation like this before, so I'm not entirely sure how I'm supposed to handle it. Do I try to talk to him about it? Do I call Ella? The cops? Eventually, I just decide to storm off. I push him out of the way, my pulse racing and my blood hot. I'm infuriated by what I've just witnessed. I want to kick something, punch a wall, tear someone's limbs off. I'm so mad.

Tyler heads back over to the shed, and I don't know what he says to his friends when he gets there, but all of a sudden they burst into howls of laughter. I can hear it echoing behind me and I can't help but wonder if it's me they're laughing at.

"Dude, come on," someone calls. The laughter in the shed stops. "That's low. Chill out."

"Shut the fuck up, Dean," I hear Tyler say, but I don't bother to turn around. I'm too pissed off to even look at him.

I hear footsteps running, and I glance up to the guy when he catches up to me. "You're Dean?"

"And I'm going to have a wild guess and say you're Tyler's stepsister," he says. There's a hand resting in his brown hair as he looks at me. "You're the only person here that I've never seen before and Meghan says that this mysterious stepsister just so happens to be at this lame party. So am I right?"

I force a smile. "Yeah. Hey, you don't happen to know which number Tyler's house is? The one on Deidre Avenue? I need to get home, but I . . . I don't know the address."

"Would I happen to know where my best friend lives?" Dean grins. "329."

"Best friend?" I glance back over to the shed. Five seconds ago they were cursing across the yard to each other.

"Complicated," he says, and then points to the house. "I can give you a ride home. My car's parked just down the block."

"Have you been drinking?"

"If I'd had anything to drink, I wouldn't be offering to give you a ride."

I heave a sigh. "Thank you."

He heads back to the house and I follow by his side, my mind awhirl. And to think I thought Tyler couldn't get any worse. I slow down for a second to look back at the shed, and with the door still open, I get a clear view of him reaching back into his pocket and pulling out the remainder of his joint. Just as he presses it to his lips and sets it alight, he notices my stare.

For the briefest of moments, he grimaces and drops his eyes to the floor. Someone forces a beer into his free hand, but he doesn't acknowledge it. Instead, he just stands there as though he's frozen in place and can't possibly move, his shoulders sunken and his head low. And then he breaks free of his paralysis and shifts his way to the back of the shed, as far away from me as possible, so that the only thing I can see is an orange glow blazing in the darkness.

* * *

As Dean is driving me home, it suddenly hits me that I'm about to have a lot of explaining to do. Not only did I bail on Dad's plans by convincing him I was sick, I also left the house and went to a party instead. Right now he's probably already calling the cops to report me missing. And to make matters worse, I'm returning home in a dress that barely covers half my body.

"My dad is gonna kill me," I murmur as I rest my head on the window. "I was meant to be sick."

Dean glances at me. "Did you make a miraculous recovery or something like that?"

"Something like that." I sit up and reach for my phone—it's second nature—but I discover I have no pockets and no phone. I left it at Tiffani's. "Crap."

"What's up?"

"Nothing." I heave a frustrated sigh and scour the dashboard for the time. It's almost eleven. I stuck around at the party for barely an hour. If I'd stayed any longer, I would have only found more reasons to despise Tyler and even more reasons to question my sanity. "Are you heading back there?"

"Yeah," Dean says as he pulls onto Deidre Avenue. "I'm kind of Jake's designated driver," he chuckles. "Gotta make sure the guy gets home."

"What about Tyler?" I ask, and then I mentally curse myself out for even caring.

Dean smiles a little. "Tyler doesn't really go home."

"What does he do? Does he just pass out in the street or

something?" I fold my arms, contemptuous but also slightly curious. "Spend the night in a jail cell?"

"Not exactly," Dean says. "He normally just goes back to Tiffani's place with her."

"Oh." Gross. "I can't believe he does drugs." Even grosser. "Did you know?"

There's a long silence. "Everyone knows."

Jake's earlier expression and Meghan's hesitant glances suddenly make sense now. They both knew what Tyler was up to.

"Why don't any of you stop him then?" I find it insane that these people are supposedly his friends, yet despite being aware that he's doing coke ten feet away from them they aren't doing anything to help him or stop him. "I mean, does his mom even know?"

"Trust me, I've tried," Dean says. He pulls up outside Dad's house and cuts the engine. "But getting through to Tyler is like getting through a brick wall. It's literally impossible. The guy just doesn't listen. We all just gotta ignore it. I think his mom knows about the weed, but definitely not the coke."

"He's disgusting." Shaking my head in disbelief, I reach for the handle and push the car door open. With my other hand, I quickly open up the small clutch purse I borrowed from Tiffani and rummage through until I grab the first bill I find. It's five dollars, and it's crinkled to the point of being void, but it's enough to cover the cost of the journey. I hand it to Dean. "Thanks for the ride."

"What's this?" He stares down at the wrecked note with a perplexed frown before glancing back at me.

"It's to cover the gas." I urge the money into his hands, but he refuses to accept it, so I sigh. "Take it."

"Eden, don't sweat it, honestly," he says with a laugh. "Just tell Ella I said hey and we're good."

I narrow my eyes at him, skeptical. Back in Portland it's the social norm to hand over a couple bucks to contribute to the cost of the gas if someone gives you a ride. If you step out of the car without offering a cent, you're pretty much blacklisted from the circle and you'll be lucky if you're ever offered a ride again. Maybe they give each other free rides down here, or maybe Dean's just too nice for his own good. Either way, I toss the bill onto the dashboard and jump out of the car before he can give it back to me.

"Keep it!" I call, twirling around and slamming the door shut behind me as I rush toward the house.

That's when I notice that the lights are all on inside. Dad will either be extremely understanding or absolutely livid. Most likely the latter. Maybe I can slip in through the back without Dad and Ella even noticing. Run up to my room, pull on some PJs, and then convince them that I've been there the entire time. Or just break down into tears and beg for forgiveness.

Bracing myself, I pull Tiffani's dress as far down my thighs as it's willing to go and stretch it a little to cover a few more inches of my body. Every little helps. I pull off the irritating fake eyelashes too and toss them onto the lawn. I carry with me the noticeable waft of liquor and there's nothing I can do to get rid of it. I just have to face the fact that I lied and deserve to be cast into the pits of hell.

The door is unlocked when I reach it, so I slip inside as quietly as possible and creep across the hall. But I'm not as discreet as I think I am, because Dad calls my name from the living room.

I bite down on my lip and step toward the door, peering

around the frame only slightly. I keep my body well hidden. "Hey."

"Hey?" Dad repeats, blinking as he stares at me in a flabbergasted sort of way. "Is that what you're going to come in here and say? HEY?"

"Hello?" I try instead. I've never been one to get myself into trouble, so all this sneaking around is entirely new to me. Mom's grounded me twice in sixteen years. Dad hasn't been around to ground me in the first place. "I'm home."

"Yeah, I can see that you're home," Dad says, his voice gruff and scolding as he gets to his feet. Ella watches from the couch. "Which is where you were meant to be the whole night. You weren't feeling great, but now it seems you're feeling absolutely fine. What's up with that?"

"I was at Tiffani's house," I blurt. This is partially true. "Girls' night. I felt a little better, so I went. I thought you'd be okay with it."

"Tyler's girlfriend?" Ella chirps. She too gets to her feet.

Unfortunately for Tiffani, yes. "Yeah."

"Speaking of Tyler," Dad mutters, "where the hell did he sneak off to?"

"I don't know," I lie. Right now, he's smoking joints and snorting coke and drinking beer and laughing at slurred jokes that aren't even funny. "He was still here when I left." It would be so easy just to blurt out to Ella that her son is a pothead. That would teach him not to be a jerk to me. But for some reason I feel as though it's not my place to tell, so I continue to cover for him. It's as though I can't stop the words from spilling out of my mouth. "Maybe he went to get food or something."

"His car's still here," Ella points out. She looks disappointed, like she was hoping he would be the child who walked through the front door and not me.

"Maybe a walk?"

"I doubt that," she says. "He won't answer my calls." It must be hard for her having to deal with a kid who is almost impossible to handle.

"Eden," Dad says. "I smell alcohol. I don't like you lying to me."

I stare at him, wondering what he's referring to: lying about being sick, lying about being at Tiffani's, or lying about not knowing where Tyler is. For some reason, there's a sudden wave of anger fusing through my veins and I have no idea why. My face contorts. "And I don't like you walking out on Mom, but things don't always go the way we want them to."

I don't wait around to hear Dad's reply. I ball my hands into fists and quickly dart up the stairs and into my room. The tequila churns in my stomach, reminding me that I could barely survive the party for more than an hour. The loud music has given me a headache and I can still recall the powerful reek of weed. Now I really do feel sick, and this time it isn't just an excuse.

* * *

I awake in the morning to the sound of Ella's voice bouncing around the house and Tyler's voice echoing twice as loud. I stare at the ceiling for a little while, listening to their yelling and wondering what time it is. And whatever time it actually is, it feels way too early for this. Tyler must have found his way home from Austin's.

With the sunlight streaming into my room and the sound

of someone mowing their lawn difficult to ignore, I decide to get up and pull on some clothes. As I'm doing this, I hear loud footsteps on the stairs and cursing. It can only be one person, and this one person just so happens to decide to enter my room.

"Did you know there's this thing that exists called—oh, I don't know—privacy?" I fix my intruder with a firm glare before I finish pulling on my hoodie.

Tyler cocks his head to one side as he shuts the door. "Here's your stuff." In his hands he's holding my clothes that I left behind at Tiffani's, and he lays them down on my bed. Surprisingly, his voice his calm now. Five seconds ago it was loud enough to deafen a small child. "And your, uh, phone." He edges a little toward me and I take it from him, slowly, as I stare up at his face. He's struggling to meet my eyes.

"Thanks," I say, bluntly. I'm still unbelievably furious at him.

Silence captures my room for a long moment. He slowly turns to leave, but before he reaches the door he spins back around again. "Look," he starts, "about last night—"

"I already know that you're a jerk and that you do drugs and that you're pathetic as hell," I say. "You don't have to explain it to me."

He frowns, his lips forming a firm line as he furrows his eyebrows and takes a few hesitant steps toward me. "Just—just don't say anything."

I fold my arms, gazing at him curiously. For once, he doesn't look terrifying. "Are you asking me not to snitch?"

"Don't tell my mom or your dad anything," he says, and his voice is so soft and almost pleading that it's leaving me slightly confused. At least the begging side of him is nice. "Just forget about it."

"I can't believe you're involved in that stuff," I murmur,

glancing down at my phone—four missed calls from Dad—and then tossing it onto my bed. "Why do you even do that? It really doesn't make you look cool if that's what you're trying to do."

"Not even close."

I throw my hands up in exasperation. "Then what?"

"I don't know," he mutters. "I'm not here for a lecture, okay? I just came to give you your stuff back and to tell you to keep your mouth shut." He throws a hand into his hair and glances away.

Maybe I'm sleep deprived or maybe I'm just insane, but I somehow gather up the courage to ask him the question that's been playing on my lips since Friday. "Why do you hate me so much?"

This takes Tyler by surprise. He suddenly looks perplexed. "Who said I hated you?"

"Um," I say. "You kind of insult me every chance you get. I get that it's weird having a stepsister all of a sudden, but it's weird for me too. We got off on the wrong foot, I think."

"No," Tyler says, shaking his head as he laughs. "You don't get it at all." Quickly scanning my room, he narrows his eyes and finally turns for the door again.

"What don't I get?" I call after him.

"Everything," he shoots back.

7

On Tuesday, I set my alarm for sunrise and make a point of heading out for an early morning jog before everyone else wakes up. Tiffani's words about the tight dress are still echoing in the back of my head, so I venture further than the neighborhood, tracing a route down to the coastal highway and back again, pushing my body to its limits. I'm dismayed to discover that the beach has a layer of fog covering it, but the air is still warm. By the time I get back to the house, Dad is awake and brewing some coffee.

"Nice jog?" he asks as I enter the kitchen.

I heave a sigh, pressing my hands to the edge of the worktop and catching my breath. "Yeah," I say, but it's closer to a pant. "Almost four miles. It was super foggy down by the pier."

"I'd pass out after the first," he jokes. "Oh, the famous fog. It's called the June Gloom. Coffee?" He holds up the jug.

"I'm good." I might love coffee, but 7AM is just too early. The only thing I could do with right now is a long, hot shower. "Anyone else awake?"

"Ella's getting dressed," he says, turning back around to fetch a mug, "but the guys are still sleeping." After my abrupt remark on Saturday night, he has lightened up and is trying his hardest to be overly nice at every chance he gets. He knows now that I haven't forgiven him, that I'm still upset with him for leaving us. He has a lot of sucking up to do.

"Does she have work to go to or something?" Yesterday she didn't seem to have a job. When Dad left for his, she simply cleaned the house, made small talk with me, argued with Tyler a little, and then drove Jamie and Chase to wherever they needed to go.

Dad gives me a small smile. "Ella's a civil rights attorney."

I blink. I wouldn't have taken her for an attorney—she seems to lose every argument with Tyler, giving up after only a few minutes. "Shouldn't she be at an office or something?"

"She's on a career break," Dad says, but he doesn't give me any opportunity to press the subject further before he asks, "You said you're going to the beach today, didn't you?"

"Yeah," I say, "with Rachael." And Tiffani and Meghan, but I doubt Dad cares about every single detail.

"If you need a ride there, Ella will take you," he offers, which is ridiculous, because I only met her four days ago and am far from comfortable enough to be asking her for rides.

"Rachael's already giving me a ride," I say. "Thanks, though."

"Alright." He takes a long swig of his coffee, then tucks his shirt into his suit pants and adjusts his tie. "Right, I'm going to head off and try to beat this LA traffic. Some mornings I win, others I lose."

"Why the shirt again?"

"I'm the supervisor."

"Oh." Finally, an answer to why this house is so luxurious. Dad's been a civil engineer since before I was even born, and the years of experience must have finally landed him a better-paid position. Obviously.

"I'll be home at six," he says, and then gives me a two-finger wave as he passes me.

I roll my eyes and head over to the faucet, pouring myself a glass of water, and then I make my way up to my room. I hear Ella swinging open the master bedroom door as I walk down the hall, so I quickly dart up the staircase before she can see me. However, there's still no sound from Tyler, Jamie and Chase's rooms.

I grab a shower—a long, hot one, long and hot enough to relax my muscles and leave my body feeling great again. I remember to shave my legs this time.

"Eden," Ella says as she enters my room without knocking, leaving me desperately clinging onto my towel. "Sorry—I—"

I tighten my grip on the fabric and offer her an awkward smile. "It's fine." *Although*, I think, *it's really not fine*. I'm half naked in front of a stranger.

Ella clears her throat, dropping her eyes nervously to the floor and keeping them fixed on the carpet. "I was wondering if you'd like any breakfast. Or did you have some with your dad?"

"I'm good for now," I say. "I'm not that hungry."

Ella smiles, nods, and then leaves. At least she's making an effort. I was expecting her to be like a stereotypical wicked stepmother. But so far, she hasn't handed me any mops.

With my hair damp, I braid it and then slip back into bed. I'm not going to the beach until the afternoon, and I can't stop myself from yawning after waking up so early, so a quick power nap is the only way to go.

"Tiffani and Megs are already there," Rachael says the second I get inside her car, five hours later. She arches her eyebrows and looks me up and down. "You look like you just woke up."

"I did," I say. "Twenty minutes ago."

"Okay, I get that it's summer but waking up at—" she taps the clock on the radio "—12:20PM is a little lazy, don't you think?"

I roll my eyes, working my fingers through my hair to ensure I've fully undone the braids. I'm left with mermaid waves—perfect for the beach and up to Rachael's standards. I pull my floral kimono tighter around my body. "I was up super early."

"Why?"

"I went for a run."

Rachael snorts. "Okay, my earlier statement is now dismissed. Have you been to the pier yet?"

I slip on my sunglasses and turn to face her, watching her closely as she focuses on the road. "The thing with the Ferris wheel? I saw it this morning. I jogged down the highway."

"Yeah, that's the pier," Rachael confirms. "We can check it out later if we have time."

It's extremely hot out today, with only a slight breeze finding its way in from the Pacific, but it's refreshing so I don't complain, especially now the fog has been burned off. Portland isn't exactly a city known for its beaches, mostly because it has none. There are the odd few so-called "beaches" by lakes or along the Willamette River, but nothing on the scale of the beach here. It runs along the edge of the city for miles before meeting up with Venice Beach, and has a constant flow of visitors.

Rachael finds a parking spot in the lot by the pier, and I grab my bag and step out. It took me ten minutes back at the house to convince myself to even put a bikini on, and now that I have I know it's the worst decision I've ever made.

While Rachael fetches her towel and speakers from the trunk, I make sure my shorts are tight and my kimono is fully spread over me. There's absolutely no way I'm taking my clothes off.

"Okay," Rachael says as she walks around to meet me at the front of the car, her sunglasses pushed up as she squints at her phone. "Meghan says they're by the volleyball courts next to Perry's, sooooooo they're over there somewhere." She points off to the right. It must be difficult to find the people you are looking for on a beach this big, but thanks to technology the struggle is minimized.

I follow Rachael from the lot onto the sand, my flip-flops flapping around my feet in the most uncomfortable of ways, and we walk for a good five or so minutes before finally spotting Tiffani and Meghan. It's hard not to—they're on their feet and waving their arms around like maniacs.

"Guys!" Tiffani calls. "You just missed some cute guy ask Meg for her number."

I glance over at Meghan, and she sheepishly drops back down to the sand again, color flooding to her cheeks. "He's from Pasadena," she murmurs, biting her lip.

As Tiffani settles back onto the sand too, I follow suit with Rachael by laying down my towel and getting comfy. I cross my legs and smile. The beach really is huge, with rows of tiny stores behind us and cycle routes and guys hurling volleyballs at one another.

"So Rach," Tiffani says, raising a brow from behind her sunglasses, "what happened with you and Trevor on Saturday?"

Rachael smirks, rolls her eyes, and then looks away. "Nothing," she says, but she's still smiling.

"Nothing my ass," Meghan shoots. "I'm guessing third

base this time, because a home run two weeks in a row isn't your thing. Am I right or am I right?"

Rachael stays silent for a long moment and then finally whispers, "You're right," before laughing. She pulls off her lace cover-up and tosses it to the side, lying down on her back and getting comfortable. I notice how perfect her figure is, how long her legs and how flat her stomach. The perfect body to compliment her mint bikini.

"Eden, what even happened to you at the party?" Tiffani asks, and I'm so distracted by Rachael's legs that it takes me by surprise.

"What?"

"Where did you go?" She sits up her equally perfect body and looks at me from behind her shades. "Who'd you go home with? What's his name?"

I almost choke on my own saliva. "Nooooo," I say, shaking my head. "I didn't feel that great. Dean took me home." How many more times am I going to use the sickness excuse?

"Couldn't handle the tequila?" She grins, laughs, and then gets onto her knees to straighten out her towel. "By the way, the guys suggested heading outta town tonight. Maybe Venice or into the city, but Dean also thought about heading out to Hollywood so you can see the sign, Eden, because you can't come to Los Angeles and not see the Hollywood Sign up close and personal. We're all going."

"Hollywood's a good idea," Rachael says. "I'm in the mood for some illegal trespassing."

I'm a little skeptical about the whole idea. "Illegal?"

All three of them offer a small smirk, then Tiffani continues to speak, albeit mainly to Rachael at first. "We're only going to take three cars to make it easier, so wherever we decide to go, Jake's gonna pick me up and Dean said he'll get you and Meg." She tilts her head in my direction. "And you can go with Tyler, because you're leaving from the same house, anyway."

I stare at her. In fact, a laugh almost escapes from my lips, but I somehow manage to suppress it. Sure, Tyler and I sharing a car may seem convenient, but putting the two of us in a confined space for longer than a minute is bound to get my blood heated.

"How about a Perry's round?" Meghan asks. She reaches for her purse.

"Get me a caramel Frio," Rachael says.

Meghan shifts her eyes to me. "Eden?"

"Um," I say. I'm not quite sure what sort of store Perry's is, and I've never heard of a Frio in my life. "What is there?"

"Just get her the same as me," Rachael cuts in as she leans back and props herself up on her elbows, tilting her face up to the sun. She leaves no room for argument.

Meghan heads off with Tiffani by her side, leaving Rachael and I alone to bask in the sun while they get drinks for us all. At least I'm assuming it's drinks. I have no idea. It could be ice cream. Either way, I'm not looking forward to it.

Clearing my throat, I decide to distract myself. "Okay, I think I've got this right," I say, crossing my legs and turning to face Rachael. She sits up to listen. "You guys are best friends, right?"

"Right . . ." Rachael agrees, but her tone is cautious as she waits to see where I'm going with this.

"And then Tyler and Dean and this Jake guy are best friends too?"

She thinks about it, pursing her lips as she carefully

considers her answer. “Kind of,” she says. “There’s a little tension between Tyler and Jake, but they ignore it most of the time.”

“Why’s there tension?” I remember talking to Jake at the party, and despite his awful conversation skills he seemed pretty friendly.

“Because Tyler started dating Tiffani in freshman year and back then Jake had this huge crush on her and there were arguments and fights, but he got over it,” Rachael explains. She rolls her eyes. “Immature stuff. They still sort of hate each other, though.”

“This tension aside,” I continue, “you guys are all, like, one big group of friends? That’s what it seems like, so I just wanna know if I’ve picked this up right.”

“You’re right,” Rachael says. “We’ve all been friends since—hell, I have no idea—seventh grade or something. We all went to middle school together. Now come on!” She throws her hands up in the air. “Let’s create some tan lines.”

“I’m kinda fine just sitting here,” I say, and I smile as wide as I can to discourage her from saying anything more. But it doesn’t work.

“Oh, shut up,” she jokes as she lies back down again. “You’re not gonna tan that great if you’re sitting there with half your skin covered up.”

I glance down, tightening my grip on my kimono and holding it closer to me. “No, really, I’m fine.”

“Got your Frios!” Tiffani announces as she creeps up behind us, and I’m thankful for her interruption. Leaning over my shoulder, she hands me a plastic cup with cream overflowing from the lid and then hands another to Rachael, tossing the straws at us afterward.

I stare at the cup for a few seconds. It looks like the most fattening beverage to ever exist. The cream just makes me feel queasy, so it's almost impossible to smile up at her. I must look so ungrateful, but I just can't help frowning. I wait until they're all looking at me, and then I slip the straw into the drink and take a sip of the iced beverage, ensuring that they notice. *Smile and nod,* I think. So that's exactly what I do. I pretend that it's the best damn thing I've ever tasted in my entire life, and then the second they look away, I lay it aside. Later, when it's melted from the heat of the sun, I'll dramatically act as though I completely forgot about it.

"The creepy dude who always serves us gave us a discount," Meghan says as she settles down onto her towel, crossing her legs. She scoops up some cream from her own drink with her index finger and slowly tastes it. "Only because Tiff flirted with him."

"I did not flirt with him!" Tiffani objects with a sharp gasp.

It's then that I rummage around in my bag for my earphones, untangling them once I find them and finding a decent playlist. I lay down and stare up at the sky. Earphones in, music loud, shades on, drink to the side, pretty girl chitchat out.

We spend around five hours at the beach and decide against a small trip onto the pier, so by the time Rachael and I get back to Deidre Avenue, I'm starting to get hungry. Thankfully, Ella has dinner under control.

"Your dad's going to be a little longer tonight, so we're having it later," she tells me when I get home. "Did you have a nice day at the beach?"

"Yeah," I say, and that's as far as our conversation goes. I also leave a trail of sand behind me as I dart upstairs to shower again and get ready for Venice, LA, or Hollywood. Tonight's itinerary has yet to be decided.

So now I'm fully showered and dressed and ready to go. When I'm double-checking my winged eyeliner in my mirror, I hear my dad's voice from somewhere downstairs. He's home, which means dinner should be ready right about now. I make my way downstairs, and as I get closer to the kitchen I realise that Dad's voice is raised.

"Do you want to know what I just witnessed?" Dad asks, and his voice is so gruff that it's obvious he's super mad.

I edge toward the kitchen arch, hanging back behind the wall and peering into the room. Ella's standing by the oven, Dad opposite her, with Tyler right bang in the middle of them.

"So here I am," Dad yells, "heading down to Appian Way to drop off some paperwork on my way home, and guess who I happen to spot at the beach?"

Ella throws Tyler a glance. "I told you not to leave."

"So I think, 'Hey, he's grounded,' and I head over there to ask him what he's playing at," Dad continues, "and he's sitting around some table with these guys who looked ten years older than him, and I stood there and WATCHED him toss ten-, twenty-, fifty-dollar bills onto this table."

Ella's eyes narrow. "Tyler."

Tyler only shakes his head, smirking in disbelief. "This is bullshit."

"Shut the hell up," Dad snaps, rolling up the sleeves of his shirt and loosening his tie. "So I'm standing right there watching him gamble and throw away cash, and guess what happened when he lost the bet?" Dad pauses for a moment. "He started swinging."

"That asshole was cheating," Tyler mutters, gripping the

worktop and leaning back against it. His eyes are dark. "I wasn't gonna let him get away with it."

"Do you want to get arrested for assault?" Dad steps forward to fix him with a glare. "Spend your life in juvenile hall? Is that what you want?"

"Tyler, you have to stop all of this," Ella says quietly, pressing a hand to her forehead and heaving a sigh. She looks more upset than angry. "I don't want you to get into trouble."

"This isn't Las Vegas," Dad cuts in. He steps even closer into Tyler's personal space, his cheeks flushed red. He's furious enough for the both of them. "What the hell were you playing at?"

Tyler presses his lips into a firm line. "Live a little."

"I'm done with you," Dad states, shaking his head. He throws his hands up in defeat as he turns around and heads outside through the patio doors, perhaps to get a breath of fresh air.

Ella opens her mouth to speak, but Tyler chuckles before she can say anything and then makes for the hall. I step back into the corner as he storms past, hoping that he doesn't notice me. But, of course, he does.

He spins around, halting as he studies me. "I've gotta give you a ride, right?"

I'm not sure getting a ride from someone with behavioral issues like him is a good idea. He's most likely a reckless driver, ignoring speed limits and running over the occasional child. "I think so."

"I'm leaving right now," he says, his tone still harsh from the argument, "so either come or stay here." With his eyes still narrowed, he exhales and makes his way to the front door. Ella calls after him, warning him not to leave, but he ignores her and heads outside.

I glance back into the kitchen. Ella appears on the verge of tears and Dad is pacing the back yard. The two of them don't seem like very good company for the evening, so there's no chance of me choosing to stay here. Sighing, I briskly jog over to the front door and catch Tyler's attention just before he reaches his car. "Wait up!"

The dinner's ruined by now, anyway.

8

Tyler's car is parked diagonally across the sidewalk and parking strip, and I can't help but wonder what sort of rage he was in when he pulled up like that. Perhaps it was similar to the mood he's in right now. He throws open the door and then pauses to look at me. He just stares.

"What?" I ask as I near both him and the car.

"Well?" he prompts. Raising his eyebrows, he gives the vehicle a nod. I run my eyes over the white bodywork for anything significant, but there's nothing of interest. "Do you even know what car this is?" He looks at me as though I'm stupid, like I don't know what an airbag is or something, and to prove a point I walk around to the back of the vehicle and study its logo. Four interlinked metal circles.

"An Audi?" I guess.

"An Audi R8," he finishes with an obnoxious smirk, his expression smug.

"Okay," I say. "Do you want me to applaud you or something?"

He laughs as he places a hand on the top of his door. "Girls are clueless. You'd probably pass out if you saw the figures on this thing."

"Get over yourself," I murmur, shaking my head and

reaching for the door. I carelessly slide inside to discover that there are only two seats, and everything is leather and metallic, and perhaps he is right about this car being expensive, and so I keep my mouth shut.

"Call Tiffani," he says as he joins me inside, slamming the door behind him. With a sharp flick of his wrist, he tosses his phone onto my lap and starts the engine.

"You mean your girlfriend who you like to either be all over or completely ignore?"

The corner of his lips pull up into a smirk and my stomach churns in disgust. I have never in my entire life met someone with this many flaws, who thinks that everything is a joke.

"You're an ass," I mutter, gripping his phone in my hand and angling my body away from him. I stare out the window as he over-revs the engine and sends us flying down the avenue.

"Call her," he says again. "I have no idea where we're going."

I heave a sigh and sit up, turning the device around in my hands and staring at the screen for a while. "Passcode?"

"4355."

Quickly I type in the digits and unlock his phone. I pull up his contacts. "Is that your favorite number or does it stand for a word or—"

"It spells out hell," he bluntly answers. But despite his monotone, he keeps his eyes on the road and tightens his grip on the wheel. "Call her."

Obeying his request, which is more like a demand, I scroll through his list of contacts until I find Tiffani's number. I take notice of the unbelievable amount of numbers he has saved, the majority of which are girls'. And then I call his girlfriend.

"Baby, what's up?" Tiffani says once she picks up, and I scrunch up my nose at the use of the pet name.

"It's Eden," I tell her. "Tyler's driving. Where are we all going tonight? Has it been decided yet?"

She speaks back within a heartbeat. "Hollywood Sign. We all agreed that we have to show you it. It's amazing." I bite down on my lower lip as excitement radiates through my body. I've always wanted to visit it, and although Venice sounds great too, I'm glad they've chosen the sign. "Have you guys left already?"

"Yeah." My voice hitches when the car jerks roughly to one side, Tyler's steering skills proving to be absolutely pathetic. I wonder how he even got his license to begin with.

"I'll text everyone and see if they're ready and we'll all just meet you out there," she says sharply. "Put me on speaker for a sec." I move the phone away from my ear, doing as she asks, and then hold the device by Tyler.

"Yeah?" he says. He glances down at the screen for only a moment before slamming on the brakes when we approach a stop sign that he obviously hadn't noticed.

"I haven't spoken to you all day!" Tiffani's voice loudly echoes through the speakers. I catch Tyler roll his eyes in complete disrespect. "Did your mom let you out of the house?"

He wrenches up the parking brake and fixes me with a firm glare, slowly shaking his head before saying, "No, I was stuck inside all day."

"That sucks," Tiffani says. Poor, poor girl. She's totally oblivious. "I can't wait to see you! We won't be too long. Just wait for us by the Sunset Ranch."

"Sure."

"Love you."

"Yeah," he says, and then takes the phone from my hand to

hang up the call. Yawning, he leans back in his seat and runs a hand through his hair.

I snort, widening my eyes in disbelief. Every day, every hour he gives me more and more reasons to detest him. "You're unbelievable. Stuck inside all day?"

With a soft grunt, he releases the brake and lets the car roll across the intersection. "That's what I'm going with."

"You're really going to lie to her like that?" I try to meet his eyes as he glances at me, but I'm also keeping my attention on the road, since he doesn't seem to be doing it. "You were at the beach gambling and fighting and you're just going to act like you were inside all day? I feel so bad for her."

He laughs, his voice so deep that it gives me a momentary chill. "Yeah, you're definitely Dave's daughter. You gotta learn to mind your own business, kid."

"Stop calling me kid," I warn. "You're only a year older than me and you've got fewer brain cells."

"Alright, kid," he says, but he's smirking. "Your dad's an asshole."

"At least that's one thing we can agree on." I sigh heavily, filling the silence. There was once a time when I could tolerate my dad. Back when I was younger, I thought he was great. But then I guess he got bored of Mom and bored of me and bored of his life with the two of us, and so he walked out and never came back. And now he's just some loser with a temper and wrinkles and graying hair. "I don't even know what his problem is. I get that you must be super annoying to live with, but it's like he looks for reasons to yell at you."

Tyler taps the steering wheel impatiently. "Tell me about it."

"My mom's better off without him," I muse, and then

instantly backpedal. "Not that it's unfortunate for your mom or anything like that. What about you? Where's your dad?"

Out of nowhere, he slams on the brakes. "What the fuck?"

I blink, stunned by his aggressive reaction and unable to muster up a reply. I try to babble an apology, but my words only come out ragged and uneven. "Sorry—I—"

Clenching his jaw and revving up the engine, he steps on the gas and the car accelerates so fast that my body is thrown back against the seat. "Don't talk," he spits.

"I didn't mean to offend you—" I try, my pulse racing as guilt consumes me. *Maybe his dad has passed*, I think. *And I've just reminded him of it.*

"Shut the hell up," he growls through gritted teeth, and I decide then that I'm not going to say anything more. I fear that if I do, he'll just continue to speed up.

Folding my arms and keeping my eyes away from him, I pay attention to the Los Angeles scenery as we leave Santa Monica on the freeway. I don't mind not talking. Every time I do, he either gives me a cocky answer, a sarcastic reply, or an unnecessary insult. He increases the volume of the music, a selection of R&B songs from his phone, and leaves it blaring loudly for the entire journey, profanities drilling into my ears. The silent tension between us is so awkward, like we should be talking but can't bring ourselves to do so. We're stepsiblings yet it feels as though we're arch-enemies, and I know it shouldn't be this way.

"We're almost there," he mutters an hour of reckless driving later. The lengthy silence is so unbearable by now that I can't even look at him. I've just spent the time trying not to think about the fact that we haven't said a word to each other in over sixty minutes, focusing my thoughts instead on how pretty our surroundings are.

We pull onto a long street named North Beachwood Drive, and before me the Hollywood Sign stands tall on the mountains, overlooking the city in the evening sun. I bite my lip and close the sun visor to get a better look, and I feel almost nervous as I stare at the global icon that I have only ever seen in movies. Seeing it in real life is a completely different experience.

Continuing straight ahead, the road changes from a residential street to a narrow canyon road running along the bottom of the mountain. We pass a sign for the Sunset Ranch that Tiffani mentioned, and shortly after, we pull into a small parking area by the side of the road. Everyone's already there, and I have no idea how they beat us.

"You took the freeway, didn't you?" Meghan asks when we get out of the car, and Tiffani immediately prances over to throw her arms around Tyler.

With his attention being fought for, he somehow manages to reply, "Yeah, did you guys go through Beverly Hills?" Tiffani's pressing her body to his and drawing his lips to hers, but Tyler doesn't seem that interested. Not quite smiling, he leans down and kisses her for the briefest of moments before drawing away and stepping back. I think I'm the only one who's paying attention to them, and when he notices me watching, he lowers his head and stares at the ground.

Jake steps forward while locking his car. "Easiest way to speed and not get caught. We didn't want to keep you waiting for an hour."

"It's incredible," I murmur, shaking my head as I stare up at the bold letters. I squint to avoid the sun. "Thanks for showing me it."

All six of them laugh at once, including Tyler. I receive a few eye-rolls too.

"We haven't shown you it yet," Rachael says. She's holding a few bottles of water in her hands. "We're taking you all the way up."

"Up?" I glance up the mountain again, wondering how steep it is. It looks like hard work.

"Yeah, up," Dean says. There are even more bottles of water in his hands. "We better get moving if you want to see it before the sun goes down. It takes about an hour to get up there. And it's hot. So here." He hands me a bottle, passes one to Meghan, and a third to Jake.

"Who remembers the route?" Rachael asks as she hands Tyler and Tiffani some water.

Tyler snorts, dropping his hand to Tiffani's waist as he points to the trail behind us. "It's not that damn hard, Rach. Sharp left and then right."

I notice a sign for the Hollyridge Trail, and I figure this is the path we'll be taking. Tyler and Tiffani stay at the front, with Jake, Dean, Meghan, Rachael and me behind them, and we begin our ascent. The trail is wide and decorated with the wonderful blessing that is horseshit.

"That was the worst hour of my life," I hiss quietly to Rachael as we tag along slightly behind the rest of the group. "Remind me never to go in a car with Tyler ever again."

She laughs, her feet scuffing the dirt as we head upward. "What happened?"

"He almost killed us because I asked where his dad was," I admit. My eyes find their way to him. He's leading us up the trail with Tiffani behind him. "Is his dad, like . . . dead?"

Rachael almost chokes on her water as she takes a sip, and

then she stops walking for a moment to fix me with a horrified look. "God, Eden, no. Mentioning his dad around him is like stepping in front of a loaded gun. You're asking to be killed."

We start walking again. "Why?"

"He's in jail for car theft or something," Rachael tells me, her voice lowered. She keeps constantly glancing up to check that no one can hear us. "Tyler's super sensitive about it."

My eyes drift back up to him. Somewhere deep inside of me, I feel a little bad for him. Maybe he was close with his dad and now he's no longer in the picture. That must be tough. And a divorce on top of that must be even harder.

It doesn't take us long to reach the sharp left turn that he rudely reminded Rachael of. The trail also goes straight ahead, but we make an almost complete turn around to the left and keep going up. The horseshit disappears after this point.

Dean was right about it being hot, and I'm thankful for the water he gave me. But despite the heat, I don't mind the hike. It's good exercise, and the views of Los Angeles are totally worth it. We stop every so often for a breather, and to just stare out over the city, taking in the sheer size of it and how beautiful it looks from above. It's so peaceful up here.

Eventually we come to a fork in the trail that opens up into two concrete roads, and we take the right.

"Shouldn't we have gone left?" I ask, noticing how we're walking away from the sign rather than toward it. It makes me wonder if they're planning on playing a cruel joke on me.

"No," Jake says. He slows down and matches his pace to mine, hovering by my side as everyone else ignores me. "Going left takes you back down. You go right and you walk around the back of the sign."

I take a long swig of my water and then point my bottle to the road ahead. "Isn't this illegal?"

"Drinking water?" Jake says. "Not that I know of."

I roll my eyes, laughing a little as I watch Meghan pull Rachael up a steeper part of the road. "Is it or isn't?"

"It's only illegal if you cross the fence," he tells me. "You can get pretty close from behind it." He tilts his head back to the sky for a few seconds, and when he glances back down he meets my gaze. "Sorry about how lame I was on Saturday. I lose all conversation skills after a couple beers."

I smile a little. I'm surprised he even remembers talking to me, and I'm blushing slightly that he's apologizing for it. "You weren't lame. Your questions were."

"Let's just start again," he says, and then holds out his hand. "I'm Jake. You must be that cute girl who's here for the summer. Eden, right?"

I feel my cheeks growing even hotter. I anxiously bite my lip and tilt my head so that he doesn't notice. I still manage to shake his hand. His palms feel warm against mine. "Nice to meet you, Jake."

"So," he says, "how's Los Angeles treating you?"

"It's amazing." I notice that either everyone else is speeding up or Jake and I are slowing down, because the gap between us and the rest of the group is increasing. I catch Tyler throwing a disapproving glance back at us. I scrunch up my nose and glare after him for a moment. What's his problem? I try not to let it get to me. "I love it."

Jake's eyes smolder as a wide grin plays on his lips. "Is your boyfriend waiting for you back in Portland?"

"No," I say, and I glance sideways at him. "If you're trying to be subtle here, it's really not working."

"Dammit," he mutters. He lets out a hearty laugh. "Subtlety and conversations aren't really my strong points. But I do have some other strong points. Let me take you out some night and I'll show you them."

He looks confident as he quirks up an eyebrow and waits for a reply, but I'm not sure how to be as smooth as him. I'm not someone who gets asked out by guys a lot. The closest situation I can think of is the one time a guy from algebra class asked me if I would help him understand the basic foundation of quadratic equations back in freshman year. Even then I said no, because he was known for his excessive sneezing. His name was Scott. Behind his back, it was Snotty Scotty.

"Maybe," is the cop-out answer I give Jake. Maybe I'd agree if we'd said more than a few sentences to each other, but right now he's still a stranger to me. Maybe another time. Maybe later.

"I can deal with a maybe," he says. "Hey, look, we're almost there."

My eyes move to the road ahead and I notice how it winds to the left, where a tall wire fence begins. Tiffani skips ahead to the bend, grabbing Tyler's hand and pulling him along behind her. "Eden, come see this!" she calls, and Jake nudges me forward.

Rachael reaches back for my elbow and hauls me up the final part of the route with her, half skipping, half jogging. We've made it to the sign in fifty minutes. The fence follows the path around, and when she pulls me around the corner it hits me all at once that I am standing behind the Hollywood Sign above Los Angeles.

My breath catches in my throat, the silence around me allowing me to focus on the moment. I press my hands to the fence, my eyes wide, my pulse racing. From behind, the view is breathtaking. The letters are absolutely huge, standing above the city. They're much bigger than you think they are.

"Worth the hike?" Dean asks beside me. It pulls me out of my trance. The only thing I can do is slowly nod, my eyes never leaving the view in front of me.

"It's so beautiful," I say quietly.

"We haven't come up here in about a year," Meghan muses as she runs her hands along the wires. "Feels longer."

Out of the corner of my eye, I notice Tyler reaching up to the top of the fence and gripping it firmly. I also notice the number of cameras around us. "What are you guys waiting for?" he asks, and then pulls himself up and over in one swift movement. He lands softly on the other side. "C'mon."

I stare at the cameras for a while, and then the row of signs clearly stating that access to the sign is restricted, and then Tyler. He's staring back at me, his smile lopsided and his eyes narrowed.

"We have, like, ten minutes before they send out the helicopter," Tiffani says as she begins to climb. "Eden, touch the sign and then we'll get out of here."

I stare doubtfully at the two of them. Helicopter? "Really, it's okay. I don't need to touch the—"

"Just touch the fucking sign," Tyler snaps, locking his eyes on me. Tiffani lands on the restricted side of the fence beside him. She places a hand on his chest and pushes him away from the rest of us.

"We won't get caught," Rachael reassures me quietly just before she climbs over with Meghan and Dean. "We do this all the time."

"Don't worry," Jake adds. "If we get caught, we'll all go

down together." He reaches for my hand and places it on the wire. "But we gotta be quick."

Succumbing to the type of peer pressure that my fifth grade teacher used to warn me about, I reach up to the top of the fence and somehow swing my body over it. I lose my balance slightly on the landing, and I only realize then just how steep the mountain truly is. The others have already started making their way down to the sign, but I wait for Jake and he shows me a way down that won't break my neck.

"I love this place," Dean says as he lingers by the first "O." "I wonder how many people around the world would kill for the opportunity to do this. We're lucky."

"Dude, stop getting all sentimental, it's just letters on a mountain," Tyler mutters. "This city is stupid as hell and so is this sign."

"You're so negative," Tiffani murmurs.

Ignoring them, I follow Jake up to the "H." He steps back and nods, a warm smile on his lips. "You first."

I feel nervous for some reason. Perhaps it's the fact that I'm about to do something that so many people dream of, or perhaps it's because I could fall to my death any second. I take a deep breath and step forward, and then I touch the white-painted metal of the "H" of the famous Hollywood Sign.

And I feel the exact same way as I did two seconds ago. "Oh," I say. It occurs to me then that we are all so infatuated by nothing more than pieces of metal on poles.

Jake places his hand next to mine. "How about that date then?"

I might have said yes at this point, simply because we're literally standing underneath the Hollywood Sign and it's the perfect place to accept a date, but Tyler is yelling, "What the hell, man?" before I even get the chance to open my mouth.

"What?" Jake pulls an irritated face, stepping back from the sign to meet Tyler's eyes as he approaches us with his hands balled into fists.

"What the hell did you just say to her?" Tyler's expression is hard, jaw clenched, eyes dark. He steps closely in front of Jake, his forehead tilted down as he narrows his eyes into tiny slits.

"Tension," Rachael mouths when I glance at her for help. I do vaguely remember her saying something about there being this unspoken tension between the pair. Right now, it no longer seems unspoken.

"Bro, get outta my face," Jake mutters. He retreats and shrugs, throwing up his hands and turning to the side.

"No," Tyler objects, shaking his head as he takes a step around Jake, straightening up in front of him again and jabbing a finger into his chest. "You two are not happening. I'll kick your ass if you even think about it."

"Tyler, baby, chill," Tiffani says, and she forces her body in between the two of them. With her hands on Tyler's chest, she tries to push him back, but his eyes are still locked on Jake. "Don't be an asshole. Stop trying to start a fight."

Dean joins in, stepping in front of Jake and shaking his head in disapproval. "C'mon, guys. Quit it."

Then my attention is torn away from the potential fight to the faint drill and the pumping of motors and the whirling of blades, and as the sound grows louder, I find myself glancing up to the sky.

And it is then that I find myself under the eye of an LAPD helicopter.

9

Tilting my head back to the sky, I squint at the vehicle hovering above us. We all stop at once, our words tapering off and our expressions faltering.

"Shit," Tyler yells, and then there's a tremendous clang as he slams his palm against the metal of the "H." He throws his hand back through his hair, shaking his head. "How the hell do they always get out here so fast?"

"Don't trip!" Tiffani yells to us all. She reaches for Tyler's hand and pulls him along with her, but instead of heading back for the fence they make a beeline down the mountain.

"Let's get outta here," Jake calls from beside me, and he steals a good look at the helicopter before he decides to start moving. "Gotta race to the bottom before the cruiser gets here."

"Those two aren't waiting around, are they?" Dean jokes, laughing and nodding toward Tyler and Tiffani's shrinking figures as they dart quickly between the dirt and the rocks and the shrubs. "Poor guy can't afford to get arrested again."

"Again?" I echo, but they all ignore me and make their move, Rachael and Meghan beginning their descent while clinging onto each other as though any misjudged footwork would cause them to fall to their deaths. It probably would.

"Be careful," Dean calls over his shoulder to me as he too follows the vague outline of a trail and widely sidesteps—or slides—his way down.

With the sound of the helicopter still vibrating loudly around us, a wave of adrenaline rushes through my veins and my pulse beats painfully beneath my skin. Here's when running every morning comes in handy. Despite the steepness of the terrain, I rush into action and follow Dean's path. The ground is uneven and borderline painful to walk on at points, and soon I'm struggling to maintain my balance, praying that I don't get arrested and hoping that I don't die.

"Hanging in there, Eden?" Jake throws over his shoulder from beside me, hopping down from one rock to another, laughing. I don't understand how he can possibly find this amusing.

"Trying to!" I call back. Just as I finish, my foot slips on a steeper part of the slope we're carefully edging our way down, and I gasp.

A firm hand latches onto my elbow. "Careful," Jake says firmly as he steadies me. He places his hands on my shoulders. "You alright?"

"I don't want to go to jail," I blurt, and then glance up at the helicopter, panic written all over my face. When I look back down, I spot the rest of the group reaching solid ground again.

Jake laughs, but only as he slowly takes another step. "You're not going to jail," he says, and then drops his hand to mine and pulls me along behind him. "The worst we'll all get is a citation."

Despite the reassurance, my stomach remains in knots as my body is hauled almost numbly down the rest of Mount

Lee. Jake doesn't trip, doesn't slow us down, and doesn't get us caught. I'm entirely thankful when we finally near the bottom after passing some houses and crossing over a trail. I spy the sign for the Sunset Ranch, and it suddenly becomes my favorite sign in the entire world.

"No cruiser," I murmur, and I can almost feel my whole body breathe a sigh of relief. Dad would quite literally cremate me in my sleep and flush away my ashes if I returned home with a trespassing citation.

"Yet," Jake finishes. He lets go of my hand as he jumps down onto the road, and I follow suit, trailing after him around the corner. "We're not clear yet."

When we find our way back to the small parking area where we left the cars, I notice Tyler's is already gone. Jake leads me over to his—a red Ford of some sort. "Meghan and Rach must have gone with Dean," he says as he unlocks the car and slides inside. Tiffani must be with Tyler.

"Where do you think everyone else is going?" I ask as I settle into the passenger seat, and I can only hope that he's a better driver than my stepbrother.

Jake shrugs as he starts up the engine and reverses out onto the road. "Who cares?" *I do,* I think. "What do you wanna do? You hungry?"

For a long moment, my eyes settle on his features as he drives and I can't help but wonder how our escape from the Hollywood Sign has ended up turning into a date. The others are gone and I've been paired off with Jake. But despite my doubts, I am a little hungry. "Is there any good food around here?"

"There's a Chick-fil-A ten minutes away on Sunset Boulevard," he suggests. "We could grab something quick."

"Sure," I say. "We don't have Chick-fil-A in Oregon."

His face falls. "What?"

"We're not allowed to pump our own gas either," I add, and I find myself getting distracted by the idea of home, wondering what Amelia is doing right now and if my mom is lonely by herself in our small house. "Oregon sucks."

"So you must think LA is great," he concludes. "We have signs on mountains and Chick-fil-A and we can pump our own gas without being arrested. Mythical." I laugh a little, as does he, and it's nice to have some male company that isn't my dad and isn't Tyler. The two of them are far too obnoxious and grouchy.

I slump back into the passenger seat and rest my forehead against the window, glancing up to the sky to check on the position of the helicopter, but it seems to have disappeared. And so I can breathe freely again.

"So do you like the city then?" Jake asks a short while later. He increases the air conditioning but lowers the music.

"Yeah," I say. Admittedly, I haven't seen much of it yet, but so far everything is pretty amazing. "More interesting than Portland, that's for sure."

"I've never been to Portland."

"You don't want to." After I say this, I reconsider. "Actually, Portland isn't that bad. We have a great indie scene, but it rains from fall until the end of spring, so that sucks, and there are a lot of strip clubs. The people are great though." I smile only slightly as my eyes fall to my lap. "Well, most of them."

The thing about Portland is that I associate it with so many things I hate. Portland is where my parents fell out of love. Portland is where it seems to rain endlessly. Portland is where my so-called "friends" are. Portland, for the most part, is okay as a city. But my life in that city just isn't that exciting, or even that happy. Santa Monica is a breath of fresh air in comparison.

"Strip clubs?" Jake widens his eyes as he grins. "I really need to visit this terrible city."

I roll my eyes. Guys are all the same. "What's Los Angeles really like, besides the obvious tourist things?"

Jake thinks for a moment as he taps the steering wheel with his thumb. "Well, the gap between rich and poor is drastic. You've got all these big shots living in these huge houses and driving Lambos and then you've got people sleeping on the streets whose only goal in life is to survive the night. It kinda sucks. But in general, the people here are great."

"I never thought about it like that," I say.

We head back down North Beachwood Drive, heading straight until we pull onto Sunset Boulevard. It's an extensive street with cinemas and restaurants and a high school and a whole lot of traffic. I study everything in awe.

When we arrive at the Chick-fil-A drive-thru, Jake pulls up to the speakers and glances sideways at me. "What d'ya need?"

Because Chick-fil-A is non-existent in Oregon I have no idea what food they serve, so I flash my eyes over the menu and choose the first healthy option I see. "The side salad." Jake nods but keeps staring at me expectantly. "That's all," I say.

"Just that?" He raises his eyebrows but quickly sighs. "What is it with girls and salads?" I offer a small smile and he turns to order. "Can I get the spicy chicken sandwich with Coke and the side salad with . . ."

"Water," I say. Again, another stare of disapproval.

"With water," he finishes for the employee nonetheless. "Thanks." We roll forward to the window, and he reaches into his pocket for his wallet, says, "I've got it," and then proceeds to pay for both our food. I say thanks.

We edge forward to the next window, and while we're waiting behind the car currently being served, he stares at me with a sort of perplexed expression.

"I hate junk food, if that's what you're wondering," I say, which is partially false. It's not the food I hate: it's the effects.

He rolls his eyes as we pull up to the final window to collect our bag of food and our drinks, and he passes them over to me to hold while he merges back out onto the boulevard. "You're telling me you hate that spicy chicken sandwich in there with French fries that are quite literally the best things you will ever taste in your entire life?"

"Yes," I answer shortly. "Yes, I hate that terrible spicy chicken sandwich with those awful fries."

"You haven't even tried them before." He shakes his head in dismay as he chuckles, and then he reaches into the bag and fumbles around for a few long seconds to grab his fries while trying to keep his eyes on the road at the same time. When he finds them, he sets them down in the center console and tosses one into his mouth. "Want one? They're good."

"Nope, I need to try out this Chick-fil-A salad and see if it beats Portland's corner shop salads," I muse casually, smirking at him as I pull out the small tray and tear off the plastic. "Definitely looks alright."

Jake stuffs some more fries into his mouth. "You're missing out."

"On heart disease?" I ask. "Good."

He stops chewing to glance at me with a defeated smile on his lips. He nods in surrender.

We head back to Santa Monica—it's getting late—and I devour my salad on the way while Jake finishes up his sandwich, somehow managing not to crash in the process. We take the freeway as the sun sets around us, and the traffic, despite how much I hate it, looks really beautiful at dusk. The music is loud but not too loud, easy for us to talk over and simple to ignore when his mainstream music taste grows unbearable to listen to. The journey is much smoother than it was three hours ago with Tyler.

"You're staying at his place, right?" Jake asks once we're back in the city.

I snap out of the trance I've found myself in. "Whose place?"

"Tyler's," he says. "That's where I'm taking you to, right?"

"Oh," I say. "Yeah. I don't know why he got all up in your face earlier."

"Because he's an ass—" He cuts himself short, clearing his throat. "I probably shouldn't put him on blast in front of his sister."

"Actually," I say, "I agree with what you were just about to say."

He studies me for a long moment, as though he can't figure out if I'm being sarcastic or not, and he eventually decides that I'm being totally serious. "I didn't expect that."

I shrug. "Me either. I didn't expect to hate my stepbrother."

He doesn't reply, mostly because I think he doesn't know how to, and so we spend the five-minute ride to Deidre Avenue in silence, except for his crappy music. All of the lights in the house are on when we pull up outside.

"Thanks for getting me off that mountain and taking me

home," I say once he turns down the music and shuts off the engine. "And thanks for the food."

"No problem, but now can I get your number so I can take you out?" He gives me a playful yet determined smile, his eyes sparkling. "And I promise it won't involve French fries from Chick-fil-A next time."

"Well, you did buy me that salad," I murmur, having a mock debate with myself, teasing him a little as I drag out his wait for an answer. "So I suppose I can give you my number."

His face lights up as he clenches his hand and fist bumps the steering wheel. "Yessssss. What are those digits, girl?" With his other hand, he fishes his phone out of his pocket and hands it to me, and I enter my number.

By now my cheeks are a flaming red. "Don't worry, I didn't give you a fake number or anything."

"Hmm," he says, and he looks me up and down as I open the door. "I'll call you tomorrow to make sure."

"Smooth again," I say, rolling my eyes and stepping out onto the sidewalk. It's dark now. "Thanks."

I gently slam the door shut and he salutes me goodbye through the window before he drives off. I listen to the sound of the engine, the noise of the tires until they fade away. After standing on the sidewalk in the dark for a few minutes, blushing to myself like an absolute creep, I finally turn around and head for the house. It's only then that I notice Tyler's car is parked at the end of the driveway. I thought he would have stayed out longer.

It also occurs to me when I reach the front door that Dad has no idea where I went. I conveniently disappeared right before dinner at the exact time Tyler did, and surely it's not that hard to connect the dots.

Barely breathing, I slowly push open the door and step inside the hall, softly closing it again behind me with an inaudible click. I can hear the TV in the living room, and so I dart past so silently that I can't even hear my own feet as I tiptoe up the stairs. I'm not worried about the fact that I went out. I didn't do anything wrong—besides touching the Hollywood Sign, which just so happens to be illegal—and Dad can't stop me from going out, anyway. I just don't have the energy to talk to him.

"Eden?" a voice whisper-calls from the top of the stairs as I rush up them, and I pause to glance up. Tyler's staring down at me, his eyes narrowed. "Where the hell did you go?"

"Where the hell did *you* go?" I shoot back. I stand up straight, climb the remaining few steps, and then stare back at him evenly once I'm level with him. "You just ditched the rest of us. Nice teamwork."

He looks tired, like he hasn't slept in days, or perhaps he's high. Either way, he groans. "I don't work well with cops, alright? I can't get caught again."

"Again," I repeat for the second time today. I'm still wondering what other criminal activity he gets up to besides throwing himself into restricted areas and snorting cocaine. "When did you get home?"

"Twenty minutes ago," he says. "Mom finally stopped grilling me about the whole beach thing earlier."

"Cool," I say bluntly, and then make my way into my room. He follows me. "What do you want?"

"Nothing," he says, and I watch as he quickly averts his eyes. I figure this is the perfect opportunity to question him about his little escapade earlier, because it was totally uncalled for.

"What was your problem with Jake?" I fold my arms across my chest, furrowing my eyebrows as he immediately turns around and leaves. And just like he followed me, I do the same in return. I end up in his room for the first time and I'm surprised he doesn't automatically demand that I get out. "I asked you a question."

"I'm not answering it," he mutters. "Wait, I will." He swivels around, his chest puffed out and his jaw clenched tight. "That guy is the second-biggest asshole I've ever met. Don't waste your time. He'll screw you over."

"Who's the first?" I ask. "Yourself?"

He stares back at me for a long moment. "Close enough."

"Okay, well, Jake's actually really nice," I say, taking a step back as I inconspicuously study the room. "Unlike some people around here. And you don't really get a say in whether I want to hang out with him or not."

"You're kidding, right?" His eyes widen and he gives a short, harsh laugh. "Alright. Don't say I didn't warn you."

"Why do you even care?" I press, aggravated at the way he's getting pissed off. Maybe if he was nicer to me I'd take into consideration the fact that he hates Jake. But he's not nice, so I don't have to.

"I don't," he snaps.

"You clearly do," I retort, but it feels pointless arguing. He's never going to admit the truth.

Wandering to the opposite side of the room, he stuffs his hands into his pockets and comes to a halt by a collection of haphazardly stacked DVDs. "What's your, um, favorite movie?"

I'm blinking at him now. What's my favorite movie? Really? I know he's trying to avoid my persistent questioning, but he could have at least come up with something better. "*Lady and the Tramp*," I finally admit, mostly because I've given up on finding out why he cares if I hang out with Jake.

"The Disney movie?" There's a laugh threatening to escape his lips, but when I nod and he realizes I'm completely serious, he clears his throat to get rid of it. "Why?"

"Because," I say, defensively, "it's the greatest love story of all time. Romeo and Juliet have got nothing on Lady and Tramp. They were so different yet they made it work. Lady was totally normal and Tramp was totally reckless, yet they fell in love." I pause to breathe, replaying the movie in my head. I find myself smiling. "And plus, the spaghetti scene is totally iconic."

"Totally," Tyler mocks. Now he is laughing, and it only reinforces my earlier realization that he does absolutely nothing besides give me migraines. I don't get it at all. How can he go from being so angry and nasty one second to relaxed and playful the next? "And I'm pretty sure Lady wasn't normal. She was boring and didn't know how to have fun. Tramp's my kinda guy."

"What, because he roams the streets the same way you do when you're stumbling home drunk at the weekends?" I smile sweetly at him, secretly hoping to annoy him the same way he irritates me. But he takes my remark as a joke, so I roll my eyes and look away from him.

I study his room. It's mostly navy, his bed unmade, mounds of clothes lying in the far corner and a can or two of beer decorating his bedside table. I wouldn't expect anything less of him. The closet is open and on the top shelf I spot the sleeve of a varsity jacket hanging over the edge, like it's been thrown in there carelessly. "You play football?" I ask.

"Huh?" Tyler says, and he follows my eyes to check what I'm staring at. "No. That's Dean's. I'm not really the football type."

"Dean plays football?" I'm surprised Tyler doesn't. He fits the total alpha male footballer position perfectly, like those stereotypical quarterbacks they have in every single high school movie. "And you don't?"

"Yeah," he says as he walks over to closet. "So does Jake. I used to play when I was younger, but I stopped back in middle school."

"Why?" I'm staring curiously after him, and I try to remind myself that this person infuriates me and that I shouldn't care, but it's no use. There are so many things I don't know about him and, honestly, it's intriguing. I can't help myself.

"According to some people, football is a waste of a time," he tells me, but his voice suddenly adopts a much harder tone. He lingers by his closet for a little while. "'Why waste your time on sport? Throwing footballs around isn't going to get you into Ivy League. Stay inside and study instead so that you can actually be successful,'" he quotes, but he's not laughing or cracking a smile. He's just staring at the ground.

"Who told you that?" Now I'm even more curious. For starters, Tyler doesn't strike me as the type of person who'd apply for an Ivy League school. In fact, I doubt he even likes school. People like him never do.

"Just someone," he murmurs with a small shrug. "So that's why I wasn't allowed to play."

I raise an eyebrow at him, but he still has his back to me. "Allowed?"

Immediately, he shifts uncomfortably and stretches up to tuck the sleeve of Dean's varsity jacket back onto the shelf.

"I mean, that's why I stopped," he says quickly, correcting himself. He might think I won't pay close attention to him, but I do. I notice and absorb every single thing he says, and I have done since the moment he first stormed into the barbecue.

But he's clearly unsettled, so I decide it's best not to question his use of the word "allowed." It suggests that whoever told him that football was a waste of time was someone with authority over him. And I get the sense that he greatly dislikes this person. Probably a teacher.

I focus on Tyler again, and with his back still turned to me, he pulls out a clean shirt from the closet and slips off the one he's wearing. Just as quickly, he swipes on the new one. But in those few seconds, I spot a small tattoo on the back of his shoulder, written in calligraphy. "I really have to give Dean his jacket back. He's been bugging me about it for ages."

He's adjusting his T-shirt, and I'm just staring at him, almost without realising at first. I notice how bulky his arms are, how tanned his skin, how defined his jaw. I shouldn't be noticing these things, but I am. I swallow.

"What does your tattoo mean?" I ask, my voice slightly croaky. I keep my eyes trained on him as he spins back around, surprised by my question. "I'm going to ignore the fact that you clearly got it illegally."

He plays dumb. "My tattoo?" When I raise my eyebrows and purse my lips, he gives me a proper answer. "Uh, it says *Guerrero*. It's Spanish for 'fighter.'" He looks almost nervous that I've asked him about it, and he silently scratches at the back of his head for a few moments.

Now I'm interested. "Why Spanish?"

"I'm fluent," he tells me. "Both my parents are. My dad taught me when I was a kid."

The mere mention of his dad reminds me of what Rachael told me earlier. His dad's in jail, so I do the respectable thing and don't ask any more questions. "I don't know any Spanish," I admit, biting my lip. "I speak French. Like the Canadians. *Bonjour.*"

"*Me frustras,*" he says in reply, and I have no idea what it means. "*Buenas noches.*" He smirks when he notices my puzzled expression. "That means 'Goodnight.'"

"Oh." I turn for the door to make my exit, but not before offering him the smallest of smiles. "*Bonsoir.*"

10

When the weekend rolls around and marks the end of my first week in Los Angeles, I finally get another chance to call my mom during a break in her hectic work schedule. She's working full-time, including night shifts and overtime, as a nurse at Providence Portland Medical Center, trying her hardest to support us both on a single income. Although Dad's payments help, it's still a struggle for her.

"Hey, Eden," Mom murmurs into the phone just before it goes to voicemail. "How are you, honey?"

"You sound tired." I frown. It's horrible knowing the pressure she's under yet being unable to do anything to make the situation better. "How long was your shift?"

"Twelve hours," she says quietly, but quickly continues before I can say anything. "A patient brought in her guide dog today and it was the cutest thing I've seen since you were a baby. It kept the kids in the waiting room entertained. I almost felt heartbroken when it left. So I was thinking that when you come home, we should totally get a dog. It'll keep me company when you go off to college next year. What do you think?"

I smile at her childlike enthusiasm. "Okay, we can get a dog. German Shepherds are gorgeous."

"Are those the intimidating ones?"

"Yes."

She pauses for a long moment. "I'll start looking." When I laugh, so does she, and then I hear her yawn across the line. "Have you settled in yet or is it still awkward?"

"Still awkward," I say. "I'm waiting for Dad to have an actual conversation with me, but it doesn't look like that's going to happen anytime soon."

"Douchebag Dave," Mom murmurs away from the phone, but I hear her anyway. "I wish you weren't stuck there with him. I honestly feel so bad for you. You know you didn't have to go."

"It's actually not that bad," I say. I shrug even though she can't see me, but I really wish she could. It's hard without her, hard having to be stuck an entire state away from the only person who's been there for me for all my life, hard having to resort to phone calls every couple days because it's the closest I can get to her. "There's this group of friends who I'm hanging out with. They're all really nice except for one."

"Which one?"

"The one that's my stepbrother," I say, and then laugh, because it's really absurd that the one person I dislike is the one I'm supposed to not dislike. "What are you doing tonight?"

"Ordering myself a bucket of fried chicken to enjoy while I spend my Saturday evening alone on the couch watching whatever crap comes on, because I'm in my late thirties and I'm already divorced and I work long hours and I look very unattractive," she kids, her voice light before she falters. "I miss you. I hope you're having fun and I hope you're behaving."

My chest feels heavy. I feel bad for leaving her alone. "When I come home we're going to get that dog and we're going to watch *Pretty Little Liars* together and we're going to order all the fried chicken you want. You only have seven weeks to wait."

"That's a hell of a long wait, Eden Olivia."

I smile to myself. "Try not to miss me too much and it'll go faster."

"Okay," she says. "I'll try not to miss my only daughter while you go and enjoy your weekend. Talk to you soon, baby." She hangs up the call while she yawns for a second time, and then the line falls into an endless, echoing silence.

Mom deserves so much better than the life she has.

"Who were you talking to?" a male voice demands as my bedroom door swings open.

My heart almost stops and, quite clearly startled, I flash my eyes up to the intruder of my personal space. It's Tyler, eyes narrowed, as per usual. "Did I say you could come in?"

"Who were you talking to?" he asks once more, firmer this time. "You got a boyfriend back in Portland or some shit?"

I stare at him, willing myself not to burst into laughter as he stares evenly back at me with his lips in a firm line. "Were you eavesdropping?"

"My room is right next door," he says, stating the obvious. "The walls are thin as hell."

I pull a face as I get to my feet. "Okay, well, I was talking to my mom." His features relax and I glance at the clock on the wall by the door. It's almost 8PM. "Shouldn't you be out doing something?"

"That's actually what I gotta talk to you about," he murmurs. Taking a deep breath, he shuts my door and wanders into the middle of the room. I raise my eyebrows at him. "You're not doing anything tonight, right?"

"No," I say. "Everyone's busy." Rachael is in Glendale for a few days visiting her grandparents, Meghan has the flu, and Tiffani spends every third weekend with her dad, who doesn't let her make plans that don't involve him.

"Alright, you're coming with me," Tyler states. "Party down on 11th Street. Don't mention it to your dad." He turns to leave, but I call him back.

"Who says I want to go to a party with you?" I cross my arms across my chest. Just this morning he was yelling at me for blocking the staircase. "Sorry, but you're sort of the last person I want to hang out with."

He grits his teeth. "Get ready."

"No."

"Yes," he says. "What else are you gonna do? Sit here all night in your room like a damn loser with no social life?"

I press my lips together. He has a point. Sort of. "What will I wear?"

Immediately a triumphant smile crosses his face and his eyes light up. "Anything. It's not the same kinda party as Austin's. This one's more . . . chill. You could turn up in a pair of sweats and you wouldn't be out of place."

"Chill?" I arch a brow again. A bunch of ideas float around my mind.

"Yeah," he says. "Are you up for some predrinks while you're getting ready? My stash is running a little low, because Mom's constantly searching my room, so all I got is beer and some Jack and a little vodka. You know what, I'll surprise you." He smiles. And it's a genuine smile, not a sarcastic one and not a smirk, without a single trace of egoism.

He heads back through to his own room, leaving me baffled. For someone who hates me so much, he seems pretty persistent that I attend this "chilled" party with him. But as long as he isn't muttering insults at me or shooting death glares in my direction every so often, I don't mind. And if accompanying him is what it takes to get on his good side, then so be it. I like the softer side of him he's briefly shown me and I hope he'll remain in a good mood for the night, because I think I might just find him less annoying and more likeable if he does. It's a chance I'm willing to take.

Thankfully, I've already showered. Mid-afternoon, I got so bored that I resorted to watching hair tutorials on YouTube and trying to follow along, only to be greatly disappointed when my results looked nothing like all those British beauty gurus promised me. Eventually I found one that worked, so my hair has been in a cute messy updo for the entire night, so I consider it done and ready to go.

"I'll probably be ready in twenty minutes," I tell Tyler when he waltzes into my room, two drinks in his hands, one a bottle of Bud Light, the other a glass of what appears to be Coke.

"No problem," he says as he hands me the glass, his cold fingers brushing mine. I flinch at his touch, but he doesn't seem to notice. "Here."

"Vodka and Coke?" I guess.

"Yeah," he says, almost sheepishly, as he pops off the cap of his beer on the edge of my dresser. "Always a safe bet. You like it, right? If you want beer, I can get you some—"

"This is fine," I gently cut in. He's rambling a little. "I like it."

"Okay, good," he mumbles. Tilting his head back, he takes a long swig of his beer and then glances around my room. "Just, uh, come get me when you're ready."

"Are you guys drinking?"

Both my head and Tyler's snap over to my open door to find Jamie staring back at us, his expression glum as his eyes run over the drinks in our hands. Tyler tries to hide his behind his back, but he's fifteen seconds too late.

"No," he lies as keeps the bottle out of view, despite how pointless it is. His tone is gentle. "You know we're not twenty-one. Why would we be drinking?"

"I can see it right there," Jamie points out, and he nods his head at the glass I'm still holding. "Does Mom know?"

Tyler places a hand on the back of his neck as he strains it to one side. "It's only a little. Can you give us some space?"

"Twenty bucks," Jamie says, but there's a mischievous grin playing on his lips as he holds out his hand. He blinks at Tyler with an expectant look in his eyes.

"I gave you thirty the other day," Tyler claims. Nonetheless, he places his beer on my dresser and reaches into the back pocket of his jeans to pull out his wallet. "Because you wanted that video game, remember? Don't think that I forgot, because I haven't."

"Hmm." Jamie thinks for a moment. "I'll take ten then."

Tyler's laughing. It makes me wonder if they do this a lot: Tyler buying Jamie's silence. "Fine, ten." He passes Jamie a ten-dollar bill and then gently pushes his head away with the quick flick of his wrist. "Now get outta here."

Jamie brushes Tyler's hand away. Stuffing the bill into his pocket, he quickly darts across the hall and back into his own room, calling, "I would have taken five."

Tyler chuckles and reaches for his beer to take a long swig. He swallows it with a sigh. "Kid treats me like an ATM." He turns his smile on me and then edges out onto the landing. "Get ready," he says.

I close the door after him and then drift into my bathroom. After freshening up and applying a not-too-heavy layer of makeup, I pull on a pair of skinny jeans and a tank top with a red hoodie thrown over my shoulders. After all, Tyler implied I would be out of place if I made too much effort, so I'm relieved that I can wear Converse this time rather than heels.

"Okay," I say as I enter his room. "I'm ready and my drink is finished, so we can go now."

Tyler's wearing jeans and a faded gray T-shirt. He's standing by the window, lining up three empty beer bottles on the ledge, and he glances over his shoulder at me. "It's about damn time." All at once he knocks them over and then makes straight for me, pulling out his car keys from his pocket.

"What are you doing?" I shake my head in disapproval, and I almost reach over to grab them from him, but I stop myself. "You've just drunk all those beers."

"Jesus," he says. "Fine, I'll get us a ride. Happy?"

"Yes," I say as he tosses the keys onto his bed.

He pulls out his phone and calls someone so quickly that they must be on speed dial. The person on the other end of the line answers almost immediately, and I watch Tyler's face while he talks. "Yeah, yeah, I'm just coming, Declan. Who's driving tonight?" Pause. "Give me Kaleb. Can you ask him to get over to my place as fast as he can? Couple doors down, actually." Pause. "Thanks, man. See you in twenty."

"Kaleb?" I ask once he ends the call.

"Kaleb's alright," he says, and then laughs a little as he shifts over to his bedroom door. "He's in college, but he still looks like a high school sophomore. He knows how to have a good time, though." Pushing open the door, he stealthily edges his way out onto the landing and then down the staircase, with me creeping along behind him. We make our way into the kitchen before slipping out through the patio doors.

"Shouldn't I have told my dad I was going out?" I ask, following Tyler around to the front of the house. "I mean, I get that you need to sneak out, but I'm not on lockdown. He's going to kill me when he realizes I've left without telling him."

"Don't get worked up about it," he tells me. "Just drink a lot and in a couple hours you won't care."

Purposely staying away from the living room window, we head down the street, almost six doors down, and then hover on the parking strip. Although Tyler may be dumb in too many ways to count, he's smart enough to know how not to get caught. If I'd been doing this on my own, I would have most definitely been stupid enough to get picked up right outside the house, which is also right in front of Dad and Ella. So I have to give him props.

"Is it a big party?" I ask, looking up at him as he leans against the trunk of a tree.

"Not too big," he says with a shrug, but then he starts chewing his lower lip as though he's nervous, and I figure he doesn't want to talk to me. This annoys me, because we end up standing in silence for five minutes until a Chevy truck loudly pulls up next to us.

The window rolls down and a small guy leans forward and yells, "Get in, bro!" but all I can do is stare at him. Tyler's right. Kaleb looks like a kid, like his features have yet to fully develop, and I can't possibly imagine him walking around a college campus.

Tyler steps past and pulls open the passenger door while I force my body up and into the backseat of the beat-up truck. It stinks of tobacco smoke inside and there's a stack of McDonald's cups littering the floor.

"Who's this?" Kaleb asks as he studies me in the rearview mirror. He's extremely pale, with short, dirty-blond hair.

"My, um . . ." Tyler starts, but for some reason he struggles to get the words out. He leans forward to increase the volume of the rap music that Kaleb's playing. "My stepsister," he finally says.

"Didn't know you had one." Kaleb looks at me even harder in the mirror. It makes me feel uncomfortable, but finally he looks away and puts the truck back in drive. He doesn't wait for Tyler to reply before he moves on to another question, thankfully changing the subject. "So how've you been, dude? Feels like I haven't spoken to you in weeks!"

Because Kaleb is a stranger to me, I keep out of the conversation (I don't think they want me in it, anyway) and allow them to talk away to each other for the ten-minute journey to the party. Tyler keeps thanking him for the ride, and Kaleb keeps saying it's no problem, and then they keep nodding their heads to the awful music.

All the while, I stare at the lyrics on my shoes.

When we finally arrive at the party and pull up to a stop outside the small house, it's a completely different scene from that of Austin's party a week ago. There's no one in sight. It doesn't look like a party at all.

"Are you sure this is the right house?" I ask the second I slide out of the truck and Kaleb locks up.

"Yeah," Tyler says, nodding to the door as he starts walking toward it. "Remember it's a smaller party. Twenty people, max."

A small party means it won't be so easy to just blend in,

to linger in the background and pray that no one notices the stranger in the room. I'll stick out. People will realize that they've never seen me before. And I'll hate every moment of it.

The second Tyler swings open the front door, I'm deafened by horrendous house music. The beat drops drill into my ears and I can feel them giving me brain damage. The place reeks of weed too. Nonetheless, the party is much less crowded and I don't feel like I'm suffocating as I trail after Tyler into a room that has been set up to store all the alcohol. Kaleb doesn't follow.

"Tyler, you made it," a guy says when we walk in. Surprisingly, he looks totally sober. "Who's this?"

"My stepsister. Eden, this is Declan. She's hanging with me for the night if that's alright with you."

"Woah." Declan's blue eyes widen as he passes Tyler a can of beer. "Dude, when the hell did ya get a stepsister?"

"Last week, bro," he murmurs, but quickly turns to smile at me. "What do you want?"

"Anything," I say, running my eyes over the table. "Actually, I'll just take another Coke and vodka."

Tyler rolls his eyes as he grabs a cup, makes up the drink, and then hands it to me. All the while, Declan watches us. "I'll show her around," Tyler tells him, and then he places his hand on my shoulder and directs me toward the door. He nudges me back out into the hall, but he doesn't join me. Instead he quickly turns to Declan and pulls him over to the corner of the room.

I watch as Tyler murmurs something to him, to which Declan nods in reply. Their voices are so low that it's impossible for me to hear, but Tyler heaves a sigh and finds his way back over to me, stepping out into the hall by my side. Several people greet him as they pass, but he keeps his attention mainly on me. "Alright, you see these people?" We stop by the door to the living room, and he uses his beer can to motion toward the group of people lounging on the couches. They all look deflated, and many of them appear to be in their twenties.

"Yeah?" I don't see where he's going with this. "They look bored."

Tyler stifles a laugh and turns away from the door. "They're far from bored. Hey, check out this guy." He points his can to the floor, and down by the hall table, a small orange and white cat is cowering. "Aw, man." Laying his beer down, he bends and scoops the cat up into his arms, ruffling the fur on the back of its neck. "Why not date this little guy? It's probably got bigger balls than Jake."

"Put it down," I say forcefully, but the cat seems to be enjoying the attention, because it begins to playfully climb up Tyler's arms.

"What can I say?" he says as he rubs its ears, and it purrs in satisfaction. I can feel my lips twitching into a smile as I watch them. "I'm a pussy magnet."

I pull a face and turn away from him, but he laughs, places the animal back down on the ground and switches it for his beer. It darts off into another room. "Look, even that cat has had enough of your bullshit."

Tyler rolls his eyes, but his smirk soon fades. "Go talk to some people. I'm heading out back for a while."

Heading out back? I know that reference. I know what's out back. I know what he's up to. Immediately my mood changes. "Are you kidding me?"

He stares back, his expression nonchalant, and he takes a swig of his beer. "Huh?"

"Don't act stupid," I hiss as I step closer to him, leaning in so he can hear me, my drink almost crushed against his chest. "I didn't come with you to this bullshit party so that you could just leave me by myself while you stand around in the back yard smoking joints and making pretty little coke lines to snort."

"It's none of your business," he shoots back, stepping away from me. "Go make some friends and leave me to do whatever the hell I want."

He tries to head off down the hall, but I follow close on his heels and quite literally shove my body between him and the back door when we reach it. "You're not going out there. It's so stupid."

All of a sudden, a wave of fury comes over him and he slams his beer into the wall, crushing the entire can against the plaster as the liquid inside showers to the floor. "Get out of my fucking way."

"No!"

He lurches forward, wrapping his long fingers around my wrist and squeezing it tightly, almost numbing my entire arm. His body is so close to mine, and his eyes are so fierce that I find myself shrinking beneath their force. "Eden," he whispers slowly. "Don't."

"No," I object once more, shaking off his grasp. I will myself not to back down despite the crushed beer can and my numb wrist. "Why do you do it?"

"Because I need to, okay?" he almost yells, and he quickly glances around to ensure no one is listening.

"You don't *need* to," I say. "You *want* to."

For a long moment, he just stares at me in silence. It's like he's wondering what to do next, what to say, how to get around me. And then he shakes his head, runs a damp hand through his hair, and breathes, "You don't get it."

I want to ask him what it is that I don't get, but he gently shoves me to the side and wrenches open the door. He slips out, slamming it shut behind him. I'm furious, and if I hadn't been humiliated the last time I went outside and interrupted him, then perhaps I would do it again. But I know it's pointless to go out there, so I storm back through to the front of the house and take a moment to think about what I'm going to do.

"Eden? What the hell are you doing here?"

I spin around in the direction of the voice, and I am utterly stunned and completely grateful to find Jake standing behind me, his lips parted as he stares at me. "Jake! I came with Tyler but he's . . . Well, he's pissing me off."

"Eden . . ." He places a hand to his forehead and steps closer to me, leaning in by my ear as he lowers his voice. "You know this is a stoner party, right?"

"A what?" I blurt, and he tells me with his eyes that I need to shut up, so I bite my lip.

"Look around you, Eden," he whispers, his breath hot on my skin. "Everyone's high."

My eyes slowly drift around the hall, to the open door of the living room. Tyler was right. These people aren't bored. Their eyes are all bloodshot and dilated, half of them staring at the ceiling while the rest laugh hysterically. The longer I watch them, the more it becomes obvious. A stoner party. Tyler really brought me to a damn stoner party.

"What are you doing here then?" I demand, folding my arms in disgust.

"Friend of mine needed a ride home," Jake explains, narrowing his eyes as he searches our surroundings. "I came to get him but looks like he already got his ass outta here. Which is something you should really do. Eden, these aren't the kind of people you want to hang out with."

"Please get me out of here," I whisper, my eyes wide. "I can't believe he brought me here."

"He's an asshole, that's why."

Funny. Tyler said the exact same thing about him. It's their word against each other's, and it's up to me to choose whose side I'm going to be on. And right now, it's Jake's. Because if I had to decide which one of them was the asshole, I would have to point to my stepbrother.

11

I can't help but feel furious that Tyler genuinely thought it was a good idea to invite me along to a stoner party. Did he really think I'd have a good time with a bunch of people sitting around getting high? It was miles away from a good idea, and I wondered why Tyler even invited me. What was he thinking? *Was* he thinking?

Jake is less stupid. He's got enough brain cells to know what's good and what's bad, and it's because of this that I've ended up in the passenger seat of his car. And wanting to hurl my fist through the windshield.

"I'm actually meant to be meeting Dean in fifteen minutes," says Jake, glancing at me with a sort of bummed expression in his eyes. "You can come hang with us or I can take you home. Choice is yours."

The idea of going back home after being stuck inside all day alone doesn't strike me as fun, and right now all I really need is some decent, non-drug-related human company. And thankfully, Dean is sweet. "Are you sure it's okay if I come with you?"

"Sure it is," he says. "Nice choice."

I heave a sigh as my body cools down a little, and I sink into the seat and adjust the air conditioning. It's easier to feel relaxed in Jake's car than it is in Tyler's, simply because I don't feel like I'm on the verge of death each time we turn a corner. "Who were you looking for?"

"Dawson Hernandez," he says, and I'm not sure why I even asked. I don't know anyone here. "Sophomore. I gotta watch out for him."

"Where are we meeting Dean?" I ask, changing the subject, hoping to forget about this wonderful stoner party. The more I think about it, the more I feel sick.

"Some band he likes—La Breve Vita?—is playing a free gig downtown. We're gonna check it out."

Admittedly, I've never heard of this band either. But given that they're playing a free show, they must be pretty unknown. "Okay," I say. "Sounds good."

It doesn't take us long to hit the busy downtown nightlife of Santa Monica on a Saturday evening, and the club signs are electric, the music loud, the people drunk, the prostitutes plentiful. We pull up in a small parking lot around the back of an even smaller building, and I can't quite figure out if it's a club or a bar or a restaurant or a weed dispensary. Either way, we head inside.

The room looks like someone's basement, and is dim and crowded and stuffy and hot. There's a tiny stage, and on this tiny stage there are four figures, either strumming or drumming or singing. I step over some crushed plastic cups.

"You finally got here!" Dean's voice echoes over the music from somewhere. He steps around from behind us, his face aglow from the flashing spotlights. "Eden? I didn't know you were coming."

"Found her when I was looking for Dawson," Jake explains, and I watch as Dean's expression falters and they exchange a knowing look.

"At Declan's party?"

"Yeah," Jake says, and he tilts his face up to the stage, laughing as though I'm not even present. "She had no idea."

The song finishes, the small crowd cheering and applauding before the singer gestures them to be silent. He steps forward to the microphone, clutching it in his hands before pacing the stage with it. "Thanks for coming out tonight, guys. You're all fucking awesome. All of you. Even that middle-aged virgin at the back who's only here for the free beer. You're great, man. You're fucking great." He breathes a heavy laugh into the microphone, gazing at his audience as they throw in some chuckles.

"You're better off here," Dean whispers to me, his eyes fixed on the stage. "I love this band."

"Alright, before we move on to the next piece of the set," the singer says, "I gotta remind you all to not give a damn what anyone else thinks. Your life is your life, your music is your music, your choices are your choices, and your vodka is your vodka. Don't waste your time doing dead-end bullshit. Do shit you wanna do. Go clubbing every night, throw yourself out of a plane, visit Bulgaria. I don't care. Do shit that makes you feel happy as fuck, because LA BREVE VITA! Enjoy the set. *Tanto amore.*"

The crowd erupts into further applauding and whooping as the drumming starts again, the guitarist and the bassist and the singer all joining in sync.

"Is La Breve Vita Latin or something?" I ask, turning to Dean. He seems more likely than Jake to know the answer.

Dean laughs and shakes his head. "It's Italian. So am I. Well, half."

"No way," I say. I raise my voice to compete with the music. "Did you live in Italy?"

"No, I was born here," he admits, a small smile on his lips as he glances between the stage and me. "My mom's Italian. My dad met her while he was on vacation in Naples and she moved over here. I've never actually stepped foot in Italy. Weird."

"That's so cool," I gush, because it is compared with my own parents' magnificent love story. Mom and Dad ended up at a house party together, drunkenly made out, and then went for hot dogs together the next day. Romantic. "Do you speak Italian?"

"Not much. Just a little," he tells me sheepishly. He continues to nod his head in time with the music.

I glance at the stage and then back to him again. "So what does La Breve Vita mean then?"

"Life is short." He grins, his smile so wide that I wonder if it hurts. "That's why I love them. They stand for living your life to the fullest. And they have kickass songs."

We laugh, but Jake doesn't. Quite frankly, I forgot he was even here until he clears his throat and steps in front of me. "Eden," he says, "are you thirsty?"

My eyes fall to the plastic beer cups on the ground, and then I study the dingy bar in the corner, and then I smile. "I'm good."

The band's set goes on for over an hour. All three of us enjoy it, but especially Dean, and by the time we're piling out of the door I feel like I've had a good night. Chilling out at the back of a small gig and listening to indie tunes beats getting drunk at a stoner party. I'm glad I came, and we find ourselves stopping by a small store for tacos before heading back to the parking lot.

"I could give you a ride back, Eden," Dean says as he stops

by his car. There's only two there, his and Jake's; the rest are gone by now. "I'm passing Tyler's place anyway."

Jake halts to stuff his hands into his pockets, his eyebrows furrowing. "I'll take her home," he says firmly. "I'll talk to you tomorrow, bro. Watch yourself."

Dean offers a single nod. "No problem. Catch you guys later."

As he slides into his car and starts up the engine, Jake and I are left alone in the lot, comfortable in the silence. Although it's not exactly silent. There's still the irritating thudding of house music bouncing from the clubs nearby. Dean waves as he drives past and away from us.

"So," Jake says, and then laughs lightly, "what do you wanna do now? 'Cause I really don't want to take you home yet."

"What time is it?"

"Just after midnight." He stares down at me with his eyes smoldering, his lips parted. Throughout the week that I've been here, I've grown comfortable around him.

I've also noticed how attractive he is.

"So you want me to take you home?" he offers, but it's an empty suggestion. "Or we can hang out for a little while longer, if you're up for it."

I think about how tired I am, which isn't very, and I think about how mad Dad probably is, which *is* very. I don't want to go home quite yet. "Can we keep hanging out? I want to avoid my dad."

Slowly, a smile spreads across his lips. "It's getting late, so how about a movie at my place?"

"Only if it's a Disney movie," I say.

"Will *The Lion King* suffice?"

"What kind of a question is that?"

Jake rolls his eyes, shaking his head as he turns away from me and walks toward his car. "C'mon, get in. We've got a movie to watch."

Jake's house is in the Wilshire neighborhood—he tells me that mine is within the North of Montana region, which is, according to him, the city's expensive neighborhood—and we pull up outside a pale-bricked detached house surrounded by shrubbery. It looks pretty big but nothing close to the size of my dad's house, or Rachael's, or Tiffani's, or any other house that I've seen so far. This neighborhood seems more crammed together, like the developers were low on space so decided to just pile houses on top of each other.

But it's a really nice place, and as Jake is leading me upstairs to his room I admire how cozy the house feels, with the overflowing rows of photo frames and trophies and ornaments and other sentimental memories. Dad's house lacks this kind of warmth.

Eventually, Jake notices me admiring every display. "Uh, my mom's a little crazy."

"No," I say, "it's cute."

He groans, reaching into a room and flicking on a light. So far the house has been quiet, so I'm guessing his parents are asleep. "It's a mess, but whatever. I'll go get the movie." Brushing past me, he disappears into another room at the other end of the hall while I enter his.

There's a mound of clothes in one corner, a bed in another, and a large TV mounted on the wall. I also spot a football perched atop the chest of drawers, and I run my eyes over the helmet on the floor.

"Tyler mentioned that you played," I muse when Jake appears again, DVD in hand.

"Yeah, halfback," he says without much interest. "Alright, time to feel sorry for Simba."

We get the movie set up, keeping the volume down low so as to not wake anyone, and soon we find ourselves collapsed in a heap on his bed. It's almost 1AM by now, and I'm starting to yawn. Even Jake seems too worn out to even pay attention to Mufasa's death.

"You know," he murmurs while he fidgets with the pillows, "I don't just watch *The Lion King* with any girl."

I sit up, my heart aching as I watch the awful scene unfold before me, and I wave him away with my hands. "Shhh. Mufasa's dead, Jake. Show some respect."

"God bless Mufasa, may he rest in peace in animation heaven," he says solemnly. He bows his head and then props himself up on his elbows with a small smirk on his face.

I can't remember when we turned the lights off, but I suddenly notice the darkness and how the TV is lighting up his face, illuminating his features and drawing my attention to his eyes. "That was a great eulogy," I say.

"Thanks." He pushes himself up further, sitting upright and staring back at me with interest. "So let me get this straight. You're from Portland, which is a cool city, apparently, and you can't pump your own gas and you order salad from Chick-fil-A and you end up at stoner parties and you love Disney movies. Nice."

"That's pretty accurate," I agree, nodding in approval.

"Don't go home," he says. We're talking over the movie, but by this point I'm no longer watching. I'm now staring at his lips as he talks, noticing how they curve as he smiles. "Just stay here for the night."

"My dad will quite literally have a seizure if I don't come

home," I murmur, but it's not a bad idea. We're both exhausted, and having Jake drive me home just doesn't seem like a safe option. He's likely to fall asleep at the wheel.

"Just stay," he says again, his eyes smoldering so intensely that it's beginning to give me goosebumps. "I've got *The Jungle Book* downstairs somewhere."

"I do like *The Jungle Book*," I whisper, fiddling with my hands in my lap as I glance down. But when my eyes flicker back up again, Jake's lips, which I was busy staring at a few moments ago, are now edging toward mine, and my breath catches in my throat.

It's a good long second before they finally brush my mouth, my chest tight as shivers surge through my body, his warm breath tickling my cheek as he pauses for a moment, his face hovering by the side of mine. It's as though he's waiting for me to pull away or kiss him back. I don't even have to think about it.

My lips find his, slowly locking in place as my eyelids flutter shut, and I feel his hand move to the small of my back. There's a soft silence, with only Simba's quiet voice as the soundtrack.

I've kissed guys before, but not in these circumstances. I kissed those guys while playing Spin the Bottle, while playing Truth or Dare, while being forced into a closet with them during Seven Minutes in Heaven. But this isn't a game or a dare or a playful interaction. It's real and it's happening right now and I have no idea what I'm doing and why I'm kissing a guy from California who I met a week ago while I'm watching *The Lion King* in his bed. I might not know what I'm doing, but I know that I like it.

And just as his mouth drifts away from mine after a long

minute or so, I feel him murmur against the corner of my lips, "You probably shouldn't mention this to Tyler. He'd kick my ass."

My eyes flicker open to meet his soft gaze, a small smile creeping onto my lips. "I wasn't planning on it."

12

And so it's only one week into my summer and I'm already waking up next to my stepbrother's arch-nemesis. *Way to go, Eden.*

As my eyelids are flickering open to the sight of the sunlight streaming in through a gap in the blinds, I roll over to face the guy by my side. Jake's stirring, his muscles bulging as he stretches, contracting in such a way that I suddenly become wide awake.

"Morning," he mumbles. His voice is quiet as he sits up, rubbing his eyes and squinting at the window. He's still fully dressed, and so am I.

"I slept here?" I blurt, which is a stupid question considering I quite blatantly did. This wasn't supposed to happen. Not only did I sneak out, I didn't come home either. Dad is going to murder me. "I need to go home," I say, adjusting my updo and getting to my feet. "Like, A.S.A.P."

"But babe—" he starts, but is interrupted by a knock on the door. I don't know what time it is, but I do know that it's not the middle of the night, so I'm not surprised when a woman enters the room.

She studies us, folds her arms across her chest, looks me up and down, and then fixes Jake with a glare. "I knew you were sneaking a girl in here last night," she says scornfully. "Does this one have a name?"

"Mom," Jake hisses as he gets to his feet.

"No, Jake." She shakes her head in disapproval, pointing behind her to the door. "She has five minutes to get out of here."

I hear him groan as she leaves. Until this exact moment, I thought Jake was a nice guy. A guy so nice that I kissed him back last night. But now, all of a sudden, his mom's attitude has left me with a few questions. My stomach churns.

"Do you take girls home often or something?" I murmur. Swinging my legs over the edge of the bed, I reach for my Converse and pull them on.

"No," says Jake, almost immediately. "She's just kidding."

I glance over my shoulder, furrowing my eyebrows to let him know I'm disheartened, to let him know that I'm not going to just brush off his mom's words easily. He might not watch *The Lion King* with any girl, but that doesn't mean he doesn't watch *Aladdin* with them. "I need to go," I say.

"Okay," he finally says, figuring out that I'm serious. If I waste any more time here, Dad will file a missing person report. "Let me grab my keys."

For a long while, I stare at him as I contemplate which decision to make. I can't conclude what's worse: a guy taking me home or arriving at Dad's house in a cab. Either way, I'll look like I've had a scandalous night.

Jake pulls on a shirt and snatches his keys from the windowsill. I can't help but wonder if it's a daily routine. "Okay," he says again. "Let's make a move."

We slip out into the hall, silently but quickly walking down the stairway in hope of avoiding another run-in with his mom.

Quite frankly, I don't think she's impressed. And I don't think my dad will be either.

"What day is it?" I ask for the sake of conversation once we're safely inside Jake's car.

"Sunday," he says. But by now his tone has softened, grown glum in a way that makes me wonder if he's mad, his eyes half shut. It could be his mom's interruption or my unwillingness to hang around with him all day that's leaving him bummed out. But I need to get home and I need to get there as soon as possible.

"Okay," I say. I divert my eyes to the road. Today, I'm far too tired to make the effort.

By the time we pull up outside my dad's place, Jake has loosened up a little. He slowly turns off the ignition before turning to face me, a small grin playing at the corners of his lips. "We should do this again," he says. "Stay at my place again next weekend. It's my parents' anniversary, so they won't be there."

"I mean, sure, we can hang out," I say, albeit rather hesitantly. My opinion on him is too mixed right now.

"You can stay for the entire weekend."

"I don't think my dad will—"

He cuts me off, firmly telling me, "Just think about it," while he stares at me. Eventually, he smiles again. "Good job I was at that party last night, huh? Talk about being in the right place at the right time."

"Thanks for getting me out of there," I murmur. I'd forgotten about that terrible party until now. I wonder if Tyler managed to get himself home.

Jake shrugs and his smile grows wider. "Thanks for letting me. I had a good night."

"Yeah," I say. Throwing a glance toward the house, I figure it's time to head inside and face Dad. "I should go."

"I'll see you later," he tells me as I open the door and step out. As I'm closing it, I wonder if he's being sincere.

Yanking my hood over my head, I send a quick prayer to the skies above and then stuff my hands into my pockets. I'm hoping the hood hides my disgraceful hair and smudged makeup. I look like I've been partying on the Las Vegas Strip all night. Although I doubt many people in Vegas go out to party dressed in a hoodie and jeans.

I don't hear Jake drive off, but I do know that he's gone by the time I reach the front door—a front door that I am oh-so-greatly dreading walking through. Conveniently, I don't have to.

It swings open before me, making me jolt in surprise, and as I'm recovering, a firm hand hauls me over the threshold. Too manly to be Ella, too built-up to be Dad. And so my earlier question has now been answered: Tyler did get home.

"Um." I shake his grip off me, stepping to the side as he quietly shuts the door behind me. I haven't even said anything and already he's glaring down at me as though I've just set his room on fire. It's like no one can ever please him.

"You're kidding," he says. "Right? You've got to be kidding."

I stare. I sigh. I play with the drawstrings of my hoodie. I stare some more. "I could say the same to you," I finally mutter. I'm past the point of caring anymore. I try to be nice, I get it thrown back in my face, repeat. Not anymore. "You took me to a party with all your pothead friends and crackhead losers. Are you insane?"

"Shhh," he hisses sharply. He holds up a finger, narrowing

his eyes down the hall to ensure no one has heard me. "Keep your voice down."

"Sorry," I say, seething with sarcasm. "I forgot your mom has no idea about how pathetic her son is."

A wave of fleeting emotions captures his eyes in a peculiar way that I've never seen before. Something flashes within them, but I can't quite pinpoint what. He almost looks hurt, but I can't be sure, because already his eyes are narrowing again. "Dave!" he yells, his voice coarse. He smiles. "Eden's home."

"Seriously?" Now all I want to do is punch him in the face.

The smile on his lips alters to a smirk as he claims his victory. "Face the consequences."

"Your consequences," I correct. "You forced me to go to that party."

"Yet I remember you agreeing to it."

"I'm surprised that you even remember anything. Was it a sober night for you? I doubt it." I push down my hood and sigh, gritting my teeth as I hear footsteps coming from the kitchen. If Dad doesn't kill me, I'm pretty sure Tyler will.

"Good luck," he says, laughing under his breath while he leans back against the wall. He folds his arms across his chest and watches in amusement as Dad approaches.

"Where the hell have you been?" is the first question Dad fires my way. All I can say is that his expression isn't too impressed. "Do you even know the time? It's almost noon. Where have you been all night? The least you could have done was answer your phone. I've been worried sick, Eden."

"I'm sorry, I—" It's at this point that I face the ultimate crisis—come clean or lie my way out of it. But I don't have the courage to own up and I don't have the experience to think of a slick cover-up, so neither option really seems to be an option at all.

As Dad's eyes bore into mine and his eyebrows arch as he awaits an answer, I frantically glance everywhere else, and my gaze lands on Tyler. He's still smirking, still watching, still enjoying me struggling to save myself from Dad's wrath. But I'm too panicked to even glare, and the longer I helplessly stare at him, the more his devious expression begins to fade.

"She was at Meghan's place," he says suddenly, his eyes locked on mine, his face tight. He looks to my dad. "I already told you that."

Dad looks baffled for a moment while he thinks, but his eyebrows only end up furrowing. "No you didn't."

"I'm, like, pretty sure I told you last night when I got back, because she asked me to let you know." Tyler cocks his head, pulling a perplexed expression as though Dad has suffered amnesia. "Remember?"

"No."

Tyler shrugs. "Man, I must have forgotten," he says, and then diverts his eyes back to me. They're soft now. Gentle. "Sorry, Eden. My bad."

There's a long silence. Dad looks completely puzzled, Tyler appears nonchalant, and I'm still trying to figure out what just happened. If I witnessed it properly, Tyler just helped me out. Helped me. Remarkable.

I find it hard to believe that one day he might make sense to me. I think that right now, he's almost impossible to understand. One minute he seemed delighted at the idea of me getting caught, the next he jumped in and covered for me. Why? It's giving me a headache, the way he switches between hating me and getting along with me. Honestly, I wish he'd just decide already. It'd save me the hassle of trying to figure it out.

"Next time, don't leave in the first place without telling me," Dad says. He seems irritated, but just when I think he's about to walk away, he says, "By the way, we're going out for a late lunch. All of us. That means you too, Tyler. Dress nicely."

The thought of a "family" meal doesn't particularly bother me anymore. However, Tyler's intense stare does. And so when Dad heads off to the kitchen, presumably to find Ella, I seize the opportunity to make sense of the past five minutes.

"You get off the hook so easily," Tyler murmurs, but I ignore him.

Instead, I ask, "Why did you do that?"

"Do what?"

"Lie for me." He seemed quite content with watching me get busted; then his attitude miraculously changed and he decided to step in and save the day. And I have no idea why. "I don't get it."

He shrugs, his eyes still calm again. His mood swings confuse me. "I owed you one," he tells me. "For taking you to that party last night. I didn't think it through. Sorry." His apology is sincere, which I find surprising, and he's not yelling at me for once, which is even more surprising.

"Why did you even invite me along in the first place?" I ask, my voice riddled with contempt. "Did you honestly think I'd want to be around that stuff?"

"I'm sorry," he says again, this time even quieter, and for a second I consider accepting his apology, but then he ruins the entire thing when he decides to mutter, "So you were with Jake, huh?"

I guess he saw the car. "What does it matter to you if I was? You have your opinion of him and I have mine. I don't want to talk about it again, because it's got nothing to do with you."

"I need to take a shower," he says, bypassing the matter even though he was the one to bring it up. He narrows his eyes again, but with delicacy. "We'll talk about this later. After this bullshit meal that we've gotta sit through."

"We'll talk about it later?" I repeat. Until now, I never took Tyler as a conversationalist. Especially when it's a conversation about the guy I was locking lips with last night.

"Yeah," he says. He turns around, and as he makes his way up the stairs, he throws a glance over his shoulder. He's smiling. "And remember what your dad said. Wear something nice."

13

We arrive twenty minutes late for dinner. The first ten minutes can be blamed on Ella, because she ended up changing her outfit twice before deeming herself appropriately dressed. The second half can be blamed on Tyler. He held us up over the simple fact that he wasn't getting to take his car. Dad and Ella planned on taking the Lexus and the Range Rover, saying there was no need for Tyler to take a third car. After all, he's grounded. And eventually he gave up the fight and dragged his slumped body into his mom's car. The entire time, I wondered how being forced to sit in a Range Rover could be considered a punishment.

"Here you are, Mr. Munro," the classy waitress at the classy restaurant says in a classy accent as she leads us to a classy table with classy cutlery. Classy, classy, classy. Five years ago, Dad would have taken Mom and me to a greasy burger joint.

He thanks the waitress and we all sit ourselves down. Dad, Ella and Chase are across the table; Tyler and Jamie are on either side of me. The restaurant is large, yet there are only a small number of tables, which are extremely well presented and spaced out. Nothing is worse than being in a restaurant surrounded by other tables all within inches of each other.

"This is nice, having us all together," Ella comments once

we finish ordering our drinks. I go for water and Tyler unsuccessfully tries for a beer. "We should do this every Sunday."

Dad nods, glancing sideways at her with a familiar expression in his eyes. Once upon a time, he used to look at my mom that way. "Agreed."

"Disagreed," Tyler throws in. He smiles, bows his head, and then folds his arms across his chest. Neither Ella nor Dad pays attention. By now, they've probably figured out that he's always going to have something negative to say every so often, so there's no point even acknowledging it. I'm starting to do the same.

The drinks arrive and we order. I end up pointing to the first option I see. Everything is far too sophisticated and bizarre-sounding to comprehend. I've probably ordered a whale's testicle.

"How long do we have to sit here for?" Tyler asks five minutes later, interrupting our parents' conversation and staring at them from across the table, his face blank. He loosens his black tie, undoing the top button of his white shirt. "I've got better things to do."

"Stop being so moody," Ella murmurs, and then she clears her throat and her voice becomes solemn. "Did you take your meds today?"

"Mom," he says sharply, quickly glancing sideways at me just before his eyes narrow back on Ella. "I'm gonna go get some air." Pressing his palms on the table and pushing himself up to his feet, he slides his chair away and heads for the door.

"Just leave him," Ella says, sighing as she places a hand on Dad's arm. He looks as though he's about to charge after him.

"You say that every single time," he huffs. To begin with, I understood why it was so easy to get irritated by every single thing that Tyler did, but by now it's apparent that Dad quite simply dislikes the guy. Period.

Ella momentarily frowns but then forces a smile onto her lips and rubs Dad's back. "Just cut him some slack."

I want to ask about the medication she mentioned, but I bite back the urge, not letting my curiousity get the better of me, and instead I silently wonder about it—although it's really none of my business. It could be treatment for erectile dysfunction or something equally private and as personal, but given the way Tyler and Tiffani are all over each other, I highly doubt it.

Ella decides to move the subject away from her eldest and most reckless son, focusing on Jamie instead. "Jay, how's that biology project coming along?"

"It's okay," says Jamie. He shrugs and stares sheepishly down at his lap. "I still need to finish the osmosis diagram."

"I hated diffusion and osmosis and active transport," I say, forcing myself to get involved in the so-called "family" meal. "Just wait until AP Biology. It gets worse."

Dad smiles in approval because I'm making an effort to join in, but then nods to Jamie. "Can you go and find your brother? The food will be here soon."

"I'll go," I blurt without thinking, and I'm surprised at myself for even offering. "It's really hot in here. I need some air too," I lie, and then get myself out of there as fast as I possibly can. Perhaps I'm still curious.

When I get outside I scan the entire lot, but there's no one around. Only a car pulling in and another pulling out. It's the middle of the afternoon, so the sun is hot against my back, my eyes squinting through its brightness. I zero in on the Lexus and the Range Rover, which are parked side by side. Ella struggled to get the Ranger Rover into the small space and Tyler ended up having to park it for her. It's then that I notice a figure sitting in the driver's seat.

Without a single question or even a word planned to say, I head over there, but cautiously. Tyler's the type of person who would slam the vehicle into reverse and kill me instantly, so I feel slightly anxious when I eventually reach the window and gently tap my knuckles against the glass.

His head snaps around, his features sharp as he furrows his eyebrows. A few long moments pass before he decides to roll down the window. "What?"

"Are you coming back inside?" I bite my lip and take a step back. After I say it, I realize how pointless it was to even ask.

"Screw that bullshit, I'm not heading back in there," he mutters, and then turns away from me.

I press my lips together, tilting my head. I mirror his glare. "You're kind of melodramatic, don't you think? It wasn't that big of a deal. She only asked you a question."

His eyes widen, but his frown remains. "Are you stupid? For real—are you? You don't understand SHIT, goddamn Eden Munro."

"There you go again," I say, rolling my eyes, my voice rising in agitation, "overreacting about every little thing. I'm trying to understand what the hell is wrong with you, but you treat me like shit every time I talk to you, so forget it. Now I'm going back inside, because I'm not a self-centered douchebag who throws tantrums when things don't go my way." Resting my case, I spin around and head back across the lot.

But I hear Tyler softly call my name, and when I glance over my shoulder, he looks more relaxed. "Come here," he says, but I don't budge. There's no reason why I should listen to him. "Come get in the car and I'll be honest with you and then we'll go back inside."

Tyler offering to tell me the truth for once is too good to miss. And if it helps to get him back inside, then I ought to listen. I heave a sigh and turn around, marching back over to the Range Rover and pulling myself up into the passenger seat without letting my guard down. "Okay, what?"

With his tie hung over the back of his neck and one hand resting on the steering wheel, he stares at me for a long minute. I wait for him to speak, but instead I watch his lips curl into a smirk. "Alright, you want honesty? Okay. I'm being totally honest right now when I tell you that we're getting the hell out of here."

Before my mind can even process his words, he shoves the car into drive and slams his foot on the gas, and there's a horrendous screeching as it spins its way across the lot. He doesn't even look before pulling out onto the street, and we fly out of the parking lot in a frenzy, forcing the cars around us to slam on their brakes.

"Are you SERIOUS?" I yell, reaching for my seatbelt and yanking it on as quickly as I can. Right now, I fear for my life.

"Not serious," he says. "Just honest."

"Take me back," I demand. Sitting sideways with one hand on the dashboard and the other on my seatbelt, I frantically glance between Tyler and the road: Tyler because I'm shooting him death glares, and the road because I don't trust his driving skills.

"You really want to go back?" The car swerves from side to side. "Look me straight in the eye and tell me that you want to go back to that place and eat that gross food and sit with your dad for an hour. Tell me that you honestly want to do that."

He stares at me, only occasionally stealing a quick glance out the windshield.

"No," I admit. "I don't. But I know I have to, so go back before they kill us both. Are you even allowed to drive this?"

In between his hard braking and rapid acceleration, he manages to reply, "Are you even allowed to look like that?"

I throw my hands up in exasperation. I've just about had it with him. "Okay, there's no need to insult me."

"It wasn't an insult, Jesus Christ," he mutters, running a hand through his hair and slamming on the brakes just before we roll into the back of the Porsche in front of us. "We aren't going back. We're going home to the house so that I can get a beer and tell you that Jake's playing you, okay?"

"Thank you, Tyler," I say acidly. "Thank you for getting me into even more trouble."

"Last night was on you," he argues, while growing frustrated with the length of time that the lights are remaining red. "Sure, I took you out, but it was you who chose not to come home, so don't try and call me out for that one."

I give in. "Fine. But new problem: Your mom is going to flip out when she sees that her car is gone. How'd you even get the keys?"

He laughs as the lights flicker to green, and he over-revs the engine. "Chill out, they'll all fit in your dad's car. And I still had them from when I was parking. Now stop distracting me, I'm trying to drive."

I press my lips together, staring at his clenched jaw as he finally decides to actually focus on the road. "Try harder."

It takes us twenty minutes to finally get back to the house, and I'm surprised that we make it there in one piece. Tyler called Ella on the way to tell her that we "couldn't care less" about eating with them and that we were heading home. He hung up before she could say anything back.

"Go to my room," he instructs as we get out of the awkwardly parked car and head toward the front door. Thankfully, he has his keys on him. "I'm gonna grab a drink and then we're gonna discuss that asshole you're so keen on."

I hesitate behind him at the door as he swings it open. "I don't want to discuss anything with you," I say. He has no say over my decisions, and I can't figure out why he thinks that he does.

He just sighs nonchalantly. "Go upstairs and go to my room. I'll be up in two minutes." He saunters down the hall toward the kitchen as I make my way to the stairs.

As I'm heading up them, I call down, "Just to clarify, I'm going upstairs to my room, not yours."

"I'll be in your room, then, in two minutes," his voice gently yells back, and I find myself shaking my head in defeat as I reach my door. For someone who doesn't care about much, he can be very persistent.

I kick off my shoes and quickly shove my mound of dirty laundry into the bathroom and shut the door. Other than that, my room isn't too messy. Tyler doesn't notice anything when he wanders in with a bottle of beer clutched tightly in his hand.

"Okay, where to start," he muses to himself. He pauses to take a swig of the beer and then holds up his hand. "Let me simplify it for you: Jake Maxwell is the biggest player of the year."

"Funny," I say, "I thought you were."

Tyler looks almost offended. He clears his throat, shaking his head. "No, there's a big difference between Jake and me. Girls want me; Jake wants girls. You know, I don't purposely go out of my way to find other girls. I just kind of bump into them at parties or whatever, maybe flirt a little, sometimes kiss them if I'm drunk and Tiffani isn't around. That's it." He watches my confused expression for a moment while he takes another long drink, and then he finishes off with a sigh. "Jake, on the other hand, is a player. He leads chicks on for weeks and sometimes even months, sleeps with them, and then never talks to them again. Guy does this with like three girls at a time." He laughs, but it's a somewhat solemn laugh. "I can guarantee you that the second you put out, he'll disappear. He always does. Pulls out either the 'Sorry, I'm not feeling it anymore,' or the 'I can't talk to you anymore, because my mom's super strict and says I can't date until college' card."

I stare at him. He's going to such lengths to scare me away from Jake, but so far Jake's been the one who's treated me much nicer. "Why are you telling me this?"

"Because I am," Tyler says.

"That's not a valid reason."

He only smiles. "Neither was my reason for leaving the restaurant."

* * *

As expected, Dad and Ella are livid when they get home that evening. Not only did they have to pay for two wasted meals, they're also extremely "upset" that we ruined our first family event, according to the pair of them. Tyler is reminded that he's grounded, and I'm banished to my room for the night. And it's a long night.

I video chat with Amelia for a while and she fills me in on all the Portland gossip. Our English Lit teacher, Mr. Montez, was apparently caught shopping for rubbers in Freddy's the other day by some seniors. Mr. Montez is in his fifties, so this information makes me feel nauseated, yet Amelia doesn't stop laughing for at least five minutes. But other than our teacher's personal life, there's not much other news, so we end up discussing college. Amelia's all set on studying biochemistry at Oregon State University, an hour south of Portland, in Corvallis. Unlike her, I can't wait to get the hell out of Oregon. I start babbling to her about how great the University of Chicago's psychology program is, but the chat disconnects while I'm mid-sentence. The Internet connection has cut out. I stare at my laptop for a few minutes while it tries to reconnect, but it only buffers endlessly and hopelessly. That's when I hear someone knocking on my wall—the one separating my room from Tyler's. There are three taps.

With an eyebrow arched suspiciously, I push my laptop to the side and crawl across the floor, cautiously edging my way toward the wall. I don't know if the knocks are accidental or on purpose, but either way I find myself tapping back. I knock once and wait. Four knocks come back.

I don't know what the hell Tyler is doing, but I highly doubt he's learning Morse code, so I figure he's just determined to irritate me even more than he already has.

"Can you stop?" I ask, my voice loud enough for him to hear me through the walls but quiet enough for Dad not to notice.

"I turned off the Internet," Tyler's muffled voice says back, and it sounds almost like there's laughter stuck in his throat. "Your conversation was giving me a headache. 'God, Amelia, isn't Chicago just so freakin' awesome? School is my favorite thing in the entire world! It's so great! I love psychology and homework and studying!'"

I glare at the door to my bathroom as I cross my legs and

press my back to the wall. "I didn't even say that." To express my annoyance, I elbow the wall.

And so he knocks back again, this time repeatedly rapping his knuckles against the plaster for a good fifteen seconds before he pauses to say, "I could do this all night. I heard no one gets any sleep at college, so this is good practice for you. I'll turn you into an insomniac in no time."

"Has anyone ever told you how frustrating you are?" I fold my arms across my chest and roll my eyes in aggravation, but somehow I'm almost smiling. I can't figure out why, to begin with, but when he talks back, I realize I'm smiling at his playfulness. It's not often that I get to hear it.

"Hmm, I don't think anyone ever has," he tells me. I wish I could see past the wall, see his face. Is he smiling like I am? Is he laying on the floor or standing up or sitting down? What do his eyes look like right now? "How am I frustrating? Enlighten me, college girl."

He sounds like he's grinning, but I can't be sure. I just tilt my face up to the ceiling and press my ear to the wall, so that I can hear his soft voice better. His friendliness is rare. "For starters," I say, "you disconnected the Internet and now you won't stop knocking on my wall."

"Technically, it's our wall." He knocks again. Just once.

"Either way, it's extremely annoying. Please stop."

"No can do," he tells me. He starts to tap his knuckles against the wall again, relentlessly and loudly.

I punch the wall then, creating a thud, and Tyler finally laughs.

I return back to my bed after that, shut down my laptop, and get under the comforter. I can't help but wonder what Tyler is doing on the other side of the wall. Is he laying in bed staring at the ceiling too? Is he texting his friends? Is he looking for a good movie to watch?

It's beyond midnight when I finally fall asleep, after thinking too much about Jake and what Tyler said about him, and reminding myself of the way Jake's mom treated me in the morning. She acted as though I was a statistic, just another girl in her son's room. She wasn't surprised. And so I can't help but wonder if what Tyler said was true.

14

By morning, I'm too tired to even eat some breakfast. I stare at the floor, my face a picture of exhaustion, and I slowly attempt to finish off the toast Ella's made for me.

"Are you okay?" Dad asks. He tucks in his shirt and adjusts his hideous tie.

"Yeah," I say. Every few hours I kept waking up because I swore I could hear more knocking. "Just tired."

I receive a single nod. "Any plans for this week?"

"Nope."

Dad has always been a terrible conversationalist, asking dumb questions and making stupid remarks just to fill silences. Half the time, I pray he doesn't talk to me at all. "Okay," he says. "I'll be home late tonight."

I don't bother to reply. I just lower my head and get to my feet, heading over to the dishwasher and slipping my plate inside as he shuffles out into the hall. Week two of eight, and already I'm struggling to survive in this place. Dad sucks. This merged family sucks. Summer sucks.

"Morning," a voice says as I slam the dishwasher shut.

I spin around, and the second I lay eyes on Tyler approaching, I pull a face in disgust. "Ugh," I spit.

"You're supposed to say good morning back," he tells me,

and bumps me to the side with his shoulder as he passes. He's wearing black shorts and a multicolored loose tank top, and I can't help but stare at his arms and the way they bulge when he throws open the refrigerator.

My eyes narrow. "You kept me up all night."

He glances over his shoulder, his eyebrows furrowed. "Huh?"

"The knocking."

For a long moment he just stares at me, his eyes shifting through several different moods, and then he laughs. "I wasn't knocking. Didn't your dad tell you the house is haunted? Demons everywhere."

"Oh, shut up," I say, rolling my eyes. "Couldn't you get to sleep or something?"

He turns around with a bottle of water in his hand, kicking the refrigerator door shut behind him. "Not exactly." He smirks as he folds his arms across his chest. I notice his tattoo again. "I was hoping you'd wake up and knock back."

"Sorry," I say. "I wasn't in the mood for communicating with you through the wall at 4AM." There's an emboldened vein running down his left arm, but I try not to pay attention to it. Amelia and I have always gushed over guys with veiny arms and veiny hands and veiny necks. Veins are attractive, somehow.

"Ouch." Slowly, he bites his lip, his eyes gently meeting my gaze. I know we're only playing around, but he looks serious all of a sudden. "What about tonight?"

"What?"

"Tonight," he says. "Will you knock back?"

I tear my eyes away from his chest and throw my hands up in surrender, giving up on the odd game we're playing. "No, Tyler, I don't want to knock back and forth. It's just weird."

"Damn," he mutters. He shrugs his broad shoulders and diverts his attention to his watch instead.

I'm just about to escape to my room when the sound of the front door swinging open causes me to pause. Perhaps Dad forgot something, or perhaps Ella is heading out to buy some groceries.

But it's neither one of our parents. It's just Dean. I can tell by his gentle voice as I hear him stick his head into the living room, saying, "Morning, Mrs. Munro," before entering the kitchen.

He, too, is dressed super casual and has his car keys in one hand and his phone in the other. Giving me a nod, he turns to Tyler. "Ready?"

"Dude, you're twenty minutes late," Tyler complains, which I find surprising. He doesn't particularly look like he'd care much about punctuality, but apparently he does.

"My bad," Dean says. "I had to stop for gas."

Tyler's eyes fall to me disapprovingly. He snorts. "You left me to hang with this fucking loser. Let's just bail already." There's a long silence. Both Dean and I narrow our eyes at him, and under the pressure he quickly backpedals. "Chill, guys. Just a little sibling rivalry, right, Eden?"

I blink. "We're not siblings."

"And thank God for that."

I choose to ignore his stupid remarks and head over to the patio doors, pushing them open and allowing a warm breeze into the house. Behind me, Tyler and Dean call that they're off to the gym. It doesn't surprise me. It's evident that they work out a lot. I contemplate asking Tyler later which gym he uses, because I'm considering signing up to one for the remaining six weeks that I'm here, but I decide to stick with my morning runs instead. Quite frankly, I don't think Tyler would appreciate his so-called sibling rival tagging along with him.

* * *

By the time Wednesday rolls around, everyone is back in town. Rachael is back from a weekend with her grandparents that she claims was so traumatizingly boring that she was on the verge of setting their house on fire; Tiffani is home again after staying at her dad's place, which she stated was the equivalent to living with Shrek; and Meghan feels great again after throwing up for three days in a row.

Instead of meeting up to gossip at the beach or over coffee or even at the promenade, we end up catching up over manicures.

"Honestly, my grandpa made me play bingo with him," Rachael continues to moan. She's been venting to us about her awful weekend for the past fifteen minutes. "Every single night. 'Rachael, time for bingo!' Here's a thought, Gramps: Hell no."

"My dad started pulling out the old albums from, like, 1801," Tiffani says, cringing. She's perched on a chair with her hands pressed onto the table, with a nail technician huddled over them.

Rachael and I were up first to have our nails brought back to life, and now it's Tiffani and Meghan's turn. I can't help but constantly glance down at my hands, admiring how glossy my nails are, and then get comfy in my reserved spot on a chair in the corner of the salon. I should do this more often. It's really not that bad.

We've traveled into Venice for these beauty treatments,

because Tiffani claims this is the best nail bar around. I don't mind traveling out of Santa Monica to come here, because Venice Beach looks amazing—at least from the four minutes that I got to see it.

Rachael paces back and forth across the room, checking her nails every few seconds. I can't blame her. "I'll take historic photo albums any day over bingo."

"I'll take either over throwing up," Meghan comments from Tiffani's side. Thankfully, she's a little shyer than Rachael and Tiffani, so I'm not the only one barely offering input to the conversation. "My insides feel like acid."

"At least you're feeling better in time for your birthday," Tiffani says. Side by side, she and Meghan have their technicians filing away at their nails. Tiffani throws a glance at Meghan. "Are you throwing a party?"

A frown grows on Meg's lips, and she shrugs. "You know how strict my parents are."

"Oh my God, Meghan!" Rachael explodes, halting mid-pace and throwing her hands up into the air ecstatically. "I have a free house on Saturday night; you can have a party at my place!"

"Another party?" I murmur, but luckily none of them hear me. I've been here for just over a week and already I've been to two of these trashy parties where unlimited booze, drugs and sex seem to be a general theme. I'm just not that into them.

"Are you sure?" Meghan looks at her from over her shoulder. She looks doubtful and a little guilty, and I can understand why. Rachael's risking her house getting trashed.

Rachael rolls her eyes. "Obviously, Meg. It's no problem. Let's do it."

"I'll get Tyler to spread the word," Tiffani offers, and when she mentions his name something flutters in my stomach. I wonder what he's doing right now.

"Tell him not to invite Declan's crowd," Rachael says, and she shoots Tiffani a firm look. "I don't want anything illegal in my house, because if anything's left behind my dad will kill me."

"I'll make sure he knows."

I vaguely remember Declan being the person who threw that horrendous stoner party at the weekend. Thank God Rachael has the common sense not to invite the potheads.

"You guys can all come over on Saturday morning and help me get the house ready," she says, and then squeals in excitement. The nail technicians flinch. "This is gonna be so good!"

It doesn't sound that good. I'll hate every second of it. I'll hate the alcohol, I'll hate the drunk strangers, I'll hate the noise, I'll hate Tyler. He gets even more irritating when he's been drinking, and I'll be the one who has to drag him home across the street at the end of the night.

"Meg, you should invite the cute guy from the beach," Tiffani teases, but it's almost sincere. "And Rach, I already know you're going to invite Trevor." Rachael's cheeks flush with color and she quickly turns to face the windows. As Tiffani giggles, she rests her eyes on me. "And I'll have Tyler, so there's just you, Eden. We'll need to find someone for you."

For a second I feel guilty for not being a good friend by telling her that Tyler's just not that into her, but my lips have a mind of their own and soon I'm blurting, "I'll just hang out with Jake."

And then there's a simultaneous "What?" from all three of them.

Tiffani even draws her hands away from the table so that she can spin around to stare at me, and I can feel all of their eyes on me at once. "Jake? Our Jake?"

"Oh my God, what have we missed?" Rachael demands, her eyes wide and eager, her bottom lip drawn into her mouth. "You don't just say you're going to hang out with someone at a party, okay? There's always a reason behind it. Are you crushing on him?"

"We hung out on Saturday night," I admit, and my cheeks are now tinted rose as my eyes drop to the floor. I wish I hadn't said anything. "And I, um, stayed at his place."

"Jesus," Meghan breathes. She blinks at me before exchanging glances with both Tiffani and Rachael. "It only took him a week to get the new girl?"

"Meg," Rach hisses, but quickly locks her eyes on me again. "How far did the two of you get?"

"What?"

"You know . . ." She glances unsurely over to Tiffani, and Tiff decides to finish for her by obnoxiously asking, "Did you suck his dick?"

I splutter, almost choke, and fail to compose myself. I manage a quick, "No," and then shake my head. "We watched *The Lion King*."

Rachael tilts her head. "Is that a code word or . . .?"

"No. We literally watched *The Lion King*."

"Oh," she says, and then bursts into laughter.

"Rachael, just stop talking," Tiffani says. She turns back around and places her hands down on the table again and allows the nail technician—who is understandably a little lost—to continue.

"But didn't anyone tell her about the Maxwell Base?"

Meghan says, and by this point I just wish I could run out of the salon and go straight back to Santa Monica. I feel mortified and way out of my comfort zone.

"The Maxwell Base?" I force myself to repeat.

"Instead of third base, it's known as the Maxwell Base," Meghan informs me. "Because our good friend Jake Maxwell just so happens to get head a lot. It's traditional, and it looks like you're up next." She and Tiffani laugh.

"You guys are so gross," Rachael says. "Eden, don't listen to them. You don't have to do anything."

"We're gross?" Tiffani gasps, pressing a hand to her chest in mock disbelief. With a shake of her head, she locks her gaze back on me. "Eden, here's the honest truth: Meghan's specialty is jerking guys off and Rachael's is blowjobs." I can see the two nail technicians rolling their eyes and shooting each other a look. I bet they can't wait for us to leave. "You'll find them in the spare bedrooms at any party with any guy. Usually with Rach, it's Trevor. I'm the classy one."

"Hey!" Rachael and Meghan both protest, but they don't exactly object. Rachael does, however, quip, "I didn't know hooking up in the American Apparel fitting rooms was now considered classy."

"That doesn't count," Tiffani argues, biting her lip as the nail technician finishes off her right hand. "At least I'm in a relationship with the person."

The entire conversation is completely awkward, but I find myself glancing up from beneath my eyelashes to see if Rachael or Meghan will muster up a reply. The two of them just exchange a quick glance, their lips forming two perfect frowns, but they say nothing.

I catch Rachael's eye and raise my eyebrows at her, questioning their sudden silence, but she only offers me a minute shake of her head, as though to tell me that now isn't the time.

And then she clears her throat and decides to put the conversation in reverse, saying, "So Saturday should be fun, right?"

15

I receive an urgent text from Rachael at 3:27PM that Saturday. Her parents have only just left—four hours later than planned—and we now only have five hours to prepare the house for a reckless high school party. Rachael wants us to come over right away, and for me, this is easy to do.

"I'm going to Rachael's," I tell Dad as I'm untangling the laces of my sneakers by the living room door. "Guy drama," I add. "We'll probably just order food, so I don't think I'll be back for dinner."

He mutes the TV, glancing over at me, almost considering whether he should object. "Remember we're taking Jamie and Chase to the Dodgers game tonight. We're leaving in an hour, because it's just north of downtown. Can you fend for yourself for the night?"

"Oh, yeah." Perfect. No need to lie about why I'm heading across the street. "I won't be back before you leave, so have a good time. Bye, Ella."

Ella smiles, her head resting on his shoulder and her hand on his thigh. I'm trying to like her, but I really can't. "Have a good night with your friends."

I nod my head in farewell and close the door behind me, heading outside and across the road. Now I've been here a couple weeks I've got used to the sunshine and the street has become familiar, but I'm still not sure where I stand with the girls I've been hanging with. Are Rachael and Meghan my friends now? With the amount of time I've been spending with them, I feel like they are. Tiffani, on the other hand, has yet to make it clear if we're friends or not. Sometimes I think we are, others I think she hates me.

I walk through Rachael's front door at 3:31PM and, as expected, I'm the first to arrive. She's dragging a vacuum cleaner along the wooden floor, searching for an outlet, and looking exasperated and worn out. We haven't even started yet.

"I couldn't start anything until they left," she explains, the vacuum cleaner trailing behind her. "They would have gotten suspicious if I'd randomly started cleaning."

"It's fine, Rachael," I say slowly, my voice gentle. "Calm down, we've still got five hours."

"FIVE hours, Eden!" she yells. She kicks the vacuum cleaner to the side and throws her hands into her hair. It's wavy today and it really suits her. "Five hours to tidy and clean and move the ornaments and buy booze and food and update my iTunes! Why did I offer to do this?" She stares at me, her eyes wide, and I can't help but laugh.

"Rachael."

More staring. "What?"

"We're helping you, remember?" I arch my brows, nodding encouragingly in an attempt to calm her down. The only thing she needs to worry about is getting caught by her parents. "Tiffani and Meghan are on their way, right?"

"Right," she breathes. Pressing a hand to her chest, she uses the other to pull down her sunglasses and then swivels around to plug in the vacuum cleaner.

"Right," I echo. "So we'll help you tidy and then we'll all go to the store and then we'll help you sort out a playlist. We've got enough time."

Without replying, she starts up the vacuum cleaner and forcefully rams it into the flooring. I decide not to question her about the sunglasses or her mental stability.

"I'm here!" a voice yells from behind me over the noise. I turn around to find Tiffani, her hands overflowing with crackers and dips. I feel guilty for not bringing anything. "Is she wearing sunglasses inside?"

I only shake my head in pity. "She's a little stressed."

"We'll take the kitchen," Tiff tells me, rolling her eyes at Rachael's frantic vacuuming. "Let's leave her be."

I follow her through to the kitchen, where she dumps the crackers on the counter. There's not much to tidy, only some plates and some knives, which Tiffani quickly tosses into the dishwasher. I open up the back door and peer outside. Tidy enough.

"So how many people are coming?" I ask as I shut the door again.

"Around forty," Tiffani says. I can still hear Rachael vacuuming the other side of the house. "We've tried to keep it small. Declan Portwood's crew isn't invited, so that eliminates around fifteen people who usually turn up to parties."

"The people who do drugs in the back yard, right?" I ask, just for clarification.

"Something like that," she says quietly, and then arranges the crackers in a row along the counter, neatly aligning them with the dips.

"Isn't Tyler in that circle?"

She immediately stops what she's doing. Her eyes flicker over to meet mine, and it's then that I realize I shouldn't have said anything. It's evident from her expression that it's a topic that shouldn't be brushed upon. "No," she says, unconvincingly.

I know perfectly fine Tyler is friends with Declan and all the other potheads and crackheads. I should know; I went to a party with them all. "Yes he is," I argue.

"What the fuck are you trying to prove to me?" she snaps. Her outburst takes me by surprise. I didn't mean to provoke her. Getting on her bad side is the last thing on my mind.

"I was just saying," I murmur. We exchange a long glance before she looks away. Clearly her mood has shifted, and her eyes are narrower. She returns to setting out the crackers and dips while I just watch, not quite sure of what to do.

"I don't like talking about it," she confesses after a moment of tense silence. "It's embarrassing having people know what I put up with."

She doesn't like talking about it because it's embarrassing for her? Shouldn't she be worried about Tyler's well-being rather people's opinions on her? I frown. "I think he should get some help."

And then she glances over at me again, this time with a patronizing smile on her lips. "To be honest with you, Eden, I highly doubt he cares what you think."

I don't know how to reply. The only thing I can think about is how irritated I feel and how I want to bite back at her. Thankfully, I don't have to muster up anything, because Meghan slides into the kitchen with a concerned expression forcing creases onto her forehead.

The first thing she asks us is, "Can someone tell me why our friend is vacuuming a coffee table while wearing sunglasses?"

We spend two hours prepping Rachael's house, which I find increasingly pointless the more I think about it. It's most likely going to end up trashed by the end of the night. We vacuum, we hide Dawn's ornaments that Rachael says have been in their family for decades, we mop the floors, we lock her parent's room. The other three bedrooms—Rachael's and two spares—are all open, for optimism.

Once the house is declared suitable for a party, we head out to gather in the necessities—alcohol and condoms. We wait outside a cheap liquor store in Rachael's car as Tiffani makes her way inside, swinging her hips and pouting. Fifteen minutes later, she rushes out with a cart overflowing with a variety of beer and spirits, including the most deathly of all: tequila.

"It was the Indian guy," she says as we help her load the bags into the trunk. "He asked for my number this time. So I gave him yours, Meg."

We make a stop by a grocery store called Ralph's, and we spend thirty minutes pacing the aisles and grabbing whatever soft drinks and chips we can find. Rachael wants to ensure there's an unlimited supply of snacks to go around. And once we're completely stocked up on alcohol and potato chips, and the car is weighed down so much that it struggles to get going, we agree that we have successfully got everything ready within our five-hour time frame. In fact, it's only taken us three. There's time left over for a quick trip to the promenade, and I pick out an outfit for the night with the help of my three friends. Tiffani picks the color, Rachael decides on the style, Meghan pinpoints the details. I end up coming home with a coral keyhole dress, which is very tight and very short but is apparently up to standard.

"I hope your parents don't call mine," Rachael murmurs

once we get back to her house and start unloading the car. She has no reason to be worried. Dad and Ella will be ramming nachos into their mouths while watching a messy football game.

"They're watching the Dodgers game," I say. "We're lucky they like football."

Rachael, Tiffani and Meghan all stare at me, and slowly Rachael asks, "Eden, you know that the Dodgers are a baseball team, right?"

"Same difference."

She shakes her head, laughing as she nods across the street. "Go get yourself ready," she says. "It's almost seven. I told people to come any time after nine. The same goes for you, Tiff. Me and Meg can handle the rest of this."

Before we go our separate ways, I agree with Tiffani that we'll come back just before nine. It's a rule that if your friend is hosting a party, you must be there before everyone else. Meghan is staying at Rachael's to get ready. After all, the party is for her.

When I get back into my own house, thirty seconds after departing Rachael's, I carefully carry my new dress upstairs toward my room. But it's not long before a brooding figure stops me at the top of the stairs.

"Looks like it's just you and me," Tyler says as I near him. It's the first time I've seen him in two days. He disappears often, and Ella doesn't even question it. Maybe once upon a time she did, but it seems that now she's just given up on asking for explanations. My dad, on the other hand, is still adamantly trying to enforce rules that just don't exist in Tyler's mind. "They're at the Dodgers game. The Angels are totally gonna lose."

"I know," I say. "Can you move, please?"

"Sure." Surprisingly, he steps to the side to let me by. I furrow my eyebrows at him as I pass, and I even hesitate before I enter my room. He looks tired. "What?"

"You're coming to Rachael's tonight, right?" I ask, even though I already know that he is. It seems that he's a permanent fixture at parties.

"Yeah," he says. He tilts his head, his eyes slightly narrowed. I can't quite figure out what sort of a mood he's in right now. He can go from relaxed to furious and back again within the space of a minute. "You're gonna be there too, right?"

"Yeah."

"Cool," he says. "What time are we heading over there?"

"What do you mean 'we'?" I almost snort as I push open my bedroom door, my dress still resting over my arm. "I'm walking across the street on my own. Not with you. You can head on over there, Tyler, any time you want."

"Chill," he mutters. Pressing his lips together, he shakes his head and saunters downstairs, leaving me in peace to get ready. It's okay for him to waste time. He's a guy. They take ten minutes to get ready: to shower and pull on a fresh shirt.

So while I hear him turn on the TV downstairs, I head into my bathroom and throw myself into the shower to carry out tedious womanly duties involving shampoo and razors. My hair doesn't take too long to dry afterward, and I decide to go for loose curls tonight. I don't put in too much effort, mostly because there's no one in this city that I'm trying to impress, so once I've got a comfortable amount of makeup on, I slip into my dress and a pair of heels and check the time: 8:49PM.

I step out of my room at the exact same time Tyler does.

He looks as though he's ready to leave. He's wearing a white T-shirt underneath a black leather jacket, and despite how simple his outfit is, it looks extremely attractive on him. The more I think about it, the more I realize he always seems to look good whether he's wearing boots or sneakers or a shirt or tank top. There's the strong scent of cologne lingering in the air too, which only adds to how perfectly put-together he looks right now. It reminds me of the cologne Tiffani was complimenting him on that day in the American Apparel fitting rooms. The Bentley one.

And so I give in. "I'm about to go over. Are you coming with me?"

Slowly he runs his eyes over me, making me feel super self-conscious about the keyhole aspect of the dress. Finally he murmurs, "I actually gotta head out real quick."

"Where?"

"Just somewhere," he says, and it's abrupt, like he doesn't really want to answer me. "Just go over. I'll be there in twenty minutes."

"But where are you going?" I press. There's something in his eyes that's making me feel uneasy. Suspicious, even. He can't look at me, his hands balling into fists by his sides, his lips almost twitching.

"Damn, Eden." He throws a hand up in frustration, turning away from me and storming back into his room. So I follow him into the dull room with the closed curtains and no lamps on, and I squint at him through the darkness.

"Why are you getting mad?" I question as he runs his hands through his hair. For some reason, he's getting really stressed out. "I'm just asking where you're going."

"I'm going to meet someone, alright?" he almost yells at

me, his entire body rigid as he locks his eyes on mine. "I've got shit to pick up and you gotta back off about it."

I stare at him, noticing his eyes and the way they shift so quickly, changing shades and growing deeper. I can even see his chest moving, almost feel his heart racing. "You're meeting Declan," I state. It's not even a question. It doesn't have to be—it's obvious. "He's not going to the party so you're going out to meet him instead. Right?"

His shoulders sink, his eyelids collapsing shut as he exhales. I listen to his breathing as he shakes his head. And when his eyes flicker open again, he's livid. "Just go to the fucking party already."

"No," I say firmly, standing my ground. It's about time someone did something to fix the problem rather than ignoring it. "I'm not letting you go out to meet him."

"Eden." He swallows, the quiet force of him saying my name only infuriating me even more, and he takes a step toward me, leaning down a little so that we are level in height. His eyes pierce mine in a way that is almost terrifying. "You can't do anything about it."

"You're right," I say, my voice growing harder, if not a little shakier. His face is in such close proximity to my own that I feel as though he's stealing my oxygen, and I find myself struggling to keep the words coming out. But I force myself to keep going, because I can't back down now. "I can't do anything about it, because you don't CARE. You don't care about the fact that I'm worried that you're going to overdose one night or have a bad reaction or end up dead. You don't care about the fact that you're seventeen and hooked on coke. You don't, do you?" He doesn't speak, only stares back at me, his eyes somehow growing even narrower. "You only care about looking cool at parties, trying to impress people with this whole badass image you're trying to pull off. It's PATHETIC."

Tyler shakes his head. "That's not why I do it."

"Then why? Is it because you're trying to fit in with those lame friends of yo—"

"Because it's a distraction!" he snaps. He presses a hand to his forehead and exhales as he squeezes his eyes shut. There's a long, intense silence. "It's a fucking distraction," he softly murmurs. He opens his eyes again, fierce as ever, and his acidic tone is back as he turns back to look at me. "And right now, I could really do with a goddamn distraction."

The anger at him, the fury, the irritation at everything he has ever said to me, it all somehow comes together at once within me. It's like a sudden surge of adrenaline and insanity rushing through my veins and triggering something I can't quite comprehend. His words have only just left his lips when I reach out for him, grasping his face in my hands and feeling the warmth of his skin. I slam my lips into his, overwhelmed by the sensation as my eyelids flutter closed and a deafening silence consumes us. It's agonizing the way my heart thuds against my chest, but exhilarating the way his lips feel against mine. And then the reality of the situation comes flooding back, and it's only a matter of seconds before he'll become enraged at me again, and I slowly pull away from him.

I take a step back, feeling sick to my stomach as Tyler stares at me, his eyes wide. I'm waiting for him to explode, for his firm voice to ask if I'm insane, to which I will have to reply yes.

"That wasn't me," I babble, my words catching in my throat as I stutter some kind of an explanation. "I don't—I don't know what that was. I—I don't—I'm—I'm sorry. I was trying to—to distract you—I—"

I'm cut off when his lips come crashing back down on my own. He's so strong that he knocks me off my feet slightly, pushing me backward until my back hits the wall of his bedroom, his hands cupping my face, his thumbs skimming my skin, his fingers winding into my hair. His lips are fast, eager, forceful. Yet so incredible. I immediately sink into him, my entire body trembling beneath his touch. I can feel his anger; I can feel the intensity. I don't know why I'm not pulling away. I know I should, I know this shouldn't be happening, but there's something so mesmerizing about the entire thing that I just can't stop. He drops his hand to the small of my back, pulling me against his body for only the briefest of moments.

And then he stops.

Just like that, he tears his lips away from mine, releases his grip, takes a step back. The moment ends as quickly as it began.

"Shit," he breathes, so softly and so quietly that it perfectly sums up exactly what just happened. Because I'm thinking the exact same thing.

Oh shit.

16

Tyler's eyes pierce mine. Mine are wide, utterly shocked, full of surprise at myself, but warm. Tyler's are different. They're a vast ocean of a thousand emotions, flickering through different shades so fast I can't keep up. And then they dilate with the darkest emotion of them all—quite simply, fury.

"I'm going to Rachael's," he mutters. Zipping up his jacket, he runs a hand through his hair and then turns away from me. It doesn't take him more than a few seconds to leave the room without so much as a glance over his shoulder. But I don't care. I'm too stunned to even possibly care.

There is no logical explanation for what just happened, and Tyler doesn't seem to want to figure one out. I stand there blinking for what seems like an eternity, until the sound of the front door slamming shut snaps me out of the numbness.

My mind is awhirl and my pulse is still racing as the realization sinks in: slowly, and then overwhelmingly. I've just kissed Tyler.

My stepbrother. I've just kissed my stepbrother. I've kissed the guy who infuriates me, the one who makes my blood heat up whenever I see him. The guy who has a girlfriend. A girlfriend who just so happens to be my friend.

What the hell, Eden?

Bile rises in my throat and I clasp a hand to my mouth. I feel like I could throw up, and as my lip trembles, I deeply inhale. I may have kissed him, but he kissed me back. And with a lot of damn energy, too.

My mind snaps back to Rachael and Meghan and the party that they're hosting across the street. The party that I was supposed to be at fifteen minutes ago. I need to get over there and I need to act normal.

As normal as a girl who hadn't just kissed her stepbrother would look.

Exhaling, I tell myself to keep it together. At least until the end of the night. But given the fact that Tyler is going to be there too, I doubt I'll be able to. Am I supposed to talk to him? Ask him what the hell just happened between us? Ignore him? I don't know.

Stumbling back to my own room, I glance at myself in my mirror before grabbing my purse and bracing myself. At least Tyler is going straight to Rachael's and bypassing his meeting with Declan—if I do try to talk to him, he won't be under the influence of narcotics.

I make my way downstairs and outside, and I lock up with the spare key. My chest is still heaving. I can already hear the faint vibrations of music from Rachael's house, and I know it's only going to grow louder as the night goes on, as more people arrive and as they get drunker.

As I'm crossing the street, a car pulls up full of guys that are complete strangers to me. But they can't say the same about me, because one of them steps out of the car with a crate of beer in his arms and catches my eye. "Eden, right?"

"Yeah," I say. I don't really stop walking; I just slow down slightly. I'm really not in the mood to socialize.

"I've heard about you," the guy says, the smallest of smirks playing at his lips. He kicks the car door shut, the beer resting in one arm as he holds out his other hand for me to shake. "Tyler's sister, right?"

I almost throw up. The word makes me feel nothing but disgust at myself, disgrace at the incestuous act I've just committed. I'm pretty sure it's either illegal or immoral. The only thing I can murmur in reply is a quick "Stepsister," and a nod, and then I'm off again. I rush up to the front door and push it open, deafened as the music consumes me, but at least it drowns out the thoughts that are racing through my mind.

"Where the hell have you been, Eden?" Rachael yells across the hall to me from the living room. She waves her glass at me. I wonder what she's drinking. When she approaches me, I can smell the booze from her as she speaks. "People are beginning to arrive and you only just turn up? Meg has been looking everywhere for you."

"Sorry," I say. It's all I can say. "Where is she?"

"Making drinks." Rachael bobs her head in sync with the music, her smile perking up into a wide grin. I suspect that she started drinking the second Tiffani and I left. "Go get yourself one!"

There's a comfortable amount of people here, around fifteen or so, spaced out and thankfully mostly sober as of now. The rest will pile in over the next hour. And with everyone relaxed and calm, it's easy to see them all clearly as I make my way through the house and into the kitchen. It's here that I find Meghan. And, unfortunately, Tiffani. I can almost taste the bile again.

"Finally!" Meghan says, her dark hair framing her face as she bounces over to me. She, too, has definitely been drinking for a lot longer than twenty minutes. As she draws me into a hug, Tiffani rolls her eyes at me. I look away. "Here, take this!" She thrusts her glass into my hand, nodding enthusiastically before twirling back over to the counter to fetch herself a new drink.

"What is it?"

"I don't know," she says. The guys from the car enter, which draws Meghan's attention away from me as she tells them where to dump their booze, and from the corner of my eye I can see Tiffani smiling at me.

She edges through the new crowd that has formed, a wine glass in hand and looking as sophisticated as ever in the white dress she's wearing. The back of it reaches the floor. "Rachael and Meg have been driving me crazy," she says, her tone light as she breathes a laugh. "They're totally tipsy."

"Yeah," I say. My voice is weak. I can't look her in the eye, but I do build up the strength to ask, "Is Tyler here?"

"He's trying to shotgun as many beers as he can," she explains, but her tone is disapproving as she stares out the kitchen window, watching the scene unfold. Hearing her talking about him only makes me feel all the more guilty, to the point where any second now I might just burst into tears. "I'm waiting for him to wear himself out and come back inside."

My eyes drift over to the window, and I see two guys standing with a pile of beer cans around them. It's Tyler and some other guy I've never seen before, and I watch for a few seconds as Tyler stabs a hole in the can with his car keys before pressing it to his lips and consuming its entirety within a matter a nanoseconds. And the two of them go on to repeat this. Over, and over, and over.

"Oh," I say. I fix my eyes back on Tiffani, ignoring the guilt that keeps forcing its way into my head. I kissed her boyfriend. The words keep playing over in my mind, endlessly, as though I'm not already aware of what I've done. "Surely that can't be good for them?"

"It's not," she admits, shrugging. Her frown deepens as she takes a sip of her wine and it almost morphs into a grimace. I find her drinking wine unusual. It's as sophisticated as the dress, and they combine to create an elegant aura that I simply can't compete with. She looks like an adult compared with me. "He's so annoying. Why's he standing out there getting drunk? He's supposed to be in here with me."

I think I know why Tyler is on the verge of liver damage and alcohol poisoning. If his head's as big a mess as mine is, then booze really is the only way to distract himself. I'd resort to it too, but I'm too concerned about the fact that I might throw up, so I just fake a smile to Tiffani and head out of the kitchen with Meg's drink still in my hand. I'm not in the mood to drink and socialize and dance anymore, so I discard it the first chance I get. I focus my attention, instead, on Rachael. She's way too happy and way too twirly and way too spinny. It's like the alcohol has gone straight into her bloodstream, so I find myself falling into the role of babysitter for at least an hour.

"I'm totally sober, Eden," she pathetically tries as I haul her up from the ground for the hundredth time. She's struggling to maintain her balance as she prances around on the wooden flooring in her platform heels, and every few minutes she just slides straight down into a heap.

I steady her again, rolling my eyes as she waves me away. "Of course you're sober."

"I can take it from here," a voice says rather loudly from over my shoulder, and someone reaches out for Rachael's arm. They catch her just before she takes another tumble.

"Trevor!" she quite literally screams. Throwing her arms around him, she almost dislocates his neck before smothering his cheeks in kisses. He throws me a thumbs up from beneath her embrace, and I can do nothing more than pray for him. Rachael's a nightmare tonight.

Relieved of my guardian angel duties, I swivel my sober self around to ease my way through the large crowd—everyone must be here by now, and the house is packed and stuffy—but a large figure steps in front of me. It's Jake, with his stupid eyes and his stupid hair and his stupid smile.

"Where've you been, stranger?" He chuckles as he throws an arm over my shoulder and takes a sip of his beer. I can feel him pulling me to the side. "I've been calling you all week."

Admittedly, I have been ignoring his constant texts and calls all week. All I've been thinking about is the Maxwell Base. "Sorry, I've been super busy," I lie. I've spent the week reading and working out. And kissing my stepbrother. "When did you get here?"

"Twenty minutes ago!" He has to yell over the noise of the music, his voice loud and clear and annoying. The corners of his lips pull up into a smile as he leans toward me, his breath tickling my skin as he moves his mouth to my ear. "Remember my parents have been out of town since Thursday," he murmurs. It's a little slurred. "You can come home with me tonight. Stay at my place."

I've heard enough about him by now to know that I don't want to get involved, that I don't want to be just another girl he can add to his list. "No thanks," I say, smiling. Maybe if

I'm sweet about it, he won't care. "I live twenty feet away, it's easier to just go home."

He looks a little agitated when I say this, but he quickly shakes it off. "Well," he says, "at least chill out with me. I'll get you a drink."

"I don't want a drink." My tone is blunter than it was when I was talking to Tiffani. Right now, I'm too distracted and too confused and too mad at myself to even put in the effort to be nice to anyone. "Sorry, Jake, I'm just a little sick. I'm not in the mood tonight." This is partially true and it's the only excuse I can think of to get him to leave me alone.

"Okay." Taking a swig of his beer, he shrugs and heads off.

The people around me are all slowly crossing the tipsy borderline, and the more people stumble over, the more making out there seems to be. I also notice that Rachael and Trevor are nowhere in sight. I can place a bet on where they are.

So while they are upstairs doing whatever it is that Rachael and Trevor do, I take it upon myself to make sure the house is looked after, since I seem to be the only one sober enough to do so. I occupy my mind by pulling the passed-out girl out of the bathtub. I distract myself by cleaning up the spilled drinks. I focus on handing out water to the guy who's throwing up in the back yard. And all of this works pretty well on helping me forget about what happened with Tyler.

Until I see him for the first time in three hours.

As I'm picking up empty cups from the bottom of the stairs, he stumbles straight past me. He is completely gone by this point, intoxicated beyond imagination as the alcohol floods his veins. He bends over as he falls to his knees and presses his palms to the floor. For a long moment, he stares at his fingers as his head sways back and forth.

With caution, I slowly approach him. I'm not sure what I'm supposed to do. So I start with the basics, quietly saying his name. My voice hitches in my throat as I do so, but he still somehow hears me through the alcohol clouding his mind. His eyes flicker up to meet mine, and they are heavy and dilated and tired and rolling all over the place. And they are dark.

"Baby." Tiffani's soothing voice comes from my side, and she steps in front of me to place her hands under his arms as she yanks him back up onto his feet. He immediately falls to the left, hitting the side of his face against the wall as she struggles to hold on to him. "Tyler," she says, but he quite simply ignores her, too wrapped up in his fuzzy world to process anything. She throws his arm over the back of her neck and helps him over to the stairs, where she sits him down. And then she promptly slaps him across the face. "Sober up," she huffs. "You're a nightmare."

It's the drunkest I've seen him, and it appears it is for Tiffani, too. She looks exasperated as she exhales, her hands on his jaws as she tries her hardest to hold his head up. He can barely keep his eyes open at this point.

She throws me a glance over her shoulder, her forehead creased. "Ella will kill him if he goes back over there like this," she murmurs, shaking her head at him in disgust. Tyler tries to mumble something, but it doesn't make sense. "I'll take him home with me for the night."

I give her a clipped nod as Tyler slides off the stairs and onto the floor, his body sprawled out across the ground. "Why is he so drunk?"

"He wouldn't stop drinking," Tiffani explains. She seems to be in a sober enough state despite the earlier wine, and she kneels down by him, grasping at his shoulders as she carefully tries to sit him upright. "He must have taken at least six shots in a row at one point." She looks almost helpless as her small figure attempts to push him back against the wall while his hands pull at the material of her dress. "He normally knows his limits. This is so embarrassing for me."

"I'll go get some water for him," I offer, and slip into the kitchen as fast as I can. All the while that I'm there fetching him a glass of water from the faucet, I can't help but realize that he chose to get this wasted. And there's only one reason as to why he would do that: It's because of what went down between us. I triggered it.

Just as I switch off the faucet and turn around, I bump into Dean. "It's nice to see a sober person for once," he says, nodding at the water in my hand. I glance down at it and then at the beer in his hand.

"It's for Tyler," I say. "What about you?"

"Well, I'm a little tipsy," he admits shyly as he reaches up to scratch his head. He shrugs. "Tyler's pretty wasted."

"I know," I say with the same blunt tone I've had all night. "Enjoy the rest of your night, Dean." I squeeze past him, through the other bodies that are gathered in the kitchen, through the stack of empty beer boxes, and back into the hall.

Tiffani has resorted to sitting herself down, her back against the wall with Tyler's head in her lap as she folds her arms across her chest. I can't tell if Tyler's asleep or dead. I hand her the water.

"Thanks," she says, and she's genuinely grateful. "He's making a fool out of me, so I'm gonna get him out of here. I don't want anyone else to see him."

"I'm sorry if he's ruined your night," I apologize on his

behalf, and I'm not sure why. Probably because it's my fault he's this drunk in the first place.

"He's always ruining my night." She sighs as he reaches up to touch her eyebrows, gently grabbing his hand and moving it away. He groans. "You're such an asshole, Tyler, you know that, don't you?"

"Tiffani?"

She glances up at me, her face taut. She's pissed off at him. "Yeah?"

"In the morning, when he wakes up," I start, my eyes falling to his face as he rolls over, his eyes closed but his lips parted, "can you tell him that I need to talk to him?"

17

On Monday, it's the Fourth of July. Only the nation's biggest celebration of the year, when fireworks are in high demand and the population seems to double within each city as thousands show up for the festivities. I don't know how Independence Day is remembered in Los Angeles, but in Portland we normally head down to the Waterfront Blues Festival every year to watch the fireworks over the Willamette River. Before Dad leaves for work, he tells me that we're going to watch the fireworks in Culver City. But I doubt it'll beat Portland's display.

"You can come and see the parade down on Main Street with us, if you'd like, Eden," Ella suggests as I saunter into the kitchen in my pajamas. Chase and Jamie are already seated at the table; Chase's eyes are glued to the TV on the counter as he shoves bacon into his mouth, while Jamie pours himself a bowl of cereal.

It's always a little awkward being left with Ella without Dad here, because three weeks ago these people were strangers to me. And now I'm supposed to think of them as my second family, as people I'm supposed to feel comfortable around. I don't, so the only thing I can do is pretend. "Okay," I agree. "Is Tyler home yet?"

I haven't seen him since the party on Saturday. As soon as Tiffani hauled his wasted ass into someone's car to go home, I left too. There was no point forcing myself to stay when there was nothing worth staying for. So I came home, climbed into bed, and fell asleep before Dad and Ella even got home. I don't know if they noticed the raging party across the street, but if they did they certainly didn't mention it the next day. They only questioned me about Tyler's whereabouts, so I had to tell them that he spent the night at Tiffani's. Ella's expression did contort slightly.

"Yes," she answers now, while she clinks dishes together in the sink. "He came home late last night. I think he's still sleeping."

I didn't hear him come in, and I'm surprised that he even did. He must have spent the entire day at Tiffani's place trying to recover from the hangover that he most definitely suffered through. Maybe today I'll finally get the chance to talk to him about what happened on Saturday. I can't go on ignoring it. It's not something that can be forgotten about.

"Is he coming to the parade with us?" I ask as casually as I possibly can, because I don't want to appear too concerned about him. I can't even begin to imagine how Dad and Ella would react if they knew. So I act nonchalant as I sit myself down next to Chase.

"I don't think so," Ella says. She pulls the plug out of the sink and dries her hands on a small towel as she turns to face me. "I think I'm just going to leave him to sleep."

The parade starts at 9:30AM. I didn't expect it to be so early, but I have twenty minutes to get ready before I head off with Ella and my two stepbrothers, leaving the third at home, asleep in the room next door to mine. I try not to think about him too much.

Instead, I focus on trying to spy a parking spot with Ella, but it's close to impossible. The streets are packed with cars and people and stalls on every corner selling American flags. We end up parking nine blocks away, walking the distance to Main Street. It's completely closed off for the event as the public line the sidewalk with their flags and painted faces. The four of us find a spot to stand in nearer the end of the street, but we have a great view when the parade finally reaches us. There are horses and marching bands and vintage cop cars and giant posters and fire trucks and street performers and floats, and by the end of it all I'm sick of the colors red, blue and white. But it's a nice start to the day, nonetheless, and it gives me a two-hour insight into how Santa Monica celebrates the momentous occasion. But I still think Portland has a much better Fourth of July vibe to it and I can't help but wish I was there instead, back home with my mom and Amelia, getting ready to head down to the edge of the river to listen to a whole bunch of different bands perform.

The traffic is crawling slowly at the end of the parade, so Ella decides to wait around downtown for it to clear. We kill time by going for lunch at a small café. Chase trails his flag along with him and I look like an adopted child: Ella and the boys are blond; I'm dark brunette.

"Did your dad tell you about the fireworks tonight?" Ella asks me once we finish ordering sandwiches, folding her arms on the table as she smiles over at me.

"Yeah," I say. "Where's Culver City?"

"Around twenty minutes away. This city hasn't done fireworks since 1991," she says, shaking her head in pity, "so we normally go out to Marina del Rey, but they're not putting on a display this year. We've heard the Culver City fireworks are great, though. A lot of people are heading down there tonight."

"Is Tyler going?" Once I say it, I glance down. Maybe I'm being too obvious, so I quickly rephrase the question. "I mean, we're all going, right?"

"Of course. Are you excited, Chase?" She grins down at him in a warm, proud sort of way. As Chase nods back enthusiastically, I realize I've never noticed her look at Tyler in such a way, and it suddenly makes me feel unsettled and, somehow, sad. He's just a reckless kid who makes it impossible to be proud of him. I wish he wasn't like that.

After I pick at my lunch and we visit a few stores, we eventually head back to the house mid-afternoon. Tyler's awake by now. I know because I can hear him moving around his room; there's a constant rhythm of footsteps. It's like he's pacing back and forth.

I decide to make a start on getting ready for tonight's events, so I grab a shower and hang around my room for a while, comparing outfits and waiting for my hair to dry. I even play some music, and I'm waiting for Tyler to knock on the wall again and tell me to turn it down, but there's nothing but silence on his end.

After I resort to blow-drying my hair, I grow thirsty, so I decide to head downstairs. I tidy up a little first, turning off my music before I leave, and then I make my way down the staircase.

For some reason, the house is silent and I wonder if everyone's gone out, but when I get into the hall, something catches my eye from the kitchen. It's Ella and Tyler. But they're not standing around making food or having a conversation. Far from it. I edge toward the archway, silently watching from afar, and I peer around the corner.

Tyler's head is buried in Ella's shoulder. She has her arms wrapped around him while she rests her chin on his shoulder, her eyes shut. But he's just breathing heavily against her, his shoulders sunk low and his arms hanging by his side. There are some sighs or some sniffs, almost a mixture of both, and I can't tell if one or both of them are crying. Ella's just holding him. Holding him as though her life depends on it.

"I get it," she murmurs, but her voice is cracked. "You're allowed to feel like this, Tyler. You have every right to. It can all become too much sometimes."

It's obvious something's wrong. I just don't know what. I'm waiting for Tyler to say something in reply, but he never does. The only thing I hear is the sound of the front door opening at the other end of the hall and my dad's voice calling, "Guess whose work let out early?"

Immediately, Tyler draws away from Ella, quickly lifting his head and walking to the other side of the kitchen. He exhales and runs both hands through his hair. I notice how swollen his eyes look just before he wrenches open the patio door and steps outside.

Ella presses a hand to her chest as she stares after his departing figure, her lips trembling. But she manages to get over it before Dad can see, and she jumps into action and starts operating the coffee machine.

"Enjoy the parade?" Dad asks me, and I straighten up. I clear my throat and just nod as he passes me while loosening his tie. He grins and makes his way into the kitchen, where he's greeted by his wife's beaming smile.

I wonder if he knows it's fake.

"We're all going in the same car," Dad announces two hours

later once we're all ready to leave for Culver City. "There's only three seats in the back, so you're all just going to have to squeeze up. Chase, you'll have to duck down onto the floor if we pass the cops."

Tyler folds his arms across his chest and rolls his eyes as he leans against the wall of the hall. He's back to normal again. A smirk on his lips, his eyes challenging. I'm still curious as to what was wrong earlier and the questions are eating away at me, but I know I can't ask. It's just not my place.

"Why can't I just take my own car?" he asks.

"Because you're grounded and you're not getting your car, that's why," Dad shoots back without so much as a glance toward him. "You and Eden, keep your phones on so we can find you at the end of the night. Jamie, Chase, you'll stay with us."

"Is that the end of Dave's stupid-ass safety explanations?" Tyler mutters, a smug grin on his face, his eyes narrowed. The expression is almost permanent by now.

Dad doesn't look impressed. "Just get in the car."

Tyler laughs as we all make our way out to the Range Rover and clamber inside with four of us squashed uncomfortably into the backseat. We're not even in a suitable position to wear seatbelts, so I sit there with Chase on my left and Tyler on my right, and we're all so packed in that my body is pressed against Tyler's. I look at my feet while he stares out the window, and the hair on my arms begins to stand up as the heat from his skin warms mine. I bite my lip to keep myself quiet, but when I notice his shoes halfway through the journey I simply have to speak. He's wearing white Converse, just like I am.

"I didn't know you wore Converse," I muse, quiet enough beneath Dad and Ella's conversation that they can't hear me.

He glances sideways down at me as his soft eyes meet my gaze. "Yeah."

And that's all we say during the entire journey to Culver City. The traffic is unbelievable, so we end up being stuck in the car for forty minutes until we finally come to a stop outside the local high school. It turns out the firework display is here, and Ella was right about there being a lot of people going. We have to pay to get into the school parking lot, and then we have to donate even more to get into the event itself. At least we don't get pulled over on the way here for overloading the car.

"If any of your friends are here, you can go find them," Ella tells Tyler and me as we all make our way inside the school, following the signs to the football field. "We'll call you at the end if we can't find you again, okay?"

"And behave yourself," Dad adds, but he's only looking at Tyler. Because Tyler is the only one he needs to worry about, because Tyler is unpredictable, because Tyler is reckless.

"Yeah, yeah, we will," he mutters, and then waves our parents away. He speeds up to get away from them, swiftly edging his body through the flow of people in front of us before he disappears.

"I know that Meghan is here," I tell my dad, but my eyes are still focused ahead, searching for the back of Tyler's head. "I'm gonna go find her."

"Be careful," he warns me, but then gives me the go-ahead with a curt nod.

I weave my body away from them, speed-walking in Tyler's direction through the hallways of Culver City High School. I can hear the faint echo of a marching band in the distance and it makes me feel as though I'm on my way to a high school football game. Which I kind of am.

The display is being held above the football field, and when I get to the back door of the school and spill outside with the crowd, there are already thousands of people in the stands and on the field. There are food stalls around the track and the sun begins to set in the distance as the crowd thickens. There's no way I'm finding Meghan.

All around me there are families and elderly couples and groups of college kids milling around, while others have chosen to set up chairs and blankets on the field to ensure they can watch the show in comfort. Whereas I'm now alone and wishing that I'd just stayed with my dad.

"I didn't think you were the type to go off on your own," a voice says beside me, loud over the noise of the band and the conversations around us. It's Tyler, and he's staring at me with a curious glint in his eyes and a small smile playing on his lips. "We can talk now."

"Now?" I echo in disbelief. Out of all the places and times he could have chosen, he chooses the middle of the Fourth of July celebrations.

"I didn't mean right here," he murmurs, looking past me as he studies the field, the people, the stalls. "Come on." He keeps his face low as he turns around and eases his way back in whatever direction he came from while I anxiously follow at his heels.

We're heading away from the field and back toward the main school building, pushing our way there against the flow of people. My heart is in my stomach as we get back inside. I don't know if he's going to be furious at me or if he'll be willing to accept my apology, and the thought of the former is making me feel as though I could throw up again.

I'm so preoccupied with nerves that I almost miss him

take me down a hallway that clearly has a sign stating "NO ENTRY." Only certain hallways are open to allow the public to get out onto the field; the rest of the school seems to be shut off. But Tyler disregards these rules, and I feel too nauseated to even bother arguing with him. We soon reach the end of the hallway that we've been sneaking along, and Tyler comes to a stop.

The noise from outside is barely noticeable now, and given that the lights in these hallways are all off, the only thing lighting up Tyler's face is the dusk sun streaming in through the windows. I can see the field from here, but it's not the field that I'm interested in. It's the person in front of me.

He stares at the wall for a few moments before he turns to face me, all smugness gone from his expression. And thankfully, his eyes are gentle. He swallows. "What the hell happened on Saturday?"

"I don't know," I admit, my voice catching in the back of my throat as my stomach knots. "I'm sorry. You were just—you were annoying me and I didn't want you to buy more drugs and I just—I just did it. I didn't mean to. I'm sorry, okay? It's really weird and it's making me feel sick and we just need to pretend it didn't happen."

He stares at me as he runs his tongue across his lower lip. "I wish I could say the same about me."

"What?" Now that I've blurted what I've needed to blurt, I feel slightly more at ease. That is, of course, until he looks at me in a way I've never seen him look at me before. And my entire body ignites again, just like it did on Saturday.

"I kissed you back," he states bluntly. "I'm not going to apologize for that."

"Why?"

For a short moment, his eyes smolder at me as he decides whether or not to answer. They're soft and calm, yet his voice is sharp. "Because I knew exactly what I was doing."

"Why did you do it?" My voice is almost a whisper as my heart hurls itself back and forth against my ribcage, creating a dull ache in my chest as the knot in my stomach grows tighter.

"Because I've wanted to do it so fucking badly," he snaps. He spins his body around, turning his back to me as he heaves a sigh and presses a hand to the wall.

"You've wanted to?" I repeat. Now I'm just lost and confused and feeling sicker than ever. "What the hell are you saying?"

"You want the honest truth?" I nod even though he can't see me, and he lets his head hang low as he shakes it at the ground. "I'm saying that I'm fucking attracted to you, alright, Eden?" The moment the words escape his lips, he swivels his body back around, his eyes no longer gentle as storms grow within their depths. "And I know I shouldn't be, because you're my damn stepsister, but I just can't help it. It's stupid as hell and I know you don't feel the same way, because you're fucking apologizing for Saturday." He pauses for a split second as he glances down at the ground. "I really wish you hadn't said sorry for it. Because apologizing means regretting."

I'm stunned into silence. Tyler, the guy who's treated me like a doormat since the day I got here, is in fact attracted to me? It doesn't make sense at all. "I thought you hated me," I manage to reply, because it's the only thing running through my head.

"I hate a lot of people," he says gruffly, "but you're not one of them. I hate the fact that you turn me on. Like, a lot."

"Stop," I say. I take a step back from him, shaking my head and holding up a hand. "You're my stepbrother. You can't say that."

"Who makes up these bullshit rules, huh?" He viciously laughs, turning to look out the window before fixing his eyes back on me. "Three weeks ago I didn't even know who you were. I don't see you as a sister, okay? You're just some girl I've met. How the hell is it fair to label us as siblings?"

Now I could really throw up. My mind is spinning, my thoughts drowning in questions. "You have a girlfriend," I whisper. "Tiffani's your girlfriend."

"But I don't want her to be!" he yells, and he's quite clearly irritated that I've even mentioned her. He runs a hand back through his hair and pulls on the ends. "I don't want to be with Tiffani, okay? Don't you get that? She's just another distraction."

"What the hell is up with you and distractions?"

"NOTHING," he shouts. Exhaling, he presses his lips together and lowers his voice again. "I've said what I've needed to say, you know what I think of you, you've made it clear you think differently, I'm done. Enjoy the fucking fireworks." He storms past me, both hands now in his hair, and the vein in his neck is clearly defined.

"Wait," I say. Staring after him, I watch him pause in the dull hallway. But he doesn't turn around. He only stands there, his shoulders rising in sync with his breathing. "You didn't give me the chance to tell you that I find you interesting."

18

The strained silence that lasts for the longest of moments is interrupted by the sound of fireworks. The sky outside the window erupts into a vivid canvas of colors and swirls. Both Tyler and I tilt our heads to see, and the lights reflect off our skin, the side of his cheeks glowing a soft orange, which soon fades away as the colors drain from the sky. They are quickly replaced with more, but Tyler has already turned away from the window. Instead, he focuses on the color of my eyes rather than the color of the fireworks.

"Interesting?" he repeats, his voice dry. "That's all you can say?"

The sky crackles and pops and hoots while the celebrating crowd below cheer, their tilted faces illuminated. The entire field is visible from up here, up in this out-of-bounds hallway. "We're missing the fireworks," I murmur weakly. I sound pathetic and I'm aware of it. Nothing will ease the frantic throbbing of my heart.

"I don't care about the fireworks," he snaps. His voice is low, but it rises as his bitter hostility toward me grows. "Are you fucking kidding me right now? Interesting?"

I don't know why he's so offended by the word. Interesting is good, interesting means different. I've never come across a person who has grabbed my interest like he has.

"Your walls," I say, my voice wavering. I bite the inside of my cheek and gnaw at my mouth as I try to steady my tone, to compose myself so that I can muster up coherent sentences. "Your walls interest me."

"I don't know what you're talking about," he splutters, his Adam's apple rising in his throat. Something shifts within the flashing of his eyes. He knows exactly what I'm talking about.

"I didn't realize it until now," I state quietly. With a soft shake of my head, my eyes drop to the floor and then back to his. "You've got walls up and they interest me."

"You know what?" he hisses. His lower lip juts out as his chiseled jaw clenches. "I don't care. Think whatever you want about me."

"Think whatever I want?" My eyes narrow into tiny slits as I hold my stare, yet he struggles to hold his. He keeps glancing erratically off to the sides, to the floor, to the ceiling. But never back to me. "I think that you infuriate me," I say. "I think that you are an arrogant jackass who can never simply be nice to someone, because it doesn't fit in with the act you're putting on."

He pinches the bridge of his nose, his eyes tightly squeezed shut as he takes a few deep breaths. I watch his chest rise as the air enters his abused lungs. The smoking isn't good for him. "You have no idea what you're saying."

"Let me finish," I order sharply. The anxiousness has faded, replaced with confidence fueled by adrenaline. "I also think that you're a jerk. Your ego is too big for your own head and you think that you look cool by being a badass. But really, Tyler? You just look pathetic."

Tyler's face falls, his taut expression crumpling as his lips twitch slightly. "Alright, now I just look like a complete moron coming up here and telling you that I'm attracted to you. You could've let me down easier."

"I thought someone as badass as you could handle it."

He stuffs his curled-up fists into the pockets of his jeans and averts his gaze to the windows. For a short while, he just stares at the sky with a sad look in his eyes. In between the explosive noise of the fireworks, I can hear his breathing deepening. He blinks and glances over his shoulder at me. "And I thought you'd figured out that I'm not really a badass."

The moment the final syllable rolls off the tip of his tongue, my entire mindset transforms. He's vulnerable, and I am completely right. His walls are a mask. It's all an act, a role he's trying to play. The crude comments and leching over Tiffani and the addictions: They're fake. It's all fake. There's more to him. Like today in the kitchen with Ella. He wasn't a badass then, and he wasn't a badass when he was joking with Jamie. Sometimes his façade slips. And sometimes I've been there to see beneath it.

It's the way his eyes sometimes soften, offering a true glimpse of what he's about to anyone who is willing to look. And I don't know why it hasn't hit me until this moment. It is so, so obvious. Our irrelevant arguments and pathetic small talk and constant glares seem so . . . so inevitable, like we couldn't stop, like we enjoyed the bickering. Somehow. We have sneered at one another since the day I arrived, fighting to try to find each other's weaknesses. Mine is my insecurity. Tyler's is the truth.

And beneath it all lies attraction.

Tyler is attracted to me, and I am attracted to Tyler.

The realization makes my heart skip a beat, my blood running cold as I lift my eyes to his. It's like I'm seeing him for the first time all over again, and now that I'm not seeing him as some jackass who rudely stormed into a barbecue, I can study him in a new light. His eyes are mesmerizing, his jaw is perfectly crafted, and his plump lips form a mischievous crooked smile. Not only that, there are so many things about him that I'm dying to find out. Mostly, I just want to uncover the truth about him. I need to know who he really is, not who he wants me to think he is. He's pretending, just an actor playing a role. I need to know what happens backstage, after the show ends and the curtains come down. Who's left?

Tyler notices my stare boring into him, and he looks perplexed.

"I think," I say, drawing in a sharp breath, "that I'm attracted to you, too."

My words take him aback. He slowly turns his body completely around to face me and he removes his hands from his pockets. Utter surprise dominates his expression. His widened eyes meet my gaze from five feet away, and he bites down on his lower lip. "You are?" He arches an eyebrow as though he can't decide if I'm playing a game or not.

In all honesty, I really wish I was.

I shouldn't be attracted to my stepbrother.

"I am." It almost hurts to admit it. But at the same time, there's a sense of relief that relaxes the tightness in my chest. I can no longer meet his eyes. "I'm sorry."

"Stop apologizing," Tyler demands. He warily approaches me, his steps slow as he relaxes his fists. His gray T-shirt is tightly fitted to his body, and I find myself analyzing every detail of his outfit as he moves nearer. Gray T-shirt, dark jeans, and the white Chucks that match mine. "Don't regret anything."

When I glance up from the ground, where his feet have suddenly appeared next to mine, my breath hitches as I realize how close he is. His face is dark as he peers down at me, his eyes soft and gentle again. Over his shoulder, the sky continues to light up with every color of the rainbow. He lifts his hand to my elbow and skims the tips of his fingers against my skin. Delicately, he traces a line down to my wrist before moving his hand to my waist. He gently grips my body.

"What's happening?" I whisper. The atmosphere is too charged to speak any louder and I can feel myself becoming breathless. I want to object, to push him away, because I know that this is wrong. But I don't. I don't, because I like the feeling of his skin against mine.

My eyes are locked somewhere between the tip of his shoulder and the window, but they're not quite focused. He must pick up on how rigid I am, because his thumb begins to soothingly rub circles by my hip. His breathing is slow, and the scent of firewood and mint captivates me, drawing me in and charming me completely. He moves his lips toward the edge of my jaw. Softly, he places them against my skin, moving in a slow line toward the corner of my lips. He stops when he gets there.

"Let me kiss you," he murmurs. He breathes against my cheek, hovering in trepidation.

"But you're my stepbrother," I whisper, my throat dry. My voice quivers and I just can't control the anxiety that is rattling every inch of my body.

I sense Tyler swallow. "Just don't think about it," he tells me, right before he takes the plunge and presses his lips to mine.

And this time around, it's even better than before. His lips are soft and moist as they lock with mine. I can almost feel his nervousness, like he can probably feel mine. The fireworks are still exploding. His grip on my waist tightens as he pulls me against his body. I don't mind. I like the feeling.

"Hey!" a loud voice yells from somewhere along the hallway, but it doesn't quite register in my mind. And quite frankly, I wouldn't care even if it did. "Cut it out, guys."

But we ignore the faint cry, too caught up in our wrong embrace to pay attention. My lips part as Tyler carefully wraps a hand around the back of my neck. He holds me close against him as his other hand drops from my waist to the small of my back. He dominates the kiss, controlling the speed and the intensity. But I don't mind this either. I like this too.

The voice in the background grows louder, as do the footsteps that come along with it. "Get out of here before I arrest you both for trespassing."

But I am still too wrapped up in Tyler. The heat from his hands radiates against my skin as he moves from a fast, light pace to a much slower, much deeper kiss. He tilts my chin up to get a better angle. I sure as hell don't mind this, and I sure as hell like it.

"Alright, wrap it up," the voice orders. It's suddenly piercingly loud and gruff. My eyes snap open, my body stiffening beneath Tyler's touch as a police officer meets my frozen stare. His arms are folded and there's a frown etched on his lips. "Cut it out already!"

"Dammit," Tyler hisses as he finally tears himself away from me. With a hand thrown back through his hair, he slowly turns around to face our intruder. He folds his arms across his chest, his hands balled into fists. "You got a problem?"

"You are trespassing," the officer states matter-of-factly,

shrewdly eyeing us in a rather degrading manner. It's like he's just discovered mice in the school cafeteria.

"Trespassing?" Tyler repeats, but his tone is contemptuous. "Don't you have better things to do? Like sorting out those drunk fights out there on the field?" He gives a curt nod in the direction of the windows, where the finale of the firework display is underway. These fireworks are bigger. More dramatic, more colorful. Below, the football field is still heaving with the local public and police officers. Events on such a large scale as this are bound to be policed. It's the same in Portland.

"Enough with the attitude," the officer snaps. He takes a challenging stance, his legs spread wide and his hands on his hips. "This school is closed apart from the designated hallways. You are trespassing and I am giving you the chance to leave by yourself before I have to make you."

"Make me?" Tyler echoes sharply. I begin to take a step in the direction we came in, but I pause to reach out for the hem of his T-shirt. It doesn't look like he's about to move. He's too busy fixing his eyes on the man opposite. "Can't you just give us a second? We'll get out of here, but you kind of interrupted something."

"Tyler, just come on," I murmur. I'm a little out of breath from all the kissing, and it's exhilarating. I want to do it all over again.

"Yes, I figured I interrupted something," the officer remarks, and he takes the time to glance between the two of us in disapproval. It causes my cheeks to flood with color. "I'm not asking to reason with you. I'm asking you to leave, and I expect you to do it. Don't try to waste my time, son."

"It's a goddamn hallway," Tyler mutters as he throws his

hands up in frustration. "It's not like we're sneaking around the White House. Just give us five minutes."

"Can't you take no for an answer?" the officer asks, shaking his head in disbelief at Tyler's persistence. "Didn't your old man ever teach you how to obey orders?"

I might not know much about Tyler, but I know that the mere mention of his dad is a sure-fire way to set him off. And that's exactly what happens.

"Are you a fucking asshole or what?" Tyler hisses, his tone suddenly venomous as he puffs out his chest and steps toward the officer. For a second I think he's about to take a swing at him, but thankfully he doesn't.

"Alright, that's it," the officer grunts. He moves one hand to his belt as he yanks out a pair of cuffs, his receding hairline allowing me to see every wrinkle on his forehead. And right now, there are a lot of them. He looks completely worked up. "I have asked you to leave but you are refusing orders and your attitude is downright inappropriate, so I am arresting you under Section 602."

The color drains from Tyler's face at the exact same moment that my mouth falls open, and right then, the officer's eyes flicker over to meet mine. "Both of you."

19

"You couldn't have just kept your mouth shut?" I hiss to Tyler. I keep my voice low in fear of getting ourselves into even more trouble, which is something I really can't afford to do right now. Pressing a hand to my forehead, I slowly rub my temple.

"Cop was a prick," Tyler mutters in return. He's awfully disgruntled as he slumps further down against the wall, his lips forming a firm scowl that I doubt will fade any time soon. He stares out of the holding cell at the busy station, glowering at each officer in contempt. "They all are."

"We wouldn't even be here if you'd just walked away." My forehead is creased with worry as I mentally prepare a list of possible punishments that Dad will sentence me to. Grounded for the rest of the summer? Sent home? Forced to do his laundry?

I glance around the cell. There's a woman throwing a tantrum in the corner, throwing her body around and slapping the floor as though it'll help her get out of here. There's also a man built of muscle standing in silence with his back against the wall and his huge arms folded across his chest. I refrain from meeting his eyes.

From our spot on the bench, Tyler and I sit close by each

other but not close enough to touch. He groans under his breath and drops his head, leaning forward to prop his elbows up on his knees. "My mom will get us out of it," he murmurs. He exchanges a quick sideways glance with me, but I'm not entirely convinced.

"What? Because she's an attorney?" I snort. It's impossible to be positive in this terrible situation, but the more I think about it, the more I realize Ella knows the law like the back of her hand. She has to. And with knowing the law comes knowing the loopholes.

"Because she's done it before," he says as he straightens up again. He interlocks his hands and twiddles his thumbs, his eyes focused on his lap. "She always gets me out of it."

"Before," I echo. I roll my eyes before focusing on what's on the other side of the metal bars. There are desks overflowing with paperwork and telephones that apparently never stop ringing. There's also a security officer standing watching over us all from afar, his wrinkled face pulled tight, his eyes narrowed. I tilt my head to face Tyler again. "How many times have you been arrested?"

The corners of his lips quirk upward into a smirk. "Once. Twice. Maybe a couple more than that."

"What for?"

"Um." He scratches his head as he rolls his tongue over his lower lip. I can't help thinking about his mouth again. "Stupid stuff," he finally admits. He shrugs as he gets to his feet, straightening up and stretching his arms. I gaze at him, not quite caring about what he's about to say. "Fighting," he says as he cracks his knuckles, "vandalism, disrupting the peace." He chuckles as he throws a cautious glance over his shoulder. "And trespassing," he finishes.

"At least you haven't killed anybody," I say lightly, but I don't know why. A week ago I would have turned my nose up in disgust at him for even being arrested in the first place, no matter what for. But now the enigma that is Tyler Bruce is winning me over and my opinion on him has greatly altered within three days.

"Not yet," he corrects. He presses his lips together, pursing them slightly as his eyes narrow back into their usual state. "I've got someone in mind." My lustful gaze immediately turns to horror. Tyler mimics my expression before letting a sharp laugh escape his lips. "Eden," he says, shaking his head and quickly rolling his eyes.

"I haven't figured out your sense of humor yet," I defend, folding my arms across my chest and heaving a sigh. He's still a puzzle to me. "I didn't even know that you had one."

He smiles again and gives me a clipped nod. "Good one."

"Bruce, Munro," a voice barks. It startles the two of us and Tyler promptly spins around to meet the disapproving eyes of a Culver City police officer on the other side of the bars. "Your parents are here." Our cell companions laugh.

"We're going to die," I tell myself quietly as my breathing quickens. I try to swallow the lump in my throat as I will myself to keep it together. "Oh my God. We're actually going to die."

"Shut up," Tyler orders, his voice even quieter than mine, and he fixes me with a stern look as I stand. "Let me do the talking."

Thankfully, our arresting officer—Officer Sullivan—is no longer around. Perhaps he's back out on the streets, searching for more Fourth of July celebrators' nights to ruin. He seemed stubborn that way, like he had a deeply rooted grudge he wanted to take out on everyone else. The second officer is a lot younger and a lot less frightening. His name is Officer Greene, and he unlocks the cell and swings open the barred door for us.

"Follow me," he commands with a sigh. I trail along behind Tyler through the bustling station as officers brush past us with little respect. Officer Greene leads us out of the main office and into a smaller one, and lo and behold, there are my dad and Ella.

Dad's hands are on his hips as his scornful eyes fix on the pair of us, and I fear he might pass out. He looks pretty riled up. Ella is angled slightly in front of him, and for the first time I see her with a completely solemn expression. She firmly presses her lips together, her hands clasped in front of her. Whenever I've seen her furious at Tyler, there's always been a hint of motherly sympathy in her features. But right now, there's nothing. She has her attorney face on.

"What the hell are you two playing at?" Dad snaps. His face continues to grow a hot red as he huffs, but Ella quickly steps forward to cut in before anyone can muster up a reply.

"Officer . . .?" She pauses to squint at Officer Greene's badge.

"Greene," he finishes for her.

"Officer Greene," she says. Clearing her throat, she extends her arm to shake his hand. "Can you explain to me why they have been arrested for trespassing? By the way, I'm an attorney." She arches her brows as she awaits an answer, and Officer Greene shifts his weight from one foot to the other, a little surprised, knowing he can't bullshit his way around her.

"Trespassing under Penal Code 602," he states without leaving her eyes, "within Culver City High School. Only the specified areas of the campus were open to the public for this evening's celebrations and they were found in a hallway in a closed block."

"Really?" Ella almost laughs at how pathetic it all sounds, and I'm stunned to see her so in control. She's normally rather quiet, only ever raising her voice at Tyler. "They stumble into the wrong hallway and you arrest them?"

"Ma'am, I was not the arresting officer," Greene informs her. "Officer Sullivan doesn't have much patience and your son here was showing a bit of attitude when asked to leave. They were given several chances to do so."

Tyler snorts but quickly stops himself and drops his head to the ground before anyone can call him out. Ella does, however, shoot him a fiery glare.

"I was in that school tonight," she continues, fixing her attention back on Officer Greene, "and I do recall seeing 'NO ENTRY' signs. But 'NO ENTRY' signs are not the same as signs warning that trespassing is an infraction and, therefore, neither of them were properly informed that they were committing an offense. They cannot be arrested on the grounds of your colleague's short temper."

The entire time that Ella is speaking, Dad glowers at me. I can't quite meet his eyes and I try to focus anywhere else but on him. To my right, Tyler is biting back laughter as he presses a hand to his mouth. I'd totally kick him in the shin if there weren't a cop standing next to us. He manages to compose himself, but the second he lifts his head and meets my eyes he starts laughing again. He bites the back of his hand as he stares at the ground.

"How about we save both of us the paperwork and I let this one slide?" I hear Officer Greene say, and immediately my eyes flicker over to him. He offers his hand to Ella.

"Respectable decision, Officer," Ella comments, and they shake on the agreement. I see her exchange a brief glance with Dad, and he nods as though they're telepathic.

"Alright," Dad says. "You two, out to the car. Right now."

Tyler's laughter has subsided by now, and he shrugs at me as Dad barges through the middle of us. "Someone's mad as hell," he mutters under his breath. He nudges my arm before turning around, the two of us following close on Dad's heels and out of the station. Ella doesn't join us.

It's dark when we get outside into the station parking lot, and it's growing late, too. As we approach the Range Rover in silence, Jamie peers through the tinted windows at us. I pull open the door to find Chase asleep at the other side.

"What'd you do this time?" Jamie asks, but his eyes are on Tyler, not me.

"Something I shouldn't have," Tyler mutters in reply, and he throws me a knowing smile.

I climb inside, Tyler behind me, and we all have to shove Chase further along until he's pressed against the door at the other side. Jamie only heaves a tremendous sigh. I look up at Dad to find him gripping the steering wheel in silence, and I'm just about to ask him if he's okay when Ella comes storming over to the car. She throws open the passenger door, gets in and slams it shut again.

"Nice going, Mom," Tyler says. He leans forward and rubs her shoulder. "You're killing 'em."

She quickly shakes his hand off her and barely even glances at him in the rearview mirror before opening her mouth to speak. "Don't even talk to me, Tyler," she warns, her voice scolding. "One of these days I'm just not going to turn up. I'm so disappointed in you."

"I'm disappointed in you too, Eden," Dad chips in gruffly. He shakes his head and starts up the engine, slowly backing out of the parking lot. "What the hell were you doing inside in the first place? I'm pretty sure the event was outside."

"No," Tyler quips. "The event was definitely inside." He runs a finger inconspicuously down my thigh, stopping at my knee. It creates the oddest sensation.

"Cut it out with the attitude," Ella snaps. She must be livid, because she never snaps. "I just had to sign for both of you to get out of there when I could have easily just left you all night, okay? So here's an idea, Tyler: Just sit there and be quiet for once in your life."

That shuts him up for the journey back to Santa Monica, but it doesn't stop him from skimming his thumb over my palm or playfully bumping his knee against mine or staring at me. I'm surprised no one notices. I certainly do, and I try my hardest to ignore him, despite the shivers running through me at his every touch.

It's almost midnight when we get back to Deidre Avenue. Dad is worn out from the driving, but he still manages to carry Chase into the house and put him to bed without waking him. Jamie disappears into his room too.

"I don't even know what to say to you, Tyler," Ella murmurs as she locks the front door. She presses her palm against the glass panel, but she doesn't turn around to face him. "I've just—I've had enough." Her voice is pained, and she sighs as she turns around and walks toward us. "Eden, just go to your room. Get some sleep."

When she gives me a small smile, I realize she's really asking for privacy. I nod, glancing between both of them before heading for the stairs. Dad passes me on my way up and we both pause.

"I should call your mom," he says quietly. It feels odd hearing him mention her. Out of place, even.

"Don't." I pull a face and pout. Mom is already stressed enough with her work; she doesn't need me being arrested piled onto her too. "It'll only worry her."

"It's worrying me, Eden!" he starts to yell, but it fades to a whisper midway through. He glances around to make sure he hasn't disrupted anything, and then he presses a hand to his forehead. "What the hell is going on with you? I know you've been going to parties. I'm forty, not sixty. I don't care about you enjoying yourself. Hell, it's summer. What I care about is the impact it's having on you. You've already lied to me a bunch of times, and now this? Who are you even hanging out with?"

Dad's abruptness takes me aback. I thought he was oblivious to where I was going and what I was doing, but it seems he's more aware than I thought he was. "Um," I say. "Rachael from across the street. Tiffani. Um. Tiffani . . . Parkinson, I think?"

"Tyler's girlfriend?" Dad asks, but he doesn't even give me the chance to nod back. "Are you hanging out with the whole group of them? Dean Carter? That Jake guy?"

"And Meghan," I mumble. I didn't take him as a dad who paid attention to which people were in which friendship circle. "We're all friends."

"Well," he says slowly, rubbing the back of his neck, "at least they're nice kids. Look, you know what, just go to bed." Unbuttoning the top of his shirt, he shakes his head in defeat and continues on downstairs.

I don't know what the hell that was, but I don't want to stick around and wait for it to happen again. Darting into my room, I kick off my sneakers and spin around to close my door, but Tyler is standing there. I almost choke.

"Hey," he whispers as he takes a step into my room. His eyes glance around as though it's the first time he's ever been in here.

"Hi." His eyes fall back to mine, and I can't quite tell what he's thinking about or how he's feeling. My open door casts a shadow over his face, so I can't see the shade of his eyes and the emotions within them. "What'd your mom say?"

"Nothing," he says, his voice low. "Sorry for taking you down with me. I should have just left when the cop told us to."

"It's fine." My anger has fizzled away to nothing by now. We didn't end up being charged, so I plan to pass it off as a simple misunderstanding between the officer and us.

Tyler opens his mouth to speak again, but the sharp shrill of a phone cuts him off. I can hear the vibrations through his jeans as he reaches into his pocket. His lips falter into a frown when he looks at the screen. "Tiffani," he murmurs. He looks like he's contemplating declining the call for a moment, but he shakes his head and shoots me an apologetic glance. "Sorry, I gotta talk to her. She'll get mad if I ignore her."

And just like that, everything inside me sinks. Everything drowns. My chest almost collapses on itself, tightening in ways unimaginable as I force myself to keep breathing. Anxiety hits me again in one big wave. I've been so caught up in him these past couple hours that I completely forgot he has a girlfriend.

"I'm sorry," he says again, grimacing at the screen once more before looking back up to take in my frozen posture. I feel sick again and he seems to notice, because he takes a step toward me but then quickly changes his mind. A tremendous sigh echoes around the room and he squeezes his phone tighter. “I’m really sorry. I have to,” he whispers. Dropping his eyes to the carpet, he slowly turns around and leaves.

I stand there feeling completely numb while he accepts the call, murmuring, “Hey, what’s up?” just before the door of his room clicks shut.

But his voice has no energy to it at all.

It’s as lifeless as I feel.

20

"Eden!" my best friend's voice yells ecstatically down the line the next morning. Her tone is so high and so sharp that I have to draw my phone away from my ear for a moment. "Finally!"

"I know, I know." I heave a sigh, which more than likely echoes across the connection. "I've been so busy."

"You keep missing my calls," Amelia states. There's a hint of irritation in her voice, which I can't blame her for. I haven't spoken to her in over a week. "How was your Fourth of July?"

I bite down on my lower lip. Yesterday is what I'm calling to talk to her about, but her question leaves me a little tongue-tied. I somehow manage to muster up a quick, "Good," between several uneven breaths.

"Just good?"

"Well," I say. I bite even harder, my cheeks warming with a rose hue as I stare down at my comforter. "I got to ride in a cop car for the first time last night."

There's a long silence, like Amelia is waiting for me to yell "Just kidding!" at her. But I don't. "What?"

I begin tracing circles on the fabric. "For trespassing."

"Is this even Eden that I'm talking to?" There are some annoying thuds as she taps her knuckles against her phone. "Hello? Eden Munro, is that you?"

I let out a small laugh. "It wasn't my fault. My ste—" I stop short as the words catch in my throat. I can't bring myself to say them, because saying them only reminds me of the reality of the situation. "I mean, Tyler," I correct slowly, "got us arrested. We would have been fine if he hadn't opened his mouth."

"That's the oldest brother, right?" Her words make me cringe, and it takes me a few seconds to compose myself before I confirm.

"Did you go to the festival?" I quickly ask. My fingers tighten around my comforter as I listen for her reply.

"Of course," she says with a sharp gasp, as though she's appalled that I even needed to ask. We always go the Waterfront Blues Festival. "It felt so weird without you there."

I frown as I run a hand through my hair. "Who were you with?"

"The usual," she tells me, right before she begins to rattle off some of their names. "Chloe, Eve, Annie, Jason, Andre . . . You know, just everyone." Hearing the names of my friends from Portland casts a tidal wave of homesickness over me. I miss hanging out with them all, and it's even worse hearing about them all spending the summer together while I'm stuck here.

But then a further thought crosses my mind. It reminds me of why I left Portland in the first place, why I finally gave in to coming here for eight weeks. It's because some people in Portland aren't worth missing. I take a short breath before quietly murmuring, "Alyssa and Holly . . . Were they there?"

"Yeah." Silence ensues until I hear Amelia exhale, and when she speaks again her voice is soft and quiet. "Don't make it awkward for me, Eden. All three of you are my best friends, but it feels like I'm supporting both sides of the warfronts. It feels like I'm committing treason whenever I talk to one of you."

I try to ignore the pain in my chest by ignoring her. "So were the fireworks good?" The enthusiasm in my voice sounds fake as I force a smile upon my lips.

"They were amazing!" Amelia squeals. She's always been hyperactive, always getting excited over the simplest of things. "We had a bonfire after it. We were out all night, making s'mores and drinking beer and listening to music. I'm half asleep right now, so I don't know if I'm making sense." She pauses. "I hope I am."

"You are," I confirm as I press my back harder against the wall. I try to keep my thoughts from wandering. "The bonfire sounded fun."

"It was!" More squeaks, more squeals, more heavy breathing. "Landon Silverman took me home."

My eyes widen slightly. Landon Silverman is pretty damn hot. "The senior?"

"Yeah," she sheepishly admits. I can picture her blushing, blinking repeatedly like she always does when she's embarrassed or shy. But the shyness disintegrates as quickly as it arrived, and she nonchalantly says, "We got to third base in the back of his truck."

I almost choke. If this is a joke, it isn't funny. "You're kidding, right?"

"I wish I was," she murmurs. "His package isn't much of a package. And I had such high expectations. It's a tragedy."

"Sounds horrific, Amelia," I say, stifling a laugh. She reminds me of Rachael. They have similar humor and similar hobbies involving males.

"What about you?" she pries, the curiosity dripping from her voice. "Canoodled with any Californian boys yet?"

"I did make out with this guy . . ." Off goes my pulse again, speeding up and beating rapidly beneath my skin. I take a deep breath. "Last night."

Amelia almost bursts with excitement. "Oh my God, who?"

I hit a mental standstill. Do I tell her? Do I tell my best friend, the best friend who I tell everything to, about what happened with Tyler? I feel like I should fill her in so that I can hear her advice, but I just can't force the words out of my mouth. This complication with Tyler feels too scandalous, too wrong. And I know that Amelia must surely feel my apprehension over the line, so I quickly blurt, "Some guy called Jake." Nice save.

"Is he hot?"

I shrug to myself as I pull Jake's face into my mind, analyzing his features and tilting my head while I decide. "Yeah. He's blond."

"Blond?" Amelia gasps in horror. "You're canoodling with a blond guy?"

"Stop using that word," I order through giggles. It is impossible to have a conversation with her without cracking a smile.

She takes a deep breath before yelling, "BUT YOU ARE LITERALLY CANOODLING WITH A BLOND GUY!"

"How shocking," I remark.

"Is that Californian water beginning to affect you? You hate blond guys," she states as though I'm not already aware of that. She's the one who prefers blond hair. "Do you want me to call your mom, because I honestly think you need medical assistance. What happened to 'dark-haired guys are better?'"

I roll my eyes. "Are you still drunk?"

"I don't know," she says. "Probably."

And with that, I tell her to go get some sleep before bidding her farewell. She promises to drop by my house later to check on my mom, and I'm thankful. Mom's probably feeling pretty lonely lately.

When I get off the phone, I decide to go for a run to clear my head. The weekend's events with Tyler have left my head all over the place, and I feel an overwhelming sense of doubt. I don't know what I'm doing and I really don't know what I'm getting myself into. All I know is that it's not simple.

I get myself dressed and tell Ella that I'm heading out, and I begin my jog south across the city for a change, instead of west to the coastline. The weather is gorgeous and the city is busy, but I don't pay too much attention to the details. Normally I steal glances at people's faces as I pass; I read license plates; I notice small independent stores that look interesting. But not today. Today, my thoughts are all about Tyler.

So while my mind processes one hundred and one fleeting thoughts at once, I somehow manage to conclude some specific facts about him: (1) Tyler is a jerk; there is no doubt about that one, (2) he is a jerk who has serious anger issues alongside possible behavioral issues, (3) he's only a jerk because he wants to be a jerk, because (4) he's definitely hiding something, (5) his favorite hobbies include getting wasted and getting high, (6) he has nice abs and I like the color of his eyes, (7) sometimes he can be really sweet, like when he's joking around with his brothers, (8) he can annoy the hell out of me occasionally, but it's okay, because (9) he is a great kisser. And finally, (10), I'm attracted to him much more than I'm willing to admit.

Over the sound of my music I hear the honk of a car, which crashes my train of thought. My eyes flash to my left as a vehicle pulls up by the sidewalk, so I slow to a halt and pull out one earphone. It's not until I take a few steps closer that I realize I recognize this car—it's Dean's, and he's not alone.

As the window rolls down, Tyler offers me a small smile and raised eyebrows. He purses his lips and then says, "I knew it was you."

"What gave it away?" I ask as I pull the other earphone from my ear and lean down. I press my hands on the car door, my breathing heavy. I don't know how long I've been running for.

Tyler's eyes light up for a moment, and he laughs under his breath and glances at his lap. "We just got outta the gym," he tells me, but it's not the reply I'm looking for. I was expecting an answer to my question. "We're heading back to my place and you look like you're about to die, so you may as well just get in the car."

My eyes drift past him to Dean. His cheeks are flushed red from working out and he gives me a quick nod.

"I am not dying," I protest indignantly, panting. I'm insulted that he said such a thing. "I can run for miles, okay?"

"Okay," Tyler mimics, but his tone is playful. His smile turns lopsided and suddenly he reaches for the car door and pushes it open, forcing me to remove my hands and take a step back. He gets out of the vehicle and straightens up next to me on the sidewalk. For a long moment, he holds my gaze. "I'll jog back with you."

"But I like to run on my ow—"

He steps in front of me and leans through the car window to grab his bag, cutting me off mid-sentence as he says, "Bro, you don't mind, right?"

Dean shakes his head and then asks, "Another session on Wednesday?"

"Yeah," Tyler agrees. "See you then, man."

As the window rolls back up, Dean drives off, leaving me alone in the blistering heat with Tyler by my side. I can see the sweat on his biceps and the way his tank top clings to his toned chest, and I can't help but gulp.

"Just so you know," he says as he begins to walk, and I follow suit, "it was your ass that gave it away."

My lips form a surprised "o" and I automatically glance down at my attire. Maybe today was a bad day to wear my fitted boy shorts. I feel self-conscious all of a sudden. "Um."

He ignores me, quickening his stride as he stares at me from the corner of his eye. "I can probably walk faster than you can run," he taunts.

"I highly doubt it," I murmur. I take a quick swig of my water and place the earphone back into my ear. Lately, I've been a little obsessed with La Breve Vita after Jake took me to their gig.

"I bet I can beat you back to the house," Tyler says, his eyes narrowed playfully as he swings his gym bag from his fingers. His tone is challenging. "Are you game?"

I snort. "I'm totally game."

Before he can say anything else, I cheat and burst into a sprint the moment the words leave my lips, my breath regained again from the short rest, and I feel fit and healthy and strong as my feet hit the concrete, the sun against my face, the breeze cooling my legs. I feel confident in myself for the first time in a long while. And it feels nice.

"Sucker," Tyler calls as he races past me, but I only laugh and speed up until my pace matches his. And then our silly race seems to get forgotten about as we slow ourselves back down to a gentle jog.

"You sure do run a hell of a lot," he says between breaths as we cross over an intersection, tracing a route back to Deidre Avenue. "Do you do cross-country or something?"

"No," I say, keeping my eyes trained on the road ahead. "I just like running. It's the best way to work out."

"Personally, I prefer lifting," he comments. I glance over and catch him casting his eyes in the direction of his arms. It's ridiculous how cocky he can be sometimes, but I'm getting used to it. "Alright," he says, and then throws up a hand as he brings himself to a stop. "I give up. I'm not a runner." He exhales a few times and presses his palm to the brick wall of a building as he tries to catch his breath. "You win."

Triumph washes over me. A wide grin captures my lips as I cock my head, studying him. "You're damn right I won."

"That sounds like something I would say." He laughs as he lifts his head, his eyes locking onto mine. Neither of us wants to be the first to look away, so neither of us do. "We're hanging out tonight," he states. I get the feeling that I wouldn't be able to object even if I wanted to, and I stand there, my eyes dilated with attraction as I listen to the words roll off his tongue. "Let me take you out. Have you been to the pier yet? Pacific Park?"

"No," I admit a little sheepishly. How have I been here for three weeks and not yet stepped foot onto the pier? The closest I've been to it is when I'm at the beach. But it looks amazing from afar.

"Then we'll go to the pier," he decides.

A lump rises in my throat as his lips curl up into a mysterious smirk, his emerald eyes sparkling, an untold story hidden within his eyes.

And it occurs to me exactly then that I am entirely on point.

Dark-haired guys are so, so much better.

21

I'd like to pretend that I'm staring at Ella's lasagna. But I'm not. I'm gazing past the food, my eyes boring into those of the guy sitting across from me with his chin resting on his hand. The guy who is quite literally the epitome of nonchalance right now. I bite my lip as I run my eyes over his jaw, over his lips, over his drawn-together eyebrows, over the sparkle within his eyes. Every so often, he smirks when no one is looking.

"So Eden," Dad says, raising his voice a little to get my attention. My eyes immediately plummet back down to my plate and my hands fumble anxiously with my cutlery as I fork up another bite of lasagna. "You're being so quiet tonight." He wiggles his brows and points his knife at me, a slight chuckle in his throat. "What are you thinking about?"

"I was—um—I was just—I—uhhh." The words keep on stuttering past my lips like I'm a three-year-old attempting to string sentences together, so I shove the food into my mouth and offer a closed smile instead.

"How's the lasagna?" Ella asks us all, her eyes widening a little as she hopes for a positive response. I'm just glad that she's changed the subject. We all nod our heads in appreciation of the dish she's slaved over. Even Tyler sits up slightly and sends her a small smile. She made a separate lasagna for him—four cheese, and definitely vegetarian.

"It's great, Mom," he says, and her face lights up with a warm glow.

My eyes drift between the two of them, watching their eyes soften as they exchange a glance, and I wonder how their relationship is configured. A lot of the time Ella just seems disappointed in him, but there are also brief moments where they seem to share a sense of silent understanding.

"It tastes so great that . . ." Tyler continues as he pulls the plate toward him, scooping up a large portion and lifting the fork to his lips. He leans forward over the plate as he takes a huge bite, but half of it falls from his mouth and lands on the table. Sheepishly, he laughs and wipes the sauce from his lips with his thumb. "It tastes so great that now I'm totally full," he says after he swallows.

Dad arches a brow from the opposite end of the table. "You're in a good mood tonight, Tyler," he says.

Tyler presses his lips together as he folds his arms on the table, his eyes moving from Dad to me. As he catches my gaze, he tries his hardest to suppress a smile. But I see it. "I guess I am." He clears his throat and pushes himself up, getting to his feet and carrying his plate over to the dishwasher. When he turns back around, his face is blank. "I'm gonna head out."

"Where?" Ella immediately looks up, and she turns around to face him. Even Jamie glances up to hear Tyler's excuse. "You're grounded."

"But I'm seeing Tiffani," he completely lies, and he's such a good bluffer that even I believe him for a moment. And then I remember. "Didn't you say you're hanging out with Meghan, Eden?"

I'm about to say no, but then he shoots me a stern look. He wants me to lie. So I say, "Yeah," and then steal a glance at Dad to see if he's buying it. Right now, I think he is.

"I can give you a ride there," Tyler pushes, his voice slightly strained as he keeps his eyes firmly locked on me. He gives me the slightest of nods as he waits for me to play along.

"Thanks," I blurt. If I attempt a longer answer, I'm bound to trip on my own words. So I smile a silly little smile and place my cutlery onto my plate as Ella stands to clean up.

But Tyler has no problem smirking back at me, like he's forgotten our parents are in the room. Either that or he simply doesn't care if they see or not. "Ten minutes?"

If only they knew we aren't actually talking about him giving me a ride to Meghan's place. "Ten minutes is fine."

"I'll just meet you at the car." He throws me a wink before sauntering out of the kitchen in his black jeans and white T-shirt. I stare after him, watching the way he rubs the back of his neck as he leaves, gazing after his tall figure and adoring the way he tilts his head down as he walks.

Seconds later, I excuse myself from the family dinner, apologizing to Ella for not having time to help her clean up, and then dart up to my room to adjust my hair, brush my teeth, drown myself in perfume, pull on a sweater . . . All the kind of necessary actions that a girl must take before heading out to an amusement park on a pier with her stepbrother.

When the ten minutes are up, I make my way back downstairs and outside to the white and black car parked out on the road because there simply isn't enough room for three cars on the driveway.

Tyler rolls down the window as I approach the passenger door, and he leans across the center console to glance up at me from beneath his shades. "I'd open the door for you, but I think your dad would have something to say about it."

I glance over my shoulder. Dad is standing by the living room window, trying to hide himself behind the angled blinds but failing miserably. I raise my hand and wave across the lawn to him, and his body quickly disappears. "Yeah," I say as I open the door and slide inside. "I think he'd wonder where your new manners suddenly came from."

"Hey!" he protests, throwing his hands up defensively as I put the window back up. When I pull my seatbelt on and turn to face him, I notice how he's pulled a red flannel shirt on top of the white T-shirt. I take a second to gulp. "I'll have you know I'm a true gentleman."

"Really?" I say skeptically.

"Really," he confirms. Switching on the engine, he plays around with the AC and then shuts his sun visor. He glances sideways at me. "Alright, I'm not. I've just heard that that's what you're supposed to do. Always get out of the car and open the door. Right?"

I smile. "Something like that."

Shaking his head and shrugging, he puts his foot down on the gas and we recklessly jolt off down the neighborhood. It doesn't surprise me; I'm used to his terrible driving skills by now.

It's when we're nearing the oceanfront that I finally decide to ask, "Why did you lie to your mom? Why didn't you just say we're going to the pier?"

I catch him roll his eyes as he snorts, "C'mon, Eden, keep up. We don't want them to get suspicious."

"What about Tiffani?" However much I want to push her to the back of my mind, I simply can't. I feel so guilty every time I'm around Tyler. As if the whole stepsibling dilemma isn't problematic enough already, I'm also sneaking around with my friend's boyfriend.

"I've got it covered. She thinks I'm hanging out with the guys." He says this so casually that again I wonder if he even cares about her at all.

The pier is extremely busy when we get there, with cars packed into the lot and families strolling around and groups of friends and couples holding hands while walking along the boardwalk. It makes me feel a little envious, and it's tempting to just stretch forward and interlink my fingers with Tyler's. But I'm not brave enough to do so, and especially not in public.

"Alright," Tyler says, clearing his throat with a sharp cough before nodding his head toward the bustling amusement park to our left. "So this is Pacific Park. And I am going to show you Pacific Park, because I used to love this place when I was a kid and I want to be the one to introduce you to it." He speaks so earnestly that I can't help but stare back at him with a smile on my lips and warmth in my cheeks.

We casually saunter down the boardwalk, listening to the soft sound of the ocean and feeling the heat of the evening sun on our faces. All the while, we enjoy each other's presence and talk about simple things around us. We try to figure out why the rollercoaster is yellow; we comment on the food trucks; we talk about the position of the benches. Why is that one facing the water and why is the other facing the city?

"This guy right here used to scare the shit out of me," he admits when we reach the entrance to the park. Above the huge "PACIFIC PARK" sign, there is an enormous purple octopus. Awkwardly, he shoves his hands into his pockets and quickly shuffles through the gates. "It still kind of does," he says.

"Ahhh." I nod my head as I catch up to him, playfully widening my eyes. "Not so badass anymore, are you?"

"Well," he says, his voice rising an octave, "would a badass tell you that he's in love with cotton candy?" Removing his hands from his pockets, he gestures toward a food cart. It serves a wide range of traditional favorites, from hot popcorn to ice cream to pretzels and, of course, cotton candy. Tyler's face is one big smile as he buys us some.

When he hands me the stick, I take note of his gentle smile when he turns back around to collect his own. "Are you sure you *used* to love this place?" I ask with a knowing edge to my voice.

His eyebrows quickly shoot up. Pursing his lips, he pulls off a chunk of his cotton candy and draws it into his mouth. "We need to go on the coaster," he mumbles as the sugar dissolves on his tongue. He doesn't quite answer my question. My smile grows into a grin.

I follow him through the flow of people until we settle down on a bench just beneath the yellow rollercoaster that circles the Ferris wheel. As I eat the cotton candy, I watch the wheel spin around and around and around.

"Eden," Tyler says, the quiet force of his voice drawing my eyes to his. His expression falters. "I wouldn't mention this to anyone. It's just easier if we, um . . . keep this whole thing a secret for now. God, please say you're good at keeping secrets."

"I am," I confirm, but the reality of all of this makes me feel nauseous. I don't want to sneak around, making excuses and lying. But I know it's necessary right now. "And I know that you're good at keeping secrets, because you clearly have a lot of them."

His lips quirk upward into a crooked smile as he devours the remainder of his cotton candy. Standing, he tosses the stick into a nearby trash can and then points to the rides above us. "It's time for these guys."

It frustrates me how he never answers a question, but his silence speaks louder than words. He never replies because he knows I'm right, because he knows that I'm figuring him out despite however much he wishes I wouldn't.

And so the two of us spend our Tuesday evening waiting in line for kids' rides but enjoying every second of it. The West Coaster, the Pacific Wheel, the Pacific Plunge . . . I'll remember them all, because I'll remember this night. I'll remember Tyler's hysterical laughter when I thought my seatbelt was broken on the Pacific Plunge and he leaned over to help me get it into place, with our hands awkwardly fumbling over each other; I'll remember his sarcastic remarks on the West Coaster when others screamed their lungs out at the slightest turn; I'll remember the way he said the ocean looked pretty cool from up there on the Pacific Wheel, but when I glanced at him, he wasn't even looking at the ocean. He was looking at me.

It's late by the time we leave the park, and the signs are glowing through the darkening sky and the stream of people is beginning to thin as we head back to the car. There are a couple people taking pictures next to the vehicle in the emptying parking lot when we get there, and they awkwardly scuttle off, knowing that they've been caught.

"It happens all the time," Tyler tells me when we get inside. He pats the steering wheel, tracing his finger around the Audi logo. "I don't know why. It's LA. There's, like, Lambos and shit on every corner in Beverly Hills."

I bite my tongue to stop myself from saying anything, but soon I can't help myself. "How did you even get this car?"

He's silent for a little while and runs his fingers over the steering wheel, like he's trying to piece together the best way to answer me. "Because I got my trust fund early. And when you suddenly have all this money, you're not really going to be rational about it, are you? I'm a teenager, of course I'm gonna go out and blow it all on a supercar." He laughs, and I can't tell if it's genuine or if it's at himself for doing such a thing.

"Why'd you get it early?" I press, mostly because I'm curious. My eyes stare at his mouth, and I study the way his lips move when he speaks, the way his jaw shifts.

"Because apparently money can make you feel better," he mutters sharply. He heaves a sigh and his hands freeze over the wheel. "It's a big trust fund," he admits. "I mean, my mom's an attorney and my dad . . ." His voice tapers off for a second before he swallows and continues, his eyes drifting over to meet mine. I stare back inquisitively, yet I feel a little guilty for prying into his personal matters. It's none of my business when and why he got his trust fund early. "My dad had his own company," he tells me. "Structural engineering. All up and down the west coast."

Oregon is on the west coast, and I can't help but wonder if I've heard of it. "What was it called?"

"Grayson's," Tyler answers stiffly, his jaw tightening as something shifts in his eyes. He glances away for a moment. "Because we were the Graysons."

At this, I rotate my body to face him, crossing my legs on

the seat. I know I'm about to push him onto a sensitive topic, but I find it interesting learning about a person's background, the foundation on which they are built. Especially Tyler. "Before the divorce?"

"Before the divorce," he repeats, shrugging his shoulders. Slumping further down into his seat, he throws a hand into his hair and lets it rest atop his head for a moment as he tugs on the ends. "I used to be Tyler Grayson. Mom didn't want us to keep his name."

I don't know how to reply. Perhaps it's because I've been so focused on his lips that the only thing I can think about is the way they felt when they were locked with mine. A lump rises in my throat, but I quickly force it down.

My silence must tell him everything he needs to know, because he slowly pulls himself up from his slumped position. His hand drops softly from his hair to my knee and a shiver shoots down my spine. He licks his lips, slowly, teasingly, and in a way that makes it feel like torture.

"Can I kiss you again?" he murmurs, without breaking our fixed gaze, his eyes soft and calm as he waits for an answer, his lips parted.

But just like he never answers me, I don't answer him. Instead, I push myself up and slowly move across the center console, trying not to dislocate my leg as I perch my body on top of his. I straddle him in the limited space, my beating heart against his chest and my back pressed against the steering wheel. It's not ideal, but it's enough.

Without hesitation, he reaches up to cup my face in his hands, and with gentle force, he captures my lips. It's like yesterday all over again but better, his lips moving with a sense of urgency. He dominates the kiss again with confidence, doing things that I didn't know were even possible. And the more he keeps on kissing me, the more I don't think I'll ever be able to get over the exhilaration.

As his lips break away from mine and move to my neck, I run my hands through his hair. The softness tickles my fingertips as he kisses my neck, slowly yet firmly, and I grasp his jaw and tilt his face up. My heart is racing as I draw his ear to my lips, and I dare to whisper, "You don't even need to ask."

22

When Tyler and I got home at the exact same time last night, we bluffed our way out of our careless mistake by saying that he gave me a ride home again. Ella believed us. She asked Tyler if he'd enjoyed his night with Tiffani. He said yes. She asked me if I had fun with Meghan. I told her I had.

And then Tyler and I exchanged a momentary knowing glance, an unspoken secret held captive within our eyes, a secret only we knew and understood.

Dad has a late start for work today, so he's still lingering around the house when I get back from my run. I'm exhausted. Instead of tracing a new route around the city like I set out to do, I ended up jogging down the beachfront from Santa Monica to Venice. It was refreshing listening to the waves of the Pacific Ocean instead of my music for a change. Almost relaxing, despite the way my lungs were aching.

"What time are you leaving?" I ask Dad as I slip into the kitchen after showering and pulling on fresh clothes. My hair is haphazardly piled into a messy bun atop my head.

Dad barely gives me a second glance as he rams a stack of paperwork into a briefcase. He rubs his temple and grabs his car keys from the worktop. "Right now. I've got an important meeting with our suppliers that I can't fu—mess up." His cheeks flush with color as he brushes past me, briefcase in one hand, keys in the other.

"Can you drop me off at the promenade on your way?" I'm craving some steaming-hot coffee, but Dad and Ella's coffee machine just doesn't do it for me. My legs are so stiff from my jog that I can't possibly force myself to walk all the way to Third Street. Tyler can't give me a ride, because he's at the gym with Dean, and Ella already left to take Jamie and Chase celebrity hunting. Apparently Ben Affleck is around today.

Dad suppresses a groan. "Come on, then."

I dart back upstairs to pull on my Chucks and get some cash before rushing back down to my waiting father, who is impatiently tapping his foot by the front door. I edge past him. He locks up and follows me over to the Lexus, his face a picture of complete stress and discomfort. If I talk to him, I think he might cry, so I decide to keep quiet for the short ride. But the silence only lasts for ten minutes.

"So." Dad clears his throat. "Are you having a good summer?"

"It's okay." Talk about the biggest understatement of the year. The summer isn't okay. The summer is like a lucid dream that I don't seem to want to wake up from. Everything about these past few weeks has been so new and so wrong, yet so thrilling and so right. "Here's good," I murmur, and point to the sidewalk of Santa Monica Boulevard.

He pulls up by the curb and I step out. Before I get the chance to close the door behind me, Dad leans over the center console and offers me a small smile. "Be careful," he says. "LA isn't as safe as Portland."

"Actually," I say, leaning down to meet his eyes, "the rate of rape crimes in Portland is now higher than the US average. Good luck with the meeting."

Dad's eyes widen as I gently slam the door shut. I don't look back. With my tan satchel hanging from my shoulder, I fumble with the strap and make my way to the Refinery, the small coffee shop on the corner that Rachael and Meghan took me to at the start of the summer, the one with the naturalistic vibe and the to-die-for caramel shots. It's quiet when I enter. There are only half a dozen people huddled over steaming mugs, some reading, some with laptops, some talking to a friend.

The girl behind the counter catches my eye and her lips curve up into a welcoming grin. I make my way over to her and run my eyes over the menu on the wall behind her. It's written in chalk, which only makes me appreciate it even more. "What can I get for you?"

"Just a regular vanilla skinny latte, extra hot with a shot of caramel." I reach into my satchel for my wallet and place five bucks on the counter. I feel guilty for adding the extra shot, but Amelia's spent months convincing me that it's perfectly okay to indulge in my favorite beverage every so often.

"No problem," the girl says as she gathers my change from the cash register. "I'll bring it straight over to you."

I take my change and head over to a small table against the wall. Setting my satchel down, I sit and get comfy. It feels so relaxing to just sit here, to chill out and study the people around me. I love to people-watch. I always wonder what their life story is. Where did they grow up? How many siblings do they have? What's their favorite flavor of ice cream?

Most importantly, I wonder if their summer is as complicated as mine.

"Here you are," the girl says softly from my side as she places the mug in front of me a few minutes later. "Enjoy."

I thank her and then wait until she disappears again behind the counter, and when she does, I grasp my drink and take the longest of sips. It's piping hot. It burns my throat slightly, but I don't mind. It tastes amazing.

Sinking further into my chair, I fish around my satchel for my earphones and my phone before plugging myself into the sound of La Breve Vita. I close my eyes, nod my head in sync with the beats, and breathe. I'm so glad I ended up at their gig. I love them. Their lyrics have depth and each song tells a story about our past mistakes, about our futures. The bridge in most tracks is in Italian.

I'm totally caught up in the music when I feel something shift in front of me. My eyes snap open and my heart almost hurls itself out of my chest as a pair of eyes stare back at me. I immediately jump upright and my earphones fall to the table.

"Hey," he says.

"You scared me," I gasp as I place a hand to my chest and struggle to catch my breath again.

It's only Dean. He looks like he's just attempted to run a marathon but passed out before he even saw the finish line. His cheeks are red, his face sweaty, hair ruffled. "My bad," he apologizes with a rueful smile. "I was getting some coffee when I noticed you sitting here."

My eyes fall from his to the to-go cup clasped in his hands. I glance back up again. "Did you just get out of the gym?"

"Is it that noticeable?" He wipes his forehead with the back of his hand and then laughs.

I shake my head and take another sip of my latte. "No." Mid-drink, a thought crosses my mind and I quickly swallow so that I can ask, "Is Tyler with you?"

My eyes scour the small shop, searching for a pair of green

eyes and a pile of black hair, but Dean says, "No, he's headed to Malibu to get his car waxed," and my search is cut short.

"Oh," I say. Disheartened, I stare at my latte and run my finger around the rim of the mug. "That doesn't surprise me."

"So what are you listening to?" Dean asks. He leans forward over the table to tap my phone, and when La Breve Vita appear on my screen, his face lights up. "No way!"

I shrug sheepishly. "They're so good."

"What's your favorite song?"

"Oh, Dean, that's a tough one," I groan. I tilt my head and rest my cheek on my palm as I run through all the band's songs from all three of their albums until I come to a conclusion. "I think it has to be 'Holding Back.'"

Dean leans back and folds his arms across his chest. He presses his lips together as he shakes his head. "Unbelievable."

"What?"

He falls still. His brown eyes meet my gaze for a long moment and his lips slowly and carefully twitch into a small smile. "That's my favorite too."

I grin back at him while trying not to, biting down on my lip. "It's an incredible song."

"It totally is," he agrees. The smile on his face widens into a beaming grin and he stares at me, as though he's content with just watching me awkwardly sip my latte. He sits down opposite me. "Your coffee is on me," he says, finally. He reaches into the pockets of his jeans and pulls out his wallet. For a few seconds he rummages inside it and then places a crumpled five-dollar bill down on the table in front of me. "Five bucks to reimburse the expense. Your five bucks."

I part my lips as I reach over to pick up the crinkled note, holding it between my thumb and forefinger as I squint at it.

There's black ink scrawled across the Lincoln Memorial on the reverse side. The more I focus my eyes on the writing, the quicker I realize it says "EDEN'S GAS MONEY." My mouth parts even wider as I lift my eyes to meet Dean's.

"You kept it?" I ask. "And you wrote on it?"

"So that I remembered to give it back to you."

"But I don't want it back."

"Too bad," he says. With a sheepish smile, he reaches down to close my fingers around the note and then pushes my hand away.

I only shake my head with a laugh as I stuff the bill into my satchel by my side. I return to my latte, taking several long gulps, as does he with his.

Dean blows out air through his mouth as though his drink is too hot, and then asks, "Where are you heading next?"

"Probably just back home." When I meet his eyes again, he's arching a brow curiously at me. "As in here in Santa Monica," I clarify. "Not Portland."

"That's what I thought," he says as he gets to his feet. He grabs his coffee and presses the cup to his lips, taking a cautious sip before nodding out the window. He blows some more air. "Do you need a ride?"

I've discovered by now that there's a benefit to being in a new city without a ride: You don't have to ask, because people offer them to you out of pity. "If that's okay," I answer. I don't have my licence yet, anyway.

"Totally fine," he says. "C'mon."

I take a final drink of my latte before stuffing my earphones back into my satchel and swinging it onto my shoulder. Dean's already made his way to the door and is leaning against it, holding it open for me as I step outside. The bright morning has dulled down slightly. I tilt my face up to the clouded sky in surprise. "Where'd the sun go?"

Dean shrugs as he trains his eyes on the traffic. "Contrary to popular belief, rain does exist in the Golden State." He nudges me forward when there's a gap in the traffic and we briskly rush across to the other side of the boulevard. I notice his car wedged into a tight spot and I wonder how he managed to maneuver the car into that position in the first place. "It's rare, but sometimes there's summer rainstorms that last for, like, an entire day. It comes out of nowhere and it's super heavy."

As he unlocks the car, I open up the passenger door and slide my body inside. "Rain doesn't faze me. It's a fixture in Portland for eight months a year."

"That must suck."

On the ride to my house, we talk about silly things like rain and snow and coffee shops and syrup flavors. I love caramel; Dean loves cinnamon. But my mood deflates when we get there and Tyler's car isn't parked on the driveway. I haven't seen him since early this morning and I'm really starting to miss him, however pathetic and desperate it seems.

"Thanks for the ride . . . again," I say almost shyly. My cheeks flush as he tells me it's no problem at all, and then a brilliant idea crosses my mind. It's so great that I grin, laugh, and almost snort. I reach into my satchel and fish around for the five-dollar bill, my five-dollar bill, the one with Dean's messy handwriting scribbled across Abraham Lincoln's memorial. When I finally find the battered note, I place it on the dashboard. "For gas money," I say.

Dean lets out a loud laugh and shakes his head. "Until next time," he says. He salutes me goodbye as I step out and head inside the house.

Tyler's car may not be here, but the Range Rover is, which means Ella is home. The house is silent as I advance down the hall. I peer around the living room door and Ella is sitting cross-legged on the leather couch with a stack of photo albums by her side.

"So did you meet Ben Affleck?" I ask as I step into the room.

Ella's blue eyes flicker up to meet mine while she shuts the album that's in her lap. "Well, there were a lot of people, which meant a lot of cars, and so I told the boys I wasn't paying for the parking fees. I dropped them off at their friends' houses instead."

I laugh and then nod toward the pile of albums. "What are you looking at?"

"Oh, just nothing," she says quickly. "Just old photos. No one was here and I thought I'd—I thought I'd grab them from the attic and look at them while you were all gone. The boys all hate it when I look at their baby photos." She stifles a laugh as she glances down, brushing her fingers over the tattered cover of the album in her hands.

"Can I see?" I move over to the couch and push the albums over to make room for myself, and then I sit down by Ella's side and pull my legs up onto the leather.

Ella looks almost nervous as she slowly opens up the album again and moves it in between us so that it's resting half on her knee and half on mine. "These were when Chase was born," she tells me.

There's a collection of photos of a newborn baby wrapped in a blue blanket within a plastic hospital cot. In all of them, Chase is crying, his cheeks flushed almost violet. Ella flicks the page to reveal more hospital photos, but this time Chase is in the arms of a middle-aged woman I don't recognize, and then in the next picture he has been handed to a man of similar age.

"The boys' grandparents," Ella informs me, a little stiffly. More pages go by and I notice that there are several blank spaces with faded outlines where photos were once placed, and then Ella stops at a particular page, which she laughs at. "Oh, God, my long hair."

Chase looks a few weeks older now, with his eyes wide and alert as a younger version of Ella holds him up to the camera, her long blond hair framing her face and her smile wide, as though the photo was snapped mid-laugh. She looks so young and so happy and so carefree. It's as though in that moment, her life couldn't have been more perfect. A smaller child stands at her side, clinging to her purple sweatpants with pursed lips. I can tell it's Jamie from the blond hair, and he must be around three years old in these photos.

"They're a little bare," she apologizes as she switches the album around for one of the others. "This is Tyler's."

My interest grows even more when she says this. Adjusting myself to ensure that I'm comfortable, I bite my lip and gaze down at the black album as Ella flips open the first page. Empty. She turns over some more. Empty. And finally, six pages in, we come across the first two photos. There's a tiny baby in an incubator, so small and so fragile and so pink.

"He was four weeks premature," Ella tells me. "He was supposed to be born in July, but he was born in June instead."

"I didn't know that." We flip over some more empty pages until there's a photo of Ella lying on a bed in a dark room with Tyler curled up against her body. She appears even younger here, merely a teenager, perhaps only a year older than myself. Her long hair is thrown up into a scruffy ponytail and her eyes are full of fatigue. She looks exhausted, but I don't comment on it.

On the last page of the album, Tyler is no longer a tiny infant. He's a few years older, standing on his own two feet in a tiny black tux. He's grinning at the camera and I smile back at him, the dark hair and green eyes feeling so familiar to me. He hasn't changed at all.

"That was on the day of my wedding," Ella says quietly.

It feels slightly awkward hearing her say these words given that I'm her new husband's daughter, but I find the whole thing interesting all the same. "When did you get married?"

"When I was twenty-one. Tyler walked me down the aisle, because I don't talk to my parents. He was only four, but he loved it." And then she shuts the book and places it to the side.

"That's it?" I ask, slightly in disbelief. "Only eight photos?"

"It used to be full," she admits. She sounds sad as she talks, but she glances sideways at me and gives me a small smile, as though she's fine. "Tyler burned a lot of them."

My eyebrows knit together. "Burned them?"

"He set up a fire in the back yard," she explains with a shrug. "There were a lot of photos he didn't want to keep. I let him do it because I thought it would make him feel better."

Before I can press the subject any further, she clears her throat and reaches for another album. It's most likely Jamie's, but she hasn't even opened up to the first page when we hear the sound of the front door opening and closing.

"Ella?" a voice calls. I think we're both expecting it to be Tyler, but the voice is feminine, and I recognize it.

"In here, Tiffani!" Ella calls back, confirming my thoughts. I wonder what she's doing here.

It takes a few seconds for Tiffani to reach the living room. When she does, she pushes the door open and tilts her head. "Oh, hey, Eden."

"Hey." I can barely make eye contact with her, like I'm a drug pusher and she's a federal agent.

"Is Tyler around?"

Ella hands me the photo album and gets to her feet, smoothing out the creases in her outfit as she takes a step closer to Tiffani. "Hmm, I haven't seen him all morning," she says. "Have you tried calling him? Maybe he's still at the gym."

"I've been calling him since last night," Tiffani states bluntly. "He keeps rejecting all of my calls. And speaking of last night, where was he?"

Ella's eyebrows furrow. "Wasn't he with you?"

It's at this exact moment that my heart stops beating and my blood runs cold. My lips part as I stare up at the two of them, and the only thing running through my mind is this: We have totally fucked up. I don't know why Tyler thought our excuses last night wouldn't backfire and I don't know why I agreed to go along with them.

And just when I think I'm going to drop dead, I hear the front door again. This time it is the person we're expecting. I hear him before I see him, his deep voice murmuring, "What are you doing here?" as he makes his way down the hall.

Tiffani turns around at the door of the living room to face him, her expression cold. "Where were you last night?"

"I told you," he says. I can see half of his face from over Tiffani's shoulder, and I watch him quickly swallow. "I was with the guys."

"Tyler," Ella snaps, stepping into his view. I can see him mentally curse. "You told me you were with her. Where did you go last night?"

"Oh my God," he says. "What does it matter?"

Ella spins back around to meet my eyes. I'm still holding my breath at this point, and I fear I might turn blue. "Eden, where did he go?"

They all lock their eyes on me. Ella's stare is stern, Tiffani's expression is livid, and Tyler's eyes are wide, like he's begging me not to screw up, pleading for me to think of something. "Um, he dropped me off at Meghan's and then he changed his plans," I lie, praying that my thought process is logical. "He hung out with the guys instead."

"See," Tyler murmurs, reaching for Tiffani's elbow as he takes a step toward her, but she shakes him off.

"Don't talk to me," she spits, placing a hand on his chest and shoving him back into the hall. "Eden, come with me. We need to talk to Rachael and Meghan. Right now." The look in her eyes warns me not to object, so I don't. Instead, I shove the photo albums off to the side and scramble to my feet. She grasps my wrist when I near her, yanking me out of the living room and into the hall. She purposely barges into Tyler as she pulls me past him.

I can tell that he is furious as he glares after us, his hands balled into fists as we disappear out of the front door. I don't even have time to fetch my shoes, so I'm hauled across the lawn in my bare feet before Tiffani gives me no option but to get into her car.

And the second she gets into the driver's seat and shuts the door, she bursts into tears. It's a full-blown sob, and she buries her face into her hands and weeps against the steering wheel. Her chest rises and lowers at an erratic pace as she struggles to breathe.

"Are you okay?" I ask, but then angrily roll my eyes at myself. Of course she's not okay. Turning around to face her, I stretch out my arm to soothingly rub her back. It doesn't seem to do any good. "What's wrong?"

There are some more long sobs before she lifts her head and wipes her eyes with her thumbs. Her breathing is still uneven as she puts the car in drive and pulls on her seatbelt. "You're not going to believe it," she whimpers as her mascara leaves trails down her cheeks. "Rach and Meg are meeting us at my place. I need to just—I need to vent."

We drive in silence down to her place, and I'm thankful that she lives in the same neighborhood. I don't think I'd be able to cope with the sound of her crying for anything longer than ten minutes. But those whole ten minutes, nonetheless, are spent with my stomach in knots. I'm pretty sure Tyler is the reason for her tears.

Rachael and Meghan's cars are already parked on Tiffani's driveway when we get there, and they quickly step out of their vehicles and come rushing over to us the second we pull up.

"Aww, Tiff! Did it go wrong?" Rachael is the first to pull her into her arms, offering her a tight hug. "Remember, he's my neighbor, so I can easily sneak across in the middle of the night and cut his balls off if you'd like."

Now I know it's definitely Tyler's fault, and I wonder if perhaps she's just upset that he ditched her to hang out with his friends. But even that seems too pathetic to be sobbing over. It must be something bigger.

"How many times have we warned you?" Meghan asks,

taking Tiffani's hand in hers and leading her up to the front door. "Tiff, you know this isn't the first time."

"Those other times were rumors," Tiffani groans, letting out another tremendous sob. "This time there's proof!"

"Proof of what?" I ask as we all shuffle inside the house. No one has yet explained why she's crying.

"Oh my God, Eden, please stay in the loop," Rachael mutters as she shoots me a glare, and then glances back at Tiffani with a sympathetic pout. She still doesn't answer my question, and soon we're all hauling ourselves up the huge staircase and into Tiffani's room, where she collapses on her bed.

"Start from the beginning," Meghan says softly as Tiffani inhales and exhales repeatedly. We're all sitting before her on the mattress, like she is our queen and we are her servants. In a way, this is true.

"I already told you," Tiffani snaps, a little agitated. "I was getting the mail in the morning when Austin Cameron drove past and pulled up. He asked if I enjoyed my night with Tyler and he kept winking at me like the fucking pervert that he is. I asked him what his deal was and he said he saw us late last night by the pier. I wasn't at the pier."

If I thought I wasn't breathing before, I'm certainly not breathing now. My mouth drops open as I stare at her. I realize that Tyler isn't the reason that she's crying.

I am.

"Did you tell Austin that it wasn't you?" Rachael asks. She pats Tiffani's knee as though it will comfort her.

"Of course I told him," Tiffani murmurs in between even more sobs as she starts tearing up again. "He said he definitely saw Tyler 'getting it on' in his car in the fucking parking lot.

He automatically assumed it was me, because obviously he's going to assume that—I'm Tyler's girlfriend."

"You shouldn't be," Meghan murmurs. "He doesn't deserve you."

Tiffani squeezes her eyes shut for a moment before taking a deep breath. "I asked Austin if it was definitely Tyler's car, and he said he was positive, he'd recognize it anywhere. He said it was definitely his license plate. So of course I asked if he remembers seeing anything about whoever this girl was, but he told me it was only outlines." A sudden growl erupts in her throat as she hurls her fist into the closest pillow. "Why the hell does Tyler have tinted windows? I thought they were illegal and now I'm starting to understand why. They let the cheaters cheat!"

Oh my God, I think. *This is all my fault.*

"He told me he was with the guys, but he told his mom that he was with me! He's a fucking liar!" More fist slams and punches and clawing as she destroys everything within reach. I can't even begin to imagine how she'd react if she knew it was me. "The entire time he was just hooking up with some whore! I feel so sick. I'm actually going to throw up. Oh, God." She clasps her hands to her stomach and drops her head low.

"You need to just break up with him, Tiffani," Rachael says, her tone slightly condescending, as though she's speaking to a small child experiencing their first kindergarten romance.

"But I just can't!" she wails as her hair falls over her eyes, and off go the tears again. She pulls her comforter up to her face to dry her cheeks off. It doesn't take long for the material to get soaked straight through. "I need him."

"Maybe Austin just misinterpreted it?" I try, forcing the

words out of my mouth. My throat is completely dry, but I try my hardest nonetheless to keep my voice from cracking or trembling. *Act clueless,* I tell myself. *Act innocent.*

"Okay," Rachael says, straining her neck to give me a disapproving look. "Eden, I know he's your family and all, but please don't defend him."

"I'm not," I try to object. I feel as small as ever, and the truth is, I'm not defending Tyler. I'm defending myself.

For twenty minutes, we listen to Tiffani rant and vent and curse until she calms down. The entire time, I sit in silence in fear of saying something that'll give myself away. Rachael suggests different methods of retribution while Meghan offers to go out and get ice cream, but Tiffani says no, because, "If I'm fat, he'll only want to cheat on me even more." This comment doesn't sit well with me. Is she trying to imply that bigger girls aren't attractive? That guys don't go for girls that have a bit of body to them? I don't know. But it still pisses me off.

Eventually she claims that she just wants to sleep, so we take it as our cue to leave. She needs space, and I'm certainly grateful to finally be getting out of there. Rachael offers to give me a ride back home again, saving me from having to walk across the neighborhood barefoot.

"Call us again if anything else happens," Meghan says as we all hover by the door. Tiffani is still sprawling out across her bed, rolling over every so often. "You have to keep us updated."

"I will," she sniffs. "Can I talk to Eden for a second?"

Rachael and Meghan exchange glances with me, and I contemplate begging them not to leave me here alone with her. But before I get the chance to even plead for mercy,

Rachael says, "Sure. I'll wait for you in the car, Eden," and they both leave.

The room falls into silence as Tiffani buries her face into her comforter. Her words are muffled as she speaks. "What we say in this room stays in this room. Don't even think about telling Tyler anything we just said."

"I won't," I almost squeak, my eyes drifting out into the hall as I stare longingly at the staircase. "I hope you're okay."

"I'm not," she says. "But Eden?"

"Yeah?"

Pushing her body up, she crosses her legs and stares across the room at me with her swollen eyes. Somehow she presses her lips together, her jaw clenched, eyebrows furrowed. Something flickers within her blue eyes, something new that I've never seen before, an expression so twisted and so sharp that for a moment she frightens me. "I know you weren't with Meghan last night, because I was."

23

Tyler is standing in the hall when I get back to the house. His arms are folded across his chest, his jaw clenched, eyes fierce. He looks as though he's about to step foot into a boxing ring, ready to knock some brain damage into his opponent. The problem is that I don't know who the enemy is.

"What'd she say?" he spits in contempt. As he approaches me, he drops his arms and curls his hands into fists. "What did you say?"

I shake my head as I peer around his tall frame, glancing into the living room. Ella is gone and so are the photo albums. "Where's your mom?"

"Picking up Chase," he says quickly, his voice gruff. "Now what the hell happened?"

I take a deep breath, my eyes trained on his hardened features as I try to make sense of everything. I'm scared to death. "Someone saw us last night," I splutter, and bile rises in my throat once more. "Austin Cameron . . . He told Tiffani."

Tyler's eyes widen in shock before faltering back into a cold glare. "Are you kidding me?" he growls. A wave of adrenaline seems to flow down his arms, and he hurls one fist at his other palm, creating a loud slap as his knuckles smack his own skin. "I will floor that motherfu—"

"They don't know it was me," I cut in quickly, my voice quiet and raspy as I interlock my fingers over and over again. My eyes fall to the floor as my chest tightens. "She's devastated, Tyler."

She's not just upset; she's furious. I feel like she might be on to us. She now knows that both Tyler and I lied about where we were last night, and despite my horrendous attempt at trying to explain, she made it clear that she plans to figure out what I'm hiding. In retrospect, I probably could have come up with something better than I did. But I was under pressure, so I rambled that I'd lied because Dad and Ella would only let me leave the house if they knew I was going somewhere safe. Convincing? Not for Tiffani. I don't think I can possibly face her again.

Silence ensues for a moment. Tyler relaxes his fists as he heaves a sigh. From beneath my eyelashes, I watch as he rubs the back of his neck before running his hand back through his hair. "I'll fix this," he says quietly. His words make me look up again, my eyes meeting his. "Look, she's pissed off. I get it, but I can make it up to her. I'll tell her I made a mistake, I'll buy her something nice, and then she'll forget about it and everything will be fine again. And then we can figure the rest out."

I stare at him in disbelief. With my lips pressed into a firm line, I grit my teeth and glower at him. "Everything won't be fine," I say tersely, spitting out each word. "Nothing is fine, Tyler! This needs to stop."

"What needs to stop?"

"This." I throw my hands up in surrender as I motion back and forth between the two of us. I shouldn't have let any of this get this far in the first place. Now I'm in too deep. Three make-out sessions too deep. "You have a girlfriend, Tyler. I refuse to be a cheater."

"You won't be," he says firmly, but then the corners of his lips curl into a smile, and he takes a few steps toward me and reaches for my elbow. The warmth of his skin creates a wave of goosebumps down my arms as he pulls me toward him, and I glance up to meet his closing eyes as he leans down to lock his lips with mine. Immediately, I yank my arm out of his grasp and spiral away from his body. He stands there, his hands hovering in mid-air as his eyes slowly snap open to glare at me.

But I only blink at him as I try to figure out what is running through his mind right now. He's quite clearly insane. After a long pause, I finally ask, "Are you serious? Now really isn't the time. Even if you could completely guarantee that she wouldn't find out—which she will—I still wouldn't do this anyway." I take a step back and wave my hands in front of me, my head shaking, a lump in my throat. "I am not doing this."

"C'mon." He has wiped the smile from his lips, but the smugness in his eyes still remains. In disgust, I spin around and march halfway up the staircase before he mumbles, "We can figure this out."

"How, Tyler?" I demand as I twirl back around, gripping the banister and peering down at him. "We only have two options."

"Only two?"

"Two," I confirm. I stare down at his smoldering eyes, and then I picture Tiffani and her smeared mascara and muffled sobs and tear-stained pillows. He couldn't care less. "You have to break up with her."

"No," he objects, with a firm shake of his head. "I can't."

"Why not?" I ask.

To start with, I think he might ignore my question. He takes a while to think of an answer. "Because it's more complicated than you think it is, alright? Tiffani's . . . Look, don't push it." He pauses and fixes me with a look that tells me not to challenge him, so despite how frustrated I feel, I just frown and wait for him to speak again. "What's the other option?"

"We ignore whatever we have between us." It hurts to say it, but I know it makes sense. If he wants to stay with Tiffani, then we have to act like stepsiblings and nothing more. No discreet flirting, no stolen kisses, no sexual remarks. But if he wants that, then he can't be with Tiffani. Because doing both is infamously known as cheating.

"So basically," he starts as he folds his arms across his chest, "I get to be with you if I break up with Tiffani? It's you or her, right?" The conceited expression is long gone by now. It's been replaced with an aggravated glower, his eyes narrowed into small slits, his chin tilted up as he studies me. I don't think it's me he's mad at, though. I think he's angry at the situation. I am too.

"Why are you acting surprised? That ultimatum is pretty obvious," I remark dryly. "You should have known that it was going to come to this."

As he clenches his jaw, he throws his head back and runs both hands through his hair. He mutters something under his breath before he turns around and stalks into the kitchen. I stomp my way into my room and slam the door loud enough for him to hear.

It's only a matter of seconds before I begin doubting everything and torturing myself with questions. The biggest question of them all is this: Why am I even attracted to Tyler in the first place?

I honestly cannot think of an acceptable answer. The whole thing is wrong. I'm attracted to my stepbrother, for starters, and the thought of anyone finding out is too much to bear. We'd be judged and frowned upon, banished from society. But it's not just the stepbrother complication that's got me baffled. It's the fact that he has so many flaws, which I should hate, but I simply can't bring myself to. At least not now. Why am I so fascinated by a guy who doesn't seem to care about anything? I should hate him for being such an arrogant, egotistic jerk. But I can no longer despise him, despite how many inappropriate comments he makes, how many joints he smokes and how much alcohol he consumes in the space of an hour, because I'm entirely convinced by now that he's not simply doing it to look cool or to fit in with the guys he hangs out with. There's something more to it all, something intriguing about who he really is beneath the tough guy that he's trying to project. I'm so interested, so infatuated, and I'm falling for him.

I really wish I wasn't.

Ella and Chase arrive home shortly after. She sticks her head into my room for a moment to check if I'm home yet, telling me that the house is too quiet and that it's making her uncomfortable. I fake a small laugh before she heads next door to check on her eldest and most notorious son. I don't remember hearing him disappear into his room, but I know he must have had the same idea as me, because I hear his voice through the walls.

They bicker back and forth for a minute or so before Ella gives up and leaves him alone again. I wonder if it's a repetitive cycle for her. She tries to get through to him, he yells back at her, she gives up. Over and over and over again. It seems like a part of her daily routine.

She comes back up later to coax me out of my room for dinner. I'm reluctant to go downstairs, but she leaves no room for arguing, so I follow her to the kitchen. Dad and Chase are sat in their usual spots, their eyes following me as I make my way to the table. And Tyler's there too, of course.

"Hungry?" Dad asks, his tie loosened around his neck as he stretches back in his chair.

"No," I say as I force myself to maintain eye contact with him. I can feel Tyler's death stare boring holes into my skin from across the table. "How was the meeting?"

Dad shrugs. "It was alright."

"Dave," Ella says as she places a dish of barbecue ribs on the table—at which Tyler gags—before moving over to Dad and placing her hands on his shoulders. "You said it went really well."

He glances up at her as she soothingly rubs her thumbs over the back of his neck and his lips quirk into a smile as they hold each other's gaze. He used to smile at my mom that way, back when they were happy together. Those small gestures and exchanges stopped long before the divorce. "Hmm," he says as his eyes move back over to meet mine. "The meeting went great."

"Good," I say.

There's an abrupt screech as Tyler pushes his chair away from the table and gets to his feet. He shakes his head at the food and scrunches up his face in disdain. "I can't sit here. I'm heading back upstairs."

Ella's smile fades from her face within a nanosecond, her

hands resting on Dad's broad shoulders. "But yours is just comin—"

"I've got some stuff to do," he cuts in as he advances toward the hall without giving me a second glance. "I'll heat it up later."

Ella heaves a sigh and moves back over to the cooker to turn down the heat. "Well, that's two kids down," she murmurs.

Chase obviously likes the idea of there being fewer people at the table, because he grins and yells, "More ribs for me!"

Dinner ends up feeling pretty weird with just the four of us. Chase and I make small talk while Dad and Ella share more elaborate summaries of their days. When they're not looking, I offer Chase a rib or two.

And dinner as a whole runs relatively smoothly until the phone rings. We think nothing of it until Dad rushes back into the kitchen. He tosses the wireless phone onto the counter and grabs his keys. "That was Grace," he explains quickly, his wide eyes on Ella as she warily stands. "Jamie's fallen on his wrist. She says it could be broken. We better go."

Ella's face distorts as she presses a limp hand to her forehead. "Not this all over again!"

"He'll be fine," Dad tells her firmly. "Let's go get him."

Ella rushes around the kitchen to check that everything is switched off, because she can't have the house going on fire while she's gone, and then she pauses at the archway to the hall. She strains her neck around to face me. "Can you and Tyler please stay here and keep an eye on Chase?"

I quickly nod as I stand up. "Go."

She offers me a thankful smile before fleeing out of the house and into the car with Dad. As the engine fades away into nothing, the only noise I hear is Chase slurping the barbecue sauce off his plate.

I begin gathering all of the dishes into a pile as he finishes eating. "Good ribs, huh?"

"Amazing ribs," he corrects. He tosses the final bone onto his plate and smiles. "Mmm."

Rolling my eyes, I reach for his plate and add it to the stack before carefully carrying them over to the dishwasher. I almost throw the bones into the garbage disposal before noticing my mistake and dumping them in the trash instead. "So does Jamie break his wrist often or something?"

"No," Chase says. He's suddenly by my side, opening up the dishwasher for me and beginning to place all the used cutlery inside. "Tyler does."

"Oh man," I say, and then I smile to myself. "I thought he was tougher than that."

With Chase's help, we get the kitchen cleaned up in the space of ten minutes, and then he heads into the living room to watch TV while I ensure the front door is locked. Now that Tyler and I are close to being alone in the house, I decide it's the perfect time to try to talk to him again. I can't tell if he's mad at me or mad at himself, but either way he's pretty furious, and I prefer to see him in a good mood.

He's sitting on the edge of his bed when I push open the door to his room. His head is low and his hands are interlocked in front of him, his room silent.

"We're watching Chase," I say quietly, to let him know that I'm there. "Jamie's maybe broken his wrist."

Immediately his eyes flash up to meet mine, and suddenly he's getting to his feet. There's panic on his face. "What happened? Where is he? Who?"

I'm a little taken aback by his outburst, and his questions only confuse me. "What?"

He clears his throat. "I mean, how?"

"I think he fell on it," I tell him. He looks like he might pass out, so I decide to lighten the mood and say, "I heard you've broken yours, tough guy," as I wiggle my eyebrows at him. But it completely backfires.

His eyes dilate with a mixture of anger and shock at my joke. "Who told you that?"

"Um, Chase." His sudden outrage surprises me, so I look into his eyes to get a clue to why he's so mad. I can't quite figure him out. "What's wrong?"

He drops his eyes to the floor and back up again. He takes a step toward me. "What else did the kid tell you?"

"Nothing," I whisper as his eyes pierce mine.

Another step. "Are you sure?"

"Stop freaking out." He ignores me, not reacting as his fierce eyes scan my body. "I'm sure," I quickly add.

"You know what? I can't deal with this," he snaps. Shaking his head and breaking our eye contact, he turns away from me and heads for his bathroom. "I can't deal with you and I can't deal with Tiffani. I can't deal with your dumb questions and I can't deal with Tiffani's whining. I can't deal with any of it right now." As though he's out of breath, he exhales rapidly as he grabs onto the edge of the sink and stares at the faucet.

"You're getting so worked up," I say as I approach him from behind, pushing open the door further so I can stand inside the small bathroom with him.

"Watch the door," he mutters. "The lock is fucked."

It sounds like he's on the verge of tearing the sink off the wall, so I gently place a hand on his arm in an effort to calm him down. But he only flinches and steps away from me.

"I need a hit," he hisses, his eyes flashing to the cabinet above. He flings open the mirrored door and reaches up to the top shelf, his hand grabbing a wad of cash. I notice the collection of prescription pills and tablets in bottles carelessly scattered along the shelves. But that's not what I care about right now.

Tyler slams the cabinet door shut again and turns around, but I quickly step in front of him and bump into his chest, blocking the door. "Don't even think about it," I warn through gritted teeth.

"Eden," Tyler says, leaning toward me as his wet lips hover by my cheek, his breath cool against my skin. "I. Need. A. Hit. Right. Now."

I glance down at the cash clutched tightly in his hand as I take a step back. My eyes flash back up to lock with his. "Because coke is totally going to fix everything, right?"

"Eden," he says again, his voice hoarse. "Move your cute ass out of my way before you really piss me off. I gotta meet Declan."

"I'm not letting you," I snap. Now I'm furious. Of course he has to resort to drugs. It's just so typical and just so pathetic of him. What is he thinking? *I don't want to deal with something, so let's fix it by ruining my life?* Drugs are for stalling.

Tyler slams his palm flat against the wall by my ear. "It's not fucking up to you!"

But what he doesn't know is that it *is* up to me whether he goes or not, because he inadvertently told me how to stop him. So as he presses his lips together and stares at me, I reach over for the edge of the door, fumbling before I finally get hold of it. And before Tyler can even notice what I'm doing, I swing the door closed, spinning around and shoving my weight against it until it stiffly clicks into place.

The fucked-up lock, as Tyler called it, just became my best friend.

24

The small bathroom falls into a tense silence. My heart is beating fast and hard. Under the fluorescent lighting, I can clearly see the range of emotions flickering in Tyler's verdant eyes. There's a hint of surprise hidden in the outrage.

"Are you kidding me?" He glances around the room as if looking for a window that's never existed, like if he stares at the four walls for long enough an exit will suddenly appear. But there's exactly that: four walls, and a locked door.

"No," I say, feeling impressed with myself for making a split-second decision, and making the right one. The right decision was to prevent Tyler from leaving. I don't even mind that I've dragged myself into this claustrophobic complication with him and that we might be locked in here for hours. Perhaps the only way to unlock this door is to take it off the hinges, or ram it down, and perhaps we might have to wait it out until morning when the neighborhood handyman can come to our rescue, and perhaps I just don't care.

Tyler, on the other hand, does care. Getting out is his only concern, and the locked door is the one thing that's in his way. He steps around me, his shoulder brushing mine as he nudges me to the side. His long fingers wrap themselves around the handle of the door and he vigorously shakes it, willing the lock to collapse in on itself, but his efforts achieve nothing.

"Just give up," I say as I study the way the veins in his arms tense as he yanks at the handle before finally accepting the fact that tonight he will not be meeting Declan Portwood.

He places both hands on the back of his neck before straining to face the ceiling, letting out several slow breaths as he attempts to calm down. I like the way he sighs, the way his eyelids flicker shut for a moment as his shoulders and chest rise and drop back down, sinking low as the oxygen leaves his body. And when he has gathered his thoughts, he tilts his face down and turns to fix with me with an indignant, aggravated look.

"I'm sorry that I actually care," I tell him. He's awaiting an explanation and perhaps a real apology, but he's not going to get either. "You're just going to have to find another way to distract yourself. An alternative. One that won't kill you."

He glances around the room again, still hoping to discover a way out, but only ends up meeting his own eyes in the reflection of the cabinet mirror. He can't look at himself for long, at the fire within the depths of his eyes, and soon he's staring at the floor. "You were becoming my distraction," he mutters, but his voice is not as gruff as it was several minutes ago. "But apparently I can't have you."

I don't know how to reply to him. Words rise in my throat, but somehow I find I can't speak. Instead, I take a deep breath, and when I finally form a reply, my tone is gentle and quiet, like we're at risk of being overheard, even though we're not. "Why am I a distraction?"

Tyler looks up then. He stares back at me with apprehension, his head tilting to the side as though he has to remind himself of what the answer is. But eventually he parts his lips to speak, and carefully murmurs, "Because you make things a little easier. Because I get to focus on you instead of everything else."

I observe the curl of his lips as the words roll slowly off his tongue. They paralyze me, my body frozen in my spot by the shower, and it hits me just how real all of this is. "Then don't stop," I say, with a slight tremble in my voice. I take a cautious step toward him, not quite sure where I'm going with this. It just feels right.

He's still staring back at me, his eyes still locked with mine, but he's blinking fast and breathing heavier and I know that he still wants one thing and one thing only. I reach up to touch his jaw, and his skin is burning hot as the fire in his eyes.

"Focus on me," I whisper.

"Then distract me," he orders. He lifts his hand, delicately reaches for my fingers on his jaw, and moves my hand away. I flinch at the coldness of his hands in contrast to the warmth of his face. Two complete opposites. Like him and me.

"We can talk," I say. The atmosphere around us has shifted from tense to calm, loud to quiet, and I almost whisper for fear of breaking the comforting stillness. "We've never once just talked."

"Okay. Let's talk," he says. Carefully stepping around me, he presses his back to the shower door and slides down to the floor. He extends his legs and heaves a sigh, his head hung low, eyes closed. I wonder what he's thinking about. Me?

"Can we talk about Tiffani?" I ask this question with extreme caution, diving into the complicated topic as gently as I can. "Calmly this time."

The mere mention of her name creates tension and it forces

Tyler to look at me, as though he's trying to figure out if I seriously just brought her up. I see an odd flash in his eyes, but then he glances away. "Fine," he says through gritted teeth.

I step over his legs and drop down onto the cold tiles, pressing my back against the door, pulling my knees up to my chest and hugging them to my body. "Why won't you break up with her? You don't even like her. You said so yourself."

Tyler trains his eyes on me. They slowly fall to my lips, to my hands wrapped around my knees, and then return to mirror my gaze once more. I wonder if he's considering whether to give me an honest answer or if he's just trying to buy time while he invents a lie. "I can't break up with her."

"But why?" His reply only irritates me more. Unless she's holding him at knifepoint, then I see no reason he can't just end the useless relationship that he clearly cares little to nothing about.

Tyler shakes his head and places a hand on his face, rubbing his eyes with his thumb and forefinger before groaning loudly. "Tiffani's really good at acting like she's the nicest girl around. But she's not. The second you do something wrong to her, she turns into a psychopath. She knows too much about me. I can't risk it. At least not right now."

"Psychopath?" I lift my head and look at him, perplexed. "What does she know?"

"It's . . ." His words taper off, and he looks uncomfortable, almost pained. He places his palms flat on the tiles by his side. "Okay. Example: Back in January, she heard I'd been hanging out with this girl during lunch period every Tuesday, which I totally hadn't, and she went crazy. I slaved over an essay for English Lit for two weeks straight, because I had to get my grades up, and she told my teacher that she wrote it. My entire grade dropped and I got suspended for cheating, which is so dumb. The same day she used her mom's email to email my mom, telling her that she was concerned for my well-being because I was smoking joints in the school basement. That part is true, and Tiffani's the only one who knew. Mom didn't talk to me for almost a month. I would have dumped Tiffani back then, but she made it clear that I shouldn't ever go there. So I never have. Breaking up isn't an option. There are so many more things she can do, because she has the upper hand in all of this."

There's a brief silence, and then I ask, "What else does she know, Tyler?" I'm trying to absorb his words, attempting to make sense of them. I try to imagine Tiffani doing those things, and at first I can't, but then I remember the look in her eyes this morning when she told me she knew I was lying. She terrified me. Somehow, I believe Tyler. She definitely has the potential to do those things.

Tyler isn't quite meeting my eyes. "Do you remember the first day of summer?"

The sudden change in topic, from Tiffani's controlling nature to the start of the summer, takes me by surprise. "Yeah. Dad was annoying and the barbecue sucked and you rudely stormed into it."

"Yeah, that." I'm waiting for him to laugh. He doesn't. In fact, he just looks even more uncomfortable than he already was. "I was super pissed off."

"Why?" I remember eavesdropping on his argument with Ella that night, but I don't remember them discussing why he was mad in the first place. He looked furious when he pulled up outside the house.

There's another silent pause. "I was mad at Tiffani," he finally admits. By now he's not even looking at me. He's just staring at the tiled flooring. "I've been thinking about getting involved in something for a while, and she found out that night," he explains, but his voice is quiet and a little raspy, and I realize he's not going to tell me what it is he's thinking about getting involved in. I can tell it isn't something he can be proud of. "She said she won't tell anyone as long as I stay with her until graduation. That's why I was sucking up to her for a while at the start of the summer. You know, in American Apparel and stuff . . ." His cheeks flush with color in sheer embarrassment of having to talk about it, but I don't mind. I'm just glad he's being honest with me. "As long as she's happy and I don't break up with her, she won't tell, because that's what she does, Eden. She likes to blackmail people into doing what she wants, so that she can look cool and stay on top of the rest of us." He exhales and shakes his head. "She told me she used to get bullied when she was younger, so I guess when she started at our school, after she moved here with her mom after the divorce, she wanted to make sure no one stepped over her. She wants to be better than everyone, cooler than them all. Having me by her side helps to boost her ego. That's why I'm stuck in this mess." When he stops talking, he groans. "I hate this."

"Wow," I say. It's all I can muster up right now. Tyler's been right all along. He really doesn't want to be with her, and he's not just saying that to make me feel better. He genuinely is stuck in a complicated situation, and I can't help but feel like I've made it worse for him. "I don't know what to say."

"I'm not breaking up with her," he says gently, finally glancing back up to look at me. He looks sad. It makes me feel sorry for him, because I honestly don't know what advice to give him. "Not yet, at least. I can't risk it right now."

"Then what are we going to do?" The floor is cold against my skin, but I try to ignore it, focusing my attention on the person across from me as I try my hardest to understand him.

Tyler fixes me with a stern stare. "I just don't want to make anyone suspicious," he tells me.

"Suspicious about what?"

"Us," he says firmly. With another sigh, he unfolds his arms and runs a hand back through his hair, tugging on the ends, and I notice the familiarity of the action. It's something he does subconsciously, a sign of his anger or distress, something that perhaps offers him some comfort for a split second. "We need to just act normal for now until we figure this out. That's another reason I can't break up with her. People would wonder why. So for now, she has to stay in the picture, because Tiffani is my normality."

"But it's wrong to do this to her," I say quietly. I envision her tear-streaked face again this morning as she sobbed uncontrollably against her comforter, releasing the brunt of the hurt she felt. We inflicted that upon her, and although it feels so long ago, it's only been a matter of hours. Maybe she's still distraught, and right now Tyler and I are hovering on the edge of a dangerous line that should not be crossed. Tyler might be in a relationship with Tiffani that he can't get out of and she might have forced him into that, but it doesn't give us the right to cheat.

"Eden," Tyler says. When I meet his eyes, his head is cocked and he's studying me. "Talk about something else. Talk about Portland."

My eyebrows furrow as I cross my legs, placing my interlocked hands onto my lap. "You want me to talk about Portland?"

"I want you to talk about yourself," he says. His eyes are smoldering now, bright and vibrant, locked with mine and unwilling to break our shared gaze. "Tell me something that no one else knows."

There is honesty within his eyes, somewhere within the fire that's still burning, and I know that I can trust him enough to share my secrets, to tell him about Portland and the people there. It takes me a minute or so to make up my mind. Only Amelia knows my secret and I'm undecided whether or not I want to make that two people instead of one, but then Tyler gives me an encouraging nod, like he's trying to convince me to jump off a cliff with him, and I give in.

I take a few deep breaths, building up the courage to speak. The truth is, I don't want to admit what's going on. "I love Portland. It was an amazing city to grow up in," I say with a sort of sad smile, as though I'm reminiscing about the good old days, as my grandparents would call them. "I had three really close friends. Amelia, Alyssa and Holly."

"Had?"

"Had," I confirm. Tyler is staring at me with keen interest, taking in my every move, every word. "When my parents got divorced I was thirteen, and it hit me really hard. I used to cry myself to sleep, because my mom would be crying and my dad wouldn't be there and I didn't know how to make her feel better and it just sucked. It really, really sucked." I pause for a moment, my next few words proving difficult to force out of my mouth, but somehow I manage, somehow I can handle it. "I started to eat a lot because I was so upset, and I put on some weight during freshman year. Alyssa and Holly had a lot to say about it."

I can see Tyler glance down at my body, and it only makes

me feel even more insecure than I did before. I try to breathe in. "You're not fat," he states bluntly, like he's mad at me for even suggesting it.

"That's because I run, Tyler."

He continues to study me, as though he's trying to figure out what I'm thinking, just like I always try to figure him out. He slowly shifts his body across the floor, almost cautiously, and then positions himself directly in front of me. My body is trapped between his legs and he places his hands on my knees, his touch making me flinch. "Keep talking."

My train of thought has been interrupted by the desire to reach over and kiss him, so I place a hand to my cheek and force myself to continue. "They made me feel like shit," I admit, because it's true. Alyssa and Holly did treat me awfully for over a year, they did throw snide remarks about my weight into every conversation, and they did cause the downward spiral of my mental health. "I had two of my supposed best friends calling me fat every day, so I started running. We don't talk anymore, but they still bitch about me on the low. It's just hard, because Amelia . . . Amelia's still friends with them. She stuck by my side the whole time, though."

"Eden," Tyler says, firmly again, like the only way to get my full attention is to use the quiet force of my name. "That's why you always say you're never hungry, isn't it?"

My lips part as I stare back at him, almost embarrassed that he's paid so much attention to me. Not even Dad has picked up on this. But then again, he's always been selfish. "You noticed that?"

"Only just now." He glances down to stare at my legs as he runs his fingers from my knees to my thighs, lightly skimming my skin. "Just so you know, I completely disagree with those girls. I'm sorry for what they did." With his head still tilted down toward my thighs as he continues tracing patterns, he glances up at me through his eyelashes, his eyes unbelievably powerful, and I succumb to their strength and the sensation of his skin against mine.

And he must feel the way my shoulders relax and sink back down with a breath of relief, and he must sense the way my entire body grows almost limp beneath his touch, and he must be sharing the same thoughts as I am, because his fingertips stop circling my skin and he grabs my thighs, leaning forward and crashing his lips against mine.

I don't know why, but I love it each time he completely dominates the situation. It's like he's doing all the hard work while I bask in the exhilaration and the adrenaline. I'm starting to get used to the way his lips fit against mine. My arms seem to move on their own accord, loosely throwing themselves around his neck as I smile against him somewhere amidst the kiss. I like that this is beginning to feel familiar.

It doesn't take long for his tight grip on my thighs to loosen, his hands wandering elsewhere, somewhere new and risky. The kiss slows down as his focus switches from my lips to his hands. They hover by the hem of my shirt for a few moments, brushing the material as though he's waiting for me to object, but I don't want him to stop. I tighten my arms around his neck and pull his lips harder against mine.

Tyler gets the message. He clasps my waist beneath my shirt with one hand as they other finds its way to my bra, leaving the thrilling trail of his touch along my body. I don't know how he manages, but he slides his hand inside the lace and cups my breast all in one swift movement. He tears his lips from mine, pulling back to meet my eyes for a moment, before moving back in again to plant a row of kisses along the edge of my jaw. His hands are still on my body, his thumb rubbing my breast in soft circles, his skin cold yet oddly sensational. Soon his other hand joins in and I suddenly grow self-conscious. I'm staring up at the ceiling through half closed eyes, my face tilted to the side as Tyler plants kisses on my neck and cups my breasts. I've never been all that fortunate in that area, especially in comparison with Tiffani, and I suddenly grow paranoid that Tyler will burst into laughter any second, but he never does.

I can feel a moan rising in my throat, and I try my best to suppress it, already embarrassed enough as it is, but then Tyler sighs against my neck and his breath tickles my skin. I move my hands to his jaw and draw his lips back to mine, but before they connect once more, our eyes lock for a moment. We catch our breath as we stare at one another, comfortable in our embrace and unable to hold back the small smiles toying at the corners of our lips.

We shouldn't be kissing on the floor of his bathroom and his hands shouldn't be on my body and I shouldn't be enjoying it. The scandalous nature of it makes it all the more exhilarating.

And all the more worth it.

25

Tyler and I escaped from the confinement of his bathroom two hours later. Our parents returned home with a son bearing a fractured wrist only to find a second son desperately awaiting their return, wondering why he'd been left alone to fend for himself. Little did they all know, Tyler and I had been in the house all along, supervising Chase from afar. I could hear that Ella was furious, probably thinking I'd bailed on babysitting and disappeared again, but when they started calling us both, they discovered we were in the room right above their heads. We had to bullshit our way to freedom.

"I don't know how it happened," I said. Not only was I lying through the door, I was also lying through my teeth.

"Me either," Tyler added.

"I was coming to find him and I fell against the door," I said. Another lie. Beside me, Tyler was pressing the back of his hand to his lips to muffle his laughter.

Dad said he'd call the neighborhood handyman, Mr. Forde, to come over straight away. But Mr. Forde obviously didn't care too much about the standard of his customer service, because he turned up on the other side of the door forty minutes later. It took thirty bucks and a lot of picking and drilling to unbolt the lock, and finally Tyler and I sheepishly made our exit.

We didn't talk to each other again for the rest of the night. It wasn't because I didn't want to speak to him. It was because he spent over an hour on the phone with Tiffani, his voice strained with the effort to come across soft and pleading as he tried his best to apologize for his "accidental mistake" that "happened in the spur of the moment", which he "completely didn't mean to do." I could hear it all through the paper-thin walls that separate our rooms. He fed her lie after lie, stacking them on top of each other as he built up a cover story, claiming that a sophomore from Inglewood wanted to see his car when he was on his way to meet the guys, and somehow the fifteen-year-old ended up in his lap. Slightly far-fetched, but Tiffani believed him. His regret was so forced and so fake that I almost wanted to tear down the wall and ask him what he was playing at. But I never did, because I remembered that the Inglewood sophomore was really just me.

And so last night I fell asleep with my mind split in two. One half was drowning in guilt, but the other was floating, recklessly in love with the idea of Tyler and the secrets that are hidden within the depth of his being.

Because, somehow, I've managed to become one of them.

* * *

"And that's why British guys are better than all these American scumbags," Rachael announces, finally, after a five-minute speech comparing the two nationalities. According to her, British guys are better, because they have cute accents and use cute words and are just overall cute, and that's as advanced as her arguments get.

Meghan voices her own opinion. She claims that the French

are better, because they kiss you at the top of the Eiffel Tower and whisper "*je t'aime*" while you share a bottle of wine.

Both of their European boyfriend fantasies are somewhat stereotypical, but I just laugh and drop my eyes back down to the sidewalk. We've just left the Refinery, so my latte to-go is hot against my palms as I slightly lag behind my two companions, my gaze following the lines in the concrete.

"Eden," Rachael says, spinning around with a sense of urgency. "You have the final say: British or French?" She and Meghan both stare at me, their expressions intense, as though I'm about to announce who's just been elected president.

I simply shrug. "French," I say.

Rachael's face distorts with disgust as she turns on her heels and stalks off for dramatic effect. Meghan grins and tells me I've made the right choice, and then we rush through the flow of pedestrians until we catch up with Rachael again, who appears to have gotten over it by the time we reach her.

"We've got to wait for Tiff on Broadway," she reminds us as we reach the promenade and head round the corner onto Third Street.

Given that it's like three hundred degrees out today, it's no surprise that there are people shuffling around, pushing past each other as they weave their way toward their next purchase. I don't know where Broadway is, but Rachael and Meghan certainly do, so I drop back and tag behind again as we sweep southbound down Third Street. Every time I come here, I notice stores that I somehow didn't notice the time before, like Rip Curl, some Australian company selling water-sports apparel, and Johnnie's New York Pizzeria, which looks adorably Italian and reminds me of Dean.

Rachael slows to a halt by H&M, pushing her sunglasses

up into her hair as she peers through the windows at the mannequins draped in floral designs. "Cute shirt," she comments. She tilts her shades back over her eyes again and starts walking, this time both Meghan and I scrambling to keep up with her. It's almost as if the alpha status gets passed onto Rachael whenever Tiffani isn't here to fulfill the role, but today the switch doesn't last long. We're meeting Tiffani any minute now.

We reach the end of the promenade and file onto Broadway, where the promenade flows into Santa Monica Place, the upscale mall cluttered with designer stores that the girls have taken me to a couple times before. We pass Nordstrom and linger on the corner of Broadway and Second. Meghan presses her body back against the windows of the store as she squints at the sun, and Rachael folds her arms across her chest and taps her foot against the concrete as she studies the traffic. For a while I watch her and wonder what she's looking for, but very soon it becomes clear.

She straightens up after a few minutes, arms dropping to her sides, expression curious. I follow her gaze. It lands on the white car that's just pulled up across the street, windows down, engine still purring as it comes to a complete halt. It's Tyler. My jaw tightens. There's so much tension between us at the moment that it's almost unbearable to be anywhere near him, especially under the watchful eyes of our friends.

"Why is she smiling?" Meghan asks as she steps in between Rachael and me, a hand resting on the top of her head, her fingers woven into her hair.

"Because she's insane," Rachael answers blankly.

The more I stare at the car, the more my jaw begins to twitch, and the more my jaw begins to twitch, the more I become frustrated with the whole situation. Tiffani is in the passenger seat. I knew she would be. The very first thing Tyler decided to tell me this morning when I woke up was that he was heading out to meet her, so it's no surprise to see her with him.

The three of us watch for a few moments as the pair talk inside the privacy of the vehicle, Tyler's eyebrows furrowed as Tiffani angles her body to face him, her hands moving as she speaks. I really wish I knew what they were saying. Tyler cracks a smile, but it doesn't quite reach his eyes, and she leans over the center console to kiss him.

"She's insane!" Rachael yells, her sudden outburst grabbing the attention of people around us, but she doesn't seem to notice as she throws her hands up in frustration. I'm surprised she doesn't hurl her coffee at the car. "A goddamn lunatic!"

I'm thinking the same thing about Tyler. I just don't say it out loud.

Something is happening inside of me, like a light switch has been flicked on, and all at once a wave of fury rushes through my veins. I try to convince myself that it's not jealousy, that I'm not jealous. But I am. My hand tightens around my cup and I almost crush it. I squeeze so hard that the plastic lid pops off and flutters to the concrete, delicate wisps of steam floating up and into the air. Immediately I draw the cup to my lips and sip at the latte as I watch the scene at the other side of the road.

Finally, Tyler pulls away from Tiffani. She's giggling like a lovestruck preteen, like she's head over heels for him again. This really aggravates me. Tiffani should hate him. They shouldn't be fixing things and they shouldn't still be together, but they clearly are. When Tiffani steps out of the car, she comes rushing across the traffic toward us, bearing a huge grin.

I'm still sipping my latte, never dropping the cup from my face, pretending to be too distracted to say anything. But as Tiffani reaches us, I notice Tyler's car still sitting there at the opposite side of the road. He seems to have noticed me too. Through the windshield, he's watching me, staring at me, until finally he smiles. It's partly apologetic, partly genuine, like he's glad to see me. I find myself smiling back, but our moment is quickly interrupted as Tiffani joins us on the sidewalk.

Rachael lets out a horrified groan and flings her coffee into a nearby trash can, as if to show her outrage at Tiffani's good mood. "What is wrong with you?"

My eyes move to Tiffani. Over her shoulder, Tyler's car revs its way down Broadway, leaving behind the gawking admirers and a plume of smoke. Tiffani, on the other hand, is unfortunately still here. Somehow her smile keeps on getting wider, so I keep on acting like I'm innocently sipping my latte. But I'm not innocent. In fact, I'm the guiltiest person around, and my coffee ran out twenty seconds ago.

"What?" Tiffani blinks her wide eyes, looking almost perplexed.

"That!" Rachael points in the direction that Tyler has just disappeared in. "I can't believe you've forgiven him just like that."

Tiffani's smile becomes a pout as she bats her eyelashes and glances up from beneath them. It's such a contrast from how she looked yesterday, when she cried out five hundred buckets of tears and looked entirely miserably. "He did explain himself, Rachael."

"You're really buying his bullshit story?"

"It's not bullshit."

There's a moment of silence as Rachael tilts her head and presses her lips together, but Meghan seizes the opportunity to speak.

"When did you get that purse, Tiffani?" she asks suspiciously. "It's new, isn't it?"

All four of us drop our eyes to the purse hooked over Tiffani's arm. It's a brown Louis Vuitton monogram purse, the leather shining under the sun. Tiffani gives us a sheepish smile.

"Well . . ." she says slowly, and then bites her lower lip. "Tyler bought it for me."

"That's what I thought," Meghan murmurs, and her eyebrows knit together as she shakes her head in disapproval. "At least we know now that it only takes a $1,000 purse to gain Tiffani Parkinson's forgiveness."

At this, Tiffani laughs. I don't. I bite the rim of my cup to stop myself from saying something I shouldn't, my teeth sinking so hard into the cardboard that I almost bore holes in it.

"He could have donated that money to charity," Rachael remarks with a twisted frown, and I agree with her comment. I'm pretty sure the homeless would benefit more from that money than Tiffani will from her leather purse. "We all knew you'd end up forgiving him sooner or later."

"And you could have stopped hooking up with Trevor six months ago," Tiffani shoots back. "We all knew you'd end up falling for him."

Meghan lets out a loud snort, to which she quickly covers her mouth with her hands. She blushes but still continues to giggle. I glance over my cup to Rachael, whose lips have parted to form an "o". She looks flustered for a moment, like she's suffering from a concussion and has forgotten how to string sentences together. I think she may be mad, but she only sighs.

"Fine," she huffs. "You can forgive Tyler."

"Thank you for your approval," Tiffani says sarcastically. "Now can we please get inside the mall already? I'm dying for a Johnny Rockets sundae!"

By this point I'm pretty impressed with myself for holding my tongue, for hanging back and acting like I'm drinking the best goddamn latte I've ever had. As we head back up Broadway and past Nordstrom and Nike, I slip my gnawed cup into a trash can.

"Hurry up, Eden," Meghan calls over her shoulder when we turn into the mall, and she pauses for a moment to allow me to catch up, which I unwillingly do.

The thing about Santa Monica Place is that it was built solely for the rich. I've noticed this each time I've been here, because it's not hard to just look at the people who are happy to flaunt their wealth. From the man in the suit peering through the windows of Hugo Boss to the woman with the sophisticated dress and heels who's eyeing up a watch in the Michael Kors window, it's clear they have money they're willing to spend. Tyler is the same.

Santa Monica Place is an outdoor mall, with four public walkways leading into an oval center, glamorous stores circling it. It's so complex and unique and modern that it makes me feel out of place, but I follow the girls nonetheless. We head up the escalators to the third and final floor, which has an open-air dining deck, and make a beeline for

Johnny Rockets. Johnny Rockets is another fast food chain that Oregon seems to be missing, because Oregon sucks and seems to be deprived of just about everything, except rain. Oregon is never short on rain.

When we reach the food court, Tiffani gets herself something called a Super Sundae, Meghan and Rachael go for the Perfect Brownie Sundae and I simply opt for water.

"The guys are on their way up," Tiffani tells us without glancing up from her phone. She texts someone—presumably one of the guys—while scooping up a mouthful of ice cream at the same time, her eyes never leaving the device in her hands. "They've finally decided what's happening on Saturday."

"What's happening on Saturday?" I blurt, my curiosity getting the better of me once again, and after I say it I realize it's the first thing I've said since I decided that French guys are better than British.

Tiffani's eyes flicker up from her phone as she swallows the ice cream she's just piled into her mouth. She stares at me for a long moment before she glances across the table to Rachael and Meghan. "Is she serious?"

"The annual beach party," Rachael says slowly, her eyes fixed on me as her spoon hovers above her brownie. She twirls it around in a circle. "The biggest and hottest party of the summer."

"Oh," I say. Quickly, I unscrew the cap of my water and take a long drink.

"They get a permit and shut down one half of the beach," she explains, although I'm not all that interested in the exact details and I don't exactly know who "they" are. "It's supposed to be over twenty-one only, but, well, you know . . ." Playfully, she adjusts her hair and pouts. "Everyone goes. There's not exactly a door to the beach where the security guards can card you."

"Security guards?"

"There's a lot of fights," Tiffani says. "And obviously you can't drink while you're there, because it's a public place and all. Unless you want to get arrested, which a lot of people do."

"So," Rachael cuts in, without missing a beat, "you get drunk before you go. Just don't get, like, wasted or anything, because you'll draw attention to yourself and you'll end up getting kicked out for being a minor."

Tiffani places her phone down on the table and draws her sundae toward her, slowly scooping up some more ice cream. She smiles as she throws me a peculiar glance and says, "I don't think we'll have to worry about Eden getting wasted."

I press my lips together and narrow my eyes at her, slightly offended, as she and Rachael stifle a laugh. "What's that supposed to mean?"

Tiffani's smile grows into a small smirk as she exchanges glances with Rachael. She holds her spoon up to her lips. "You're just not very . . ."

"I'm not very what, Tiffani?" I gnaw at the insides of my cheeks as five million words run through my head all at once. Not very cool? Popular? Sociable? Pretty? In other words, not very like them?

"Reckless," she says, and then shovels the ice cream into her mouth.

Reckless? I'm not *reckless*? I almost mimic one of Meghan's snorts but somehow manage to suppress the laughter in my throat. *Oh, Tiffani,* I think, *I can assure you I am pretty damn reckless*. If only they knew.

Tiffani swallows and stares at me, noticing my silence. "Where were you on Tuesday night?"

"Tuesday?" My voice is something between a whisper and a squeak. On Tuesday night, I was at the pier with Tyler. I certainly wasn't with Meghan, and Tiffani knows this.

"Yeah, Tuesday." She blinks at me as she awaits an answer. I don't know why she's asking me again. It's like she wants to try and catch me out, like she's hoping I'll casually blurt out the truth in front of them all.

Rachael's watching me too, intensifying the pressure of Tiffani's question. My palms sweat. Meghan snorts again, and I begin to wonder if perhaps Johnny Rockets has slipped a few grams of pot into her brownie. She won't stop giggling.

Tiffani heaves a sigh. "Where did you really go?"

"Oh my God!" Rachael almost screams, her body shooting upright as she leans across the table. "You were totally hooking up with Jake!"

Tiffani turns to her. "That's what I thought too."

My shoulders drop in relief. Thank God that's what she thought my secret was. I've been in constant worry over the thought of Tiffani figuring out it was me that was with Tyler on Tuesday, but she isn't on to us at all. "Maybe," I say with a small smile. I look away. I'd rather they thought I was sneaking around with Jake than Tyler.

At this, Rachael almost hurls her body across the table. Her mouth is hanging open as she shakes her head quickly, like she can't believe what she's hearing. I can't blame her; I wouldn't either. "Was it a home run? Eden, tell us!"

Meghan bursts into a fit of giggles and all three of us turn to look at her, confused. She bites her lip to smother some of her laughter, but she ends up squeezing her eyes closed and murmuring an apology. Until this moment, I hadn't realized she'd been texting the entire time.

"Meg, what are you even laughing at?" Tiffani questions, sounding peeved.

"I'm sorry," Meghan splutters again as she tries her hardest to control herself. "I'm texting Jared. He's hilarious."

"Who the fuck is Jared?" Rachael asks.

"The guy from Pasadena! The one from the beach," she says. She smiles at Tiffani and then adds, "He and his friends are coming on Saturday."

"Oh my God, you and Eden are ridiculous!" Rachael folds her arms across her chest and rolls her eyes. "You're both talking to guys and neither of you thought to tell us?"

"You never told us about Trevor," Tiffani says with a playful grin. "We only found out because Meg walked in on the two of you at Jason's party last year."

"Let it go," she huffs, but she's cracking a smile.

The guys show up five minutes later. I'm thankful, because we've been sitting listening to Meghan tell us everything she finds hilarious about Jared, and she's beginning to repeat herself.

There's Tyler, Dean and Jake, and I notice that Dean has positioned himself between the other two. I still don't understand how Tyler and Jake are friends, yet they hate each other. Somehow they can force themselves into acting civil. The three of them wander over to us and pull over chairs from another table. I notice how Tyler settles himself next to Tiffani, but not too close. His eyes never meet mine.

"So we've decided," Jake starts, once we've gotten past the greetings, "that we'll go to Dean's before the party on Saturday."

"A party before a party," Dean says. He grins as he quickly glances around the six of us, as though he's trying to gauge if we're game or not. "We'll take care of the booze."

"You guys just take care of looking good," Jake finishes. He pulls a face and shrugs, leaning back in his seat and folding his arms across his chest.

Rachael flings her spoon across the table at him, and he dodges it by a centimeter. "Prick," she mutters, and he offers her a crooked smile.

"You know I'm kidding, Rachy baby," he says innocently. He cocks his head as though he's challenging her to a rap battle or something.

"Don't call me that!"

While they bicker, I don't say anything. I'm mostly too embarrassed at the thought of the girls thinking I had sex with Jake two days ago, but I'm also trying my hardest to act as nonchalant around Tyler as possible. Too much eye contact could be suspicious, but none at all could also raise questions. After all, he's my stepbrother. It would be weird if we didn't acknowledge each other. So occasionally I glance over at him, hoping each time that he'll look up at the same moment, but somehow I never seem to be able to catch his eye. He's too busy staring at the table while Tiffani runs her fingers up and down his arm, and he looks like he's frozen stiff. She doesn't seem to notice. Her hands reach up to grasp his jaw as she draws his lips toward hers, but he jerks his head to the side and she ends up planting a kiss on his cheek. After that, he stares at the ground, never looking back up.

I angle my body slightly away from them and turn to Meghan for support, but she's back on her phone again, snorting and giggling at texts from Jared. I glare around the group. All of them are annoying me in one way or another, except Dean. My eyes land on him, sitting at the opposite side of the table and looking as left out as I feel.

"Freaks," he mouths. He smiles, and I think about the five-dollar bill that he wrote on and I grin back, but then Rachael's voice distracts me.

"Eden, you and Jake should go for a walk or something," she says with an edge to her voice, her eyes wide and encouraging as she stares at me. She gives me a curt nod and then turns back to Jake. "Off you go, lovebirds."

Jake raises his eyebrows, looking perplexed, like he wants to ask, "What the hell?" but manages to refrain. He stands and lets his eyes fall to me before he nods to the escalator. "Eden?"

Rachael's beaming at me, Dean has averted his eyes to the sky, and Tyler has finally glanced up, his attention caught. Tiffani is tracing circles on his neck with her index finger now, but he doesn't seem to pay attention, only glares at me instead.

Jake's still waiting, so I quickly get to my feet, murmur, "We won't be long," to everyone and then walk around the table until I reach him. I don't linger to wait for a reply from anyone, so Jake and I head off on our own. We weave our way through the food court and across the dining deck.

Jake stuffs his hands into the pockets of his jeans as we take the escalator down to the second level of the mall. He leans against the handrail. "So what's up?"

"Not much," I say. I don't particularly want to talk to him, especially after I've been ignoring his texts for a few weeks now. I was hoping he'd give up. That way, we wouldn't be in the awkward situation that we are now. "We haven't talked in a while."

"Tell me about it."

"I've been busy."

"I figured," he says.

There's tension in the air as we step off the escalator and saunter over to the glass barrier that wraps its way around the entire level. We're peering down at all the people on the floor below as they zip across from one store to another. Jake's leaning forward, his arms crossed and resting against the barrier, and I slowly run my fingers over the metal.

"You know that I have to go home next month, right?" I glance sideways but don't angle my head to look at him. He doesn't look back at me. I know this isn't exactly what Rachael had in mind when she sent us off alone, but she's given me the perfect opportunity to set things straight with him.

"Yeah, I know," he says.

"Right," I say, although my voice is laced with trepidation, worried that he'll take my words the wrong way. "So maybe we should just stick to being friends."

Jake still doesn't glance over at me, but he shrugs and stares at a group of girls on the floor below. They look like seniors and I wonder if he recognizes them. "Whatever, Eden," he mutters. "It was never going to be anything serious. Just a little fun, if you know what I mean."

I blink and take a step back from the barrier. "Wow."

"What?" Now he looks at me. He straightens up and narrows his blue eyes, acting like he didn't just say what he just said. "I thought you knew that."

"I did," I say sharply, suddenly realizing that Tyler was completely right when he told me that Jake was a player. Just a little fun, that's what Jake plays for. Nothing serious, because serious isn't cool. "I just didn't believe it until now."

I don't even know why I'm getting angry over this. In fact, I should be thrilled to get Jake off my back, overjoyed that he didn't get offended. I don't think I ever saw myself being with him, anyway. He was a good kisser, and that night was fun, but that's as far as Jake and I are going. We're simply friends. Minus the benefits that he likes to think he's entitled to.

I sigh and rub my temples. "Okay, whatever, it's cool. You bought me Chick-fil-A, so thanks."

"Cool," he says with a laugh, but he sounds a little agitated. The thing about Jake is that he seems like a nice guy, but there's a look in his eyes right now that makes me wonder if he's a completely different person when things don't go his way.

I don't know what to say back to him and it looks like he's done talking anyway, so I turn around and stalk my way back over to the escalator. He follows me. We head back up to the dining deck, where our friends are still sitting. Tiffani has somehow managed to sprawl herself across Tyler's lap. She sure does take the phrase "forgive and forget" seriously. But I notice that Tyler doesn't return her enthusiasm. She's all over him, but his hands are stuffed into his pockets and his expression is blank.

Rachael wiggles her eyebrows at me when we approach, but I pretend not to notice and fetch my bottle of water from the table instead. Tiffani finally unwraps herself from Tyler and the seven of us actually have a conversation for once, discussing the party on Saturday and what alcohol to get and who they think will turn up at beach. I just sort of nod my way through the entire thing, agreeing with everything Rachael says and hoping it's enough to get me through.

* * *

That night, after Rachael and I finally made our way home to Deidre Avenue, I picked at the mac and cheese that Ella made for dinner, set off on a run, and then collapsed into bed shortly after. An entire day of trailing around stores was simply too much for me to handle, so the exhaustion from the extensive socializing and the run combined was enough to put me to sleep long before midnight.

I don't know what I was thinking about before I dozed off, but I'm pretty convinced I was thinking about Tyler. I know that he was all I thought about when I was running. I couldn't get today out of my head. It was the way he pulled up to the mall with Tiffani and her new purse that he splashed a wad of cash on, kissing her like he hadn't been kissing me the night before. It was the way he'd smiled at me afterward, the way his eyes had crinkled, the way he was keeping everything a secret, keeping us a secret. That's what I couldn't stop thinking about.

Suddenly I'm stirring awake again, my room dark, the house silent. I stare at my wall through half-closed eyes and behind me I hear my door squeak open again, and I realize this is what has woken me. I moan into my comforter.

"Are you awake?" a voice whispers across the room. It's Tyler, and my eyes promptly fly open, my door groaning as it clicks shut again.

Now I most definitely am, I think. I don't move an inch. My eyes just rest on my dull wall as I listen to the muffled sound of Tyler's footsteps shuffling across my carpet. "Yeah," I murmur. "What time is it?"

"Three," Tyler says, his voice still hushed, like we shouldn't dare make a sound. I hear him exhale from behind me just as the mattress shifts beneath my body, my comforter lifted up as he slips into my bed. "Can I sleep with you?"

I'm still pretty much half asleep as my eyelids flutter closed again, but the corners of my lips pull up into a small, tired smile. When I don't reply straight away, Tyler starts to babble.

"I mean, not like hook up with you, just fall asleep, you know, like, rest," he blurts quickly, his breath tickling the back of my neck, his body never touching mine.

"I know what you meant," I say.

There's a long silence. The only thing I can hear is our breathing, completely out of sync. Whenever I inhale, he exhales, and it almost begins to sound like a rhythm until his breathing slows. That's when I feel his warm, bare skin press against my back, his chest hard yet somehow comfortable, his long fingers moving to touch my arm. The sensation makes my body shiver.

"I'm sorry about Tiffani," he whispers against my ear as he runs his other hand through my hair.

"You should be."

"Just let me figure it out," he almost pleads, his voice laced with something that I can't quite understand, and, quieter, he adds, "I'm trying to figure everything out."

I'm still staring at the wall. "Like what?"

"Eden," he says, "in case you haven't noticed, I'm pretty fucked up." He draws his body away from mine and rolls over to face the other way, so I finally tear my eyes away from the wall and switch onto my other side.

I stare at his back now, my gaze resting on his tattoo on the back of his shoulder blade. I lift my hand and press a finger to the ink. "I wouldn't say that. More like lost."

"Lost?"

"Yeah," I say. My voice is barely audible. "I think you're lost."

"What makes you think that?"

I trace a line from his tattoo down to the bottom of his spine and back up to his other shoulder, edging my body closer into him, craving the heat from his skin. I wrap my arm around him and close my eyes, whispering, "Because you have no idea what you're doing or where you're going," only moments before I fall back asleep once more.

And by 7AM, he's gone.

26

"I am so excited!" Rachael squeals from her closet early Saturday evening. I hear the screeching of hangers right before she twirls back into the room in her strapless bra, a collection of tops in her hand. "Okay, which one?"

I prop myself up onto my elbows on her bed and cock my head, studying the pieces of clothing as she lifts each one up individually and hooks them over the top of her door. "The white tube top."

Rachael ponders over it before she agrees with me. "You're totally right!" All at once, she scoops up the rest of the clothes and tosses them into a pile in the corner of her room and then pulls on the white tube. It works well with the cerise maxi skirt that she spent twenty minutes contemplating.

"Are you sure this looks okay?" I frown at her and then glance down at my own outfit, a mint skater skirt and a white bustier, which, admittedly, does make my chest look slightly more impressive than usual. I've stacked a bunch of bracelets on my wrist, but I still feel too casual.

"It's a beach party," Rachael says slowly, as though I'm a toddler who's still learning how to comprehend words. She drops down onto her floor to pull on a pair of tan sandals, too focused on her footwear to even glance up at me. "You look hot. I really like that top."

"You're only saying that because it's yours," I remark, but I'm smiling. Maybe I do look hot for once and maybe I do like the feeling of satisfaction that stems from this. It makes me feel like I fit in.

Rachael rolls her eyes and then gets to her feet, carefully angling herself in front of her full-length mirror to ensure she looks good. I tell her she looks incredible, but she brushes my comment away as her cheeks flush with color, and we say nothing more in relation to our outfits.

"We're so gonna be the last ones to get to Dean's," she says a few minutes later, once she's finished applying a third coat of lip gloss. She pouts at the mirror. "You ready?"

"Rachael," I say as I sit up, "I've been ready for thirty minutes."

"That's true," she muses. With a laugh, she reaches for her tan clutch purse on her dressing table and then springs over toward the bed, extending a hand and clasping my wrist. She yanks me up to my feet and then widens her eyes. "Remember," she says sternly, "drink as much as you can at Dean's, because once we get to the beach, that's it. No more booze." Her bottom lip juts out at the idea of alcohol having a time limit attached to it.

"Got it," I say. She lets go of me and twirls for the door while I pull on my sneakers. I reach back for my gray sweater on the bed and slip it on over my shoulders. Because the party is on the beach, I'm preparing myself for the ocean breeze. I steal a glance at myself in the mirror as I pass, deeming myself acceptable. "Let's go."

The two of us head downstairs and into the kitchen, where Dawn is busy stacking the groceries into the cupboards. She pauses when she sees us and tuts.

Rachael's voice becomes overwhelmingly sweet as she twirls her hair around her index finger and asks, "Mom, can you give us a ride to Dean's?"

"Rachael, you know I don't want you to go to this party," Dawn says, looking doubtful as she places a can of pineapple rings into the cupboard. She shuts the door and turns to study us, her arms folded across her chest. "You're not even old enough."

"But Mom," Rachael gasps in horror, "everyone's going. Do you want me to be a loser? Is that all I am to you? A loser?"

I want to laugh at Rachael's acting ability as Dawn arches her eyebrows at her daughter, like she's debating with herself whether she should play cool-mom or loser-mom. Eventually she must opt for cool-mom, because she heaves a defeated sigh. "Don't drink too much," she says quietly, and I think she'll cave in to Rachael's request for a ride. "You too, Eden. Do your parents know you're drinking?"

"My parents are divorced," I deadpan.

Rachael lets out a tremendous laugh, but Dawn just looks flustered. Thankfully she doesn't press the question any further, because if she did, I'd have to tell her that yes, of course my dad and Ella are completely aware that I'm going to a party to consume as much alcohol as I possibly can. Actually, they think I'm at the movies.

"Wait by the car," Dawn tells us. She wipes her hands on her pants and then presses her palm to her forehead, soothing away the headache we seem to have caused. "I'll get the keys."

Rachael throws me a triumphant grin and then the two of us hurl ourselves down the hallway and out the front door before her mother can change her mind. We hover outside on the driveway by the Honda Civic for a few long minutes. Rachael takes advantage of the wait by checking her makeup in the right wing mirror while I stare at the house across the street. Tyler's car is still parked on the road. It makes me wonder if he's still inside, still getting ready for tonight by showering himself in that stupid Bentley cologne that Tiffani adores so much. The thought makes me grind my teeth, so I turn away from the house and stare at my reflection in the car window. Rachael's done a good job of my makeup, so good that I wonder if it's even me that's peering back.

"That divorce line is an awesome way to dodge questions," Rachael says approvingly, her head popping over the car roof as she straightens up.

"I think I'll use it more often," I say.

We hear the thud of the front door closing as Dawn unwillingly walks over to the vehicle. She unlocks it and we all clamber inside, me in the backseat and Rachael in the passenger. It's not until Dawn is backing out of the driveway that I suddenly feel nervous and slightly nauseous. I shouldn't be. I've already been to a number of parties over the summer, because it's the only hobby these people seem to have, but this time I'm especially apprehensive. Perhaps it's because this is a community event, not just some trashy house party, or perhaps it's because I know we're underage yet we're going anyway, daring to blend in with the adults. But maybe it's this: I'll be there, Tyler will be there, and Tiffani will be there.

The ride to Dean's house only takes five minutes and it occurs to me only when we're outside that I've never been to Dean's place before. I wasn't even aware that he lived in the same neighborhood as Rachael and me. Dean's car is parked out front, and I think of the gas money again.

Abruptly, Dawn brings the car to a complete stop by the sidewalk and angles her body around to face Rachael. Her expression is earnest, her forehead creasing with worry. "Please don't get drunk," she says very softly. "Remember you're four years away from being twenty-one, so be grateful I'm letting you go out in the first place. Be responsible."

Rachael heaves a dramatic sigh and stares longingly at the house. "I know, Mom."

Dawn cranes her neck to face me, a small smile on her lips. "You be careful too, Eden."

"Thanks," I say, but my tone sounds almost sarcastic and for a split second I worry that she'll assume I've got a serious attitude.

Finally Rachael swings open the car door and steps out, so I follow suit and wave goodbye to her mom before leaping up the driveway after her. Thank God I'm not wearing heels; it's so much easier to do everything without them.

"My mom is so embarrassing," Rachael apologizes, and she genuinely does look mortified. Honestly, I didn't think Dawn was that bad. My mom would be the same. "I get the same thing every time I go out. It's like she's trying to make me feel guilty."

I laugh when she shudders, so she glares at me and then sticks out her tongue. Nudging her to the side, I jog up to the porch, my hands trembling slightly with nerves. I can hear music pumping from inside, voices laughing.

I throw Rachael a wary glance as she comes bounding over to me. "Do I knock?"

"Do you knock?" she echoes in disbelief. "Oh my God, Eden, no. Just go in already." Without waiting for me to ask any more seemingly obvious and apparently stupid questions, she reaches past me and throws open the door, a dazzling smile on her face as she floats over the threshold.

I follow her into the house and immediately we're in the living room, the kitchen through an archway ahead of us. The music drills into my ears as I click the door shut behind us, my eyes scanning the place as I try to figure out who's all here already. Apparently, everyone. Rachael is right: We're the last ones to arrive, and our friends all pause around the island in the kitchen to stare at us. They look like they're in the middle of taking shots.

"It's about time!" Jake yells as Dean shuffles around them all to get to us.

Meghan's standing with two cups of alcohol, one in each hand, alternating between them. She somehow manages to grin at us in between swigs. Jake's standing next to two guys I've never spoken to and I wonder why they're here.

Dean wanders over to us, a beer in his hand and a smile on his face. "C'mon, guys, you need to catch up!"

"You don't have to worry about us catching up," Rachael says, smirking as she elbows me in the ribs. "We can drink fast."

I almost want to say something. If Rachael has only learned one thing about me this entire summer, it should be that I'm a terrible drinker. Alcohol tastes like sewage, and drinking it fast is almost impossible for me, quite literally the equivalent of self-torture. Half the time the taste is so bitter and so strong that I can hardly even get it down my throat without gagging. But I keep quiet and say, "Yeah, we can drink super fast."

Dean arches a brow at me, as though he knows I'm bullshitting. "We're about to play shot roulette." He points to the kitchen, where everyone seems to have dived into deep conversation with one another, and we follow him through to where a roulette wheel is set up. Each glass looks gross, each one containing a different concoction from the glass next to it, and I can't figure out the numerous types of booze they've been using to fill them.

"Eden, I don't think you've met the guys yet, have you?" Dean asks as he pops the cap off a bottle of Twisted Tea and hands it to me, and I'm thankful that he hasn't handed me anything stronger. He nods in the direction of the two strangers standing next to Jake.

They both glance over from their conversation, their words tapering off as they both offer me an acknowledging smile. One is extremely tall, taller than Tyler, and the other is more on the short side. The tall one has a hard look to his face, like he's pissed off at everyone and could dropkick all of us in one go, and the shorter one is wearing a cap on top of his mound of brown hair.

"That's Jackson," Dean says as he points his beer to the guy with the cap, and then nods to the other. "And TJ."

"'Sup?" TJ says, but then he turns back to Jake and continues the conversation that we interrupted.

"They're on the team," Dean continues to explain. "Jackson's a wide receiver and TJ's a cornerback. Did you know I play football? I'm a linebacker. Middle linebacker, that is. Do you like football?"

I think it's the most I've ever heard Dean babble, nothing but a bunch of slurred sentences somehow strung together. "Dean," I say slowly. It's not quite the reply he's looking for. "How long have you been drinking?"

With a sheepish eye-roll, he holds up three fingers.

"Three hours?" I ask, and he nods. "You guys sure do take

this whole beach party thing seriously." With a small smile, I pat him on the shoulder and move around the island to fetch myself a straw, slipping it into my drink and taking a long sip. The music is still loud and the voices are even louder, despite there only being nine of us.

That's when I realize there are two people I haven't spotted yet. I have yet to see Tyler and Tiffani. I study the kitchen once more to make sure I haven't just missed them, but they're definitely not here. For a second I think that Rachael and I aren't the last ones to arrive after all, but then something catches my eye.

There are two figures hovering outside the kitchen window, and, of course, it's Tyler and Tiffani. I stare through the glass at them, both of them oblivious to my watching eyes, and soon my face contorts with disgust. Tyler's smoking while Tiffani wraps herself around his torso as though she's clinging on for dear life. She kind of is.

Taking a long sip of my drink, I place the bottle on the counter and head outside. No one inside notices me slipping through the kitchen door to the back yard, but Tyler and Tiffani do. They both fall silent as I click the door shut and spin around to face them. Tiffani's lips are pressed together, irritated that I've interrupted their beautiful romance. I wish Meghan were here to snort.

"Can you go back inside?" she says, and she doesn't even attempt to say it nicely. Her tone is sour, her attitude bitter. "And, like, give us some space?"

"Back off," Tyler mutters, and I think Tiffani is just as surprised as I am that he's actually defending me. She glares at him and then turns back to me.

Ignoring her twisted face, almost as twisted as my iced tea,

I roll my eyes toward the joint in Tyler's hand. "What are you doing?"

"Relax," he says as he lifts it to his lips, placing it between his teeth, and murmurs, "It's just a cigarette."

"That's all you're gonna smoke tonight, right?" I give him a hard look. "Just cigarettes?"

In the few seconds that it takes him to take a drag, drawing the smoke into his lungs and exhaling it back into the air, he just stares at me with a sense of nonchalance in his eyes. "Go back inside if you're just gonna interrogate me, sis."

Tiffani laughs, but I barely even pay attention to her, my eyes are so fixed on Tyler, everything else around him slightly blurred through the smoke. He hasn't spoken to me in such a condescending tone in weeks. Nothing gave him the right to do so back then, and nothing gives him the right to do so now. I almost want to slap him across the face, but then I notice the way his eyes harden right before he glances away and takes another drag. It hits me then that he's acting, because acting is all he ever does. His façade is back, the stupid badass front that gives him a sense of control over himself and a sense of power over the rest of us. *Of course,* I think, *Tiffani is here.* He can't have her knowing the truth about what he is, which is lost. Totally and completely lost.

"We're about to play shot roulette," I say stiffly, acting as though I didn't hear what he just said. "So if you wanna join in, then you should probably come inside."

"I'm totally game!" Tiffani announces. She pulls away from Tyler and skips over to my side, her balance not quite steady, her eyes wide with excitement. I give her a quick sideways glance, wondering what her priorities in life are. At the moment, I'm guessing Louis Vuitton purses and tequila shots and my stepbrother.

My eyes drift back to Tyler, who is now taking a sip of beer in between each puff of his cigarette. I tilt my head and ask, "Are you joining us?"

"Obviously," he says with that same haughty tone, and at that I shake my head and make my way inside to join the rest of the preparty.

Everyone is gathered into a huddle around the island, circling the roulette wheel like vultures. Jake has the balls in his hands, throwing them up into the air and catching them again, which I find rather impressive considering the fact that he's a little tipsy. He stops juggling and points a finger at Tiffani and me as he motions for us to come over.

I slide myself in between Rachael and Dean, grabbing my Twisted Tea from the counter as I pass. Dean throws his arm over my shoulders and drinks his beer with the other. He jerks around almost too roughly, to the point where my neck hurts, and then Jake kicks off the game, flicking the balls onto the wheel. TJ and Jackson pound their fists against the worktop and I swear the shot glasses almost fly into the air, but Jake grabs his drink and tips it down his throat.

"What the fuck is that?" he splutters in disgust a few seconds later as his face scrunches up at the foul taste of the brown liquid.

TJ howls with laughter and claps his huge hands together. "Mud water from the back yard!"

Jake presses his lips into a firm line as he fires TJ a furious glare, and then he shoves him to the side and pushes his way over to the sink, where he promptly spits all over it. While Jake is on the verge of throwing up, Tyler finally comes sauntering in, hands in his pockets, face blank. He joins the game: the awful game, the game of the unknown. I'm even more worried than I was a minute ago. Who knows what other cruel jokes the guys have thrown into the wheel?

"I can't wait to get to the beach!" Dean yells into my ear, and it's so loud that I quickly draw myself away from him. "I really, really can't wait!"

"We need to get really drunk," Rachael whispers into my other ear. I realize then that I've placed myself between the drunk and the drunk-wannabe. "Even Meghan is beating us!"

This is true. I don't know how long everyone else has been here for, but they're all moving over the tipsy borderline. Either they've been drinking for hours or they've been drinking extremely fast. Most likely a combination of both. As Dean said, Rachael and I need to catch up, and quickly. I glance around the circle of my friends—my friends plus TJ and Jackson—and they're all grinning and yelling at the roulette wheel and looking like they're having the best damn time of their lives. Except Tyler. I notice then that he's standing behind Tiffani, hovering a step or two back from her, like he's terrified to touch her. And he's staring at me. Only me.

The whole situation is only stressing me out. Tyler's still confused about the best way to handle our circumstances, and Tiffani's grinning, bearing a huge smile that conveys a sense of authority as she glances at everyone around her one by one. I want to forget about the two of them for a little while. I don't want to overthink the situation I'm in with Tyler, because I'll only end up ruining my night, and I don't want to attempt to figure out what Tiffani is thinking, because the only thing that's rushing into my mind is that she thinks I'm not reckless.

My grip tightens around the bottle in my hand and I quickly force the biggest grin that I can possibly manage upon my face. I spin around to Rachael. I'll show Tiffani reckless. "Okay, let's get drunk."

"I know where Dean's parents hide the good stuff," she whispers. She grabs my wrist, yanks me out of Dean's grip and we sneak away from the game. We hover by the archway to the living room for a few seconds, and when everyone gets distracted by another mud-water shot that Meghan has just drunk, Rachael gives me a thumbs up and we skip through the living room and into a small hallway, where the music sounds muffled and the air is cold.

"Are they here?" I ask.

"Who?"

"His parents."

Rachael smiles and points to the roof. "Upstairs."

There's another door and she yanks it open, opening up a dark, cold room. It's not until she pushes me down a step and my hand hits a car that I realize we're standing in the garage.

"Where's the light?" Rachael mutters as she fumbles around on the wall, searching for a switch, and when she finally finds it she flicks it on.

I'm standing next to a black BMW and I quickly take a step back from it, careful not to touch it again, and then I glance around. There are stacks of cardboard boxes in each corner, but the walls are completely covered in red and white football merchandise. There are football jerseys in glass display frames, huge flags and banners that stretch from the top of the wall to the floor, a small shelf with gold helmets in cases and a couple footballs, and then a collection of photo frames.

"His dad's a total 49ers fan," Rachael muses as she dances

toward the shelves on the far wall, which is lined with bottles of alcohol. I watch her for a second as she picks up a few of the bottles and examines them, nodding her head in approval. "I told you I knew where the good stuff is!"

Rachael's still scanning the booze, so I move around the car and run my eyes over the photos on the wall. A smile plays at my lips as I recognize Dean, draped in a San Francisco 49ers jersey and a red cap on his head, a few years younger than he is now. A man stands by his side, equally as dressed up for the game as Dean, and one hand rests on Dean's shoulder while the other holds a hot dog. It must be his dad, and they're standing outside the entrance to Levi's Stadium. There are a lot of pictures like this, of Dean and his dad. It's like every time they attended a 49ers game, they documented the moment.

One photo stands out. Instead of there being just two people in it, there are four. Dean and his dad are in their permanent pose, but on one side of them there's a boy standing next to Dean, both of them around the age of twelve. Dean's friend is dark-haired and green-eyed.

"We're going to drink this tequila and we're going to drink it straight, like total badasses, without the salt or the lime," Rachael states solemnly, her chin raised, bottle of Cazadores in hand as she twirls over to me.

I throw a skeptical glance down to the bottle before I swallow and point to the photo. "Is that Tyler?"

For a second, her eyes widen and then narrow into slits as she leans toward the photograph to get a better look. "Jesus Christ, he looks like a fetus!"

I stare at him again, the Tyler in the picture. The jersey on his back matches Dean's, but his expression doesn't. Dean's smiling wide, Tyler's frowning. In fact, he's not even looking at the camera. He's looking off to the side, his eyes heavy and his attitude far from what you would expect of a kid attending a 49ers game. Even his body is slightly angled to the side, despite the fact that Dean's arm is thrown over his shoulders. Maybe Tyler just hates the 49ers. Maybe he's a Chargers fan.

On the other side of the photograph, there's another man standing next to Dean's dad. His hair is black, his back is to the camera, and he's pointing to the name on the back of the red jersey he's wearing. It's personalized. It says "GRAYSON."

Something flutters in my stomach. I move back from the photo and my eyebrows knit together, my lips parted. Tyler's dad. It's the first time I've ever seen him, or at least some of him. I have an overwhelming need to see his face.

I turn back to Rachael. "Is that his dad?"

"Dean's?" She glances up from beneath her eyelashes while she flicks off the cap of the tequila. "Yeah."

"No," I say. "Tyler's dad. Is that him?"

Rachael fully looks up now. She stares at me and then shifts her eyes to the photograph again. "Yeah," she says again with a shrug. "The older Tyler gets the more I think they look identical. At least from what I remember. His dad is probably super old with a beard by now. Do they let people shave in jail?"

"I don't know," I say, but my attention has turned back to the picture. There's something unsettling about it. Dean and his dad look so happy, so thrilled to be at the 49ers game, beaming proudly next to each other. Yet next to them, it's quite the opposite. Tyler and his dad are standing at opposite ends of the photograph, and Tyler just looks lifeless, with his heavy eyes and slumped shoulders. It makes me wonder what the circumstances were and why he wasn't as happy and thrilled as Dean was to be at that game. "What is it with Tyler and his dad? I just know that there's something."

Rachael shakes her head and presses a finger to her lips as though to silence herself. "I don't know. We have this unspoken rule in the group. We don't talk about Tyler's dad unless we have a death wish, and we don't talk about STDs in front of Meghan, because her biggest fear in life is waking up with chlamydia."

I ignore this unspoken rule and press the matter. "What if he was adopted?"

"Adopted?" Rachael considers the possibility for a moment as she stares at the photo again. She shakes her head. "Nope, he's definitely his dad's kid. Too similar not to be. Now c'mon," she says. "We need to hurry up! We're gonna fall behind."

I frown and look away from the photograph. She's waving around the bottle that's in her hand. "Okay, okay, I'm ready."

A huge grin forms on her lips and she takes a deep breath. "It's going to taste like you're on fire, but it'll get us drunk in no time, so grow some lady balls and suck it up."

"God," I say, but I clench my fists by my side and squeeze my eyes shut, mentally preparing myself. The last time I drank tequila I made a beeline for the sink. And that was with the salt and the lime. "I'm ready."

Rachael gives me a nod before she presses the bottle to her lips and takes a quick shot. She immediately doubles over and presses a hand to her mouth, her arm extending as she shoves the bottle into my hand. "Oh my GOD," she gasps, her face scrunching up as she shakes her head, as though it'll get rid of the taste.

I almost chicken out then. What's the point of putting

myself through the torture of tequila? I stare doubtfully at the bottle while Rachael heaves next to the car, waving her hands erratically in front of her mouth, and it makes me question what I'm doing. But then I remember what Tiffani said on Thursday at the mall, about her not having to worry about me getting drunk, about me not being reckless.

My grip tightens around the bottle of Cazadores and I tilt it to my lips, throwing my head back and pouring as much of the tequila into my mouth as I possibly can. And all at once, my mouth feels like it's on fire, burning from the bitterness. Tequila looks like urine and tastes like gasoline.

I almost drop the bottle as I quickly rush for a swig of my Twisted Tea, and suddenly it tastes like water in comparison, so I keep on drinking. And drinking, and drinking, until I've completely downed the entire remainder of the bottle. I collapse back against the wall, exhausted and out of breath, and I stand there breathing heavily for a few long seconds.

"Again," Rachael says. She reaches for the bottle of tequila and yanks it from my hand, repeating the pattern of tilt-swig-die once more.

I manage to follow the cycle, and we pass the bottle back and forth to one another until we get to our fourth round and I simply can't do it anymore. The second the tequila hits my tongue I splutter it everywhere, unable to force it down my throat. It goes all over the side of the BMW, the tequila running down the side of driver's door. I throw Rachael a shocked glance.

"Eden!" she screams, but bursts into laughter immediately after and doesn't stop for another three minutes.

I'm horrified. Dean will hate me, his parents will sue, and I'll end up in juvenile hall for criminal damage. "Why is there a car in here?" I yell in exasperation, and I feel my cheeks grow red.

"It's a garage!"

"I thought this was the basement!" I scream back at her in between a fit of laughter, and I find my footing becoming unstable and my body swaying into the walls, and the only thing that I can think is this: *Tequila is a bitch.*

I know Rachael is a lightweight, I just didn't figure that I'd be equally as intolerant of alcohol as she is. Skipping dinner probably wasn't the best idea, and now that stupid tequila rhyme is starting to make sense. *One tequila, two tequila, three tequila, floor.*

When I glance down, the floor is exactly where Rachael is. She's sprawled out on the concrete, giggling and not even bothering to push herself up. She's happy just lying there looking like a dead seal.

"We need to keep going!" I say as I reach down for her arm and try my hardest to yank her up and onto her feet, but I only lose my balance and topple on top of her, probably crushing her spine.

"Yes, yes! Keep going!" Rachael shouts through hysterical laughter as I roll off her.

"What's next on the agenda, Rachy baby?" I snort. Everything seems so hilarious, so carefree, so *reckless*. I can't help myself. I'm lying on my back now by Rachael's side, staring at the white ceiling of the garage, and it's only just occurred to me that the walls are all painted. "This garage is so beautiful."

Rachael's still laughing, so hard that she's not even making a sound anymore. Her lips are parted and her eyes are squeezed shut and the only thing I can hear is the sound of her choking on the air. "What is wrong with us?"

I push myself up onto my knees and stare at her, forcing my lips into a straight line. Fifteen minutes of tequila shots and the pair of us are totally buzzed. Remarkable. "We need to keep going! Drink as much as we can, remember?"

Rachael nods with enthusiasm and struggles to get to her feet, gripping the wing mirror of the BMW for support. If I were sober I'd be worried about damaging the car, but I'm not sober, so I somehow couldn't care less.

"Jägermeister!" Rachael cheers. She grabs the dark bottle from among the collection on the shelves and turns back to me. Grinning, she holds the bottle up in the air and toasts, "To alcohol poisoning!"

Another fifteen minutes and two deadly shots later, I'm wondering why I was stupid enough to drink so much in such a short time frame. It's the type of thing your parents and teachers warn you about, the type of thing that they tell you will kill you. But none of that matters. No one ever cares about the consequences, because in the moments between taking a drink and the effects hitting you, everything always seems like the best idea in the world. This explains why Rachael is on the hood of the car, using the Cazadores bottle as a microphone as she switches between performing the national anthem and stripteasing her way onto the roof.

"Eden, you are hilarious to get drunk with," she announces with a bow after her slightly warped rendition of 'The Star-Spangled Banner'. She's standing in her maxi skirt and her bra, having tossed her tube top to the ground.

The muffled music from inside the house grows louder all of a sudden, and when I glance away from Rachael's performance for a second I notice it's because the door to the pantry has opened. Dean's standing there with his arms folded across his chest. Both Rachael and I stop laughing, freezing in position, sheepish smirks on our faces.

"Rachael," Dean says slowly, "please get off the car."

Rachael bites her lip to stop from laughing as she sits down and attempts to slide off the roof of the vehicle, but she promptly falls off the side and hits the ground with a thud. The bottle of Cazadores smashes into a million pieces. I do the honor of laughing on her behalf as she groans through a series of giggles.

"Damn, Rachael," Dean mutters. "Watch the glass." He looks stone-cold sober now in comparison with us. He steps into the garage and leans down to pull Rachael up, grimacing in disgust at the state she's in, and once he's steadied her, he searches for her top on the floor. "We're ready to go," he says, but I can tell he's annoyed at us. While I'm still laughing in the corner, he pulls Rachael's top over her head and fixes her with a stern glare. "How much did you drink?"

Rachael doesn't answer his question, only glances over her shoulder and motions for me to come over. I awkwardly place the bottle of Jägermeister down on the ground and shuffle around the car, my eyes never meeting Dean's. He heaves a sigh and directs us back into the pantry and through into the living room, where Jake is holding open the front door.

"What the hell have you two been doing?" Jake asks. Rachael and I exchange a glance and laugh once more, because for some reason we just can't seem to stop.

Dean turns off the music and calls upstairs to his parents that we're leaving while I follow Rachael to the minivan outside. I vaguely hear Meghan tell me that Dean's older cousin doesn't mind chauffeuring us around despite the fact that there aren't even enough seats for us all. Nonetheless, we pile in (quite literally—Rachael ends up having to sit on my lap), and Dean and Jake follow behind us, and soon there are nine of us crammed into the vehicle. I'm too buzzed to even care that Tyler and Tiffani are in the very back seats, her body swung over his and her hands wrapped around his neck. She's laughing over the thumping music that's playing, but Tyler's not paying attention to her. His face is angled to the side as he stares out the window and for some reason, when I steal a glance over my shoulder, he looks the soberest of us all. Immediately, he senses my stare and his eyes flicker over to lock with mine.

I feel on top of the world, so all I can do is pull a giddy smile at him. My head isn't quite balancing on my shoulders, and he notices this, because he narrows his eyes into either a disapproving or a concerned look. I can't tell which, and I don't get much time to figure it out, because he returns to staring out the window.

And so the rest of us spend the journey cracking jokes while we laugh and laugh and laugh, and it makes me feel better knowing everyone is just as tipsy as Rachael and I are. Actually, we're not even tipsy. We're drunk, and it feels good.

27

The beach party is apparently a huge deal. Half of the beach, the one on the right of the pier, is sectioned off for the event, with roads closed and security guards patrolling the area. When we all tumble out of the minivan in the pier parking lot, I'm consumed by the noise of music and voices, and the atmosphere feels electric. I squint at the beach in front of us and I notice a stage set up right bang in the middle of the sand, with huge black speakers attached, and on it, there's a DJ entertaining the crowd.

"If any of you morons get us kicked out, I'll personally kick your ass," Jake threatens. He glances around us all, fixing us all with a warning glare. "Unless you're a girl. If you're a girl, you'll get the silent treatment."

And with that, we all head for the sand, our heads hanging down slightly as we pass some security guards. It makes me wonder if I look as drunk as I feel. I really hope not. I'll be kicked out within five minutes if I do, but thankfully we stagger onto the sand and blend in with the crowd of people around us. I expect the nine of us to stick together as a group, but we don't. The guys nod us goodbye for now and head off in one direction, and I'm surprised Tyler heads off without Tiffani.

"We should totally skinny dip!" Rachael suggests, her voice loud over the music. She catches the attention of some men around us and they give her a quick nod of encouragement.

"We should totally not skinny dip," Tiffani remarks. She shoots the guys a death glare and pushes us further into the crowd, and I'm so drunk that I almost twist my ankle just trying to walk.

Sand finds its way into my Converse and it is the most uncomfortable feeling in the entire world, so I simply kick off my shoes and bend down to pick them up, dangling them from my hands by the laces. I nod my head in sync with the beats of the music and am shoved from side to side by the people surrounding us. They're all clearly adults and of age, but I don't care.

"Jared and his friends are here!" Meghan screams at us over the noise, spinning around with a panicked expression. She touches her hair. "How do I look?"

"Like you're looking for trouble!" Rachael yells, which is true.

"I'll take it," Meg says, and then she blows us a kiss and worms her way through the crowd. I doubt she'll be coming back to join us anytime soon.

I'm now waving my shoes in the air and receiving glares from the people by my side, mostly because I keep almost whacking them in the face, but I feel too free and too on top of the world to apologize. Miraculously, I find myself dancing: wild and crazed dancing, but still dancing, which is rare for me. The DJ on the stage is playing house music and everyone has a hand bobbing in the air and my head feels fuzzy and even the ocean is starting to roll to one side.

I'm enjoying myself, jumping on the sand and waving my

shoes in the air, when Tiffani grabs my and Rachael's arms and draws us toward her. She doesn't look to be having as much fun as we are, and I can't tell if it's because she didn't drink as much or if it's because she thinks the event sucks.

"I'm gonna go find Tyler," she says loudly, and when she takes a step back I can just about make out that she looks pissed off.

"Nooooo!" Rachael protests. "Stay with us!"

"I need to keep an eye on him after what happened last year," she says with a shake of her head.

I narrow my eyes at her, my laces still tangled around my fingers, and I blow some hair out of my face. The evening sun is scorching. "What happened last year?"

Tiffani only glances sideways at me with an annoyed and disapproving look in her eyes. "Eden, please stop waving those things around." She reaches for my shoes and pulls them away from me, pulling a face at the lyrics written along the side, before sighing and handing them back to me. "You look stupid, so try and act a little normal. Now have fun, you two."

Rachael gives me a drunken shrug as Tiffani elbows her way out of the crowd. She's out of breath and so am I.

"What happened last year?" I ask again once my breathing is restored. Rachael's outline is slightly blurred, so I squint at her in order to see her better, but it doesn't help. My body feels like it's rolling from one side to the other, like the ocean.

"Tyler took some sketchy stuff," she says quietly into my ear as she leans in, careful that no one hears us, even though everyone is too busy partying, "and then he passed out and we all thought he died, but then he had a seizure and we were like, 'Oh, shit, he's not dead,' and yeah. We all dragged him back to Tiffani's place and she cried all night about how he made her look stupid in front of everyone. She locked herself in her bathroom and wouldn't come out, so the rest of us stayed over to make sure he was okay and he ended up being totally fine. It was super scary at the time, and now Tiffani's paranoid that he'll do something like that again." She's out of breath again by the time she stops talking and so she takes a dramatic gulp of air and then exhales.

I know for a fact that if I were sober I'd be concerned and I'd probably go and look for Tyler myself, but I'm too drunk to do any of that right now. I might also be mad at Tiffani for caring more about her reputation than Tyler's life, but I just pull a face and return to swaying, and eventually Rachael does too.

The thing about being drunk is that you seem to lose not only your senses but also track of time. It feels like it only takes ten minutes for me and Rachael to force our way to the front of the stage, but when I look up and see the darkening sky I realise much more time must have gone by. I'm sweating by now and when I look to my right, I realize I'm suddenly alone. Rachael has disappeared.

"Oh," I say. A laugh escapes my lips and I turn around and begin to dance my way out of the crowd, feeling slightly claustrophobic now. People are looking down on me with odd expressions. It's so obvious that I'm half a decade away from being old enough to be here.

Away from the stage, people are milling around on the sand, some socializing and others trying their hardest to pick up girls. The crowd of people is thinner back here, so I stop and take a moment to breathe. I don't feel as energetic anymore, and the booze high that I seemed to be on is wearing off as the night goes on, but I'm still past tipsy and I'm still enjoying every second of it. A fight breaks out near me and the security guards come bounding over, barking demands and breaking up the scuffle, dragging the two troublemakers away from the event.

I think that's when it hits me that I'm alone. Alone, and still slightly drunk. In that split second, a flood of panic drowns my body and I instantly reach into the pocket of my sweater to fetch my phone. There's only one problem. It's not there.

I check my other pocket, and then I check my bra, and then I check my shoes. No phone, and no cash either. Everything is gone. I don't know if everything has fallen out of my pockets and is now buried six feet under the sand, or if I've been robbed. Either way, I have no means of calling anyone. Now, just like everything else, if I were sober I would be smart enough to realize that it's not the end of the world, that the house is only a forty-minute walk away. But I'm not sober and so it is the end of the world.

Tears well in my eyes and I try to blink them away, but my lips begin to quiver and soon they're rolling down my cheeks. I pull my sweater around me and stare at the sand. I'm scared people notice me crying here like the dumbass sixteen-year-old that I am. I'm too young to be out here drunk and alone and mugged.

"Dammit, Eden," a voice mutters, and the warmness and familiarity makes me stop weeping. I glance up through tear-blurred eyes to find Tyler approaching me.

"Tiffani is looking for you," I sniff. I pull the sleeves of my sweater over my hands and dab at my eyes, careful not to smudge my mascara anymore than I already have. "Your girlfriend."

"What the hell are you crying for?" He ignores my words, steps directly in front of me and lowers his head, looking up at me from beneath his long eyelashes. The emerald in his eyes reminds me of seaweed.

"Everyone left," I tell him. My eyes are starting to sting and swell up. I sway to the right. "Tiffani, Meghan, Rachael . . . My phone's gone."

Tyler grasps my arm and steadies me, but he also looks me up and down. "How drunk are you?"

"Are *you* drunk?"

"Not anymore." He presses his lips together as he thinks for a moment. Leaning forward, he untangles the laces of my shoes from around my fingers and then drops my Chucks to the sand. "Put them back on. There's trash everywhere."

When I tear my eyes away from him and glance down, I notice that he's right. The beach is littered with food packaging and crushed soda cans and lighters. *I've been dancing on top of all this crap,* I think. Quickly, I slip on my shoes, and the sand inside them feels uncomfortable again. But I feel safe now that Tyler is here, so I grin at him despite my blotchy makeup.

"Your dad is going to kill you," he mutters, but not exactly to me. He heaves a sigh as he scratches the top of his head, trying to figure out what to do.

I don't intentionally set out to make it difficult for him, but I'm feeling recharged and ready to have fun again, so I twirl away from him. I come to a stop ten feet away and turn back to face him with a playful smirk on my lips. His eyes narrow with concern as he watches, waits. People keep walking through the gap between us, but the moment it's clear I throw myself onto the ground and forward roll my way back to him.

It doesn't work too well. I end up on my side, my legs tangled around each other, my shoulder possibly dislocated. I hear people around me laughing.

"Get off the ground," Tyler orders. I feel him grab my body and yank me upright. "What did I just tell you about the trash?"

"I loooove this beach," I drawl slowly. My head feels heavy and I topple to the left, but Tyler quickly catches me and holds me upright by my shoulders. "I'm going to come back next summer just for this party!"

"Are you coming back next summer?" He looks down at me with a solemn expression and urgency in his voice, and in that split second it's like all the alcohol in my bloodstream suddenly evaporates.

"I don't know," I say. "It depends if my dad wants me back or not."

"I hope he does," Tyler murmurs, his hands still on my body, still holding me. "I know I do."

My brief sober moment doesn't last long and I'm back to swaying against his embrace, not quite doing anything purposely. His words barely register in my mind. My swaying develops into an attempt at dancing, but I'm vaguely aware that I just look like a complete fool.

"You're drawing attention to yourself," Tyler hisses against my ear as his hands tighten on me, so tight that they restrict my movement, which is exactly what he's trying to do. "You're gonna get us kicked out."

"But I'm twenty-one!" I yell at him, laughing through my words. I wiggle under his grasp and it only makes me giggle at myself even more.

"Oh my God," Tyler groans under his breath. He turns

his face to the side and stares at the sand, his jaw clenched, eyes shut. He takes a deep breath, lets go of my body, walks around me, and, in one swift movement, bends and pulls me onto his back. "You need to sober the fuck up," he mutters as he starts to walk.

My arms are slung around his neck and it's possible I'm choking him to death as I cling onto him. His firm hands are under my thighs, my legs are wrapped around his waist, and he's walking so effortlessly that the thought of me not weighing much gives me a moment of satisfaction. I rest my head on his shoulder and blow air against his neck as he continues to carry me across the beach.

"Troy-James," Tyler calls out, and the unfamiliar name makes me lift my head in curiosity as Tyler comes to halt.

There's a small group of people, three of them, standing in front of us, and they all spin around to Tyler's voice. There's two girls and . . . TJ. The guy from Dean's, the guy that's the cornerback. Troy-James. I mentally piece the obvious together and I feel exceptionally clever when I do.

"What's up?" Troy-James, or TJ, says. The hard expression he wore earlier is long gone and he looks like he's having fun. This is understandable given the fact that there are two clearly older girls hovering by his side. They both offer me sympathetic smiles.

"I need your apartment," Tyler says straightaway. "You're still on Ocean Avenue, right?"

"Bro." TJ blinks for a while and then exchanges a quick glance with the girls he seems to have charmed. He settles his eyes back on Tyler. "What are your plans, man?"

Tyler shrugs as he flicks his eyes over his shoulder at me, the movement causing me to jolt against his body, and then he says, "Sobering her up. Her dad'll kill her if she goes home like this."

"Dude, you're kind of messing up my plans," TJ mutters in a strained voice. He pulls a face and squints at us.

"My place is free," one of the girls comments, and with that, TJ reaches into the pocket of his shorts and tosses Tyler the keys to his apartment. Just. Like. That.

"Leave 'em under the doormat," he says.

Tyler manages to squeeze in a thank you before TJ and the girls head off. I feel him sigh again as he tightens his grip on my legs and starts to walk again, walking and walking until I realize that we're heading away from the party.

"Why are we going to his apartment?" I mumble into his shirt, because it's almost impossible to keep my head up now. "Why does he even have an apartment?"

"Because you're just embarrassing yourself out here," he says with a chuckle, and it makes me wish that I could see his face right now, so I could look at his eyes and wonder what's going through his mind. But I'm still too tipsy for that. "And his parents are, like, millionaires. They bought him an apartment down here for his sixteenth birthday. Who the hell does that?"

"Millionaires," I reply. He laughs again.

I don't mind leaving the party. I've already lost my phone and my money and my friends back there, and now that the alcohol is wearing off and the sun is beginning to set, I just want to go home. Of course, going home isn't an option right now. Dad thinks I'm at the movies, watching some mediocre love story, but really I'm being carried away from a party because I took too many shots earlier. I'm just thankful that it's Tyler who ended up coming to my rescue. If Jake or Dean or even Meghan had tried to escort me away, I would have put up a fight.

"You can put me down, you know," I murmur after ten minutes of nonstop walking on Tyler's part. I'm worried I'm hurting him.

"What, so you can get hit by a car? No way," he says curtly as he pauses on the edge of the sidewalk. He throws a quick glance in both directions and then drifts across the avenue. I can still hear the music from the stage.

"You're missing the rest of the party," I say, but he doesn't reply.

He carries me over to the row of apartments and condos and hotels on Ocean Avenue, the buildings that I've jogged past on so many of my runs, the ones overlooking the beach. We slow down by a four-storey building, and Tyler carefully carries me up the steps and pauses outside the entrance. Carefully, he slides me off his back. My legs feel like jelly when I try to stand.

"How are you feeling?" he asks without glancing up, too busy fumbling around with the key and the lock.

"Embarrassed," I admit. I'm gradually sobering up after my last drink, almost three hours ago, and I'm starting to become more aware of how ridiculous I've been acting. I vaguely remember spitting all over Dean's parents' car.

Tyler finally gets the door open and he reaches back for my arm to pull me over the threshold and into the lobby of the condo building, which is bright with polished flooring. "We've all been there," he muses, trying to comfort me.

"Like you last year?" My tone sounds almost contemptuous, but I don't mean it to. I'm just curious. Always curious.

Tyler stops walking, abruptly halting in the middle of the

lobby. He cranes his neck to stare back at me, his expression immediately hardening as he narrows his eyes. I bite down on my lower lip and wait for his outburst, for his aggression to take over, but it never does. He just shakes his head and yanks me into the elevator.

"206," he says quietly as he presses the button for the second floor, and he barely looks at me in the seconds that it takes for us to get there. His fingers are still wrapped around my wrist.

Unit 206 is at the front of the building. I stare down at the doormat beneath my feet, finding it more interesting than it actually is, studying the pattern. Normally I wouldn't care, but it appears tequila is creative and enjoys the art of doormats. I only stop when I'm pulled into the condo.

And God, it's really pretty.

The living room is basking in the glow from the sunset that's shining in through the floor-to-ceiling windows around the room. Everything has a deep orange cast to it and it looks really beautiful. It's the type of sunset that you only ever see in photos, and most of the time they're Photoshopped. But up here in this condo with the huge windows overlooking the beach, it captures the essence of real beauty. I stare at it for a while.

"Here," Tyler says softly from behind me, catching my attention. I finally tear my eyes away from the windows and look at him. He's holding a glass of water, which he forces into my hand. "Drink it. Now."

A smile toys at my lips as I lift the glass and take a long swig, only now realizing how dehydrated I am. It feels refreshing and cool against my throat, so I end up drinking the entire thing in a matter of seconds.

"Sit down," Tyler orders. He takes the empty glass from my hand and nods in the direction of the couch behind me. When I don't move immediately, he presses his hand to my shoulder and directs me over.

"It looks so pretty," I say once I'm safely perched on the couch. I stretch out and get comfy, my body slumped back against the cushions, my eyes focused on the windows. If I listen closely, I can just about hear the faint pumping of music. "Doesn't it?"

"Sure it does," Tyler says from a few feet away. I rotate my body to face him, crossing my legs and watching him in silence as he fills up the glass again by the faucet. He brings it over to me, his hands wet, and then he dries them off on his jeans once he's passed the glass to me.

The quietness of the room contrasts with the noise of the party across the street, but there's something relaxing about it all, about the faintness of the music and the brightness of the sun as it dips below the horizon. Tyler sits down on the edge of the couch, several inches away from me, and just stares while I drink my second round of water.

"You need to sleep this off," he tells me. He's still looking at me in disapproval, and it feels odd having our roles reversed. Normally I'm the one dealing with him. "Come on." Reaching for the glass in my hand, he takes it away from me again and places it on the coffee table. He moves his hand back to mine. I flinch, but he doesn't seem to notice. Delicately, he pulls me up onto my feet as he stands, his other hand grasping my waist to prevent me from losing my balance. "You good?"

"Good," I confirm.

He turns around then, but he doesn't unlock our hands, only squeezes his fingers around mine while he leads me through the kitchen and into a hall. We stop outside the door at the very end, and Tyler shoves it open to reveal a small bedroom. He pulls me inside.

I slide off my shoes and kick them to the side, almost subconsciously, and make a move toward the huge bed that's occupying most of the floor space, but Tyler slides his hand under my knees and scoops me straight off the ground and into his arms instead.

His face is only inches from mine, so the only thing I can do is stare at him. There's nothing else I can do. His eyes are so beautiful, so intriguing, that it's impossible not to find yourself drawn to them. He's not even looking back at me, but I can feel his heart beating through his chest and the way it's speeding up. And then, almost as quickly as he picked me up, he's gently laying me down on the bed and pulling back the sheets.

"I'll go get your water," he murmurs, almost shyly, and bites his lip as he turns and leaves the room.

I glance around me while he's gone. There's a mirror on the wall to my right, and the second I lay eyes on my blurred reflection, I gasp. I look horrific. My hair, which I spent over an hour straightening, has returned to its natural wave and feels knotted and gross. The same goes for my makeup, which Rachael slaved over. One of the fake eyelashes she applied is missing. I quickly reach for the other and pull it off, sticking it to the bedside drawer.

"Here," Tyler says, and I jump, a little startled. He's filled the glass back up to the brim again and he lays it down on the drawer, right next to the eyelash I've just torn off. "Water and sleep: the only way to sober up and minimize your hangover as much as possible." He laughs a little as he moves around the bed, heading over to the window and pulling the curtains shut.

"You should take your own advice sometimes," I comment, but I'm only teasing him. I'm still feeling a little buzzed. "Next time you're drunk, I'm just gonna chant, 'Water and sleep, water and sleep.'"

When he turns back around from the window, he's biting back a smile that's fighting its way onto his lips. He just shakes his head and then nods at me. "Get some sleep, Eden."

I let out a laugh and then finally give in. He's right, after all. I really do need to get some sleep. Grabbing the sheets, I slide down onto my back and get comfy, burying my head into the pillow as I fluff it up a little. I'm just about to close my eyes when I notice that Tyler's lingering by the door, a little unsure of himself, like he doesn't know whether he should leave the room or stay.

I lift my head up a few inches so that I can look at him properly. I'm not laughing anymore. "Are you going back to the party?"

"I don't know," he says quietly. His eyes fall to the carpet as he shrugs, but he doesn't glance back up again. "I mean, Tiffani's probably looking everywhere for me."

"Oh."

"I'll let you sleep," he says, his eyes gradually meeting mine. And then he smiles again, and it's another one of those smiles of his that I adore. A genuine smile. Sincere. Gentle and reassuring.

I lay my head back down on the pillow and roll over onto my side, squeezing my eyes shut as he leaves the room. As I'm left in the silence, all of me craves for him to come back and stay. I want him to be lying next to me, just like the other night when he crawled into my bed in the middle of the night. I just want to know that he's here with me. I want to feel his warmth and his touch. That's all I need. It's all I'm missing.

I think that's the moment I realize I'm in love with him.

* * *

A few hours later, I'm stirring awake. The heat in the room is suddenly unbearable and I wake up almost sweating, my face flushed. Immediately I reach for my water on the bedside drawer through the darkness as I sit up. It's warm by now, but I gulp it down nonetheless.

"How are you feeling?"

I immediately stop drinking, almost spluttering the water all over myself, and fire my eyes over to the corner of the room, right next to the window. It's dark, but I can still make out Tyler's outline, not to mention the vividness of his eyes. The more I focus on him, the clearer he becomes. Soon I can almost see his entire face.

"Better," I say. This is true. The room is no longer spinning and my thoughts are logical again. Now my only problem is that I'm just too hot and extremely thirsty. "What time is it?"

"Three," Tyler says. He darts his eyes to the window and laughs so quietly that it's almost inaudible. I notice that the curtains are open again, and from my position on the bed all I can see is the dark sky and the moon. There's still the faint lull of music echoing from the beach. "The party's still going strong."

I look back over to him and my eyebrows furrow in confusion. "Didn't you go back?"

"No," he murmurs. His voice falls even quieter than it already is, almost on the verge of becoming a whisper. "I was worried that you'd throw up or something. Plus it was probably best that I just stayed away from it all."

He chews on his lower lip and suddenly he appears sad, uncomfortable. It wasn't that he looked super happy before or anything, but there's this sort of shift in his expression that makes him look vulnerable in that moment. He appears worn out, deflated even.

"What's wrong?" I ask, the glass of water clutched tightly in my hands. It's warm against my skin.

"Nothing," he says. Leaning forward, he rests his elbows on his knees and interlocks his hands, staring at nothing in particular.

"I know there's something wrong." I take another sip of my water, but my gaze never leaves his face. I'm scared I'll miss something, like a flash of emotion in his eyes or a sense of aggravation, but so far he's doing a good job at remaining pretty aloof. "What's wrong, Tyler?" I ask again.

He lifts his head up and glances sideways at me. With a mighty sigh, his shoulders sink. "It's just . . ."

"Just what?"

"This time last year," he says slowly, but then his words taper off and he looks away again.

"You passed out," I finish. His eyes flash back up to mine, and he looks confused. "Rachael told me. You passed out because of the drugs."

"Just drink your water," he mumbles under his breath, and he gets to his feet. His face is dark, a shadow cast over it.

I do as he commands, finishing up the remainder of the water in my hand, and then I set the glass down on the bedside drawer. I push the sheets off me and shift my body off the bed, getting to my feet and edging my way toward him. My legs feel stiff. "Why do you do it?"

Out of nowhere, he throws his hands up in despair and I quickly take a step back, wary that I'll end up angering him. "Why are you asking me about this again?"

"Because I want the truth."

"I already gave you the goddamn truth," he snaps. His cheeks are tinted with a red hue as fury builds up inside of him. Tyler hates the truth; Tyler hides the truth. "I do what I do to distract myself."

"From what?" I almost scream the words at him, because I just want to uncover the truth about him already, because I'm fed up knowing absolutely nothing about him. "That's what I want to know, Tyler. I want to know why you need all these bullshit distractions."

People like Tyler have a reason. No one ever acts the way he does simply to distract themselves. No one. I need to know what it is that makes him act the way he does and what makes him say the things he says.

"Distractions make everything easier," he eventually hisses. His eyes are sharp, eyebrows so furrowed that lines appear across his forehead.

"Makes what easier?"

He grits his teeth together and balls his hands into fists by his sides, the veins under his skin straining from the pressure. I can almost see the gears in his mind shifting as he falls silent for the longest of moments. His voice is quiet yet threatening when he speaks again. "Stop, Eden."

"Stop what?" I take a step closer to him and I try to stare back evenly, willing myself not to back down like I have before. This time I'm determined to get the truth, and no amount of glaring on his part will throw me off.

"Stop trying to figure me out." He says each word so slowly, so firmly, that I can hear each syllable as they roll off his tongue. Because he's taller than me, he's glowering down into my face with a sort of heavy look in his eyes, and it suddenly reminds me of the photograph in Dean's garage. The photograph of him before the 49ers game. The one with his dad at the opposite end.

"Tyler," I say. I think of him like a puzzle with a million pieces that gradually need to be pieced together to get the full image. One piece of the truth at a time, that's all it takes. "49ers or Chargers?"

"What kind of a dumb question is that?" he retorts, clearly agitated. He scrunches his face up as though he can't believe I've changed the subject so easily. It's almost like he's thinking, *Did she really just go from a pain in the butt to a football fanatic?* "49ers," he says.

My lips part as I stare at him, my face blank. Inside, my mind is swirling as I try to comprehend his answer. It's inconsistent with the photograph in the garage.

"I saw a photo in Dean's house," I tell him as I cautiously approach the subject, "of you and him and your dad before a 49ers game. If you're a fan, how come you looked like you didn't want to be there?"

He just stares at me and blinks a few times. "Dean was supposed to take that down."

"Answer the question," I demand. I'm growing impatient, and everything feels so peculiar all of a sudden. I'm overwhelmed with nerves as I find myself gradually figuring everything thing out. "What was wrong that day?"

Tyler walks away from me then. Reaching out, he scoops up my glass from the bedside drawer and his hand tightens around it, his knuckles paling from the pressure he's applying. I think the glass might shatter beneath his touch, but it doesn't. He moves over to the window and just stands there, the only sound the faint lull of the music and his heavy breathing.

The pier lights are on now and they glow from behind the palm trees that line the avenue, the Pacific Wheel going around and around and around. I don't know why. It's the middle of the night. Tyler's head lowers.

"What is it with you, Eden?" he asks quietly, but his back is turned and he's staring out the window at the ground below. "You're not supposed to figure me out. No one is."

The atmosphere has shifted and I can sense his mood in the stillness of the moment. His shoulders are dropped low as he traces the rim of the glass with his middle finger. I don't want to speak again. I want silence so that I can just study him and all his features and all his flaws. I want to look at his face again and I want to catch his gaze and I want to smile and for him to mirror it. I want to see him clench his jaw as he thinks; I want him to trust me enough to tell me what his thoughts are. I want to see through him, to understand him, to accept him.

I want him.

"Tyler," I whisper. I try to draw his eyes back to mine through the quiet force of his name, but he doesn't quite turn around. He only gives me a quick glance over his shoulder. "Trust me. Please."

He's still staring down at the carpet, but now he's shaking his head, slowly, like it hurts to give in. With his eyes squeezed shut, he exhales. "Don't make me tell you."

I edge my body in front of him very carefully, stepping

between him and the window. Not that it matters; he's no longer looking out into the night as it carries on without us. I swallow the lump in my throat and press a delicate hand to his chest. "Please," I whisper.

His eyes open agonizingly slowly and I'm waiting for the emerald within them to hit me, and when they finally meet mine my breath catches in my throat. They're so dilated and so soft and so pained, and I have never once witnessed such emotion pool over him before. I've seen furious and I've seen sadistic and I've seen vulnerable, but this goes beyond vulnerability. I see helplessness.

"My dad's an asshole," he whispers, his lips barely moving. "I told everyone he's in jail for GTA. That's not true." His jaw tightens and he turns his face to the side. I watch him physically build up the courage to keep going, his nostrils flaring, and he never turns back. And then he dares to utter words that have never once crossed my mind. "He's in jail for child abuse."

Those two words cause my blood to run cold, and a shiver surges down my spine. The words are painful to hear. They're two words that should never be said together, because child abuse shouldn't exist, shouldn't be a thing, shouldn't be real. Bile accumulates in my throat and my lips part, my mouth gaping in disbelief as Tyler closes his eyes again. I'm only now realizing how hard it was for him to say what he just said.

"You?" I whisper.

He nods.

Every single detail I have collected up until now suddenly clicks together all at once, and it's so overwhelming that I feel paralyzed, unable to move. I can only think. Now I understand why he looked unhappy in that picture in

Dean's garage. Of course he was unhappy. Now I understand why he has suffered broken wrists before. Of course he got mad when I brought it up. Now I understand why so many photos were missing from his photo album. Of course he got rid of them. Now I understand why he needs distractions. Of course.

Of course, of course, of course.

It's so obvious now.

I let out a breath and force myself to ask, "Jamie and Chase?"

"Just me," he says.

"Tyler, I . . ." Something inside of me is shattering at the thought of Tyler going through something so horrific and so cruel. My voice cracks and I have to stop for a second to compose myself. My hand is still on his chest and I can feel his heart beating, slow and loud. "I'm so sorry."

"I do a pretty good job of keeping it a secret," he mutters as he steps back from me, and the devastation in his eyes is gone now. It has been replaced with a bubbling anger that is fueled by the pain within him. "No one knows. Not Tiffani, not Dean, not anyone."

"Why haven't you told them?"

"Because I don't want pity," he shoots back sharply, but I can hear the strain in his voice. With a shrug, he turns away from me and walks across the room to the other side of the bed, gripping the edge of the drawer. "Pity is for pussies. I don't wanna look weak. I'm done with being weak." There's a thunderous slam as he hurls his fist into the top of the drawer and spins back around, livid. "That's all I ever fucking was. Weak."

Everything is starting to make sense to me. I glance away

from him, out the window to the deep dark blue of the sky outside. The Pacific Wheel is still turning, people still partying on the sand. I look back at him. "You weren't weak. You were a kid."

He vigorously shakes his head as he marches back across the small room, his hands curled into fists again as he presses his back against the wall and slides down to the floor. He looks completely defeated. Again, he has shifted from anger to vulnerability. He fixes his eyes on a spot on the wall opposite him and his voice softens up again. "You know, I didn't really get it for a while," he says quietly. "I never understood what I did wrong."

I know he wants me to listen, to just shut up and hear him out, so I hold back my questions and sit down in front of him. I cross my legs on the carpet and just listen to his words, all while watching his lips as he speaks.

"My mom and my dad . . ." he starts, but he talks very slowly, like he's thinking of how to word everything as he goes along. "They were just teenagers when they had me, so I get that they probably had no clue what they were doing. They both got a little obsessed with building careers. Dad had his dumb company, the one I told you about."

"Grayson's."

"Grayson's," he echoes. Clearing his throat, he leans forward and folds his arms across his knees. "It was great to start with. The business really took off for a few years, but when I was, like, eight, some deal fell through. Dad had a shit temper. He came home one night and Mom was at the office working late and he was super pissed off and he took it out on me. I kind of let that one slide. I thought it was a one-off. But then his employees were all quitting and it stressed him out and he took it out on me again. It kept happening more often. It went from once a week to every single night. He'd tell me I couldn't do anything I wanted to do, because I needed to focus on school instead. Said he wanted me to get into Ivy League so that I didn't end up fucking up my career the same way he was. But the truth was, I didn't want to have a big-shot career or get into an Ivy League school, yet I spent every single night locked in my room trying to study so that he wouldn't get mad at me. I thought, I'm trying, right? That's enough, isn't it? But it wasn't. Every night, he still came upstairs and threw me around." He pauses for a long moment, and when he speaks again, his voice has been reduced to nothing more than a whisper. "Every single night. Four years."

"I'm sorry," I murmur once more. I really am. No one deserves to be treated like that, especially by a parent, the person you're supposed to be loved and protected by. I feel sick to my stomach.

Tyler just shrugs. "Mom was so busy, she seriously had no idea. She blames herself for it now. She tries to ground me, but it just doesn't work, because she never reinforces it. I think she's terrified of trying to be strict, you know? It's not her fault though. She did notice sometimes. She'd be like, 'Tyler, what have you done to your face this time?' And I just made up some lame excuse each time. I would tell her my face was busted because I was playing football during gym class or that my wrist was broken because I fell down the stairs. When really I broke my wrist three times one year, because Dad just loved to see how far he could bend it back."

"Why didn't you tell someone?" I'm whispering now. The silence is so fragile that I'm terrified of breaking it. "Does my dad know?"

"Because I was fucking scared of him," Tyler admits, his tone harsh, voice cold. When he lifts his hands and runs them back through his hair, I notice how his eyes darken as his temper heats up. "There was no way I could tell. The only person who doesn't know is Chase. He was too young. Mom didn't want to scare him. The rest of the family all hate Dad now."

"When did it stop?"

"When I was twelve," he says, but he pushes himself up from the floor at the same time. He's still clenching his jaw as he speaks. "Jamie came upstairs one night and saw Dad hitting me. Called the cops, even at his age. Dad was arrested that night. It didn't go to trial, because he pleaded guilty, so it was never publicized. I got to keep it a secret. I get to pretend that I'm fine." A heavy sigh escapes his lips as he walks away from me once more and begins to pace back and forth across the room. "I really fucking hate him. Really, really hate him. After a year or something I started to believe that there must have been a reason for it all. I thought I deserved it for being a worthless piece of crap. I still do. I can't even move on from it, because it's impossible to forget, which sounds so pathetic, but it's true. I'm supposed to be on antidepressants, but I don't take them, because I want to drink and get high instead and you can't do both. And you know what, Eden? You're right. I'm lost. I'm totally fucking lost in this mess."

From my position on the floor, I press my hands down on the carpet and push my body up. Once I'm on my feet, I try to analyze the emotions flickering within his eyes. There's everything at once, shifting from one emotion to another so fast that I can barely keep up.

I hear him inhale sharply right before he yells, "I depend on distractions! They make coping easier, because in the hours that I'm drunk or high or both, I forget that my dad fucking hates me!" And then, almost as quickly as the wave of anger washed over him, adrenaline kicks in. He stops pacing and reaches for the glass on the bedside table, snatching it and then hurling it across the room.

I jump a step back, startled when the glass shatters against the far wall. There's an awful sound and it pierces through me for a second. The pieces of glass all drop to the floor in a ragged pile and Tyler just stands there, staring, breathing. Satisfied, he collapses onto the bed.

"I hate him," he spits. With his eyes now trained on the window again, I approach him in an effort to comfort him. His features might be hard and his expression might be twisted, but I know he's genuinely upset. I can hear it in his voice, and I can see it in his eyes.

It's dark now, and the music from the beach is beginning to fade away to nothing as the party wraps up. The moon is floating above the ocean and there's a soft glow illuminating the condo. Tyler's face is lit up, and I slowly edge over to the bed, where he's slumped. His eyes drift up to meet mine when I step in front of him.

I'm shivering. Not because it's cold in here, but because nerves are rattling every inch of my body. Tyler's still holding my stare and he just looks anxious and I wonder if he's expecting me to bombard him with more questions, but that's not my intention. My intentions are better.

Nervously, I reach out for his face and cup his jaw with both hands, forcing him to hold my gaze as I sit myself down on his lap. He doesn't budge, doesn't move, doesn't breathe. I don't think I'm quite breathing, either. I move my lips to his but linger before I get there, and we stay like that, just him and me, for a short while. It's comforting yet absolutely terrifying at the same time, and I know he's just waiting for me to lean in, and I know I want to, but I wait. I wait until I feel his breath against my cheek.

"Thank you for trusting me," I whisper ever so carefully against his jaw, and then I finally kiss him.

Through the darkness and the silence, something ignites. I don't know what it is, I can't put my finger on it, but I feel it. I feel the way my pulse takes off and my heart aches in my chest, and I feel the way goosebumps begin to appear all over my body, the hairs on my arms rising, and I feel Tyler's lips against mine. Plump and moist and eager, just like always. I can feel him channeling his hurt, his anger . . . I can feel him channeling it into desire. It's that desire for something we both want but can't have.

He tastes like beer and tobacco, but there's something enthralling about it. It's so familiar, because it's so him, his permanent taste. He kisses me slowly and slips his hands under my skirt, squeezing my ass as he sits up. I'm still in his lap and I press my chest hard against his as I rub my thumbs against his skin, his jaw still cupped between my hands. I feel the muscles in his arms tighten as he lifts me off his lap and lays me back down on the bed next to him. My entire body feels like ice, frozen beneath him as he hovers over me, his hand sliding along my thigh beneath my skirt. For a second I worry that I'm suffering from paralysis, but my lips are still moving, still kissing, so I'm not. It's just anxiety and the fear of the unknown.

But no matter how nervous and nauseated I'm starting to feel, I refuse to tear my lips away from Tyler's. He suddenly intensifies the kiss, quickening the pace, and while my lips are locked with his I let go of his face and shrug off my sweater. I pull it out from beneath me and toss it to the side. When my hands find their way back to Tyler, they're reaching for his white T-shirt. My arms feel numb as I awkwardly fumble around with the hem, trying my best to figure out how to pull off his shirt without breaking the kiss. He notices my struggle and laughs against my lips. It's a hearty laugh, the kind of laugh that makes you smile back, a laugh that makes you feel comfortable. Pulling away and sitting on his knees, he swiftly yanks the T-shirt off and throws it over his shoulder. My cheeks flush with color as my eyes linger on his chest and his abs and the indention of his V lines, and it makes me wonder if I'm dreaming, because Tyler belongs in Abercrombie & Fitch, not here on the bed with me.

He moves his body back over mine and presses his lips to my collarbone, one hand gripping my waist, the other edging its way up my skirt again. He kisses my skin slowly as I tangle my hands through his hair, twirling the strands around my fingers. My eyes are closed and I rest my chin on his forehead as I try to steady my breathing, because I've never been so excited and nervous in my entire life. The heat from his chest contrasts with my shivering as the tips of his fingers run along the lace that decorates the top of my underwear. My stomach churns in anticipation and for a moment I feel like I might throw up.

He's so experienced and has everything down to a T., and I'm so inexperienced and have yet to discover why guys find boobs so attractive. So many fleeting thoughts come and go, like when do I move my hands? Where do I put them? Do I wait for him to advance or do I make the move myself? Does he expect me to moan? Do I moan? I can't possibly imagine myself moaning. Am I supposed to be doing something right now, like unbuttoning his jeans or kissing his neck? Who was the first person to ever have sex, anyway? John F. Kennedy was a total player, and if the beloved former president of our nation was able to seduce girls at his every whim, then I'm pretty sure that sex can't be that bad. Those girls would not have thrown themselves into the president's bed if sex was terrible. For a second I wonder why I'm thinking about our assassinated president. I bet if Lee Harvey Oswald was still alive even he wouldn't be thinking about JFK while getting it on with his wife. And he freaking killed the guy.

Stop it, Eden.

Tyler's lips trail kisses from my collarbone up to my jaw as his hands explore my body, one running from my waist to my face. He brushes my cheek with his thumb, and I can feel his affection through his fingertips and the way they leave a warm trace over my skin. I never want it to end, even when I'm losing my breath and tightening my grip on his hair. I don't mean to, but I end up tugging on the ends as I arch my back.

Thankfully, Tyler leads me through it all, never once saying anything for the rest of the night. Even when I hesitate at one point, struck with worry over what he'll think when he sees my body, he pauses, waiting until I swallow the nerves before continuing. And even when he's undoing the clasp of my bra and even when he gets up to kick off his jeans and even when he's fumbling around in his wallet, he never once says a word, but I like it this way. I like the deafening silence of the whole experience as I stumble my way through it with the person I've fallen head first for.

That's what makes all of this better.

It's because I'm with Tyler.

Not Jake and not Snotty Scotty, the guy from algebra class, but Tyler. The guy with the secrets and the weaknesses, the guy who trusted me enough to admit them all to me. I respect him for that. It took a lot for him to tell me the truth and now I only want him even more. I don't want this to stop. Tyler and I . . . We shouldn't be together and we shouldn't be doing what we're doing, because the bottom line is that we're stepsiblings, no matter how much we wish we weren't. I'm so attracted to everything about him and I shouldn't have to feel like I'm doing something wrong because of it. It's not wrong. Where's the blood relation? There isn't one.

I just know that if anyone ever found out the truth about Tyler and me, we'd be frowned upon. I can't even begin to imagine how we'd go about telling our parents. How do you break the news to a married couple that their kids are dating each other? How does all of this work?

There's no going back from this moment. There's no changing the way Tyler's groaning against my ear, no erasing the fact that I'm digging my nails into his back, no forgetting the way our hips are rolling together.

Because Tyler might have told me his secrets, but now he has a new one.

28

When I wake up later in morning and take in the sight of the room around me, I don't particularly feel different. You're supposed to be a different person; you're supposed to see everything in a new light. But I feel the exact same as I felt last night, except now I've got a headache. My body isn't in mortal agony and I don't want to cry, but I'm not exactly basking in joy either. It just feels like any other morning, a new day.

My throat feels dry, like I've been walking in a desert for a week and haven't come across a water source yet, and my voice sounds raspy as I sit up and call out for Tyler. That's another thing I thought would be different after you lose your virginity: I thought you would wake up next to the person you're so infatuated with.

A moment of panic sweeps through my body. Maybe Tyler left. Maybe he abandoned me here, took off before I woke up, regretting what happened and running away. The condo is too quiet. It shouldn't be. Tyler should be by my side like in the movies, where you wake up and the significant other kisses your forehead or plays with your hair or whispers that he loves you, or just *something*.

I glance around the room and see the small window has

its curtains pulled over again. I can't even figure out if it's morning or if it's the middle of the night or if it's two days later, because the room is dull and starved of light.

Scrunching my face up, I grip the sheets around me and glance back over to the mirror on my right. I'm completely bare. With a gasp, I yank the sheets up to cover my chest and stare at my reflection, horrified.

Where the hell is Tyler?

The bedroom door opens then, stiff against the fluffy carpet. Tyler elbows it open fully and takes a step into the room, his face a little pale. I'm just relieved that he's still here. He's fully dressed and there's a small smile on his lips as he meets my eyes.

"I was just about to wake you up," he says, his voice soft. The emerald shade in his eyes is a light green, and I know it's because he's calm. That's what I've noticed most over the weeks that I've been here: Tyler's eyes and the way they reflect his mood. Dull and light: vulnerable. Normal: cocky jackass. Dark and vibrant: he's furious to the point where he could possibly kill someone.

"I thought you left," I admit, realizing that I was overreacting. I know Tyler wouldn't leave me, because I know he wouldn't treat me like that. I hope he wouldn't treat me like that.

He gives me a hard look, appalled. "I'm not that much of an asshole." The corners of his lips pull back up into a smile as he glances away, almost shyly, like his ego has been bruised and he's lost all his confidence. "You've got nothing to worry about."

I spot the bright mint color of my skirt in his hands, and when he notices me staring at my clothes it's like he remembers why he's entered the room. "Here," he says, carefully placing the clothing on the bottom of the bed. He stands there awkwardly. He can't really hold my gaze; he can only glance back and forth between me and my clothes and the window and the floor and anything else he can look at. Color rises in his cheeks.

"Are you okay?"

Finally his eyes lock on mine and his entire face flushes pink. He rubs at the back of his neck as he strains it to one side. "Sorry," he murmurs, but I can hear the nervousness in his tone. "I'm—I'm not really used to, like, this." He pauses for a second. "We should probably talk about, uh, last night."

I'm still hugging the sheets to my chest, but by now there's a smile on my lips. I think it's the first time I've seen Tyler appear truly anxious and out of his comfort zone. Usually he's so in control of situations and so confident, and now here he is, mumbling and unable to look at me properly. But then I think about his words and I immediately wipe the smile from my face.

"Was I bad?" I dare myself to ask.

"No, no," he says quickly. He lightens up a little, at least enough to give a small laugh. "I meant more along the lines of . . . You know, where do we stand now?"

We exchange a long glance. He's biting his lip, holding his breath while he waits for me to answer. But honestly? I have no idea. If anything, it's just made our complicated situation feel all the more real and all the more intense.

"I'm not sure," I admit. "Where do you want us to stand?"

"I'm not sure." He heaves a sigh and stuffs his hands into his pockets, but it's clear he's thinking deeply about something, his face a picture of concentration. "Answer me this: Do you regret it?"

"No," I say immediately. How could I regret something I wanted so desperately? "Do you?"

"You know I don't," he murmurs, and then he smiles another one of those genuine smiles, the ones I don't think I'll ever be able to get over. He reaches for my clothes again and walks around the bed with them, stopping by my side and placing them in my lap above the sheets. He's still smiling. "We'll figure all of this out. Eventually. But for now, get dressed, because we really need to go. Troy-James just called and he's on his way home."

I purse my lips at him a little sheepishly as I hug the comforter to my body, not moving an inch. "Can you, uh, give me a sec?"

"You're acting like I haven't seen you naked," he says, but it's playful and he nods. "Be quick," he calls over his shoulder as he leaves the room.

Once he's gone I grab my skirt and pull it on under the sheets, still too embarrassed to get out of this bed undressed. I pull on my bra and my top and then finally step out onto the carpet, the room feeling as though it's spinning a little. As I slip my sweater on and wrap it around my body, I press a hand to my forehead and breathe for a few seconds. I felt fine until I stood up; now it feels like my blood is poison and it's killing me from the inside.

When I make my way through to the kitchen, Tyler is hovering by the trash can, tipping a tray of glass into it. I glance over the worktop into the living room, where sunshine is streaming in through the huge windows and casting light over everything, and I take note of how everything has been tidied to the point where the place looks immaculate, like we were never here. He must have cleaned up all the shards from the glass that he smashed last night while I was still sleeping.

With a sigh, he shoves the tray into a cupboard and turns to me, rubbing his hands together. "I called us a cab," he tells me. He steals a glance at his watch and then nods to the door. "I know it's weird, but I can't exactly ask someone for a ride without having them wonder what the hell we've been doing. We can't look suspicious, remember? The cab driver won't know us. It should be here any second."

I give him a weak nod. "Where are my shoes?" The carpet keeps my bare feet warm, but I realize I'm not exactly sure where my Converse have ended up. I quickly scan the living room for them.

"I don't know," Tyler says, and his eyes also join in the search. "But we need to get outta here."

"But my shoes—" I try to protest, upset that I've lost them. My favorite pair of Chucks, too: the ones with my favorite lyrics written along the side. The ones that I pull on to go to school, to go grocery shopping for my mom, to wear to beach parties when I'm drunk and want to kiss my stepbrother.

"I'll buy you a new pair; now come on," Tyler urges, growing slightly impatient. He furrows his eyebrows as he heads over to the door, opening it up and standing out in the lobby, waiting for me to join him. When I do, he locks up and slides the key under the doormat.

The polished tiles beneath my feet feel cold and I dash across the lobby and into the elevator before Tyler even has a chance to turn around, but when he does he smirks before joining me inside right before the doors close.

He looks at me hard as the elevator begins to move, his expression stern, but he's struggling to suppress the smirk. "I don't think we should mention last night to our parents."

"I don't think we should mention last night to anyone," I

correct, but even though we're only joking around, I tense up. I just want to sigh endlessly. That's all this is, one huge sigh, because we have no idea what we're doing.

Tyler must notice the worry in my eyes, because he reaches over and gently grasps my hand the same way he did last night when he was looking after me. I stare at our hands for a moment, taking in the way they look when they're interlocked together. I like it. When I glance up at him, he only smiles and tightens his fingers around mine.

There's a thought lingering in my head, that perhaps we'll never be able to tell anyone, and that we'll constantly be whispering, "Shhh, this is a secret," to each other. Keeping this a secret is hard, but telling is harder. We can never win.

When the elevator doors open, Tyler leads me through the lobby to the main entrance, and through the glass doors we can see a cab parked by the sidewalk. I'm hesitant about walking outside barefoot, but I quickly get over it and follow Tyler down the steps and into the vehicle. A middle-aged woman greets us, hungover smile on her lips.

It takes us almost twenty minutes to get back to the house, which is surprising considering it's Sunday morning and the traffic is minimal. I think the cab driver is taking advantage of the fact that we're young, assuming that therefore we must be naïve and completely blind. She takes at least five wrong turns, murmuring, "Oops, not this one!" each time. I'm glaring at her from the backseat as she drives, noticing the way she's purposely riding up the fare and prolonging the time I have to sit in silence overthinking everything about last night. It's making me feel nauseous, but Tyler only shrugs at me when I point to the meter with a scowl on my face. He doesn't bother to argue about it, just hands the driver twenty bucks and yanks me out of the car, which promptly zooms off the second I've shut the door.

"Where did you tell them you were going last night?" Tyler asks as we linger outside the house for a moment, not quite sure how we're going to handle our parents. I look like trash and my shoes are gone and I most likely smell of booze.

"The movies," I say.

Tyler lets out a breath and shakes his head down at me. "The movies? Where's your originality?"

"What was your excuse?" I fire at him.

"They didn't get one. I left before they could notice."

"Well," I say, "that doesn't surprise me."

He chuckles, but he still appears slightly anxious when he glances back at the house. We have no choice but to go inside—we'll have to eventually. I wish I could stay away from it, away from Dad and away from Ella, hidden somewhere with Tyler while he tells me more about his life. That would be perfect.

Ella is in the living room when we get inside. She's holding a few sheets of paper and she's studying them, a finger pressed to her lips. Jamie's sitting on the recliner with his fractured wrist resting on a pillow. He stares at us both with a peeved expression, and I think it's the first time I've ever seen him looking displeased.

"Dave, they're home," Ella says loudly without even glancing up. I was hoping she wouldn't notice us awkwardly hanging in the doorway, but it's true what they say about parents. They have eyes in the back of their heads and four ears.

Tyler glances sideways at me, his face taut. He's better used to dealing with our parents than I am, and quite frankly,

I'm hoping he'll do all the talking on my behalf. If I try to explain myself, I'll only stammer and blurt out something that I wish I hadn't, like when Tiffani heard me tell Ella I was with Meghan and it totally backfired.

Dad barges into the living room moments later in his sweats and T-shirt. I'm not used to seeing him without a shirt on his back and a tie around his neck. It makes him seem less intimidating, like he's my grandpa. "What do you have to say for yourselves?" he barks, and immediately it becomes clear that he is pissed off on an entirely new level.

"The movie was good?" I try, but even Tyler shoots me a look that says, *Don't even bother.* I should have known Dad would go insane when I didn't come home. Movies don't last until 10AM.

"You two went to that beach party, didn't you?"

Ella has looked up from her papers and placed them down on her lap while Jamie continues to watch Tyler and I struggle to get out of the shark tank. There's a sparkle of amusement in his eyes, as though this is entertaining. On my end, it's not.

Neither Tyler nor I muster up a reply. This tells our parents exactly what they need to know: Yes, we lied and yes, we went to the beach party underage. In my defense, nothing like it takes place in Portland. How was I supposed to turn down the opportunity? In hope of saving our fate, I try to appeal to Dad's sympathetic side. So I cry.

"My friends took me there after the movies," I choke out through my exaggerated sobs. My voice is raspy, but it isn't fake. I'm still dying of thirst. "I didn't even know what it was!"

Tyler's staring at me, his face blank. I'm defending only myself and apparently he believes I'm not doing a very good job. With a sigh, his eyes shift from me to my dad. "I chose to go," he says, casually honest. "What are you gonna do? Ground my ass for another five years?"

Dad glances between Tyler and me, his eyes narrowed, like he can't figure out which problem to tackle first: my fake weeping or Tyler's attitude. He chooses neither.

"Where have you been all night?" he interrogates while Ella watches, and her gaze only makes me think about what Tyler said last night, about her being wary when it comes to parenting and having to punish him. Dad seems to have no problem at all when it comes to striking up an argument.

"We all crashed at Dean's place," Tyler bluffs, although in a way it's only a slight distortion of the truth. We did crash at someone's place, only it was TJ's and not Dean's, and Tyler and I weren't exactly sleeping. "Just chill out. It's summer."

"Oh," Dad says with sarcastic realization. "My bad. I forgot that it's summer, so that means you can do whatever the hell you want. Sincerest apologies."

I can hear Jamie stifling a laugh and I want to tell him to just shut the hell up, but I know that wouldn't go down well with Dad. Besides, I like Jamie. In the you're-pretty-okay-for-a-stepbrother sense, that is.

"This isn't the first time you haven't come home, Eden," Dad mutters in disgust. My eyes quickly flicker back over to him and I force a couple more tears to well up. His hair looks grayer than it did over a month ago when he picked me up from the airport, and the more his scowl dominates his features the older he appears. Mom looks twenty-one in comparison.

"It's just sleepovers," I sniff, way more dramatically that I intended. The first time I didn't come home was when I fell asleep at Jake's place after kissing him during *The Lion King*. The second was last night, when I was too captivated by Tyler's touch, too charmed by his voice, too in love with his being.

"That's not the point!"

"Then what is?"

Dad glares at me as he struggles to muster up a decent reply. He comes up with nothing and sets his attention back on Tyler. "You're impossible, so I'm not even going to say anything. Just go upstairs. Get out of here." He glances over his shoulder at Jamie with a sort of scowl on his lips, and Jamie gets the message and stands to leave.

"Fine by me," Tyler says with a smirk, but it quickly fades when I catch his eye. His lips quirk into a sincere smile instead, a smile full of reassurance, like he's trying to tell me not to worry because everything will be okay. When Jamie approaches him, Tyler swings his arm carefully over his shoulder and gently leads him out of the room, murmuring, "How's that wrist, kid?"

In that second, I wish I was like Tyler. I wish I was able to put up a front and act like everything is a joke. I wish I got into trouble so much that being yelled at becomes part of the daily routine. I wish I wasn't still standing here in front of my Dad, subject to questioning and disappointed expressions while I have these stupid tears running down my smeared makeup.

Dad, I have realized, clearly doesn't have a sympathetic fiber in all of his being. I should have known. Every time Mom was upset, he didn't care. Every time she cried over him, he cared even less. He's never cared.

I quit the crying act and look at him hard. "Well?"

Ella's still in the room. She's gnawing on her lips as she continues to watch, never moving from her position on the couch, staying silent. I don't know if I should be glad or not, because I haven't yet figured out if she's the type to join in the yelling or the type to defend you.

"Eden," Dad starts slowly as he rubs his temples. "I didn't bring you down here so that you could sneak around and lie to me."

"Then what the hell did you bring me down for?" I explode, throwing my hands up in exasperation. "Did you want to take me bra shopping? Did you want us to sit over campfires eating s'mores? What, Dad? What did you expect?"

I cannot even begin to fathom my hatred. For the six weeks I've been here he hasn't made the slightest effort to fix things with me, to apologize for walking out on both Mom and me without an explanation, for leaving and waiting three years to see me again. And he wants to come into my life now? He wants to try and act like my parent now?

"I think we all need to just calm down. The important thing is that she's here," Ella says with a slight edge to her voice. I've concluded now that not only is she the type of mother that doesn't mind if you disappear, she's also the kind who defends you when you do.

"Exactly," I remark, trying to make my voice softer. "I'm home and I'm alive, and so is Tyler, but if it helps, I'm sorry. I'm sorry for us not coming home."

Dad doesn't accept my apology. He just stares at me in a way I'd never expect a father to look at their daughter, like he can't stand me. In that exact moment, I hate him.

"What are you looking at me like that for?" I ask. "What is your problem with me, Dad?"

"I don't have a problem," he says. He glances sideways at Ella, like he needs backup in order to fight a sixteen-year-old, but she only looks at him with wide eyes.

"Is that why you didn't talk to me for three years? Because you don't have a problem with me?" I don't know where my words are coming from. Somewhere in the back of my mind, these thoughts have been gathering ever since he left. Now that I'm furious at him they're spilling out all at once, and I can't stop them. I can see the color rising in Dad's cheeks as he takes in my words. "Is that why you walked out? Because you don't have a problem?"

"That's enough!" he barks, because he can't handle the truth. He can't handle the fact that he's a sorry excuse for a father, because he never thinks he's in the wrong. That's why he and Mom argued all the time. Nothing was ever his fault. It was always hers.

"You haven't even tried to make an effort with me." I even take a few steps toward him. My chin is tilted high, because I'm determined to let him know how I feel. "You haven't even said sorry to me yet. That should have been the first thing you said to me when I stepped off the plane."

Dad throws his hands up in defeat. "Okay, Eden, I'm sorry. I'm sorry I haven't been around," he mutters, but it's far from sincere. "There. Are you happy now?"

"What's the point of that now, Dad?" I shrug. "You're three years too late."

I want him to look hurt. I want my words to have an effect on him, and I want him to drown in guilt. But he doesn't look pained at all. He looks pissed off as he narrows his sharp eyes at me, delivering a scornful glare. "You're exactly like your mom, you know that?"

Ella looks shocked.

"Thank God," I say. "I'd hate to be like you."

Now I've got my point across, I decide it's time to storm

out before he can try and argue back with me any further. He knows I'm mad at him and it's going to take a lot of apologizing on his part if I'm ever going to forgive him.

His eyes cold, Dad turns back to Ella, and I swing around and march toward the door.

I hear Ella hiss, "What the hell, Dave? Go after her! I know she's been out all night, but you think you're going to make it up to your daughter by being all high and mighty?"

"Hey, don't blame me for this. It was your idea to get her out here in the first place. God, teenagers are a nightmare . . . Maybe once she's back home and Tyler's in New York we'll be able to get back to normal."

I halt by the door and swallow painfully. Did I just hear right? Dad just invited me because Ella told him to? It shouldn't surprise me, it shouldn't hurt, but it does. I turn around and look at them both. "You don't want me here?"

They look up at me, shocked. Ella gets up. "Eden, you weren't supposed to hear that; of course your dad—"

But I can't stand to hear their excuses. "And why is Tyler going to New York?"

Ella fires my dad a glare, but then she looks back at me and gives a tight smile. "It's nothing."

I know that it's certainly not nothing, but I'm tired of asking questions and never getting a straight answer. I'm absolutely livid and I think my heart might explode from my high blood pleasure. Mom's always been right about Dad. He's an asshole.

I stuff my hands into the pockets of my sweater—it only reminds me once more that I was robbed—and storm up to my room. My head's still spinning, even more so now, and all I crave is water and a shower and Tyler. Two of those things I can have.

Ugh.

I need to clear my head, to remove myself from the house and get some fresh air instead. I need to run. I'll shower when I get back; I'll talk to Tyler when I get back. I just need to think straight first.

I fight the overwhelming urge to throw up as I slip out of my skirt from last night and change into my running gear, fetching myself a bottle of water from the kitchen and heading out the patio doors in order to avoid Dad.

And then I'm off, falling into a steady pace as I make my way north rather than west. I don't want to go back to the beach. I want to take a new route; I want to end up some place different and new. And so I quickly find myself in Pacific Palisades, the sun beating down on me, my feet thudding against the concrete and my headache slowly easing away.

I think last night has just made everything even more complicated than it already was. Now Tyler and I are walking on eggshells, monitoring our words and ensuring not a single soul catches us exchanging a knowing smile. If we get caught, we're screwed.

My head is a total mess. In a perfect world, Tyler and I wouldn't be related through a marriage certificate. In a perfect world, Tyler and I wouldn't have to sneak around and hurt people in the process of falling for each other. In a perfect world, I'd get to brag about him to Amelia. But this world isn't perfect. Far from it.

* * *

When I get back to the house forty minutes later, still a little hungover and out of breath, I come to an abrupt halt on the lawn.

Tiffani's car is parked out front. It shouldn't be. It's Sunday morning, and they never see each other on Sundays.

I force myself over to the front door, but there's a stiffness in my bones, and I can't tell if it's because of the run or because I know there's something not quite right. I almost want to turn around and run another five hundred thousand miles in the opposite direction, but I drag myself inside the house and creep up the staircase. I notice Dad and Ella are talking in the living room when I sweep past, most likely discussing ways to get rid of their two reckless kids.

I've barely reached the landing when Tiffani emerges from my room, shoving open my door with Tyler hot on her heels. He reaches for her arm and tries to pull her back, but she shakes off his grasp.

"Oh, here she is," she says venomously, her voice dripping with acid. "You're just in time."

Tyler's eyes are wide as he stares at me from behind her, and with a minute shake of his head he runs a hand through his hair.

"In time for what?" I dare myself to ask, although judging by the furious expression on her face I don't think I want to know. Tyler looks worried, and I can't blame him. I'm starting to feel the same.

Tiffani's eyes are like ice and I've never seen her look so . . . nasty. Right now, if this was a scene in a movie, she'd be the villain for sure. "I need to talk to you both, because in case you can't tell, I am pissed the hell off." She balls a hand into a fist. "I am this close to punching you in the face, Tyler."

"What have I done this time?" He's staring at her with a perplexed look in his eyes, but it doesn't stop him from taking a step back, just in case.

"What have you done? Are you seriously asking?" Her mouth is agape, and then she takes a deep breath. "Back yard. Now."

She barges past me and knocks me against the wall. I scrunch up my face and glare after her as she descends the stairs. What's her damn problem? I glance back at Tyler. He presses his hands to his face and mouths, "Fuck."

Tiffani pauses at the bottom of the staircase and glowers back up at us. She throws a pointed glance at the living room door, where our parents are. "I can talk to you both outside or I can talk to you right here," she says slowly, her voice hushed, "and trust me, I think you'd rather I spoke to you outside."

She knows, I think. *She so fucking knows.*

The exact same thought must cross Tyler's mind, because he shoots me a panicked look and swallows. I can't think of a worse time to be confronted about all of this. I'm hungover, I'm sweaty, I'm tired, and I look like I've just escaped from rehab. I'm that trashy.

There's absolutely no chance of me getting out of this. I wonder if it's too late to run those five hundred thousand miles. Tyler's nudging me down the stairs and I can literally feel his unwillingness through his touch. His arms are rigid, fists curled. Somehow, the two of us make it through the patio doors and into the back yard.

"Sooooooooo," Tiffani says.

Tyler furrows his eyebrows. "So . . ."

"So I woke up to a text from TJ this morning," she states. She's glancing between the two of us, so I try to look nonchalant. I try to look like I didn't just sleep with her boyfriend. "And you know," she continues, "I'm getting real sick of other people talking to me about us hooking up, Tyler, because half the fucking time it's not even me."

"What are you talking about?" Tyler asks, and both Tiffani and I stare at him. He knows what she's talking about. He knows exactly.

"Don't start, Tyler. Just don't," she snaps, her voice growing louder. She's turning vicious, and I know that the chance of us remaining friends after this is pretty slim. "He made a joke about us hooking up last night, because his room was a total mess, and we both know perfectly fine that it wasn't me."

"Look," Tyler starts, taking a step toward her. "Baby, I didn't hook up with anyone, I just forgot to tidy the place up after—"

"Shut UP!" she yells, and he does. I think she's past the point of putting up with his bullshit. She squeezes her eyes shut for a second, breathes in and out, and then turns to me, a smile on her lips. "Eden, didn't you want your shoes?"

Everything stops. My heart skips a few beats, my limbs stiffen, my blood runs cold. I try to splutter some words out, but they rise in my throat only to disappear. My voice becomes a rasped whisper. "How did you—"

"Because," she hisses, "TJ asked if I'd had a good night and then said I'd left behind my Converse. Asked me what the words written on them meant." My heart completely stops beating now. "I sure as hell remember you waving yours around the entire night. The ones with the lyrics on them, right? By the way, you're not getting those back. I told him I didn't want them and asked him to toss them in the trash for me."

"But Tyler's my—"

"Stepbrother? Yeah, I know." She's growing so livid that tears are threatening to fall. Quickly wiping her eyes with the back of her hand, she straightens up and adjusts the waistband of her sweats. "I just spent the past half hour arguing with myself. I was like, 'No way, they're totally related.' But I've watched *Clueless* before, okay? You know, when Cher falls for her stepbrother? I'm not STUPID."

This is it. This is what being caught feels like.

And it feels like hell.

Both Tyler and I are at a loss for words. I don't quite think either of us ever prepared ourselves for what would happen if this ever happened, if the truth was ever uncovered. It feels like Judgment Day. I feel so small, so tiny, standing here in front of Tiffani. I can't even look at Tyler. I just feel sick, like I could hurl at any second, so I try my hardest to hold it back as the barbecue over by the pool catches my eye.

I wish I could rewind the summer, back to my first night in this city with the neighbors piled into the yard and the barbecue sizzling and Dad cracking lame jokes. I want to do it all over again, but this time around I don't want to fall for my stepbrother. This time I don't want to be in the mess I'm in now.

"You didn't really hook up with Jake, did you, Eden?" Tiffani really is crying now. Angry tears: the worst kind.

"No," I whisper.

"It was you that night at the pier," she says, and I feel like I'm dying inside. Everything is shattering as the guilt consumes me. I refused to ever be a cheater, but that's exactly who I've become. "You're a liar."

"I know," I say, my voice cracking. I'm nearly crying too. I don't want to be here. I want to be in Portland with my mom and Amelia. I want to be sleeping until noon and I want to be watching reruns of my favorite TV shows. I don't want this. "I'm a liar. I'm a bitch. I'm a terrible friend."

Out of nowhere, Tyler steps in front of me and clears his throat. He's been silent for a while, and it makes me wonder exactly what he's preparing himself to say. "You know what, Tiffani?" he says, and she looks at him with wide, hurt eyes. "I don't even want to be with you. I've wasted three years because you blackmailed me into staying with you. Do whatever you want. Tell everyone everything you know about me, because having you keep it a secret isn't worth the effort it takes to put up with you." His voice grows louder with each word. I can see Tiffani's ego taking the hit. "We're over. Sue me. Report me to the cops. I don't care. I'm done."

I certainly didn't expect this. Just the other week Tyler was claiming it was almost impossible to break up with her. She could potentially ruin him if he did. But now . . . It's like he doesn't mind, like he just wants to get away from her. Perhaps being in a relationship with her is worse than having his life messed with.

"This is all your fault!" Tiffani screams at me. Her voice is so strained that I subconsciously take a step closer to Tyler, which probably doesn't help in the slightest. "I don't even care about the fact that you're basically siblings, which I should, because it's disgusting, but no, the only thing I care about is that you've ruined everything."

I feel even worse than I did before. I stole her boyfriend. Unintentionally, but still. Shaking my head, I step out toward her again. No matter how many hurtful comments she's thrown my way, I'm still drenched in guilt. "Tiffani, I didn't mean for—"

Tyler holds up a hand to silence me. "It's over, *babe,*" he tells her instead. With a callous shrug, he points to the gate. He's being so harsh about it, and I feel terrible, both about my actions and for Tiffani. If she didn't want to kill me, I'd hug her right now, like the friend I'm supposed to be to her. I didn't mean for anyone to get hurt.

Frustrated and crying even harder, she throws her hands into her hair and screams, "But you can't break up with me!"

He laughs. He actually laughs at her. I don't think he's processed the fact that she knows our secret and has every reason to tell it to the world. "Because I won't be there to make you look cool? Because you won't get to control me anymore?"

"Because I'm PREGNANT, Tyler!"

The second the words leave her lips, the atmosphere thickens so much that it's almost suffocating. Tyler's entire body deflates and the color drains from his face. I look back to Tiffani. She's weeping now, and it's the kind of crying that looks like it hurts, the kind that causes you to lose your breath. Now I really do think I'm going to hurl.

Tyler seems to lose his voice, the only sound he can breathe out being a minute whisper. "What?"

She starts backing away from us, her cheeks stained with tears and her heart broken. I can't take it in. I feel like someone's just punched me and knocked me out, because everything seems fuzzy and dull, the way your room feels when you first wake up.

I hear the patio doors slide open, but I'm too numb to even glance over. I make out Ella's voice asking, "What's all the screaming about?"

Tyler doesn't say a word. I think he's in shock. He's just staring at Tiffani, his lips parted, his eyes an ocean of different emotions. I finally glance over to the patio doors, and Ella and my dad are staring at us. I know what they're thinking. They're wondering why Tyler looks like he's having a heart attack and why Tiffani is a weeping mess that's heading for the gate.

When she reaches it and pulls it open, she stops and turns back, sniffling back her sobs as she meets Ella's eyes. "You should know that he's hooked on coke!" she yells. "And he's started dealing too!"

"You bitch!" Tyler snarls, snapping out of his frozen state just as she disappears through the gate, which slams shut behind her.

Her words echo through my mind so loudly that it hurts. That's what she's been holding over him the entire summer. It's what Tyler was talking about when we were locked in the bathroom. It's what she must have found out at the start of the summer, when she confronted him about it and angered him and caused him to storm into the barbecue in a horrible mood. That's why he's staying off the police's radar.

Because he could go to jail for this.

If there is any way for today to get worse than it already is, then it's this. There are too many things to deal with at once as the truth spills out: the truth about Tyler and the drugs, the truth about Tiffani, and, worst of all, the truth about Tyler and me.

"Tyler," Ella says loudly yet slowly. "Please tell me I misheard that." Her hands are on her chest as she steps outside, Dad close by her side. "Please, please tell me you're not."

I'm holding my breath as I look at Tyler, waiting to see if he'll deny it. He's just standing there again, like he's so overwhelmed by everything that he's ended up paralyzed. There are probably a million and one thoughts flying around his head right now.

He lowers his head, drops his eyes to the grass, and murmurs, "I wish I wasn't."

Ella clasps her hands to her mouth, muffling her horrified gasp, her eyes flooding with tears. Everything is going wrong today. She turns to Dad and buries her face in his chest, and surprisingly he wraps his arms around her and doesn't say a word. By now, I'd expect him to be arguing. He might be silent as he comforts her, but it doesn't stop him from glaring.

When Tyler looks up, I can see the pained expression in his eyes again, the same one as last night. The guilt is almost dripping from him. "Mom," he says, his voice choked, "don't cry. I'm not, like, addicted or anything. I just—well, it helps."

Through her tears and through my dad's shirt, Ella mumbles something, but it's so muffled that I can barely make out what she's saying. Tyler doesn't either.

"Mom, breathe for a sec," he says, and cautiously he begins to walk toward her. Even though my dad has her wrapped comfortably in his arms, Tyler reaches over to place a hand on her shoulder, but she shakes it off and lifts her head.

"I said," she whispers, "get out."

Tyler's eyebrows knit together. "What?"

"Get out of this house."

I think it's at this point that we all freeze. We're all stunned. Dad's eyebrows shoot up even higher, like he can't believe that Ella is really kicking her son out of the house, and Tyler is speechless, his lips moving but not speaking. I really, really want to cry now. He can't get kicked out. It's the last thing he needs, especially after Tiffani's bombshell.

"Are you serious?" His voice is so soft, so weak.

Ella doesn't say anything, just steps back from Dad and

dabs at her eyes, sniffing. She looks devastated. "Tyler, please," she pleads gently, and then immediately bursts into tears again. "Just leave. I can't handle this anymore."

Tyler and I exchange shocked glances as Dad hugs Ella to his chest again. Neither of us was expecting all of this to happen. It's a Sunday. Sundays are supposed to be boring. I shouldn't be watching Tyler get kicked out of the house.

Tilting his head down to face the ground, he stuffs his hands into the pockets of his jeans and walks past our parents. He moves in such a defeated manner, with his shoulders low and his steps slow. Like it's second nature by now, I break out of my rooted spot on the lawn and go after him. I ignore Dad's eyes as they follow me, because I'm beyond the point of caring about what he has to say.

Tyler's already sprinted up the staircase by the time I catch up to him, and Jamie and Chase are standing on the landing, their eyes wide and curious. It makes me wonder if they've heard the entire thing, from Tyler being hooked on coke to getting kicked out. They quickly move to the side as Tyler and I push past them and into his room. He slams the door shut behind us.

I stand by the side of his bed and watch as he reaches into his closest and pulls down a navy duffel bag from the shelf. Dean's varsity jacket comes with it, falling to the floor before Tyler kicks it out of the way. For a few minutes, he rummages around his room, pulling out shirts and jeans and piling them all into the bag without saying a single word. The stress shows on his face.

"Where are you going to go?" I ask, breaking the silence. I can't imagine not having him in the house and hearing him argue about the bacon each morning. I can't imagine the room next to mine being empty. I can't imagine not seeing him smile at me when we pass on the stairs.

He glances up as he slides the strap of the bag onto his shoulder, but our eyes don't meet for long before he looks away again. "I have no idea," he says quietly, turning his back on me and heading across to his bathroom. I follow behind him. "Dean's. Maybe. I don't know. My head's a mess."

I pause at the bathroom door. My eyes are heavy, but it doesn't stop me from keeping them trained on Tyler. I take a deep breath. "You've started dealing?"

Immediately he stops moving and just stands there, the only sound him exhaling slowly. He lowers his head and stares at the tiled flooring. "Only recently."

Disappointment floods through me. I thought it was serious before, but now I'm even more concerned, knowing just how deeply involved he is with the criminal underworld. "Why?"

He shakes his head as though he doesn't know the answer, and he still has his back to me. I wish I could see his face, mostly his eyes, so I could see if he looks sorry for what he's doing. "It's easy to . . . to get wrapped up in at all. Tiffani's so mad. She'll probably try to report me, I just know it."

"I can't believe she's . . ." I can't even bring myself to say it, because I'm struggling to wrap my head around the whole thing. The only thing I can think of is this: It's a damn good job Ella doesn't know yet, because I'm pretty sure she'd have a mental breakdown if she did.

"Me either," he murmurs, and right as he's opening up the cabinet door in the bathroom, he spins around and doubles over the toilet. He presses a hand against the wall to steady himself, and heaves. It must be the shock of it all. I felt the same way too. "Fuck."

"I don't know what to say, Tyler." I honestly don't. How can I tell him everything is going to be okay when it seems like nothing will be? I rub his back in an attempt to comfort him, but it only makes me feel stupid. His former girlfriend is pregnant, and here I am, rubbing his back while he attempts to throw up over the idea of it. "Where does this leave us?"

"What?"

"Us," I say again. "What's going to happen with us? You and Tiffani?"

He heaves again, but nothing comes up, so he blows out some air and stands. Turning to face me, he finally locks his eyes with mine. He does look sorry. "I don't know. I need to figure all of this out first."

"I don't know either," I say, but my heart falls through my chest the second the words leave my lips. What the hell is going to happen now? Tyler and Tiffani just got tied back together. Where does that leave me? Tossed to the side while they figure out how to handle the situation they've just found themselves in?

Tyler edges past me and reaches into the cabinet to gather his toiletries, tossing them into the bag and beginning to zip it up. I notice there are some bottles left behind on the top shelf, and I know exactly what's inside them.

I nod to the antidepressants. "Please take them. You won't feel so down all the time."

Tyler follows my gaze, and for a moment, he contemplates the decision. I know what he's struggling with: antidepressants or alcohol and drugs. He glances back at me, sees my pleading expression, and then reaches for the three white bottles and tucks them into his bag. I can do nothing more than hope that he puts them to good use. Perhaps he'll feel better.

We stare at each other for a moment before he leaves. He still looks extremely pale, like he's been throwing up for weeks and has yet to recover. With his dull eyes mirroring mine, he leans forward and wraps his arms around me, pulling me into his embrace. It's the first time he's hugged me. Sure, I've kissed him a hell of a lot—we've even slept together—but we've never once just stood and held each other. We've never shared a moment like this, where my face is buried into his chest and his chin is resting on my head, and I can only wish that it's the first of many, because I like the way my body seems to fit perfectly into his.

And although I'm hungover and sweaty from my run, he presses his cold lips to my forehead and whispers, "I'll figure it out."

He pulls away, and in that moment he looks terrified. He has absolutely no idea what he's doing, and no matter how hard he's trying to put up a strong front, it's so clear that he's fighting the will to break down. I can't blame him, I really can't.

With a nod, he brushes past me and makes his way over to his door. I can only stare after him. I still feel numb, like I'm suffering from endless pins and needles, so I just watch as he steps out onto the landing without glancing back.

The last words I say before he leaves are, "I really hope you do."

29

Two days go by.

Two days in which I haven't seen nor spoken to Tyler, two days in which Ella has spent every waking hour moping around the house, two days in which everything feels out of place. Sometimes I hear Ella ask Dad where he thinks Tyler's at right at the moment. Dad always says he's not sure. Sometimes she even says that kicking him out of the house was the worst thing to do, because now she can't keep an eye on him. He has more reasons to get high now, she believes. I like to think she's wrong about this. I have enough trust in Tyler to hope that he's viewing all of this as the wake-up call he needed. A chance to maybe figure out his life. Jamie and Chase, however, aren't so understanding. Last night, Jamie argued with his mom. Yelled at her for kicking Tyler out, called her unfair and too strict. This morning, Chase said he didn't like the house being so boring. Said he wanted Tyler to take him out for a ride in the Audi, something they do once in a while. Chase is into cars. But today his brother isn't here to take him for a ride around the neighborhood while over-revving his engine.

Thinking of Tyler's car, it's odd not seeing it parked diagonally on the sidewalk. I imagine it parked outside Dean's house, in that same I'm-a-terrible-parker manner, and it makes me think, in that split second, about heading over there to visit. Just because Tyler has been kicked out of the house doesn't mean I can't see him. He's only five minutes away. Maybe I'll ask Rachael to give me a ride over there.

Shaking my head as I run across the lawn and over the street, I make my way to the red Bug that's waiting for me on Rachael's driveway, its engine purring. Rachael is adjusting her hair when I slide into the passenger seat.

"You're officially the worst person ever when it comes to time management," she throws at me, but she's smiling. She pushes shut the mirror in her sun visor and pulls on her seatbelt.

"I'm sorry," I say as I press a hand to my chest in mock horror, "I'm so, so sorry. I shouldn't be three minutes late. Feel free to burn me at the stake, oh holy one."

Rachael laughs and whacks my arm, rolling her eyes straight to the back of her head in the same way that Amelia often does. I feel homesick in that second. "So," she says, "what's the gossip from Saturday?"

As she drives, I stare at her. Worry consumes every inch of my being, combined with the fear that Tiffani has probably already begun to spread our secret like wildfire. *Rachael knows,* I think. *And Meghan, and Jake, and Dean. They all know.*

She glances out the corner of her eye, a playful grin on her lips. "C'mon," she says, "You have to tell me! Did you go home with Jake?"

Maybe she doesn't know, or maybe she does and is just trying to catch me out, so she can stop the car and yell, "LIAR!"

It's the first time I've seen Rachael since Saturday. After

her three-day hangover subsided, she called up the house and demanded that we go for coffee to have a catch-up, because she hasn't seen me in "two years." Now I'm wishing I'd faked an illness.

Eventually I answer her question with a quick "No," and then turn away from her. I prop my elbow against the window and pretend to find the neighborhood interesting and beautiful, but after living here for a while, it just looks familiar and normal and boring to me now. "What about you?" I throw her a quick glance, looking at her from beneath my eyelashes.

She grows flustered under my stare and leans forward, gripping onto the steering wheel and biting back a smile. "I stayed at Trevor's."

"Just stayed over?" My eyebrows arch.

"Well, that and some other unmentionable events." A laugh escapes her lips but it quickly falters into a sigh. She shrugs. "I just want him to ask me out on a proper date already."

I feel bad for her. Trevor is all I've heard her speak about the entire summer, and although he may only be her "party fling," according to Tiffani, it's obvious Rachael is seeking something more from their encounters.

"Guys are assholes," I tell her, because I'm starting to believe it.

Take Trevor, for example. Sure, he may be sweet when he's drunk, but deep down he's probably nothing but a horndog. Example two: Jake. The player. I admit to falling into the trap at the beginning of the summer, when I thought he actually cared about getting to know me, but in the end all he was really after was a new name to add to his list. Final example: Tyler. He's an asshole for the way he treats people and he's an asshole for getting Tiffani pregnant.

This fact has gradually angered me more and more over the past couple days. I didn't take him as someone who'd be so careless, who could make such a big mistake. The reality of it all is beginning to sink in, and hurts. Tyler's going to be a dad. He's too young and too irresponsible, and I know that there is absolutely no way he'll be able to handle it.

Rachael bitches about Trevor all the way to Santa Monica Boulevard. He's hot, but he's a prick. He can be really loving, but he's a prick. His parents like her, but he's a prick. By the time we park the car and reach the Refinery, I feel like I know enough about him I could steal his identity.

"I'm so freaking mad," Rachael huffs, finally giving up on her ranting. But she perks up when she orders her cappuccino, and I my latte, and then we set ourselves down by the wooden table against the windows facing out onto the boulevard. "Oh, I totally forgot!" She pulls her purse up onto the table and rummages around inside before pulling out not only twenty bucks, but also my phone. "You must have left it at my place before we went to Dean's. I found it under my bed just as I was leaving to pick you up."

I stare at her. "Are you kidding me? I thought I was mugged on the beach! I cried!"

She bursts out laughing and places the bill and the phone in front of me, but when I try to switch it on I realize it's dead. I heave a sigh just as the barista sets our coffees down in front of us, immediately brightening up my day.

"Okay, I've been waiting all morning to talk to you about this. Let's get down to the big news! Can you believe Tyler and Tiffani broke up?" Rachael explodes after taking a sip of her coffee, looking at me with wide eyes. "I mean, I've been telling her for ages that he's a piece of shit—I'm sorry, I know he's your brother and I know I'm supposed to be his friend, but seriously, he treated her like crap." Her hands move as she talks, frantic and quick, like she's a reporter announcing some breaking news. In a way, it kind of is.

"Has she spoken to you?" I set my eyes on her, wondering if Tiffani has told her the full story: the version that includes me. I try to ignore the fact that Rachael's taking Tiffani's side. Sure, Tyler didn't treat Tiffani all that great, but can anyone blame him? She was controlling him and he didn't want to be with her.

"She came over last night," Rachael says, and I listen while holding my mug to my lips, sipping slowly at my latte. "He broke up with her. How insane is that? I think she said it was on Sunday morning."

"Yeah, it was. I was there." I shift my eyes to the windows, observing the constant stream of people and cars passing by.

Rachael's eyes widen again, her entire mind focused on the drama. "Can you believe he cheated on her again?"

Immediately my eyes snap back over to her and I slowly lower my mug. I wrap my hands tight around it. My heart is throbbing in my chest. "Did she tell you who the girl was?"

"No," she says, and the biggest wave of relief flows through my body. "Do you know?"

"No," I lie. I turn away again, hoping she doesn't see the guilt in my eyes or hear the waver in my voice. "Another girl from out of town, I think."

"I just can't believe he turned around and broke up with her when it should have been the other way around." She purses her lips and gives a small shake of her head. "She was so pissed off she told his mom about the coke."

I frown. That's not the only thing she told her. "Yeah, he got kicked out."

"I know," Rachael says, "which is why I can't believe she's letting him stay at her place." Holding her coffee to her lips, she takes a long swig.

"Wait, what?"

She glances at me. "What?"

"He's staying at Tiffani's place? He told me he was going to Dean's." This new information hits me hard. I get that the situation Tyler is in just now is tricky, but I didn't expect him to just throw himself back into her arms so easily. My heart beats even faster.

"Well, he's definitely not at Dean's," Rachael says, an eyebrow raised. She shrugs. "I don't know. I thought it was weird too. But you know how Tiffani is. She's so possessive over him, no wonder she's forgiven him. She can't bear the thought of some other girl claiming him. She says they'll definitely get back together, which is so stupid, because he's nothing but a cheater, so why the hell would she want to get back together with him?" She puffs out her cheeks once she stops babbling. "She's kind of a lunatic. She just can't let go."

"She's pregnant, Rachael," I say in a hushed voice, and it slips out of my mouth so fast that I begin to panic. It's not up to me to break the news. Maybe Tiffani wanted to tell Rachael and Meghan herself.

Rachael's jaw drops and I swear she almost tilts backward off the chair, her coffee splashing out of the mug when she slams it down on the table. She immediately huddles closer to me, her eyes blinking quickly from the shock. "What?"

"She told him on Sunday," I whisper, feeling sick again at the idea of it all again. "Right after he broke up with her." The more I think it all through, the more it makes sense. Of course he's staying at her place. That's what happens when couples end up with a kid on their hands. They throw the past behind them and stick together. "She has to forgive him and he has to go back to her."

"This is insane!" Rachael whisper-yells into my ear before pulling away from me. She tries to process the news, her eyes still blinking wildly as she stares out the windows. A perplexed expression crosses her face. She looks back over to me. "Wait," she says. "She was drinking at Dean's on Saturday."

I don't reply. I just think about her words for a second, trying to recall everything that happened at Dean's before I got drunk in the garage. Rachael's right. Tiffani was more than keen to join in with the game of shot roulette, which she shouldn't have been if she was pregnant. She was tipsy when I spoke to her in the back yard.

"Wait," Rachael says again, holding up a finger, one eyebrow arched. "You said she told him right after he broke up with her?"

"Yeah. Like, five seconds after."

Rachael exhales a long breath before saying, "You don't think . . .?"

My thoughts suddenly sync with hers, and the realization of what she's hinting at hits me so hard that I feel like I've been punched in the gut.

Tiffani's faking it.

"Oh my God."

"It's not uncommon," Rachael says, pressing a manicured finger to her lips. It's as though she's just cracked a murder case. "You tell the guy you're pregnant so that he has no choice but to stay with you."

"You really think Tiffani would do that?"

"I want to believe that she wouldn't," she says quietly as

she reaches for her coffee, "but she'd seriously stop at nothing to stay with Tyler. He does a lot for her reputation. Like I said, she's a lunatic."

Or, in Tyler's words, a psychopath. But I don't think she has a real mental disorder, just some serious issues. She has to have issues if she's willing to attempt something like this.

I can't even begin to imagine Tiffani stooping to such a low, but Rachael is right. Over the summer I've learned that Tyler and Tiffani's relationship is seriously messed up. No matter what he does, she can't stand to be without him, because she can't stand not being in control. Of course she wants it all back. And how do you force a guy into getting back together with you? Fake a pregnancy.

"I know how we can find out if she's lying or not!" Rachael says enthusiastically, and I swing my legs around to face her properly. My forehead creases with worry. I don't know what's going through Rachael's head, but it's probably something ridiculous. "You know how we're all going over there on Friday?"

"I'm not invited," I say, and immediately turn back around and set my eyes on the store across the street. I wasn't even aware that Tiffani had invited everyone over, so clearly I'm not included. And I can't blame her.

"You are," Rachael says, and then nods to my phone, still lying on the table in front of me. "You haven't had that for a couple days. She's probably texted you. Anyway, it's movie night."

I grind my teeth together to stop me from accidentally saying something. Rachael doesn't understand. I know I won't be invited. Tiffani hates me. But I can't tell Rachael this, of course, because Rachael will ask why, and that's a question I'm not willing to answer. What would I even say? *Tiffani hates me because I slept with Tyler, who, just to clarify, in case you forgot, is my stepbrother. Two secrets in one! So, Rachael, I'm a shitty friend and a shitty person. Hell yeah!* .

"So on Friday," she continues, getting to her feet, "we need to figure out if she's lying or not. And I know exactly how."

* * *

Once I'm home and I've charged my phone, I find twenty-nine missed calls from Dad from Saturday night, and three from Mom over the past few days. There are also some texts from Amelia, telling me that Landon Silverman hasn't stopped texting her ever since their sexual encounter in the back of his truck a few weeks ago, and that she keeps blowing him off because he's "no longer her type." Two months ago she was drooling over him in the hallways.

But there's not a single text from Tiffani.

Unsurprising.

There's also nothing from Tyler.

Surprising.

I haven't done anything to him, so he can't be mad at me. I know his head's most likely a mess, but that doesn't give him the right to just ignore me, to toss me to the side while he figures everything out. I still care. I still want to know how he's holding up. But for the most part, I try not to let his silence get to me. Maybe he just wants space.

With Dad, Ella and the boys visiting friends on the other side of the city, I have the house to myself. So while I'm rummaging around the kitchen, I decide to call my mom back to check in on her. In all my sixteen years of breathing, she has never once gone twenty-four hours without seeing me. Somehow, she's managed to survive an entire summer.

I drum my fingers along the worktop as I listen to the monotonous tone, but there's no answer, so I try her cell. She picks up on the third ring.

"Oh, look, my favorite daughter is alive!"

Her voice fills me with a warmth that can never be replaced, the type of warmth that makes you smile no matter how bad your day is. I'm starting to appreciate it more. "Mom," I say, smiling, of course, "I'm your only daughter."

"That's why it's such an easy choice," she fires back. "How's everything going?"

Terrible, I want to say. *Dreadful, awful, out of control.* "Good."

"And how are things with the asshole who gave you half your genes?"

I roll my eyes and yank open the refrigerator. Mom's never been shy when it comes to expressing her severe dislike for Dad. "Not good," I admit. Dad's been awfully quiet since Sunday and I can't figure out if it's because he's mad at me or if it's because he's trying to be cool for once by leaving me alone to do my own thing without him stalking my every move. It's most probably the former.

"What's happened?" Mom asks, and her voice is suddenly laced with concern.

I shrug even though she can't see me, and then press my phone to my ear with my shoulder as I fumble around inside the refrigerator, shifting through packets of meat until I find the apples stored at the back. I grab one and step back. "Nothing," I say. "We've just been arguing a lot."

"About what?" Now she just sounds worried, and there's

whistling across the connection. She must be outside.

"Me not coming home," I confess. Mom's always been easy to confide in, always been there when I needed her, always been my best friend. I'm never apprehensive about being honest with her. "I've stayed out all night a couple times."

"Doing what?" Scrap the concern and the worry, now she sounds stern. "Eden? Do I need to put you on birth control?"

For a second I just fall silent, too mortified to muster up a reply. That's another thing about Mom: She's very, very straightforward. "That's it," I say, "I'm hanging up now, bye Mom, please don't talk to me ever again, I can no longer make eye contact with you, it's been nice knowing you, love you, bye."

"Eden!"

"Yes?"

I can hear her laughing down the phone. A gentle, soft laugh. "I'm sorry. It's just that you're sixteen and you're getting older and at your age I—"

"Can we please change the subject?" With my cheeks flushed, I head over to the faucet, wash my apple, and then pull myself up onto the worktop and take a bite.

"Hmm," Mom says after a long minute of hearing my crunching across the line, "you're enjoying your summer, aren't you?"

I take another bite and swing my legs back and forth over the edge of the counter, tilting my head to the side as I carefully consider my answer. I know for a fact that if I'd been in Portland for the summer, it would have been spent trying to hang out with Amelia, minus Alyssa and Holly. It's been nice to get away from their constant digs about my weight for a while. I would have also probably joined the gym, maybe even studied, and I definitely wouldn't have fallen for someone I shouldn't have. Summer in Santa Monica has been an entirely new experience altogether.

"It's been different," I eventually answer.

"So you've made lots of friends there?"

I think about this for a moment. Tiffani has totally wiped me off her list of friends, so she doesn't make the cut, and Jake has zero substance once you see past his smooth pick-up lines, so I wouldn't consider him a friend either, more like a douchebag who tried to hit on me. So I'm left with Rachael, who has filled Amelia's void for the summer; Meghan, who has been consistently sweet; and Dean, who's always been there to either rescue me from a party or brighten up my day. And Tyler, of course. Although, I think we're slightly out of bounds when it comes to the friend zone. We crossed that line a long time ago.

I exhale. "I've made enough."

"And you really like the city?" she presses, a sense of urgency to her voice. I picture her gripping her phone tightly as she holds it to her ear, the way she always does when she's eager for gossip or yelling at sales representatives when they call first thing in the morning.

"I guess?"

"Eden," she says slowly, and then pauses. "What do you think about moving down there?"

I draw my phone away from my ear and scrunch my face up at the screen, wondering if I've misheard her. Moving? As in, living here? "What the hell?" I hold my phone between my ear and my shoulder again as I slide off the counter, staring out the patio doors. "Like, permanently? Me?"

"Us," she corrects. She's quiet now, but I can still hear cars whizzing past her.

"Us?"

"I've been thinking," she says, and her voice rises an octave as she she dives into her venting mode. "How come your dad gets to just head off and start up a new life somewhere else? Why can't I do that? Why am I stuck here in Portland when I didn't even want to live here in the first place? I was happy in Roseburg, but noooooo, your dad wanted the big city life of Portland!"

"Santa Monica is a city."

"Yes, but there are half a million more people in Portland, Eden," she informs me in her matter-of-fact voice, the same voice she uses to talk to patients. "I've been looking into it."

"But why?" I almost scream the words in exasperation. For someone who hates Dad so much, it doesn't make sense for her to want to move closer to him. "If you want to try somewhere new, move to Chicago with me in two years. Or Canada. Why do you want Santa Monica?"

Silence ensues for a moment, and I impatiently dig my nails into my apple as I wait for her to answer. She takes a deep breath. "Well . . ." she starts, slightly hesitant, "while you've been gone I've been talking to a few people. I joined a dating website."

This takes me by the utmost surprise. Mom . . . dating. It's something I never thought I'd witness, simply because for three years straight she has drilled me with the fact that men are the spawn of Satan. "Are you playing a joke on me?"

"No." She laughs a little, but I can tell she's slightly nervous, most likely embarrassed too. "This summer has made me realize that I don't want to be living on my own when you go off to college and that I really, really need to throw this divorced ass back onto the market. I've been talking to this really nice guy for over a month now." She waits for a second, presumably to see if I have anything to say, and then continues when I remain silent. "His name's Jack. And guess where he lives? Culver City. Fifteen minutes away from where you are."

I know where Culver City is: It's where Tyler and I just so happened to end up at the police station. "So you want to move here because you've been talking to some guy for a month? He could be a total creep, Mom."

"God, Eden, no." She heaves a sigh and I can hear her jingling around a set of keys, and it makes me wonder what she's doing and where she is. "More like I head down to meet him over coffee, and we'll take it from there. Who knows? It could go really well, and you've already made friends there, and it would make starting a new school less daunting. It's a good place to start for both of us."

Less daunting? School with Tiffani and school with Jake and school with Tyler? I can't think of anything more anxiety-inducing than that. "I don't know," I murmur as I chew my lip and toss the apple into the trash can, barely eaten, and then run a hand through my hair. "It's such a huge thing."

"I think it could be good for you," she adds. "You won't have to deal with those girls again. The ones with the stuck-up parents."

"Alyssa and Holly," I tell her, but my words escape as a mere whisper. I try to ignore the churning in my stomach and the pounding of my heart, focusing instead on Mom's warmth as it radiates across the line.

"I passed them in Walmart the other day," she says roughly, "and do you have any idea how bad I wanted to hurl my bag of onions at them?"

I laugh, and it feels good to be giggling at her humor and

ability to lighten up even the worst of moods, and it feels nice knowing she's on the other end of the line. "I'll bet you did."

"Look," she says, but then pauses for a moment as a door swings open. I recognize the familiar creaking, the annoying oil-deprived hinges of our front door offering an irritating greeting every time we open it. "It's just an idea. We'll talk about it when you get home. Deal?"

I'm about to say "deal," but before I even get the words out of my mouth, the front door slams shut, loudly echoing across the connection. Following it, there's the squeakiest of barks.

My eyebrows shoot up. "Was that a dog?"

"Dammit," Mom mutters. "She was supposed to be a surprise."

30

By Friday, I was getting pretty tired of moping around waiting for Tyler to come back. I just wanted to see him, even if it was only for a few seconds while he came home to grab some more clothes. But he never did show up for the week, and he never did reply to my texts, and I never did see him.

It pissed me off a lot more than I thought it would. I knew I'd miss not seeing him every morning, but I never thought I'd grow frustrated and mad at him. It didn't make sense for him to completely cut me off. When I asked him if he wanted to meet up at the Refinery for coffee (as stepsiblings, of course), I heard nothing back. When I asked him if he was doing okay, I heard nothing back. When I asked him if he even remembers what happened last weekend, my phone had never been so silent. Tiffani probably has him wrapped around her finger.

Tiffani, who absolutely hates me.

Tiffani, whose house I'm about to turn up at uninvited.

Tiffani, who's most likely going to burst into flames when she sees me.

"Are you going out?" a voice asks from over my shoulder, and I swivel around from the living room window to meet Ella's curious eyes. She runs them over my outfit, which doesn't exactly qualify as attire for lazing around the house.

"Am I grounded?" I have a feeling I might be, but Dad's never mentioned it, so I'm praying he's letting last weekend slide. Even if I am, he's not here to reinforce it.

"No," Ella says. "Where are you going?"

I divert my eyes back to the window as I stand there, staring through the blinds and fixing my eyes on Rachael's car, which is parked on her driveway. She should be out any second. It's pouring rain, the dark sky casting a permanent shadow over the city, and I have to squint through the drops on the windows in order to see properly. "Movie night with my friends," I answer without turning back to Ella.

There's a silence, and I can hear her shifting across the room to leave, but then she stops walking and takes a deep breath. "Do you know if . . ." she murmurs quietly. "Do you know if Tyler will be there?"

"He'll be there," I say immediately. That's another reason I've agreed to go tonight: Tyler. If the only way to see him is by turning up at his crazy ex-girlfriend's house, then I'm willing to go through the anxiety of the whole thing. I just want to see if he's okay. Spinning back around, I meet Ella's sad gaze. "Are you missing him?"

I don't think she quite knows the answer, because she has to think about it for a second. After Tyler left on Sunday, she spent the entire night bursting into tears every half hour, and part of me wondered if she was crying over more than just the drugs. "I am," she says, finally, and then moves back into the center of the living room to sit down on the couch. She picks up a cushion and holds it in her lap, gripping it tightly. "The house feels empty without him, and I know that sounds weird, because he was never here half the time anyway, but there's just something odd."

I know what she's talking about. She's talking about the way the house is quiet and the way the vegetarian food in the refrigerator hasn't been touched, she's talking about the fact that there's an empty seat at the table each morning, and she's talking about the fact that her son is no longer stumbling home in the middle of the night, even more lost than he was the night before.

"Yeah," I say. "I get it."

"I'm just worried about him," she admits, and I like the way she's being honest with me, just like she has been the entire summer. Ella's not that bad for a stepmom, despite my first impression of her when she paraded me around the back yard at the barbecue introducing me to every single neighbor. She felt too obnoxious, too loud. Only now does it occur to me that perhaps it was fake, nothing more than a brave front, the same way her son has built up a façade to make him seem like he's fine . . . But they're not fine.

It feels like I've spent the whole summer being blind. Everything is so obvious now, and I just wish I'd been able to piece it all together weeks ago. I should have figured Tyler out a long time ago; I should have tried to better understand his aggression toward his father. It feels the same way with Ella. I was so adamant that I'd dislike her that to begin with I never understood anything about her. But now I'm starting to appreciate her for her vulnerability. Now I understand her.

Tears threaten to fall, so I turn back to the window and blink them away before Ella notices, but I think she already has. Rachael still hasn't come out of her house yet, so I glance down at my feet and swallow back the lump in my throat. "Tyler told me about his dad," I say quietly.

I hear Ella take a sharp breath and I'm almost afraid to turn around in case she's furious at me for bringing it up, but I'm alone in the house with her and it feels like the right time to talk about it. Dad's taking Jamie to get his wrist checked out, and Chase has gone along for the ride. And Tyler . . . Well. He's still gone.

"He told you?"

I crane my neck to look at her, taking in her wide eyes and furrowed brows and parted lips, and then I make my way over to the couch and sit down beside her. She stares at me in surprise. "At the weekend," I tell her, but I talk slowly to ensure nothing slips out, like the fact that I ended up sleeping with Tyler too. "He told me everything."

"He actually told you?" Ella's just blinking at me now, and when I nod she hugs the cushion to her chest and looks away. "I can't believe he told you. He doesn't like to talk about it. I'm . . ." She tapers off and just shakes her head, still a little shocked. "I just want him to be okay. That's all I want." Her voice sounds delicate and hushed, her eyes flickering between me and the wall. "Not a 4.0 GPA or a tidy room or to wash the dishes, just okay, and he's not even that."

Hearing her talk like this makes my eyes well up again, so I can't even bring myself to reply. If I open my mouth, my voice will sound choked, and if my voice sounds choked, the tears will escape. So I just sit there, holding my breath and biting down hard on my lower lip, because I really don't want her to see me crying.

"I've been in discussion with some people . . ." she says slowly, which thankfully saves me from having to speak, and I wait for what she's about to tell me. "They run events throughout the East Coast. Awareness events for . . ." She takes a deep breath and starts again. "They raise awareness of different kinds of abuse." Turning her head away from me, she draws her lips into her mouth and composes herself before glancing back over. "The organizers want Tyler to be a speaker."

"A speaker?"

She nods. "They want him to represent physical abuse. They have other teenagers standing for domestic, emotional . . . They want him to tell his story, over and over again, for a year. I don't think he'd be able to handle that, because he hates talking about it. That's why I'm just so surprised that he told you."

I take a minute to process this information while the rain batters against the windows. Last week it was so difficult for Tyler to tell me the truth, and I can't begin to imagine how tough he'd find it having to tell the story to strangers. But at the same time, he'd get to meet others who have been through the same things he has, and it just might help. "It could be good for him . . . You know, to talk about it."

"It's a really great opportunity," Ella adds, but she's staring off into the carpet, almost like she's weighing the pros and cons in her head. "He'd have to straighten himself out first though." That's a pro. This could be the kick that he needs to put him on the road to giving up on distractions, to becoming a person who doesn't depend on alcohol and drugs. "And he'd have to move to New York for a year, starting next summer." That's a con. A huge con.

I try to meet her eyes, but she's still staring at the floor. "Is that what my dad was talking about last week? When he mentioned New York?"

Another nod. "I haven't told Tyler yet. Now isn't the best

time." She glances sideways at me with a small smile on her lips, but it doesn't quite reach her eyes. That's something I've always found odd, people smiling when they're sad. There's no such thing as a sad smile. Just a brave one.

"You're a really good mom," I say, because they're the only words running through my mind as I watch her overthink the situation with Tyler, and they suddenly seem to spill out on their own accord. She only wants what's best for him, and sometimes that's not enough. But she's trying.

Her lips part in surprise. She looks like she's about to say something, but she's interrupted by the sound of a car horn blasting. The horn blows three times.

"That'll be Rachael," I say as I get to my feet. I smooth out the creases in my jeans and offer her a smile, because somehow in the past ten minutes I feel like I've gotten closer to her. For the first time, I really do see her as my stepmom. "I'll see you when I'm home."

The corners of her lips pull up into a smile to mirror mine, and this time her smile isn't brave. It's sincere.

Outside, Rachael has reversed out of her driveway and is furiously revving up her engine out front of my house instead. She rolls down the window as I approach and yells, "You were supposed to be looking for me! We're wasting valuable time!"

I throw open the door and slide inside, barely getting my seatbelt on before the car takes off down the avenue. The seat is wet from the rain. "I was talking to Ella," I say, but I don't want to leave room for her to ask what we were discussing, so I quickly add, "What's the plan?"

"Stop being curious," Rachael orders, lifting a hand off the wheel and wagging a finger at me. I scoff. Curious is all I'll ever be. "You don't even need to do anything. You'll mess it up, so let me talk."

I roll my eyes and adjust my seat, pushing it back to give me more legroom, and then I slump down and heave a sigh. "Where did this rain come from? It feels like I'm in Portland," I murmur, tapping my knuckles against the window as I try to distract myself, because nerves are rattling me. But I can't let Rachael know this, because then she'll wonder why I'm nervous, and there's no way in hell I'll be able to tell her that I'm panicking beyond despair over the fact that Tiffani is going to flip when I turn up at her front door.

So for the five-minute ride I act as normal as I possibly can. I text Amelia, rummage through the CDs packed into the glove box, adjust the heating, and, of course, listen to Rachael. She's telling me about Trevor again, and she's gushing over the fact that he's started adding hearts to the end of their texts, and she's blushing as she tells me how sweet he's suddenly being.

By the time we're nearing Tiffani's house, the nerves are almost completely gone because of my desperate need to escape Rachael's Trevor drama. I'd rather throw myself into Tiffani's arms than hear about how nice Trevor's shoulders are.

But the second we pull up outside, I revert to my original mindset. Tyler's car is parked on the driveway, side by side with Tiffani's, and suddenly I'm terrified again. I have to deal with both of them at once, and I'm certain that Tiffani will rip out my hair, and I have no clue what Tyler will say to me. That's if he even decides to talk in the first place.

I relax only slightly when I spot Dean's car and Jake's. The more of us, the better. If I make it over the threshold, at least they'll be there to make the situation less daunting. Even Jake seems like fun to hang out with right now.

"Remember, leave me to do the talking," Rachael says as she grabs her purse from the backseat. Quite frankly, I don't want to do the talking, so she really has nothing to worry about.

We lock up and run across the lawn to the front door, which Rachael promptly shoves open and drifts through. She never knocks, and this is something I'm still getting used to. That being said, not only do I feel unwelcome, I also feel extremely rude. Nonetheless, I follow Rachael into the house and a waft of fresh popcorn overwhelms me.

Immediately to the left of the open-plan area, Jake and Dean are stretched out on the L-shaped couches that run around the room. Meghan's not coming tonight, because she's grounded after last weekend, but Dean does sit up when he sees us so that he can acknowledge our presence with a nod and a smile. Other than that, both of them look bored and out of place. Jake's playing around with the remote for the TV, flicking through channels and sighing in between each one. Usually on Fridays we're at parties. Usually we're not having movie nights.

There's a laugh from somewhere to my right and my eyes immediately snap over to it. The first thing they land on is Tiffani. She's pulling out a bowl of popcorn from the microwave and then carelessly dropping it on the worktop as it burns her hands, laughing all the while and looking totally normal. Normal, not heartbroken. But it makes sense, because Tyler is standing right by her side, sighing at her ridiculous attempt to prepare food. He tries to laugh, but his lips only pull up into another one of his fake smiles. As usual, it doesn't reach his eyes.

I wonder what he's thinking about and what he's planning to do. Right now, he's stuck living at Tiffani's house, believing something that might not be true, something that Rachael is adamant on proving false. What are his thoughts? Are they going to get back together? It would be horrible if they did. Tyler's only just managed to get himself out of the grip she had on him and I'd hate to see him get wrapped up in that mess again.

The two of them are so distracted in the kitchen that they haven't even noticed Rachael and I entering the house, so I interlock my hands and twist my fingers around each other anxiously as I make my way over to the living room. I try to force a smile on my face, but my frown only ends up deepening.

Dean must notice my scowl. He sits up, his blue T-shirt contrasting with the brown of his eyes, and then whispers, "This is so awkward." He nods behind me to the pair in the kitchen. Tiffani's running a hand through Tyler's hair, her eyelashes fluttering. "They broke up but . . ."

Tell me about it, I think. We're all just as confused as each other. Have they broken up? Are they just friends now? Are they back together already? What the hell are they, besides incompatible?

Rachael's still standing by the front door, just staring at the two of them in disbelief. She cranes her neck to look at Dean and me, pointing a thumb to Tiffani while mouthing, "What the hell?" I've discovered by now that Rachael is very anti-Tyler-and-Tiffani.

Both Dean and I shrug, but really I just want to tear the plaster off the wall or smash the TV or set the couches on fire. I want to do something that will release the anger that's fizzing inside of me, and I can't even seem to figure out who I'm mad at. Part of me is mad at myself for finding myself in this situation, where I'm stuck between my stepbrother and his ex-girlfriend, or girlfriend. I don't know anymore.

"Rachael!" Tiffani's voice calls across the room, and both Rachael and I whip around to face her. She's hugging the bowl of popcorn to her chest and grinning. But it doesn't last long. Her eyes drift over to meet mine, and the second she lays eyes on me, her smile falters. "Eden?"

"It took you long enough to notice us!" Rachael complains jokingly as she pads across the carpet toward the staircase.

Tiffani's still staring at me, still glowering. "Sorry," she tells Rachael, but her eyes never leave mine. I can feel her glare boring holes in my skin and I try to glance down at the floor, but I can't, because I'm staring at the person standing two inches away from her.

And he's looking straight back.

Tyler's lips are parted and he's biting the skin on the inside of his cheek, his head tilted slightly. He looks paler than usual and his eyes are set deeper in their sockets, which makes him appear almost lifeless, like he hasn't slept for days and is about to pass out any second.

Rachael clears her throat from the staircase. "Tiff, can we talk to you for a sec?"

"Sure," she says bitterly, and with the flick of her hair, she spins around and slams the bowl of popcorn down onto the worktop.

I can feel Dean watching from behind me as she makes her way over to Rachael, and I can hear Jake watching football on the TV, and I can see Tyler edging his way over to the living room, wearing a pair of sweats and a faded T-shirt. It makes him look at home, and this makes me uncomfortable. Tiffani storms up the staircase, leaving Rachael to motion for me to join them. So I do, because although I'm terrified of Tiffani right now, I need to know if she's lying or not. But as I'm scrambling over to the stairs to catch up with them, Tyler grasps my elbow in passing.

He yanks me back, moves his lips toward my ear, and then hisses, "What are you doing here?"

"I could ask you the same thing," I mutter. Shoving his hand off me, I fix him with a glare that quickly turns into a disappointed frown. Something in his eyes shifts, the same way they were constantly altering last weekend, but before I can begin to process the change in his expression, he's already turning away from me and heading over to Dean and Jake.

I hover for a moment. I contemplate pulling him back and telling him that Ella misses him, and that there's a perfect opportunity waiting in New York for him, and that he doesn't need to stick around here wasting his time with Tiffani. But Rachael yells my name from the top of the stairs, so I have no choice but to follow the sound of her voice, leaving Tyler behind.

And at the back of my mind, there's only this: *We are never going to be able to be together.*

Upstairs, Tiffani is standing at the door to her room, her arms folded across her chest. To begin with it looks like she's blocking us from entering, but then I realize she's waiting for us to hurry up and get inside, so Rachael leads us in.

Immediately I notice that the room is different from the last time I was here. There are clothes scattered all over the carpet, and I realize that they belong to Tyler.

Rachael notices too, and, of course, she has something to

say about it. "Is your mom seriously letting him stay here?" She kicks a pair of jeans to the side.

"Yes," Tiffani snaps. She's clearly pissed off by this point, given that I'm here standing in her room, not to mention that we've just separated her from Tyler. "Now what is it?"

She glances between the two of us, awaiting an answer, while I stare at Rachael and Rachael stares at her. I'm not planning on doing any talking whatsoever. If I do, like Rachael said, I'll only mess up. So I wait for her to execute her brilliant plan, growing even more anxious for the truth.

"I'm not even going to do this subtly; I'm just going to ask you straight up," Rachael says, and the atmosphere in the room thickens as we all wait for the question I know she's about to ask. With her purse resting over her arm, she taps her foot impatiently on the carpet and locks eyes with Tiffani. "Are you pregnant?"

I stare at Rachael. That's it? That's her clever plan? It does, however, do a good job of startling Tiffani and taking her by surprise. She's so flustered by the abrupt question that she just stares at Rachael with wide blue eyes and parted lips. And then she fires her eyes in my direction.

They're like ice as she grits her teeth, grinding them together while fury washes over her. She knows I told Rachael. I'm the only person who could have. She takes a while to respond while the rain batters against the window, the sky an ugly gray. "Y-yes," she manages to stammer.

I raise my eyebrows and exchange a glance with Rachael, who nods and then directs her eyes back to Tiffani once more. "Okay," she says as she reaches into her purse and begins to rummage inside, "you shouldn't have a problem with taking a couple these then, right?" Just as the words leave her lips,

Rachael pulls out two drugstore pregnancy tests, her expression taut as she waves them in the air.

And it only takes these two items to scare Tiffani to death. She's staring at them, wide-eyed and blinking furiously, while the corners of her lips twitch as though she's fighting for words to rise in her throat. I can see her digging her nails into her palms. "No problem," she squeaks, finally, but her voice is so shaky that it becomes obvious that it is a problem.

"We'll just sit here and wait," Rachael informs her with a tight smile as she passes the two small boxes into Tiffani's trembling hands.

Tiffani studies the tests, gives Rachael a shaky nod, and then forces her body toward the bathroom. Her steps are slow and unwilling, her breathing fast and uneven. When she reaches the door, she places a hand flat against it and comes to a halt. Quickly, she spins around and there are tears rolling down her cheeks, her face red. "Fine! I'm not!" She screams the words across the room at us and she bursts into tears.

Rachael throws me a triumphant grin, but I'm in no mood to start grinning back. I feel numb. Tiffani did lie. It sickens me that she had to resort to such a pathetic act, and it worries me even more that she was planning on misleading Tyler. For how long? What was she going to do? Feign a miscarriage and hope the two of them would live happily ever after?

"What the hell is wrong with you, Tiffani?" Rachael snaps, and I'm thinking the exact same thing. You have to be a pretty terrible and desperate person to do something like this.

Tiffani's sobbing, the rain that's pelting against the window drowning out the sound of her sniffing. Everything feels so loud all of a sudden and the only thing I can think about is Tyler.

He's downstairs, totally oblivious, and still believes that he has quite possibly made a huge mistake. None of this is fair on him. He's probably stressing out over the whole situation, wondering how he's going to break the news to Ella and figuring out what's going to happen with Tiffani. But now he has no reason to stay with her, because there's nothing holding him to her.

"I'm telling Tyler," I splutter. My heart is beating frantically in my chest and I know I need to tell him as soon as possible, and I don't trust Tiffani enough right now to let her fix her own mistake, so I throw open her bedroom door. "He needs to know."

"No!" Tiffani screams, but I storm my way along the hallway before she can stop me, too furious to worry about what she'll do. She still knows our secret, but right now I'm so zeroed in on Tyler knowing the truth about her that I don't even care if she tells or not.

When I jog down the staircase, Tyler's lying on the couch staring at the TV screen alongside Jake and Dean, watching some football game that I don't take notice of.

"Tyler," I snap, loudly so that it'll grasp his attention, "I need to talk you. Right now. Kitchen." I blurt out the words as quickly as I can, and although they come out blunt, Tyler can hear the strain in my voice, and he immediately knows that something's up.

He gets to his feet while Dean raises an eyebrow curiously, but I move away and as far into the kitchen as I can go so that neither he nor Jake can hear us. Tyler comes padding across the carpet in his sweats, a puzzled look on his face. He stops directly in front of me, and I quickly steal a glance over his shoulder to ensure Dean has looked away. He has.

"Tiffani's not pregnant," I hiss, my voice hushed but frantic. "She's faking it so that you'll get back together with her."

He quickly takes a step back, appearing slack-jawed as he blinks at me. "What?"

"She just admitted it to us!"

For a long minute, he just stares at the wall as the expression in his eyes shifts, his breathing slow. I wait. I wait to see which expression he's going to end up with. I keep waiting. He clenches his jaw, his hands curling into fists, his features hardening, and soon he's livid. He looks like he's only just stopping himself from punching the wall, so I place a hand on his arm in an effort to comfort him, but then immediately draw it away when I hear footsteps on the staircase.

Tiffani comes bounding down, tears streaming down her face, her eyes searching the living room. Both Jake and Dean stare at her with parted lips, because the sight of her crying is enough to draw their attention away from the game. She spins around from the living room to the kitchen, and it's then that Tyler's eyes meet hers.

And she must be able to tell by his expression that he's furious at her, because she cries even harder as she rushes across the room to us, her eyes swollen. "Baby, please, I'm sorry," she tries, but it just sounds choked and unintelligible. "I'm so, so sorry!"

She tries to reach out to touch him, but he swiftly angles his body away from her outstretched hand and yells, "You're a psychopath!" It's so loud that everyone falls silent.

Rachael's standing at the bottom of the staircase, her eyes fixed on the scene, and Dean and Jake have paused the TV and sat up to watch.

"I hate you!" Tiffani screams, but when I glance back over to her, she's not looking at Tyler. She's looking at me. Her eyes are fierce, and I can place a bet on what's running through her mind right now. And so I think: *Here it goes. She's going to tell them all our secret, because now she has every reason to.*

I squeeze my eyes shut and wait for it, for her voice to yell out the truth and for the rest of them to gasp, but no one's saying anything. When I steal a glance through my half-closed lids, her lips are pressed into a firm line, and she just continues to stare at me. And then, for the briefest of moments, I swear she almost smiles.

And right then, I realize she's not going to tell them. At least not now. It's obvious she's planning on holding on to our secret for a little while longer.

And this absolutely terrifies me.

She bursts into tears again and buries her face in her hands, turning away from us, spinning back around to the staircase and pushing Rachael out of her way.

Tyler's still furious, and he slams his palm flat against the worktop before pinching the bridge of his nose between his thumb and forefinger. He exhales slowly, his eyes closed. "I'm leaving," he mutters when he opens them again. "I'm not staying here. She's insane."

I hear a door slam somewhere upstairs, and the five of us just exchange glances, unsure of what we're supposed to do. Tyler, on the other hand, knows perfectly fine what he's doing. He's making his way across the kitchen to grab his car keys from the worktop, his muscles bulging as he does so, and without another word he storms over to the front door and wrenches it open. The rain finds its way into the house, leaving drops of water on the carpet, just before

Tyler disappears through it, slamming it shut behind him.

Silence. Tyler's just stormed out, and Tiffani's upstairs having a mental breakdown, and we're all just sitting here in her house trying to process what's just happened.

"So I take it they're not together?" Jake says with a slight laugh.

From across the room, Rachael's staring at me with wide eyes and raised eyebrows. I don't think she was expecting it to play out like this; I don't think she was expecting me to throw myself into the middle of it. She looks like she's trying to decide whether or not she should go upstairs and check on Tiffani, because she keeps shifting her weight from one foot to the other, moving up and down the stairs while she contemplates it all.

Somewhere amidst the hammering rain, I hear the sound of Tyler's car rev to life, its engine roaring from the driveway. My conversation with Ella floods my mind, and I quickly try to remember everything she said, everything about New York. I might not know where Tyler's planning to go right now, but I do know where he should go. Home.

I hug my hoodie tight around my body and prepare myself for the run, yanking the hood over my hair and making for the door, praying that I catch him before he takes off. Without a word, I pull open the door and the rain blows into my face, freezing my nose. I hear Rachael calling from behind me, asking where the hell I'm going, but I'm too focused on Tyler's car to pay attention to her.

Holding onto my hood, I run along the stone path and come to a halt by the driver's side, and the windows are so tinted and the rain is so heavy that I can barely see him. I rap my knuckles against the glass, squinting as drops of rain roll down my face. It feels just like an October morning in Portland, only heavier.

Tyler rolls down his window an inch and yells, "Get in!"

I jog around to the front of the vehicle and quickly slip into the passenger seat, heaving a sigh when I slam the door shut behind me. I've only been outside for a matter of twenty seconds, but I'm soaked straight through. I push my hood down and blow wet strands of hair out of my face, and then I turn to Tyler.

His hair is wet and ruffled as he presses his lips into a firm line and puts the car in drive. "Ready to go?"

"No, Tyler." I shake my head. The rain sounds louder in here as it hits the bodywork of the vehicle, and the pitter-patter begins to drum in my ears. "I'm gonna go back inside."

He pulls a face as if to say I've lost my mind. "Why the hell did you just come out here?"

"Because," I say, but it comes out as a pant while I wipe the back of my hand across my face, "I need to talk to you first, so listen. First things first: Please don't ever go back to Tiffani."

He snorts, gripping the steering wheel tighter. "Screw Tiffani. She's unbelievable."

I stare at the windshield, watching the water roll down the glass, and for a moment it feels relaxing. I glance back over to him, but his eyes are fixed on the wheel. "Tyler," I say quietly, trying my hardest to draw his gaze to meet mine, and he slowly does. His cheeks are a little red, which contrasts with the paleness of his lips. "Please go home and talk to your mom. She's there alone just now, and trust me, she'll let you back into the house. She has something she needs to tell you, and it's really, really important."

He clenches his jaw then and turns his head away, staring out his side window to the lawn, but it's blurred through the rain. "I'm not welcome there," he says stiffly.

"I'm serious." I angle my body around to face him, so that I can see his eyes. They're vibrant yet somehow calm, and I can almost see the gears in his mind shifting as he considers what I'm telling him. "Just hear her out, Tyler. Go home and ask her about New York."

His eyebrows draw together as he glances sideways at me. "New York?"

I exhale before softly saying, "Talk to your mom, Tyler."

"Okay." He lets out a sigh while running a hand through his damp hair, and right then I want to kiss him again.

I want to swing over onto his lap just like I did weeks ago at the pier, I want to crash my lips into his like I did the first time in his room before we left for Meghan's birthday party, and I want to feel his touch the exact same way I felt it on Saturday.

I want to do all of these things, but I can't bring myself to.

There's something in the back of my mind that's telling me there's no point. Just because Tyler and Tiffani are clearly not getting back together doesn't mean that Tyler and I will automatically get into a relationship. We can't. There's just no possible way for us to be together, and this hurts me more than anything else. It hurts more than Dad walking out. It hurts more than Alyssa and Holly's cruel comments.

It isn't painful.

It's agonizing.

It's all I've thought about the past few days. I thought about the fact that I'm going home next month. I thought about the fact that our parents would kill us if they ever found out what we've been up to. I thought about the fact that this is wrong, and it's impossible to convince myself otherwise.

I want to be with Tyler. I do. More than anything else. I want to be with him more than I want to get into the University of Chicago. I want to be with him more than I want to be skinny. I'd do anything for it to happen. But it never will, and so there is absolutely no point in wasting our time.

Tyler notices my stare. "What?"

"I would kill to be able to kiss you every day," I admit quietly. I will myself not to break down. I know putting a stop to us is the best thing to do for us both. It'll be too hard to keep going. Too complicated. Too wrong.

"You can," he tells me, and he's almost whispering as he turns to face me, his eyes studying me delicately, like he'd snap my body in half if he were to narrow them. "Every single day. I wouldn't mind."

"Me either," I murmur. I can feel a dryness in my throat as I build up the courage to just get this over with, to just blurt it all out at once in hope that it'll hurt less. "But that's the problem, Tyler. *We* wouldn't mind. What about everyone else?"

He takes a moment to process my words and the pained look in my eyes, to understand what I'm trying to tell him. And when he figures it out, I can see the hurt flashing across his face. He has to glance away as he swallows, and when he looks back, his eyebrows are furrowed, his eyes crinkled at the corners. "We can get around everyone else," he tries, but his voice is weak and he has to pause for a moment while he finds a deeper tone. "We can figure this out. They'll understand. Maybe not at first, but they will. Seriously. We'll manage. We'll . . . We'll do it." He moves his hands as he speaks, as he babbles an endless list of reassurances at me, but none of them are helpful.

"Tyler," I say, and he stops breathing heavily for a moment while he listens. And it's then that the tears press at my waterlines, because I know exactly what I'm about to tell him next. I fear that hearing myself say it will only make it feel all the more true. "We can't be together."

And it does feel true now. It is the truth.

Tyler grits his teeth to stop his lips from trembling. He shakes his head slowly, his eyes squeezing shut as he exhales through his nose. He just sits there for a while, not really doing anything, just holding himself together as best he can. While he does, the tears roll down my face and I have to quickly dab at my cheeks to wipe them away. Crying always makes things seem worse than they are.

But I think this is the worst this situation could possibly be. So I'm allowed to cry. I'm allowed to stare at Tyler's quivering lips through blurred eyes and I'm allowed to feel like I'm dying inside. I'm allowed to, because I am. My entire body is going numb. My chest is tightening. My heart is contracting.

Tyler finally opens his eyes again. The emerald within them has faded, his pupils are dilated with pain, and he's inhaling deeply and exhaling slowly. He lifts a hand to his hair and pulls on the ends. "You didn't just say that," he says, his voice a feeble whisper.

His reaction only makes me cry more. The tears well endlessly in my eyes and fall so quickly that I can't even keep up when trying to catch them. "We just can't do this," I croak. It's beginning to hurt when I talk.

"Don't do this. I swear to God. Please, Eden," he begs

suddenly, his voice fast and raspy. It cracks at the end and he jerks his head toward the window, breathing against the glass. It steams up. "We've come this far already. You can't give up now."

"We have to." I don't even care now that I'm a bubbling mess. Each word escapes my throat as a ragged splutter and I'm unable to pull myself together. I want to be strong enough to do what's right, but I'm not. I'm weak.

Suddenly he spins around, urgency in both his actions and his words. "Tell me what you want me to do it and I'll do it. I'll make this work." One hand grips the steering wheel; the other reaches out to touch my knee.

I glance down at his fingers as they touch my jeans. I just stare at his hand as I force down the bile in my throat. I don't look back up again. "Don't make this harder."

"I need to be with you," he whispers. His fingers move from my knee to my hand, and he grasps it in his and presses his thumb down hard on mine so that I can't possibly shake him off. He interlocks our fingers. I have no choice but to glance back up, to meet his eyes as they well up, and I've never seen him look so . . . so torn apart. "Don't you get it? You're not my distraction. This is me, Eden. This. Right now. You're making me a goddamn mess, but I don't care, because it's me. I'm a mess. And the thing I love about you is that I'm allowed to be a mess around you, because I trust you. You're the only one who's cared enough to figure me out. I want to be your mess."

"I'm still going to care," I manage to say, even though by now there are so many tears flowing down my cheeks that I can barely see. "But as your stepsister."

"Eden," he pleads once more, squeezing my hand even

tighter, like he's terrified to let go. "What about last weekend? We . . . Was all of that for nothing? Has the entire summer been for fucking nothing?"

"Not nothing," I say, but I'm staring at our hands, at the way they fit perfectly together. My stomach knots. "We've learned a lot."

"This isn't fair!" he yells at the exact same time he slams his other hand against the steering wheel. He grips it so tight afterward that his knuckles turn white. "I told you everything about me. I told you the truth. I broke up with Tiffani, and now she's probably already planning how she's going to ruin my life even more than it already has been, but I don't care, because I thought it would be worth it. I thought it would be worth it, because I was thinking of you. I was putting you first. You know what the only thing running through my mind was when I walked out of that house right now? *I can finally be with Eden.*" He falls silent, taking a moment to rub at his eyes as he exhales. His chest is rising and sinking rapidly as he releases his grip on me and places both hands back on the wheel, his eyes fixed on the rain that's rolling down the windshield. "And then you come out here and tell me that you don't want to."

"Do you think I want to do this? Because I sure as hell don't, but I'm doing it because it's better for us both." I'm trying to force his eyes to meet mine again, but they never do. He just keeps staring at Tiffani's driveway, at the rain, because right now the weather outside beats the storm that's taking place in here. "I don't want to see you get worse if this goes wrong. What are you going to do if our parents find out and absolutely hate us? This isn't the right time. We can't handle this. You need to fix your life as it is, because you need to go to New York, and you don't need any of this added on."

"What the hell is in New York?" he yells, exasperated, his fierce eyes snapping back to mine. "Why can't you just tell me?"

"Because your mom wants to," I tell him, but I sound like a sobbing catastrophe. I sniff a few times as I try to regain my breath, slowing down my breathing and attempting to compose myself. It doesn't really work. "Whatever there is between us, we have to ignore it from now on. We need to stop this now before we get in too deep."

He shakes his head, eyes tightly squeezed shut. The rain is still hammering against the windows, loudly and relentlessly. "If that's what you really want," he eventually murmurs in a low voice, but I just know he's hating this as much as I am. "If you really, really want us to ignore this . . . Then I guess I have to."

I heave a tremendous sigh. I want this to be a nightmare. I want to wake up in Portland and for Mom to tell me that I've never stepped foot in Santa Monica before and that I don't have a stepbrother called Tyler. I don't want any of this to be real. It hurts too much to be real.

When he opens his eyes and turns to look at me, he just stares. I can't bear the sight of them, pooling with emotion and hurt, but I can't look away. His breathing sounds louder than the rain and it quickens as he leans toward me, and I know exactly what he's thinking, and I want to kiss him too. So I do, because it's the last time I ever will.

I pull myself up onto my knees and climb onto him, stretching out my hands and gently grasping his neck. It's so sudden, but I can't stop myself. It reminds me of when he took me to the pier, when we kissed in his car, in this exact position. And just like I did all those weeks ago, I press my lips to his once more.

But it's so slow this time, so agonizing. Tyler places his hands on my waist and holds me tight against his chest, and all while his lips capture mine for long, drawn-out seconds. Over and over again, he keeps kissing me. I almost feel him sigh against me. It hurts to be kissing him, to know that I'll never get to do it again, but it's also calming in a way. It's like closure.

The sound of the rain is drilling into our ears, and our bodies are damp, and my hair is all over the place, and Tyler almost just suffered a mental breakdown, and I've cried enough tears to fill the pool in our back yard, and it's all just so messy.

It sums up our situation completely.

And for that reason, it's perfect.

Tyler groans as he pulls away. When his lips finally tear themselves away from mine, my stomach drops, and I refuse to let go of him. Instead, I hold him there, his face by mine, and I exhale against his cheek. My eyes are still closed. I'm not sure if his are too.

"Stepsiblings," I whisper, breathing the words softly yet firmly. "Nothing more."

"Nothing more," he confirms, but then his head hangs low and he pulls away from me, so I finally have to let go. He turns his face to his window and places his hands back on the wheel. I think he's finally given up.

Reaching for my hood and pulling it back over my head, I tuck strands of wet hair behind my ears and rotate my body toward the door. I reach for the handle, pausing for a moment to see if he'll say anything, but he doesn't, so I step out of the car.

And just like that, I'm walking away from him. From us.

Quickly, I slam the door shut behind me to stop the rain

getting in, and then I make a dash across the lawn. I glance over my shoulder and rain blows into my face again, but it doesn't stop me from seeing Tyler's car peel out of the driveway and head west. Hopefully he's making his way home. I stand there, out on the lawn in the pouring rain, waiting until his car disappears into the distance.

The thing I like most about the rain is that people can't tell whether or not you're crying. And right now the tears are streaming endlessly down my cheeks and soaking into my hoodie. The wind whips around me and I turn around and run back to the front door. Thankfully, when I get there Dean is swinging it open for me. I stop the second I get inside, letting the water roll off my face, my messy bun toppling over to one side.

"Are you crazy?" he asks, but he's laughing. "Hang on, I'll grab a towel."

He rushes off into another room, probably the bathroom, while I stand dripping wet next to the living room. I notice that both Jake and Rachael have disappeared. The house still smells like popcorn and I can hear the low volume of the football presenter commentating on the game, and then Dean comes padding back over to me with a huge white towel in his arms. He unfolds it and throws it over my shoulder, and I immediately pull it around me and dry my face. I feel like I'm drowning.

Dean still has a playful smile on his lips, but the more he studies my expression, the more it fades away. Soon he's frowning. "Are you okay?"

"I'll be fine," I say, but it's bullshit. Everything hurts and everything feels broken. I don't know if I'm going to be fine, but I can't let Dean know this, so I sniff and nod to the staircase. "Are they with Tiffani?"

"Jake and Rachael? Yeah." He bites his lip as he laughs. "I look like a crappy friend standing down here instead of offering her moral support, but I was actually about to leave."

"Leave?" I echo. "Where are you going?"

"La Breve Vita are playing another gig downtown," he says quietly, and I like the way he mumbles, shy about the fact that he's totally obsessed with this band. It helps to distract me. "I was gonna catch the end of their set after the movie, but I'm going to head over there just now instead. Hey, you can come! If you want to, of course. I mean, you've probably got better things to do with your time and you seem kind of upset, but I'm pretty sure they'd help cheer you up."

"I'll come," I say gently, and I can't help but smile as I let down my hair and attempt to towel dry it. Suddenly Tyler's obsession with distractions is starting to make sense. Right now, I'm trying to distract myself with Dean, because the less your mind thinks about the things that are tearing you apart, the better you feel. "I really like them."

"Are you sure?" He tilts his head and studies me, taking note of how soaked I am.

"It's just water," I say with a shrug, and then drop the towel to the floor as I gather my hair and throw it up into a damp ponytail. Right now, I couldn't care less about how I look. My eyes and my cheeks burn. They sting. "I'll dry out on the way there."

Dean looks as though he's about to protest, but then he just grins and pulls out his keys. "You have to go back out there now."

So I steal the towel. Holding it above my head like a makeshift umbrella, I run outside to the car with Dean sharp on my heels, and we both dive inside the vehicle as quick as we can. The heating goes on full blast and La Breve Vita's third album starts up in the CD player and Dean cracks a couple jokes about the towel, which aren't even funny but I laugh anyway.

"I was right about the rainstorm, see?" He leans forward over the wheel as we make our way to the gig and he glances up at the sky through the windshield for a moment. He blows out some air and then leans back in his seat again. "It's always so crazy."

"How long does it last?" I ask. My eyes are fixed on the wiper blades as they struggle to keep up with the amount of rain that's blurring the windshield, despite already being on their fastest speed. It's been raining this heavy since morning.

"All day," Dean says, but his tone is a little off as he grips the steering wheel and concentrates on the road. "Really, it's hard to say."

The gig is in the same venue as before, with the same crushed cups scattering the floor and the same cologne wafting around the air. Through the darkness, Dean leads me over to the back again, where we linger by the far wall. No one shoves you out of the way back here. I shrug my shoulders into my hoodie, giving up on getting dry. I just started to dry off in the car when, of course, I had to get straight back out and into the rain again. But Dean's soaked too, and so is everyone else, so no one seems to give a shit.

"They're working on a new album at the moment," Dean tells me over the noise. The band is on the stage, but they've paused for a few minutes to drink some water and to tune the guitars. "It'll be released in January. I'm stoked. It's gonna be awesome!"

I smile at his excitement and enthusiasm, because it really

is adorable seeing him get so hyped up about it all. His eyes are sparkling, but then he seems to think he's embarrassing himself, because he looks away and rubs the back of his neck.

We've arrived just in time for the beginning of the next song, and the lead singer steps up to the microphone. He clears his throat and then squints at the small crowd through half-shut eyes. "It's awesome to see so many of you here tonight despite the shitty weather," he says with a hearty chuckle, "and it's even more awesome that you're here to see us. We're about to perform one of my personal favorites from our second album." The crowd cheers in anticipation of what song it might be, and I can see Dean biting his lip, his eyes glued to the stage. "We wrote this song a few years ago now, and it's actually a pretty cool story, how this song came to be." He rubs the sweat from his forehead with the back of his hand and then begins to pace back and forth across the stage, his head tilted down and his eyes on the floor. "I had this friend . . . Let's call him Bobby. So I had this friend, Bobby, and Bobby was a hell of a guy. I went to college with him and we shared the same dorm building, and Bobby was majoring in law. And you know what? Bobby fucking hated law. Bobby wanted to major in musical theatre, but he stuck to law, you know why? Because society is a piece of shit." He shakes his head and pauses for a moment before continuing. "Bobby went through hell and back to finish that major. He wasted four years doing something he didn't want to do, because all through high school people talked smack about him because of what he was interested in. You know how Bobby feels now? He feels pissed off that he's stuck with a bullshit law major. So screw whatever the hell anyone else thinks about you or your decisions. If you're gay, then hell yeah, embrace that shit! If you want to start up your own paint store, then start up your own goddamn paint store. Stop holding back from being you." He clears his throat again and steps back into position in the center of the stage, his eyes flickering up to look at us all again. "So if you haven't guessed it already, here's 'Holding Back.' Enjoy. *Tanto amore.* Much love."

I don't know what it is about this band, but suddenly I adore them even more than I did before. I already loved the song, and I already understood the message it was trying to convey, but listening to the singer be so straightforward and to the point only makes me appreciate the lyrics even more than I already did. I can relate to them a hell of a lot. Especially this song, because it makes me wonder if I've done the right thing, if maybe I should run back home and tell Tyler I've made a huge mistake, that I really do want us to be together. But in my heart, I know we have to hold back. We have no other option. Tears spring into my eyes again as I listen to the song. It's bittersweet.

I feel a huge pang in my heart, but I bite down on my lip and keep my eyes trained on the stage. The guitarist starts strumming, and then the bassist joins in, and then the drummer, and then finally the singer, and soon the song is blasting around us, deafeningly loud but all the more exciting. I can feel the music vibrating through my body as goosebumps surface along my arms, the hairs rising.

And it's then that I feel Dean's hand slip into mine.

He takes me by surprise, but his skin is warm, and he squeezes my hand tightly before rubbing soft circles on my skin with his thumb. I don't let go. It's partly because it's so sudden and out of nowhere that I'm not quite sure what to think of it, and also partly because it feels almost . . .

comforting. Dean's always made me feel comfortable. And right now, of all times, I need all the comfort I can get.

When I glance sideways at him, his eyes are locked on the stage and he's nodding his head in sync with the kick drum. But most importantly, he's smiling.

EPILOGUE

Ten months later

If someone had told me last year that I'd be finishing up junior year in Santa Monica and not Portland, I would never have believed them. I would have laughed. Yet here I am, piling my marine biology textbooks into my locker and rummaging around for my car keys. When I find them and take a step back, Rachael comes twirling over to me from the other end of the hallway.

"Another day down!" she cheers, a huge grin on her face. She lifts her hand and waves two fingers in front of my face. Yesterday it was three; the day before it was four. "Two days to go until graduation!"

"Yeah, for you," I mutter, pretending to be pissed off, but then I roll my eyes and laugh. Rachael's been counting down the days ever since Christmas and she's already perfected her method of tossing her cap, so I'm cutting her some slack, despite how badly I hate the whole idea of her graduating. "When you're in college, remember to spare a thought for your best friend who's still stuck here."

"You're our little baby," she coos as she stretches out an arm to pat my head, but I duck and step to the side, fixing her with a deathly glare. I quickly scan the hallway to make sure no one noticed, but Rachael just giggles and purses hers lips together innocently. "You have to make sure our legacy lives on," she says. "I want you to write my name on every bathroom stall to ensure that I become a legend within this building. In five years' time, I want people to know that I walked these hallways."

"Unfortunately, no one actually cares." She whacks my arm just as I slam my locker shut, but then her laughter fades and her lips flatten into an awkward half smile. I know that expression like the back of my hand, so I heave a sigh and ask the daily question. I already know the answer. "Tiffani's coming, isn't she?"

Rachael quickly nods, and when I turn around I see the same thing I see every other day. Tiffani and Jake, hand in hand, sauntering down the hallway. It doesn't faze me. Honestly, I think they're an okay couple. The rest of the school seems to agree, with the girls constantly telling Tiffani how jealous they are, to which she usually flashes a dazzling grin in reply. They've been dating for a while now. Tyler was scribbled off her "must have" list a long time ago.

"Hey, guys," she says softly as she passes, and Jake gives us a clipped nod. But they don't stop; they never stop, because Tiffani and I still aren't on speaking terms. We can be civil, the same way Tyler and Jake are (although now the tension has grown worse), but we aren't friends. Rachael and Meghan try to hang out with us separately. Thankfully, Tiffani's going to UCSB, so she's packing up and heading for Santa Barbara in the fall. Jake's going to Ohio State, halfway across the country, so I've been wondering how long the two of them will be able to cope with the distance. I give it a month.

They float off down the hall and disappear out the exit, and

Rachael turns to me, breathing out the air she's been holding in. "On the bright side," she says, "you won't have to see her every day."

This is the difficult aspect of being in a group of friends who are all a grade above you. When Rachael, Meghan, Tiffani, Jake, Dean and Tyler graduate on Thursday, I'll be left behind. I still have senior year to plough through before I get to experience college for myself. For now, I'll have to stick with my friends in my own grade, the ones I've made gradually over the past year, who may not be my best friends but are still a great group of people.

I swing my car keys around my index finger as I start to make my way to the exit. Rachael quickly follows, so I steal a sideways glance at her. Thank God she's going to UCLA. She and Dean are the only two who aren't moving away. "Are you seeing Trevor tonight?"

"I think so." Her face lights up at the mere mention of his name. They may be in a relationship, but Rachael still sees him as her crush, as though she's still fighting for his attention. She's constantly blushing around him, constantly smiling. "And I think I heard Meghan say that Jared's coming into town to visit her."

"Where is Meg?" I ask as we slip through the exit to the sprawling student lot. The scorching sun beats down on us as we make our way to our cars, the lot emptying. No one ever hangs around for long once classes are finished for the day. "I haven't seen her."

"She had to ditch classes after lunch," Rachael informs me just as we reach our cars, parked side by side, of course. Rachael throws open the door to the Bug and tosses her purse inside, but she lingers outside for a moment, staring at me from over the roofs of our vehicles. "See you tomorrow, first thing?"

When I nod, she blows me a kiss and I gracefully pretend to catch it. "Enjoy your night with Trevor!" I call just before I slide into my car and rev up the engine. The steering wheel burns my hands when I first touch it, so I end up steering with my fingertips as I peel out of the lot and onto the boulevard.

Luckily, Mom's house is in the North of Montana region, just like Dad's, and it's handy having them live close by each other so that there's no need for me to travel back and forth between opposite corners of the city. I take the Deidre Avenue route home, passing Dad's house to see who's there, and when I glance in my rearview mirror I see Rachael's car turn off the road and pull up on her driveway. We used to joke about carpooling, because our routes home are the exact same, only mine has an extra couple minutes added on top, but we've never gotten around to sharing rides. It's too late to start now.

I roll down my window to let some air into my car as I push my shades on, nodding my head in sync with La Breve Vita's newest single, an upbeat tune with a sick chorus that's been stuck in my head for days. I refuse to ever take it off repeat.

When I reach Mom's place, it doesn't surprise me that there are no cars parked out front. Both she and Jack are at work, like they usually are most weekdays when I come home. Turning onto the driveway, I cut the engine and pull myself out of my car and into the blistering sunlight again. It really is hot out today. Wiping away a bead of sweat, I pull out my keys and head inside.

I've always found Mom's house much more welcoming than Dad's. Ever since she found it on the market last year,

I've fallen in love with it. I like that it's small and only has two bedrooms. I like that it has a cute porch and a nice fireplace. It's always so cozy and homey inside, and it's the perfect place for Mom and me. And Jack now, too, of course. He moved in a month ago, and it's starting to feel normal having him here all the time.

I'm greeted by Gucci the second I step foot over the threshold. She comes bounding over to me, paws sliding on the wooden flooring, tongue out. She circles my legs, sniffing at my clothes as I reach down to scratch the back of her ears, just the way she likes it. She's a gorgeous German Shepherd. It turned out Mom was actually serious last summer when she suggested getting a dog, and arriving home in Portland to find a puppy flying around the house was definitely the best thing to come home to. Mom chose the name. She told me once that she likes to believe it helps Gucci fit in here in LA. It took me a while to get it.

Right about the time Mom was considering moving down here, a job appeared at Saint John's Health Center, a hospital right bang in the middle of the city. And if that wasn't luck, then it sure as hell was when she actually got the job. The salary is better and the shifts are more suitable, and Mom doesn't seem so tired all the time anymore. She's constantly smiling, and I know it's because of a combination of several things: Jack, the new job, and Gucci. Moving down here really has been beneficial to her.

"I hope you're in the mood for spaghetti and meatballs, because that's all I feel capable of making tonight," she huffs as she walks into the living room. She's changed out of her scrubs, but her hair is still pinned into a neat bun, her smile reaching her eyes as Gucci greets her by jumping up on her.

"She's hyper today," I comment, nodding my head at the crazed animal who's attempting to slobber Mom in kisses, but she holds her back. "Did you walk her before work?"

"No, I was running late," Mom admits as she stands, wiping the dog hair off her pants. She rolls up her sleeves and nods to the leash that's hung up by the front door. "Can you take her out just now? Just while I'm making dinner."

I agree. It's perfect weather outside, I'm bored, and I could do with visiting a few people. Leaving Mom to prepare the food, I hook Gucci up to her leash and set off through the neighborhood. Gucci tugs at the leash, her body much stronger than mine, and I feel her pulling me along just like she always does. I once tried to take her with me on one of my runs, but I only ended up out of breath and panting after ten minutes, completely unable to keep up with her, so I had to turn around and go home before I dropped dead.

It only takes us ten minutes to reach my first port of call—Dean's house. Instead of heading inside like I normally do, I try to be creative, so I pull out my phone and dial his number. I stare at his bedroom window while I listen to the monotonous ring.

"Eden," he answers.

I smile at the sound of his voice. "Come outside. Gucci wants to see you." When she hears me say her name, her ears perk up and she looks up at me with huge glossy eyes.

Dean laughs gently across the line, and even though I heard that exact same laugh last night when we were at the movies, it feels like I haven't heard it in days. I don't think I'll ever get enough of it. "On my way," he says, and then hangs up.

I shove my phone back into my pocket and pat Gucci on the top of her head. "Good work, girl." She sits by my side on Dean's lawn, her tail wagging as we wait for him to get outside. More sweat tickles my brow.

The front door swings open, and Dean steps out and pats his thighs, yelling "Gucci!" at the top of his lungs. He knows I hate it when he does this, because Gucci always hurls herself at him, her weight almost yanking my arm out of its socket before I get the chance to let go of the leash. When I do, she bounds across the grass and jumps up on him, knocking him back a step or two.

"Who is it you're dating?" I call, and when he hears me, he shoots me a lopsided smirk and pushes Gucci off him. He grabs her leash and makes his way over to me. "Is it me or the dog?"

"Most definitely you," Dean says. With his free hand, he clutches my waist and pulls me toward him, pressing his lips to mine. Dean's always been a gentle, deep kisser, and he's always been one to smile in between each one, which is exactly what he's doing now. I can feel his lips twitching into a grin against mine. "You're a better kisser than the dog, that's for sure."

I let out a laugh as he steps back and passes the leash to me. "I'd be worried if you said I wasn't."

From behind him, Dean's dad, Hugh, has propped his head around the doorframe and is throwing me a wave. He's wearing a dark-blue boiler suit covered in grease, which means he just got off work within the past fifteen minutes. Hugh owns a garage, and Dean's about to start working for him right after graduation. Dean's referring to it as a gap year before he packs up and heads for college, and I'm glad he'll still be in Santa Monica while I finish senior year.

"Am I still coming over later?" he asks.

"Of course." Tuesday nights are when Mom and Jack clear out to give us some space. Mom's even started calling it "Deansday."

"Great." Reaching into the pocket of his jeans, he pulls out his wallet and flicks through the notes. "Here," he says, and passes me the exact same five-dollar bill that we've been passing back and forth for a year now. We'll find any excuse to use it. "Five bucks for letting me see the dog."

I roll my eyes and stuff the battered bill into my pocket, tightening my grip on Gucci's leash and glancing down the avenue. "I'm going to go drop by my dad's place. I'll see you tonight."

I bid him farewell by planting a quick kiss on the corner of his lips. Gucci stares after him as he disappears into the house, so I struggle to yank her away to begin with, but then she backs down and soon we're on our way to Dad's house.

It's only five minutes away if I walk fast, which isn't a problem considering Gucci is pulling me along, quickening my pace. When we near it, I notice that all three cars are there: the Lexus, the Range Rover, the Audi. This tells me that everyone's here, including Tyler. My stomach flutters.

As I'm making my way up to the front door, I hear voices and laughter coming from the back yard, so I alter my course and make for the gate instead. Chase is in the pool, Dad is attempting to spark up the barbecue, and Jamie is kicking a soccer ball around. Gucci barks when she sees it and tries to lunge across the yard, but I grab her collar and hold her back.

"Eden!" Dad lifts his head from the barbecue and gives me a nod, genuinely looking happy to see me. We've never really sat down and talked about what happened last summer, and I'm still angry with him, but he's been trying a lot harder to get along with me recently. Maybe our relationship will never be what it was. Or maybe it'll just take time. But at least now we're trying. "Are you hungry? We're about to cook up a feast." It reminds me of last summer, of my first day here in Santa Monica and my first time meeting Tyler. It feels like a decade ago.

"Mom's already got dinner under control," I tell Dad quickly, because I'm still focused on trying to hold Gucci back. I fire Jamie a pleading glance. "Jamie, please hide the ball for a second."

He rolls his eyes as he kicks the ball up and catches it, before turning around and gently tossing it through the patio doors. Now that Gucci can longer burst it I unclip her leash and let her go. She whizzes around the yard like a lunatic.

"Is Tyler here?" I ask. It's mostly because I didn't get the chance to speak to him at school today, and I have yet to go a single day without talking to him, but I also ask because part of me wonders what he's doing right now, and what he's thinking about, and if he still loves cotton candy as much as he loves amusement park rides.

Dad doesn't glance up from the barbecue, but he does point to the house with his thumb. "Upstairs."

I leave Gucci in the yard under Jamie's supervision and make my way into the house, which is also my second home. I've spent more and more time here over the past year, and now Jamie and Chase really do feel like my little brothers. Ella can never take my mom's place, but I know I can rely on her. Dad . . . Well, Dad is Dad. I alternate weekly between my mom's place and here, so that I have the chance to live with both halves of my family, because quite frankly, I love them both.

"Eden! Are you here for the barbecue?" Ella's standing by the island, measuring out jugs of juice, but she pauses to smile at me. She's wearing her suit, the jacket placed neatly over the back of a chair behind her, and I figure she hasn't been home for long. She's been back at work for six months now.

"Not tonight," I say. "I was walking the dog and I thought I'd drop by. Tyler's upstairs, right?"

"Yes, he's packing." She sighs, but she's smiling.

Despite the way my chest aches at the thought of him moving away, I head across the kitchen and into the hall, skipping up the stairs two steps at a time. It's silent upstairs, and the blinding sun lights up each room. Tyler's door is ajar, a stream of sunlight shining through. I push it open fully.

There are two suitcases laid open on his bed, half filled with his clothes, and the rest of the room is bare. Everything else has already been shipped across the country and is waiting for him in his apartment, right in the center of Manhattan. Tyler steps out of the bathroom and gives me a small smile.

"Hey," I say.

"Hey."

There's a silence, the same as there always is every day when we talk. It's not an awkward silence. It's become familiar. It's as though we need a moment to compose ourselves in case we do or say something we shouldn't. A moment to pull on our game faces, to build up our brave fronts, to convince ourselves that we aren't still in love with the person standing in front of us.

Ignoring the way my palms grow sweaty and how my heartbeat picks up, I stare at the suitcases for a short while before finally shifting my eyes over to meet his. "Can you believe you're really moving to New York?"

It took Tyler a lot of convincing to agree to it, but here he is. On Monday, he's flying over to New York and staying there for an entire year, traveling the East Coast, sharing his story, and possibly helping others. But he's had to work hard for the opportunity. He's graduating on Thursday with a 3.3 GPA. He hasn't been high in eight months. The last time he raised his voice to any of us was last year. It's like a weight has been lifted off his shoulders now that everyone knows the truth, everyone understands him. Inevitably, the truth had to come out at some point when he let it slip that he was moving to the other side of the country. Rachael's a little nicer to him now.

"It's kind of insane," Tyler replies with a shrug, and he walks toward me with some more clothes, which he packs into the suitcase. "Car's getting shipped tomorrow, and then that's everything."

"It's going to be so weird not seeing you for an entire year." I'm so proud of him for everything he's done and everything he's about to do, but at the same time it hurts knowing he's not going to be here. No matter how much I try to convince myself otherwise, he's so, so much more than just my step-brother. How am I supposed to cope without seeing the person I love every day? Somewhere within me, I know that it might help. Maybe being separated for a year will do us good. Give us some time to get over each other.

"That's the worst part," he murmurs. Reaching forward, he closes one of the suitcases and zips it up, and then he turns back to me. His eyes are still as gorgeous as they've always been, but I try not to think about it. "Have you thought anymore about next summer?"

Last week, Tyler invited me out to New York next summer.

The events wrap up in June, but he won't be coming home until August, so he's spending his summer vacation in the city and he wants me to do the same. But that's a dangerous idea.

"Just us two," he reminds me, his eyes smoldering as he tries to suppress a smile. He takes a step closer to me, and it gets my pulse racing and my heart throbbing the same way they always do whenever he gets too close. All the air in my lungs rushes out. He stretches out an arm and pushes his bedroom door shut with a soft click.

Over the year, we've done a pretty good job of ignoring the attraction between us, and an even better job of ensuring no one finds out that there ever was one. Besides, I have Dean now. I should be focusing on him. But sometimes, just sometimes, Tyler and I forget to pretend. Like right now.

He takes another step toward me and draws me into his arms, hugging me tight against his body as I inhale his cologne. The Bentley cologne, his favorite. I already miss him and he hasn't even left yet, and as I rest my chin on his shoulder he drops his hands to my waist. And so I'm hugging him and he's hugging me back, and there shouldn't be anything wrong with it, because I'm still allowed to hug my stepbrother, but there is something wrong. There's sexual tension, and there shouldn't be.

His breath feels hot against my neck as he exhales, his cheek brushing mine. He grips my waist tighter as he moves his lips slowly along my jaw, planting a sharp kiss on the corner of my mouth. I feel him smile against my lips, and he dares himself to whisper, "I'll see you next summer, Eden."

Acknowledgements

Thank you to my readers who've been with me since the start and watched this book grow. Thank you for making the writing process so enjoyable, and thank you for sticking with me for so long. Thanks to everyone at Black & White Publishing for believing in this book as much as I do. I'm forever grateful to Janne, for wishing to take over the world; Karyn, for all your comments and your expertise; and Laura, for always looking after me. Thanks to my family for their endless support and encouragement, especially my mum, Fenella, for always taking me to the library when I was younger so that I could fall in love with books; my dad, Stuart, for always encouraging me to be a writer; and finally my grandad, George West, for believing in me from day one. Thank you Heather Allen and Shannon Kinnear for listening to my ideas and allowing me to ramble on about this book, without ever telling me to be quiet, despite however much my excitement most likely drove you both insane. Thank you Neil Drysdale for helping me get to where I am. Thank you, thank you, thank you. And finally, thank you to Danica Proe, my teacher back when I was eleven, for being the first person to tell me that I wrote like a real author, and for making me realise that an author was exactly what I wanted to be.

BOOK 2 IN THE INCREDIBLE DIMILY SERIES
Did I Mention I Need You?
ESTELLE MASKAME

Coming Soon!

BOOK 3 IN THE SENSATIONAL DIMILY SERIES
Did I Mention I Miss You?
ESTELLE MASKAME

Coming Soon!